THE
FRIEND

Charlie Gallagher

D1584788

avon.

Published by AVON
A division of HarperCollins*Publishers* Ltd
1 London Bridge Street
London SE1 9GF

www.harpercollins.co.uk

HarperCollins*Publishers*
1st Floor, Watermarque Building, Ringsend Road
Dublin 4, Ireland

A Paperback Original 2021

First published in Great Britain by HarperCollins*Publishers* 2021

Copyright © Charlie Gallagher 2021

Charlie Gallagher asserts the moral right to be identified
as the author of this work.

A catalogue copy of this book is available from the British Library.

ISBN: 978-0-00-844551-5

This novel is entirely a work of fiction. The names, characters and incidents portrayed
in it are the work of the author's imagination. Any resemblance to actual persons, living
or dead, events or localities is entirely coincidental.

Typeset in Sabon LT Std by Palimpsest Book Production Limited, Falkirk, Stirlingshire
Printed and bound in UK by CPI Group (UK) Ltd, Croydon CR0 4YY

MIX
Paper from
responsible sources
FSC™ C007454
www.fsc.org

This book is produced from independently certified FSC™ paper to ensure
responsible forest management.

For more information visit: www.harpercollins.co.uk/green

For Lynn and Pete. Who started the story.

Prologue

This had always been her happy place. The sort of place every fifteen-year-old has. A place to be free, to be among friends. To be safe.

But today was different. Today it was just her, a handful of pills and a bottle of water to wash them down.

The sound of children playing grabbed her attention. In the distance she could see two toddlers in matching blue, giggling on a colourful merry-go-round. Right next to them a young girl occupied the swing, her red hair trailing behind her. She shrieked for her dad to push her higher, wearing a smile like nothing else in the world mattered.

It wasn't so long ago that had been her: carefree, happy. Innocent. A child whose only knowledge of evil came from storybooks, from stern warnings from her parents, from Halloween. Evil wore a witch's hat; it was a stranger who would try to lead her away in a crowd or the bogeyman in a mask with fake blood round the mouth. It was obvious, you knew to scream or to run.

But now she knew the truth.

Evil isn't shrouded in black, beckoning from the darkness under the bed. It doesn't make itself known. Evil is slow, quiet and patient. It is the shadow consuming a smoker's lung, it is

1

the person who pretends to be your friend so they can silence you for ever.

Now she knew evil. And because of her, all those other girls would know it too.

She threw the tablets to the back of her throat, the water to wash them down part of the same movement. Her focus was lost as her eyes blurred with tears. Soon, for her at least, this would all be over. But evil doesn't stop, the shadow will still spread in silence.

He was never going to stop with her.

Chapter 1

One month later. A hotel just outside Dover.
Tuesday

A Tuesday night, sitting on the same barstool as so many nights before: Danny Evans could have no way of knowing his life was about to take another dramatic turn. The pub was called The Duke Inn, the name a nod to the military school that almost shared an entrance but none of the grandeur. Though a separate building, the pub also served a hotel where Danny had a booked room that was just a short stumble away. Danny was pretty certain he was not the demographic of choice. In truth, the pub was more a restaurant aimed at families, and he might well have recognised himself as the eyesore at the bar if he had taken a moment to consider his surroundings.

But now it was late. The families were gone. Only the drinkers were left. Another pint dropped in front of Danny, a shot glass followed, and his place among the drinkers was affirmed.

He swept up the shot first: neat dark rum that lingered in his throat. He swigged at the pint next, smacking his lips while the heat from the rum spread through his chest.

'Who won?' A stool scraped next to him, then creaked under the weight of a man taking the seat. Looking down,

3

Danny could only see thick thighs in grey suit trousers over two-tone shoes: tan with a streak of blue through the middle that made Danny think of a classic car interior. Danny raised his eyes to the TV screen above them. He'd picked the barstool in front of the television out of habit, but had only been vaguely aware of the football match showing. It had passed him by as a fuzz of green and an occasional word breaking through from familiar-sounding commentators, like having old friends talking to each other in a room while you sat on the periphery.

'No idea, mate.' Danny's words were his first for a while and they made the roof of his mouth itch.

'I know you!' the man said, suddenly seeming animated, pleased with himself. Danny lifted his head to look higher than the thighs: a grey suit jacket matched the trousers, wrapped round a man in his late forties maybe. He wore a white shirt that was hanging open and crinkled like it had given up a tie. An expensive-looking watch gripped his wrist, the metal strap and matching cufflinks catching the light as he ran his fingers over pursed lips that stood out from a patchy-grey beard. He was tanned too, despite it being February.

'Don't think so, mate,' Danny replied.

'Evans, right? Danny Evans!' Danny felt himself grimace. He'd come to hate the sound of his own name, especially when it meant he had been recognised. 'You played football for the town, the captain! You did a few seasons up at the Gills too, right? You're a legend round here.'

'Legend,' Danny snorted. He'd never felt further from the word.

'I'm right though, aren't I?'

'I've played a bit. Not no more, though.'

'That's a shame. I used to get up Crabble a lot, me and my little girl. You were her favourite player, a proper no-messing centre-half. "The Beast", right? They called you that after

4

someone bit a piece of your ear off and you played on. I remember the pictures, you were covered in claret.'

'That was a long time ago and it was just a nick.'

'A nick! Still living up to the name, I see. How about I get your next beer? You know, as a thank you.'

Danny waved him away. 'No need. I got paid, I got cheered, that was thanks enough . . .' He stretched out his finger to rest it against the side of his pint glass, keeping his attention on where the bubbles rose as a twisting line to rush for the surface. 'Best days of my life,' he muttered.

'I bet. Any chance I can get a quick picture? Just to send to my daughter. She won't believe me when I tell her.'

'I'm not so sure, you know. I'm hardly the model athlete tonight. I'm happy to sign something for her maybe? I might have a shirt back in the room?'

This time it was the man waving Danny away. 'Look, don't worry. I'm bothering you, I can see that. I didn't think you would still be around here. Dover, I mean. Most of the players come from all over the place these days.'

'I've no idea where I am right now, mate.'

'Are you still working for the club then?'

'I'm back involved, yeah. Coaching mainly now . . . you know.' Danny didn't really know himself anymore. His energy for the game and conversation about it was all but gone. His whole life's obsession and suddenly he could barely care less. He tried not to think about how that had happened, how quickly. It terrified him.

'Well, I'm sure you get this a lot, people like me bothering you when you're enjoying a quiet one. I don't get down here much anymore. I can't believe I got to meet you.'

'Sure. Have a nice night.'

The chair scraped and squeaked again, this time until it was empty. Just a few moments later Danny's commentator friends said goodnight too before the screen they had occupied went black. The only movement left was from the bar staff

5

who were well into their closing-up ritual. Danny dragged at his beer until his throat burned. He closed his eyes to it and instantly the room did a little spin. It was time to go.

The night sky seemed to provide a ceiling that held the sound of the passing traffic. It was steady, even at this time of night. The A20 passed right across the front of the pub, carrying traffic away from the busy ferry port that was just out of sight at the bottom of the hill and had Dover's famous white cliffs as its backdrop. There was a service station to his left, the bright lights of its forecourt only serving to thicken the shadows of the path to the hotel's main entrance. He considered a cigarette, just to warm his throat if nothing else. It was a new habit, one he might quit if he could even remember why he had started.

'Hey!' Danny turned to see the same suited man who had taken the seat next to him. He was walking after him waving a piece of paper. Danny pushed his cigarette back into the packet. He lifted the collar on his jacket and dropped his chin. It was freezing cold. He didn't like the cold. He wanted to make sure his new friend was aware of his discomfort.

'Oh, did you want that autograph?' Danny had made it far enough for the shadow to swallow him whole.

'It's not your autograph I want, Danny. I know who you are.'

'You said that.'

'I don't mean Danny Evans the washed-up footballer. I mean, I know who you really are.'

'What is this?' Danny looked around, expecting the shadows to give up another assailant. This conversation suddenly had a very different feeling.

'I know why you're currently living in a hotel, drinking yourself into a stupor every night. I know that you had to get away from your wife, from your family. I know what happened, Danny. I know about Callie.'

Danny's hands lifted out of his jacket pockets already

6

bunched into fists. He took a step towards the suited man, who didn't react – he didn't step back or raise his own hands in defence. Danny managed to keep his fists by his side. He was no stranger to being the target for a windup.

'What is this? You trying to get a smack off me? You should know, there's nothing left. Wind me up and I will lash out but there's no money. You'll just end up with a busted jaw; a local headline if you're lucky but they don't pay nothing.'

'I don't want a smack, Mr Evans. I just wanted to get your attention. I can help you.'

'We were talking, weren't we? In there. You had my attention.'

'I don't like talking in places like that, I know better. And I wanted to be sure it was you. I'm a private investigator. I was hired by someone like you, someone who went through the same thing you and your family are going through. I have information, Danny. I have answers.'

'Answers? What are you talking about?'

'I know what happened to Callie. And I know why you can't talk about it, why you lash out at anyone who even mentions your daughter's name. She wasn't the only one who suffered. There were others.'

Danny stepped towards the man, his foot scuffing the concrete, a stone kicked and rolled. The suited stranger flinched slightly this time, but still didn't step back.

'I don't know you. And I barely trust the people I *do* know these days. I suggest you scurry away before you get that smack you came here for.'

'I understand.' The man held his hands up in surrender. 'You're right, you don't know me.'

'And you don't know who I am either. Don't believe what you've read or heard. It's all bullshit.'

'Private investigators like me only believe what we find out for ourselves. That's why I'm here, because of what I have found out. Think about that, Mr Evans.'

7

Danny didn't want to think. Not now. He walked away as quickly as he could. When he emerged out of the shadow it was with a new destination in mind. The service station sold alcohol all night. He checked behind him, making sure his new friend had stayed put. When he came back out of the shop, the man was gone.

Chapter 2

Wednesday

The morning was always an extension of the night before when Danny had been drinking. The muzzy head was an instant reminder, but he knew that would pass; it was the fatigue in his muscles that would linger. It usually got worse as the day wore on. By evening, he felt lacklustre and wiped out. This morning, even the few steps to the bathroom were laboured. The sudden whirr of the extractor fan made him wince. He turned to sit on the toilet, not even bothering to stand up to urinate. As he finished, he glanced out of the bathroom and saw a white envelope on the floor by the door of his room; it looked like it had been slid underneath.

The envelope was A4 in size, face up and blank. At first it felt light enough to be empty, but it wasn't. From inside he took out a single sheet of paper. The writing was scratchy, barely legible:

Maybe I didn't get it right last night. I just wanted to talk, to help. I took the liberty of making an appointment for you to see me.

You should know, I don't usually work for free. But this is different. I know how much you and your family must have suffered.

9

I'm sorry about the time but you will understand when you get there. Those answers I mentioned, I do have them. But they're no good to me.

The Old Mill Development: CT17 OAX. Tonight, 10pm. Follow the light.

'Follow the light!' Danny scoffed. 'God left it, did he?' He turned the letter over in his hand, but there was nothing else. He opened his door and stepped out into a long, bland corridor. His eyes followed the patterned carpet up to a set of fire doors. He didn't know what he was expecting to see. There was no one about. The envelope could have been pushed through at any time. The end of his night had seen him swigging from a bottle of rum until he had passed out on the bed.

His phone's sudden vibration had him wincing again. The screen glowed with the name MARTY JOHNSON: his agent. Marty always called to confirm breakfast appointments. Danny didn't answer. Marty wouldn't be expecting him to by now. Instead, he threw his phone into the middle of his messed-up bed and turned the shower on.

'Jesus, Danny, your wife tried to warn me, but you're worse than she said.'

'You spoke to Sharon?' Danny's knife dropped to clang against the plate as he fixed on Marty. His toast would have to make do with being half-buttered.

'Of course I did. You don't answer your phone anymore.'

'What did she say?'

'That you were staying in a hotel. That you were drinking too much and that whatever hotel it was she was sure it would have a shit-hole bar to suit your new lifestyle. She wanted to know which hotel too. Obviously I said I didn't know.'

Danny took a moment to look around. The Duke Inn doubled as the venue for their buffet breakfast. Shutters had been pulled down to conceal the bottles of alcohol but from

10

their table he could still see the stool he had made his own. The interior of the place looked worse in the daylight. There was no hiding the carpets with their worn tracks to the bathrooms, the slapdash paint job in fading orange, or the fake fireplace stacked with dusty pine cones. His wife was right; she was always right.

'I needed somewhere to go, somewhere she can't find me. Just for now.'

'You can't stay here for ever.'

'Nothing's for ever, Marty. The last year has taught me that for sure.'

Marty smiled. He was Danny's latest football agent and very likely to be his last. Danny had been through several, some of them representing far bigger players than he had ever become. But Marty was still typical of all of them. He had the expensive watch, the LaCoote motif on a crisp white polo shirt and again on fitted chinos that led down to shoes with no socks. He also had impossibly neat facial hair and, at that time, was partaking in the 'man-bun' craze that seemed to fit with the BMW coupe he had parked outside. The watch was on a monthly repayment, of course, the car too, and the combined amounts were eye-watering to the point that it meant Marty couldn't rent in London like he aspired to. He would need players at bigger clubs for that. It was the unspoken truth between them but Danny didn't think it would be long before Marty gave up on him. He was starting to get used to that.

Football had always been Danny's obsession. He had never seen it as a negative thing. Until now, facing the end of his playing days with no real sense of a plan B.

'She's worried about you.' Marty spoke like he was braced for a reaction.

Danny leaned back, giving up on the toast completely to swap it for his strong coffee. 'How messed up is that? You kick something out onto the street and then tell people you're worried about it!'

11

'It's a little more complicated than that.'

'You're my agent, Marty, not hers.'

Marty held up his hands, one containing a glass of orange juice. 'I'm not taking sides, you know me better. I just want your head back in football. This is a big year for you. That coaching role at Dover Athletic, it was yours, signed, sealed, delighted. But the board are getting a little shaky. They're worried about you too.'

'Worried? They know I can do that job!'

'They know you can do anything when you're keen. And sober.'

Danny bit his lip to hold back his first response. 'Coaching. . .' he said instead.

'Coaching, yeah. A coaching role at a club like that, where you've got some sway, where you're respected, where you can make mistakes and they'll still give you time . . . They give you the kids to manage and you get some results and who knows, suddenly you're getting offers for football management. I've said it to you all along, it can be a real future for you. Plus you get a salary and—'

'Salary! If you can call it that!'

'Fine, it's not Premier League money but prove yourself at this level and the only way is up. A head coach or a manager in the Football League will do you very nicely, thank-you-very-much. Earn a contract in the Championship and you're sorted for life, whether you work the whole of it or not. Trust me, I will make sure of that.'

'Why would anyone give me a job running a Championship side?'

'They won't, not straight off the bat. That's why you need to clean yourself up, finish your coaching badges, get yourself established in this role and start doing what you do. You're smart, Danny. You know football, you know the nitty gritty, the messing about behind the scenes to get the players you want and then getting them to do what you want.

12

Players listen to you, you've captained every side you've ever played for. That ain't no fluke and it's rare. You're The Beast after all.'

'I don't feel like it right now.'

'I see that. I've seen it before with players when they get to the end of their playing time. They can't see beyond, they feel a bit lost. Your home life too . . . It's been a bit . . . topsy turvy. But I think all your issues have the same solution. Get yourself sorted, get yourself clean and back to the Danny Evans who could boss a game of football without leaving the centre circle, and everything else will fall back into place.'

Danny suddenly flashed angry, he couldn't hold it back: '"Back into place"! How can everything be back in place while . . . I had a life, Marty, a family, or are you forgetting all that? That's not just going to fall back into place, is it? It could get worse from here. Far worse.'

Marty made that face he always did when he was about to be patronising. He wasn't good at sympathy. The effort required was always obvious. 'You don't know what's going to happen. Callie's in a coma today but she might not be tomorrow. The doctors have said there could be a big change any time, right? And then you can start getting back to where you were. Look at you, Danny, you're something, even smelling like you spent last night trying to drink until that something went away. I know you are.'

'There's no guarantee Callie's coma ends with her waking up; no one's promising us that. She might never . . .' Danny couldn't complete his sentence, he'd never been able to say it out loud. He didn't need to.

'You gotta have hope though, am I right?'

'So is that what this meeting was about today? A little pep talk?'

'No. This was just about me making sure I can sit you down in front of the people at Dover Athletic and they will take us seriously. There's a good job here for you. The meeting

13

will be this week. There will be a contract for you to sign that will make you a coach. It can run alongside another playing contract if they offer you another year. But you need to take this opportunity, Danny, OK. This is it for you – after this we're all out of options.'

'I get that.' Danny sighed. 'Look, I do appreciate what you've done. I know you're doing your best for me.'

Marty smiled. 'Of course. You're my favourite client and looking after you is my job.'

'Spoken like a true agent.' Danny sniffed.

'I can't speak any other way.' Marty made that face again, the one where he was about to patronise him. 'Are you going to the hospital today?'

'I go every day, Marty, you know that.'

'Sharon said she was too.'

'She goes every day too. So what?'

Marty smacked his lips. 'Have a shower, will you? Before you head out, I mean.'

'I've had a shower!'

Marty ran his hands through his hair and tugged on his man bun. 'Another one then.'

14

Chapter 3

For Danny, walking through the William Harvey Hospital felt very much like Groundhog Day. Callie had been in here for a month now and Danny had made the same trip just about every day since. Today – as always – he walked with his head down, following the same endless polished floors that reflected the blur of different coloured uniforms as they hurried in every direction, spreading the thick smell of bleach and antiseptic as they went. The Intensive Treatment Unit was on the second floor. He took the stairs, he liked to anyway, but it would also avoid the confined space of the lift, despite heeding Marty's advice to take a second shower.

And then there was Callie.

His daughter always seemed the same too. The same bed in the same space. The ITU was made up of five areas: Callie was in the third, first bed on the left, furthest from a window that was sealed shut to ensure the ITU was stuffy to the point of oppressive. Callie was in the same position too: laid out on her back, her eyes closed, her face expressionless, with the same mechanical hiss and whirr as a machine assisted her breathing through a tube that parted her lips to reach deep into her throat. Another tube ran alongside it too. Danny had asked a lot of questions when he was first presented with the

15

horrific image of his daughter, to be told that she needed much more than just assistance with her breathing. She was also being fed a sedative to keep her asleep, an analgesic for pain and drugs to minimise the risk of long-term liver damage. Since that first terrifying image, additions had made it even more terrifying. Another tube now fed her through her nose, her wrist trailed another that monitored her blood pressure, while she was also connected to a dialysis machine via her groin. The final intrusion was a catheter that left a bag of urine visible, hanging down from under the bedsheets. They had told Danny that he would get used to seeing her like that but a month down the line and it still hit him every time.

He felt the same cold, clammy touch from her skin as he took hold of her hand.

'Hey.' Sharon's arrival made him jump. Her voice seemed strained, but still instantly recognisable to him from across the bed – as it should be after fifteen years of marriage. *Long-suffering*, she would be called if he was to believe what he'd heard recently. He could hardly argue. They'd had tough times: extra-marital affairs, addictions, depression – all his. But they had come through every one. He might have accepted that his marriage was going to fail at some point, that he was going to be out of the family home, but he had always assumed that it would be down to something he had done, his fault, which would also make it something he might be able to fix. Instead something else had torn them apart. *Someone* else. The stranger who had silently manipulated and abused his daughter, the stranger who had forced her into a desperation so strong that she would seek to take her own life with a handful of painkillers. *Painkillers*. He hadn't even been able to say the word out loud. The doctors had also detected a toxic amount of Paracetamol in her system. They suggested this might have been her first choice to effectively overdose but explained that it could take time and she might have lost patience. He could barely imagine what could have left her

16

feeling so desperate. There had been a police investigation; Callie was a victim of online grooming, she had been black-mailed to send pictures. It had all come out a few weeks before she had tried to take her own life. Callie wasn't the only victim – a number of her friends were involved too. It was a difficult time, of course it was, but he had no idea just how huge the impact had been on her. His confident, popular, sassy daughter – reduced to this. Being kept alive by a series of tubes.

He assumed the police investigation would ramp up when Callie was rushed in but all they could provide was more questions than answers. Still there were lots of missing pieces. The name of her abuser being the most obvious; a sense of justice was another.

Danny kept hold of his daughter's hand as he greeted his wife, 'I didn't think you came in this early?' he said.

Sharon was carrying coffee, the brand matching what he had passed at the entrance.

'Well, I was able to get the school run taken off my hands, so I thought . . .'

'You thought what?' She had two cups: Danny was now aware that she had come here with the intention of speaking to him after weeks of doing anything to avoid it.

'Marty told me you were heading over after your meeting so I had an idea of what time you might be here.' She put one of the cups down on the table at the end of Callie's bed, pushing it an inch towards him.

'You two have been talking a lot just recently,' Danny said, and his wife reacted with a warning look.

'We're both worried about you.'

'Don't waste your energy on worrying about me. Save it all for her.'

Sharon took hold of Callie's other hand. She had stayed the opposite side of the bed. He watched as she gently straightened out Callie's fingers like she was trying to massage some life into them.

17

'Do you ever wonder if she dreams in there? You see it in the movies, don't you . . . people in comas dreaming. I can't stop thinking about it, if Callie can dream she can have bad dreams too . . . It sounds ridiculous doesn't it?'

'This whole thing's a bad dream.' Danny gently pushed Callie's fringe where it had fallen over her eyes. She was such a pretty girl, gentle features but with a real spark to those eyes. Just like her mother.

'I can't bear it, Danny, the thought that she's having bad dreams too. I like to think of her as just sleeping, resting so she comes back stronger. I hate to think she's struggling in there.'

'I know.'

Sharon's lips twitched like she might be breaking down and Danny had to fight the urge to walk round to her and wrap her in a hug. She was quick to change the subject.

'How's your digs?' she said.

'Like a football tour stopover in Chernobyl. Only without the lads.' He forced a laugh. Sharon only managed a smile.

'Are you staying on tour? Is that your plan?' she said.

'Plan!' Danny scoffed and regretted it instantly. 'I'm not sure what I'm doing from here, not yet.'

'Marty was talking about some job opportunity with Dover. Sounds like you're moving further on with the management side? That sounds good.'

'I've got options, yeah. I'll need to get my head down.'

'Are you going to be able to do that?'

'What do you mean?' Danny snapped. Again, he regretted it. Sharon stayed calm, of course she did, it was always him that would escalate first.

'You've got a lot going on right now,' she said. 'We both have. I've been struggling to concentrate on anything, I can tell you that.'

'I'll be fine,' Danny said.

'I've been thinking that maybe we can get a loan together,

18

enough to get you the deposit for a flat, you know, somewhere a bit more permanent. I've had a look, there's a few places about that you might like, I can send you the links through . . .' She faded out to study him like she was waiting for his reaction.

'Flats? Sure, send them through. Can't hurt to look.' Danny had no intention of looking. As bleak as the hotel was, finding a place to rent was a permanent solution to a problem he had hoped would be temporary. Sharon seemed to relax a little, like maybe they had moved past the part where she might have been expecting a battle.

'Has anyone spoken to you? About . . . about the investigation?' Danny said.

'Spoken to me? The police, you mean? Not for a while now.'

'Not the police. There was some guy, he said he was some private investigator, he came to see me at the hotel.'

'Private investigator? Where would you get the money from for—'

'I didn't hire anyone. It's nothing to do with me, with us even. He was hired by someone separate from all this but he was talking about having answers for us. About whoever did this to Callie . . .' Danny's words petered out. It sounded even more ridiculous out loud.

'It was in the local papers, Danny, it's everywhere on social media, everyone knows our business, just like always. It'll be some weirdo who fancies himself as being part of the story. You didn't give him any money, did you?'

'No. He wasn't asking for money. He said he had answers. That was all he said.'

'He will . . . Ask for money, I mean. Sounds like a con artist to me. There's nothing more valuable to you in the whole world right now than finding out who did this to us, to our daughter. Anyone would know that. Tell him to do one.'

'I did.'

'What did he look like?'

'I don't know really. Older than me. Nice suit . . . It was late, I was heading back and I was a little . . .'

'Drunk?'

'I was going to say tired.'

'But you meant drunk.'

'I'm an adult, Sharon. I'm allowed to have a quiet drink when there's nothing else to do.'

'You're allowed to do whatever you want. That's always been your biggest problem.' She paused to come back softer. 'Look, I don't want to argue. I just wanted to see you were OK.'

'I need to see my boy,' Danny said.

'We talked about this.'

'You talked *at* me about this.'

'And you were drunk then, too. You think I want a two-way conversation with a drunk about something as important as our son?'

'It won't happen again.'

'The drinking will. It sounds like it happened last night and that was probably why some suit thought he would chance his arm with you. He saw a weakness and he went for it.'

'I'm not drunk now. Don't hold back, Sharon.'

'You still reek of it.'

'I just want to see my son. Maybe I drink because you're keeping me away from the only thing I have left. Did you ever think about that?'

'I have to think about *him*. Jamie is all that matters in this conversation. You should have seen him after you left. He's grown up worshipping his dad, The Beast of the football pitch, the local legend. He's spent just about every moment of his childhood with a ball at his feet and your name on his back. I really don't know what he thinks about you anymore. He's stopped wearing your football shirts, I know that much. You really hurt him.'

20

'He's twelve. I let him down, I know that, but I'm still his dad, I can make it up to him. You can't keep me away from him for ever, that's not fair. Don't make me beg you, Sharon . . .'

'I don't want to talk about this now. Not in front of Callie.'

'In front of Callie? That's the best one yet. And not the first time you've used her to shut me down either, is it?' Danny could feel his head throbbing as his anger increased. He still had hold of his daughter's hand but he let it go. He needed to get out to where there was some air. He suddenly felt like he couldn't breathe.

'Running away again, are we, Danny?'

'Just doing what my therapist told me to do. My *therapist*. The one you drove me to.' He stumbled when he made it back out into the corridor. His head throbbed. Fresh air was a long walk away. He ducked into a gents toilet to splash some cold water on his face instead.

'God DAMMIT!' Water dripped off the reflection that yelled back at him. He always got so angry when he was around her. He knew why: he wasn't angry at her, he was angry at himself for being so pathetic, for giving her so much material to throw back in his face. And he was angry that he had no control, that he could do nothing about what it was that was tearing them apart.

Danny Evans had never been the sort of man to stand still and do nothing.

21

Chapter 4

9.20 p.m. The last of the families filed out and The Duke Inn was again under the control of the losers, the forsaken. The drunks.

'Another?' said the cheery voice of the lad working the bar. He had a creased shirt and lank hair that caught the light, held back by a black hairband. Danny couldn't help but notice how the barman behaved differently when talking to Danny compared to those that came in to eat as a family: like they were mates, kindred spirits with an understanding. Not like those other *decent* people with ironed shirts and homes to get back to at a reasonable hour. At least he seemed to have finally got the message that small talk was off the table. Danny wasn't in a bar for conversation, it wasn't even about the drink. The truth was far worse: he went there because he had nowhere else to go.

Danny nodded.

'With a chaser?' Lank hair tapped his watch as if to communicate that it was that time of night – they're mates, see? They understand each other. Danny should say no. This should be a wakeup call, he should look around, realise what he had become. Instead he just gave another nod. Lank hair turned away. A couple of minutes later, a fresh pint was placed

22

in front of him, then a dark rum shot next to that. Danny reached out to press the glass where the bubbles of his beer raced to the surface. He felt a sudden sense of déjà vu. This felt like the exact same moment as last night when he had been interrupted.

'Ten p.m.' The words that fell from Danny's lips were almost involuntary. He straightened up to look around, as if the suited man might reappear to offer the same promise of answers. Instead it was the barman who made a beeline back to him.

'Did you say something?'

'Sorry . . . no,' Danny replied. He checked his watch. When he'd got back from the hospital he'd read over the note again, even going so far as to run the postcode through a mapping application on his phone. It had come up with a location he knew well enough, walking distance from Crabble – Dover Athletic's home ground and his place of work. The last line still read like a strapline from a 'B' movie: *Follow the light.* This was what had prompted Danny to screw the note up as tight as he could and throw it into the bin. Sharon was right. She was always right. That was another part of the reason she could make him so angry. This guy would be some con-artist who'd read about him in the paper or picked up what he could online. He would want something from Danny, he just hadn't pitched it yet. No one did anything for free.

But his phone was lying on the bar and when he unlocked it the mapping application was still open with the postcode showing. The phone stated he was twelve minutes away. He thought again about Sharon, about how she was always right, how she had dismissed him instantly when he had talked about this guy. But what if he did have some answers? Maybe he had found something as part of another investigation and he was just a decent bloke who needed to share what he knew. It was no skin off his nose, after all. If he was hired by someone else as he said he had been, then he would already have been

23

paid. The man had said that he wasn't in the area much so if he did have answers they would soon be leaving with him, maybe for good. How Danny would love to report back to Sharon and tell her that he had ignored her advice, made his own decision, met up with this man again and actually been given something. How she was wrong this time.

Danny sat up from his slouch. It was just twelve minutes away. If he got there and was asked for money he could just tell the guy to piss off. His wife need never know. He wasn't as stupid as she thought he was.

He stood up. His stool caught on the carpet, toppling over. No one so much as looked. He scooped it back up, his vision blurring a little when he leaned forward. He stumbled a little too. There was no way he should be driving. He reached back to the bar for the shot of rum.

'One for the road,' he muttered and made for the door. The fresh, chilly air rushed him, taking over his lungs to force a gasp. He made it to his car and sat in the darkness for a couple of minutes to assess if anyone had seen him. The last thing he needed was another drink-driving charge for Sharon to add to her arsenal. His previous conviction was only just spent and was consistently something she would bring up to throw at him. It was just a twelve-minute journey. He would take it easy – blend in.

He blinked at the display, trying to concentrate. Through the windscreen the traffic streamed past almost without a break, mainly large HGVs building up speed as they moved away from the port. Danny fired his Mercedes and crawled slowly past the windows of the bar, hoping his lank-haired friend wasn't taking too much notice of what people did after they stumbled away from the premises. He stopped at a junction, looking right to where he had a view of Dover Castle lit up in the distance. He had taken his family there plenty of times. Sharon, Jamie, Callie and him. A complete unit. A vivid memory pushed its way through the fug of alcohol: it was

24

sunny, they were sitting on long wooden benches for a jousting re-enactment in the grounds of the castle. A court jester had come out between the rounds to keep up the atmosphere, and picked on Danny. They had all laughed together, their smiles lit up by bright sunshine. It was one of many memories he had of being part of a happy family. It was just last summer. It seemed like a lifetime ago.

A horn blared.

It snatched him back to the cold February night. His rear-view mirror was full of headlights. He had got lost in his thoughts. So much for blending in.

He dropped down the hill on the Jubilee Way to go against the flow of the lorries. The last part of the road had stilts to support it where it burst out of the famous white cliffs, with the Port of Dover a muddled mess of lights and activity around its feet. The sea presented as a solid mass beyond it with an occasional pulsing light to break up the nothingness. The road curved round to bring him down to sea-level and a row of tired-looking bed and breakfasts lined the right side while a white-stone promenade washed in bright downlights made up the left. Danny soon turned away from the sea where a new development of shops and restaurants stood – a development that no doubt played its part in making the rest of the journey bleaker, as he picked up a one-way system that led him through the town centre. Here he passed boarded-up shops, many with 'TO LET' signs reaching out with the same forlorn hope as a thumbs-up from a hitchhiker.

Crabble Paper Mill was on the other side of the town. The mill had been another important part of the town once, its 'Conqueror fine paper' a worldwide brand, but no longer. He had been to this building as a kid with his school. Then it had been hot and busy, the smell of pulp like nothing he had experienced before. Now the busy yards that had once been packed with lorries waiting for their produce were filled with a housing development still in progress. The whole site was

25

earmarked for development, the old factory included. Another of the yards already contained a clump of homes that were finished and occupied, had been for years, but the houses on the side where his directions ran out were half-finished at best. He'd read in the local press about issues with contracts being sold to multiple developers, causing delays, but whatever the issues the progress was slow.

Now the yard was dark. A gate fashioned out of mesh fencing was pushed open with a thick chain dripping down to the floor. There was just one lit window in the distance standing out in the blackness.

'Follow the light,' Danny said as he peered over at it. He laughed too, an escape of nerves.

His car had been a source of weak light, but when he locked it the darkness around him thickened. The mesh of the gate stood out like a grey slab in the gloom. He moved through it, his feet tripping on the loose ground as he did. It led to a flattened area of compressed hardcore with raised kerbs and drains to shape it like a road. On the left side the structure of the original factory looked like it was still in the falling-down part of the process. A row of newly built dwellings was on the right, their exterior style carrying a subtle nod to the mill, but they still looked like an intrusion. The road that would serve them twisted left to go out of sight behind the factory. Most of the houses looked like shells, some with black eyes and open mouths where doors and windows would go. A mini-digger looked to be sleeping off a day's work on the right side, parked under a set of large floodlights that looked precarious at the top of a steel tripod. The lights were all off. This made no sense; he had heard of these places getting screwed all the time for their metals and plant machinery.

Danny, at least, was glad of the darkness. He had no idea what to expect and took some comfort in skulking through shadows towards the lit window. He would have a look at

26

least, a peek into the window to see if there was even anyone in there. There was still plenty of time to decide that this was bollocks and to just walk away. He picked out a route that followed the building line on the left, where the shadows were thickest. The ground was at its most uneven here and he felt his feet kick and trip over loose boulders and down potholes while his eyes were still not accustomed to the darkness.

He stopped when he was closer. Now he could see that it wasn't a lit window at all, but a lit doorway. This part of the row looked to be more developed than the rest. The internal walls even looked painted. The light made them glow bright enough to force him into a squint. This one had fitted windows too, and a front door that was pushed wide open.

'Yo, strange suited man with all the answers. You in here?' Danny's head throbbed where a hangover was already starting. Yet he had never felt more sober. This felt crazy, even more so as he leaned into an empty hallway with bare wooden stairs straight ahead. The floor looked like it was formed from a layer of fresh screed. It was dark grey with brown bootprints going in every direction. There was an arrow on the floor too, drawn in safety chalk yellow. Next to it was something else written in the same chalk, a single word in block capitals:

DANNY.

The arrow pointed to the right. He stepped in.

'HELLO?' He called out louder now, his voice bouncing around like there was nothing or no one to stop it. 'This ain't funny, none of it. Show yourself or I'm gone.'

No answer. The front door had a layer of protective film that was bright blue, and a peeled piece caught a breeze to flutter against the door, making Danny jerk towards from it.

'This is ridiculous, Danny!' he scolded himself but his eyes dropped back to his name and the arrow beside it. It pointed

27

towards a whitewashed door with no handle. He was going to have to open it for this to play out. He knew he wasn't going to be able to walk away from here without knowing what this joker had behind that door for him. He stepped to it, pausing with his hand resting against the wood. He held his breath for any sounds: nothing.

The door opened inwards to reveal a far darker room. The light from the entrance hall behind him did its best to push past but it was moving into a large space and was soon lost. He could see far enough to make out a layer of semi-transparent plastic sheets hanging across the middle. He could also make out a dark shape behind them where some tools or equipment might have been left. A typed piece of paper clung to the middle of the plastic:

DANNY. YOU WILL NEED TO BE CALM AND YOU WILL NEED TO READ.

Then there was another arrow. It came out from under the text to point to the bottom right corner of the paper and to a metal chair that was directly underneath. A black plastic folder was on the seat cushion. There was a light switch by the door. He pressed it and had to squint again – somehow this room was even brighter. He took a step towards the chair but stopped dead as a faint sound broke through. Sounds were difficult to pinpoint in the sparse interior. He couldn't tell a direction. It could even have come in from outside. It was a scuffle, something moving in the wind maybe.

He picked up the folder. Opening it revealed a first page that contained just two words. They were enough to raise his pulse to the point that he could feel it banging against his temple: CALLIE EVANS.

He turned the page. Next was a printed document, a block of text in the style of a report. His eyes darted across it, rushing ahead so it didn't make sense. He had to focus, slow

28

down his movements and drag his eyes back to the start to read slower, to be able to take in the words:

Callie Evans was the 5th victim discovered and shall be referred to ongoing as V5.

V5 was contacted initially using the same platform – a direct message from a social media picture sharing application. The offender's phone contained a number of conversations with V5 using this format.

Danny gripped his nose. His eyes flicked back to the printed sign:

DANNY. YOU WILL NEED TO BE CALM AND YOU WILL NEED TO READ.

Behind it there was movement. The dark shape. A sound too and there was no doubt where it was coming from this time. Danny dropped the folder face down on the chair.

'Hello?' he said. There were no nerves now; it was anger that filled his words. 'What the fuck is this?' He searched the plastic sheeting in front of him. There were two zips he could see, looking like they were holding the sheets of plastic together across the room as a divider. The black smudge moved again. It was subtle enough for him to doubt what he was seeing. Then more noise – like a gurgle. He pulled one of the zips all the way up until it curved away from the middle. The plastic parted to reveal a pair of wide eyes that fixed on him. The gurgle came again. It was more earnest now, a man trying to communicate but unable to form words. The drastically shortened shotgun barrel between his teeth would be making that impossible.

'Jesus. SHIT!' Danny recoiled. One step back became a stumbled three. He looked around again, expecting other internal doors to open, for people to burst through with an

29

explanation or even his mates with a camera and loud laughter. They'd got him, that was for sure. He would still be angry – furious even. But relieved at the same time.

They didn't come.

He looked back over the scene in front of him. The plastic sheeting hung limp where it was unzipped to the floor and the man beyond was presented like he was suspended in a web. The ends of his toes were the only part of him touching the floor while his hands were wrapped tight behind his back. He had ropes around his chest and hips, taking his weight and tilting him forward. Another rope was tight under his chin, pulling his head up so they were now staring at each other. Two sturdy-looking bench weights hung off him, one from each shoulder, to keep his head in place. The shotgun was on a tripod stand, not unlike what he had just seen outside holding up a floodlight. It looked makeshift. The barrel was deep into his mouth, his jaw locked open to take it. It was so wide that the tattoo reaching out from his chest and up his neck was distorted by pulsing veins. The tattoo was of a bird with a large wingspan – an eagle perhaps. The man made more sounds from the back of his throat. It was all that he could do.

Danny looked round for something that might help. A knife, an axe, anything that he could cut him down with. As he searched, his eyes fell back on the typed sheet that was at an angle on the floor from when the zip had been opened.

DANNY. YOU WILL NEED TO BE CALM AND YOU WILL NEED TO READ.

He picked the folder up and turned it back over:

O1 made first contact with V5. As with previous behaviours, O1 posed as a younger male and claimed to have an interest in football. It would be obvious from the

30

material V5 displayed on social media that football was among her interests. A bond formed quickly and, as we have seen before, O1 soon moved the subject matter to that of a sexual nature.

V5 resisted at first. It appears to have taken O1 a far longer time to convince V5 to share photos at all, and photos of an explicit nature only followed when she was sent examples that V1, V3 and V4 had supplied. This is behaviour that O1 has also demonstrated in other cases, the desire and ability to 'normalise' the sending of explicit materials, while labelling them as 'art' and claiming it to be 'what friends do'.

V5 submitted a photo in a state of undress. Again, O1's behaviour followed the previous pattern and the nature of his messaging became far more pressured until he received an image that was suitable for his needs. At this point, O1 immediately threatened to share this photo if V5 did not meet his further demands.

The page ran out. Danny shook his head like it might clear it. He'd never seen this report before, never heard anything like it from the police. *Where had it come from?* All they really knew was what Callie had told them – she'd been blackmailed online for pictures and she didn't know who it was. That was it. The police had said there was nothing left on her phone that helped. She'd restored it to factory settings – the police said there was nothing they could do with it. Callie said she was told to do it as part of the threats towards her. But a private investigator had been able to get more, he'd been able to get answers.

He looked up, back at the seated man. He was so tense that he felt like his jaw was locked tight, like he was the one restrained and not the man in front of him. He was finally able to speak.

'You know what this is?' Danny's words rasped from a dry

31

throat. The man was silent now and his wide eyes looked heavy with moisture. 'I think I might know what this is. If I'm right, then I think I might know who you are, why you're here.' Danny gestured with the folder. 'Like this. Is that why you're crying? Do you know who I am?'

Danny broke away to turn the page and continue reading:

As before with all V's, V5 provided photos increasingly explicit in nature in order to meet the demands made by O1. The threats increased. An example being that O1 was able to provide the email addresses of all V5's school teachers and that of numerous family members, including her parents.

Parents are Danny and Sharon EVANS. They reside at 54 Prospect Close, Lydden, Dover. Danny EVANS appears to be a minor local celebrity following a football career at Dover Athletic. O1 demonstrated awareness of this and included the potential fallout for Danny EVANS as part of his threats.

Other messaging applications in use at the time show that V5 was becoming increasingly isolated from family and friends and felt unable to talk with them. This desperation pushed her to reach out to SOPHIE CUMMINGS via Twitter. This account contained messages from a female who initially described a similar issue – that of being blackmailed for explicit messages and videos. V5 and 'Sophie Cummings' held many private conversations online where 'Sophie Cummings' advised V5 against involving any other persons. V5 and Sophie Cummings were not known to each other outside of social media.

'Sophie Cummings' is now known to have been O1 via a fake profile. This is the same method as displayed with all other victims.

The final exchange between O1 (acting as Sophie Cummings) and V5 reads as follows:

32

V5: I cannot take this anymore! This has to end. He wants a video now. Of me doing something really bad. Pls, tell me what to do . . . What can I do? U said he would get bored and move on. Why won't he leave me alone!?'

AC: I know. I'm so sorry I was wrong . . . He won't leave me alone either. There's only one way out for me . . . for us. It's what we talked about. It'll just be like going to sleep. Kill yourself, Callie.'

The book slipped from Danny's grasp, the plastic slapping against the solid floor and reverberating round the room like a firecracker. Danny flinched from every part of his body. He looked down, dumbstruck, unable to move while his pulse beat behind his eyes, each one seeming to thicken the cloud of confusion in his mind.

'She coulda spoke to me! She coulda spoke to any of us . . . I didn't know . . . We couldn't have!' He looked up at the man opposite, who was still watching him intently. He reacted by looking away, breaking eye contact for the first time to look at the floor. Danny took a moment to steady himself, to get control of his breath then bent forward to pick up the folder. He stared at the man the whole way.

The next page had just two words:

MARCUS OLSEN.

He turned the page to find another report written in the same format:

Marcus Olsen is the offender for all victims. From this point on he will be referred to as O1.

Below this was a mugshot labelled 'O1'. It was in full colour and showed a heavyset male with hair shorn close to his scalp

33

and thin lips surrounded by stubble. He looked to be mid to late thirties. He was shirtless in the photo with most of his torso visible. It showed a large eagle tattoo, its wings pushing out to cover his chest, the top of its head running up the middle of his neck to finish just below his chin. In the photo his thin lips were pushed together in a leer, and his arm was angled down to suggest his hands were in his lap. The photo overall looked like it was taken from a webcam and then cropped: poor quality, but good enough. Danny stared at the smiling eyes in the photo. When he lifted away he found the same eyes in real life. This time there was no sign of a smile. This time his thin lips were forced apart by the barrel of a shotgun.

'Marcus Olsen.' His throat was now so dry it hurt. Danny watched the man closely as he uttered the name. There was a reaction, no doubt, as much as he could with his head held tightly in place. He jerked like he was trying to shake it, like this was all a big mistake.

But Danny didn't think it was. Not for a moment.

He moved back to the folder, where the printed words continued. He read them out now, almost revelling in it.

'O1 is a twice convicted *paedophile*. His previous offending is for possession of indecent images of children including examples of the highest grading of indecent image.' Danny looked up to make eye contact again. 'Marcus Olsen the Paedophile,' he spat. He went back to reading: 'The wider investigation evidenced that he sought to identify a target who could give access to a number of further victims, behaviour that is similar to what we have found with V1 through V5 in this instance.' Danny continued, 'There is a period of four years between O1's release from prison following his second conviction and his first contact with V1. It is highly likely that there was other offending in this time. Marcus Olsen's behaviour suggests a prolific and committed sex offender whose impact on his victims has been so severe that a number have

34

opted to end their life. Further, it is apparent from his manipulation, specifically in the case of V5, that he actively seeks to groom his victims, then attempts to coerce them to end their own lives, thus removing the traces of his offending.' Danny ran ahead over the next sentence and had to pause to take it in. He swallowed a couple of times, he wanted to read this bit out loud, but it was like his throat had tightened. He fixed on the man tied down in front of him, then broke away to force the words through gritted teeth. 'In the case of V5, it is known that O1 sourced the tablets that V5 used in her suicide attempt.'

Danny laid the folder back flat on the chair, his movements deliberate and slow. He peered around again, then held his breath for as long as he could. He wanted to stop for a moment, to think, but also to listen, to be sure that he was alone. They had never worked out where Callie had got the concoction of drugs from. There's legislation to prevent the sale of Paracetamol in toxic amounts – a fifteen-year-old shouldn't be able to buy a single one. The police had still done enquiries anywhere she could have got them from. The doctors had been able to reverse the affects of the painkillers but the Paracetamol caused an acute liver injury which meant she had needed to be kept unconscious. The ventilator keeping her alive had then caused pneumonia in her lungs and they'd nearly lost her. He'd nearly lost her. And he still might.

Now all he could hear was the man opposite, his breathing heavy and erratic. He was sucking in shallow breaths like he was panicking. They fuelled another sound from his throat, a moan perhaps, whatever he could manage.

'You need to be QUIET!' Shouting, Danny found himself standing straighter; the ferocity ripped at his throat, freeing up some fluid that he had to spit out. It moved him forward too, closer to Marcus Olsen. He waited, forcing the man to lock eyes with him, which he did but just for a moment. Then the man's eyes angled down and Danny followed their

35

trajectory to see where he was looking. He felt his face twist into a wide smile.

'Didn't even know I'd done that.' Marcus Olsen was staring at the shotgun, specifically where Danny's right index finger now rested against the trigger while his left hand had taken hold of the stubby barrel close to where it met his lips, like he might be holding it steady. He focused on the feeling of the trigger against his finger. It had some slack in it. He pulled it back until there was resistance. Suddenly he felt good; powerful. This man was at his mercy. Exactly as he should be.

'Shall we see if there's anything else in there? Maybe there's another page explaining how this was all a terrible mistake after all!' Danny used his left hand to scoop it back up. The next page was a different format. It was made up of screen-shots from typed conversations involving his daughter. Callie's words were labelled with her name this time, and every time he read it he felt himself grimace. He had to step back and straighten up to be able to breathe, letting go of the weapon in the process.

The messages laid bare his daughter's desperation. She was asking to be left alone – begging. Begging for nothing to be done with the photos and videos she had sent. Begging that her parents would not be told. The conversation with 'Sophie Cummings' was shown too. Callie's desperation was even clearer here. She was more candid; it was clear she trusted this person. And why shouldn't she? She believed they had a connection – two women going through the same trauma. Danny turned the page. There was only one message on here. It showed the last exchange between Callie and Sophie Cummings. The final reply stood out behind yellow highlighter:

Kill yourself, Callie.

It was dated 3 January. A day that would always be etched in his memory. The day his fifteen-year-old daughter had

36

silently taken a taxi to a park she loved, where Danny had pushed her on the swings as a baby. And their lives were changed for ever.

Danny paused to fix again on the man responsible. After all this time, here he was. Helpless. Vulnerable. Danny must have blocked everything out completely because he was suddenly aware that the man was shaking his head and moaning. Danny was sure he would be calling for mercy, begging to be left alone.

Just like Callie had.

Danny turned to the last page of the folder. It was a note addressed to him directly. He skimmed it but nothing was going in, not anymore. He threw the whole folder aside. The slap as it hit the ground this time barely registered, like the room had suddenly filled with water to deaden the sound. The man had become still too and now stared straight at Danny.

'You know who I am, don't you?' Danny said. 'Callie . . . She's my daughter. I should be angry.' Danny had to stop, to swallow hard a couple of times and lubricate his throat to continue. 'For a moment I thought it was going to come, but I just can't *feel* anything. I haven't for a while. It's like Callie took that ability with her, the moment she slumped over on that bench it was gone. If she doesn't wake up I don't think I will either. But the one thing I can feel is scared. I'm terrified *every single day*. And then I feel guilty, it's crushing, like I only want her to wake up for me, for my sake. And you know what, that's true, because I want *us*, I want the family that I had . . . my family.' He swallowed again. 'It was everything. But now it's like one of the limbs has gone numb and we're just waiting for it to come back so we can move again. But she might not come back. Not like she was, not ever. So we might have to find a way to move on without her and I'm so terrified that we won't. That I won't. But maybe that's what this is.' Danny took a step forward and, through the numbness, he felt the butt of the weapon bump him in the chest.

37

He moved his right hand in to take up the slack in the trigger, revelling again in the feeling of the metal pushing back. 'Maybe this is how we move on.'

The man made a sound again, the loudest yet, a guttural moan from the back of his throat – begging.

Danny pulled the trigger.

Chapter 5

Thursday

6.30 a.m. Cold, fresh. An electric-blue sky merging with a frigid blue ocean. Gentle, lapping waves pushing clacking pebbles, the call of a gull and the smell of its prey. An assault on each of the senses but Danny Evans was numb to it all.

'Morning!' A passing jogger. Dover's promenade was steady with them. Each trying to get their exercise in before the day started. Danny would do the same in the off-season; he always felt better about a day that started with a run. But not today. He hadn't slept, not a wink. Hadn't even tried. He had gone back to the final page in the folder. It had been instructions for him, a short word on what should happen next. The only part that had sunk in was that he needed to leave and the rest would be sorted. *Sorted?* He didn't even know what that meant. He had watched enough cop shows to have a guess: Cleaned up, wiped down, dismantled. The body dumped where it would never be found. *The body dumped!*

He was a murderer.

He had left quickly, still in a haze of confusion that was made worse when there wasn't the release he had expected. He hadn't felt elated or happy or free. He thought he knew all about revenge, he had thought about it enough, but revenge

39

isn't an emotion, it's an act, and he hadn't considered what should follow.

It just felt like nothing.

And he was still terrified, only now he was scared that no one had done anything since he had left that place last night. That the scene he had hurried away from was still there. Marcus Olsen had barely moved when he had pulled that trigger, the tethers were too strong and tight for that. But the back of his head had. Most of it was missing. A large volume of his blood had moved as well, thrown against the wall behind him to drip and run down over the scars left by the shot.

And now Danny was surrounded by the beauty of an early morning by the sea, with cheery joggers wishing him a good day like he was one of them: a normal member of society. But he wasn't. Everything had changed.

He turned away from the sun rising over the water to make his way to his car. He felt drawn back to that building site; he could barely picture what it might look like in the daylight. The only image he could conjure now was of a brilliant white wall with streaks of different shades of red running down it. He didn't know what he could do there, he knew he should stay away, but he just wanted to see it.

The traffic was light. Danny used the same one-way system he had used the previous night. The boarded shopfronts were somehow more melancholy in the daylight. London Road took him to the outskirts where bookies, second-hand furniture stores and takeaways seemed to repeat in a three-shop pattern. The site for a snooker club where he had spent much of his youth drifted past on his left and as he rounded a corner created by the emergence of the River Dour he could see cars parked tightly together, each of their windscreens showing their asking price in a bold font – the place he had bought his first car. This was a town of memories for him, the place he had grown up, the place he had become someone: the local lad captaining the local football team.

40

Now he would have to add another memory.

He slowed as he passed the paper mill. The gate he had walked through appeared on his left. This was where he had killed a man.

Despite it being just before 7 a.m. there was some activity. A white van had pulled just inside the gates and two men hung near it, both clutching their breakfasts in distinctive takeaway bags. Beyond them he could see three other people in high-visibility vests. They were further into the site, closer to the back, closer to the house he had left. It was the only snapshot Danny could get as he rolled past but it was a snapshot of normality.

A petrol station was next on his left and he pulled in and stepped out into the cold. He kept his head down as he walked away from his car and onto the pavement, back towards the site. The white van had been moved, it was still close to the entrance but now it was side-on and its livery identified the occupants as electricians. The same men were still by it, their drinks steaming visibly. Danny was close enough to catch a snippet of the conversation: 'Lost the power to the lighting on the site again. Fucking rats just like last time. They come out the river and chew the shit out of the place! I tell you what, son, don't be putting your Maccy Dee's down for a fucking moment!' The man doing the talking laughed too loud as he slapped his mate, then laughed louder still as he caused his friend to slosh his coffee. Then the loudmouth swung his arm dramatically up towards the floodlight. 'Soon get 'em up and running, boys, just as soon as you pull your fingers out your arse!'

Danny couldn't slow his pace any more and he was soon out of earshot. He couldn't be sure which house he had entered overnight, just that it was down the far end, facing the entrance. All the front doors were shut now. Someone must have closed it after him. He remembered how he had left in a panic, sprinting back across the yard. There was no way he had

41

stopped to close the front door. But someone had, otherwise they would know by now. Everyone would know. They would have been drawn to an open front door, they would have seen what he had done and this place would surely be overrun with police.

Danny crossed the road to double back to his car, picking up his pace as he did. He needed to leave. He shouldn't have come back.

Chapter 6

Joel Norris saw the first shot coming a mile off. He was already twisting from his hips, throwing one shoulder back so it flashed across his vision, rising all the time. It was fired from the floor, right where his own weapon was now pointing. He got two shots off quickly, hitting with both, and then he turned to the sound of more assailants. Too many. He took hits to the chest and legs. Another shot flashed across his face to fill his vision with red.

His chest plate shook violently while his gun vibrated in his hand with a noise like a 1980s computer game. He locked eyes with his six-year-old daughter – she was across the corridor, concealed in the shadow of a sunken cubby. He could just make out her shaking head.

'What?' he remonstrated. 'You can't hide there the whole game!'

'Don't talk to me!' she hissed back. Too late. While his laser pack reset, the blue team pushed past him, hunting for the enemy he had been conversing with. His daughter put up a good fight. Angry red flashes burst from the cubby while she moved and dodged as best she could with her left hand stretching across her sensor to improve her odds. She took at least four out before her own pack shook and flashed where

43

a shot had finally got through. She huffed then stomped down the corridor. Joel took a few steps after her, his head lifting to the sound of a klaxon. The game was over.

'You did great!' Joel said as the house lights illuminated a sulky six-year-old fiddling with the straps of her chest plate. She'd already ditched the laser gun on the bench next to her.

'You said you were trained!' his daughter retorted. 'That's what you said. You're too big and you're too slow!' His daughter was finally free of the equipment. She ditched it on the bench next to her gun and made for the exit.

'Are you not staying for the scores?' Joel called after her as she pushed the door to reveal his wife standing on the other side, her face in a grin that quickly dropped away. She raised her eyes to look beyond their furious daughter as she stomped past. Joel just had time to shrug before the door fell back shut. He was laughing hard too as he waited for the scores. They were given out by a spotty youth who did an obvious double-take at the thirty-nine-year-old, strongly built man with closely shaved hair struggling to free himself from where the strap of the largest backpack caught on his bicep. When Joel did get himself free, he moved to tower over the kids, his hand out for his Laser Quest score sheet. He didn't care what the lad thought; raising two daughters would strip you of that concern very quickly.

The soft-play centre he exited into was a cacophony of white noise cut up by the shrill screams of a million kids. It was half-term week and packed. Joel made for a table in the café area. His wife had already sat back down. Six-year-old Abigail Norris was sitting down too, which was just as well, since standing up would have her in danger of tripping over her bottom lip. She was making an effort not to look at him.

'Where's Daisy?' Joel asked after the missing eight-year-old that made his family complete.

44

'She found a couple of schoolmates and I haven't seen her since.' Michelle Norris suddenly looked very serious. 'I hear you let the whole team down in there, Daddy?' She was containing a smile but her brown eyes had a sparkle that gave her away.

'So it would seem. We won, though!' He wafted a sheet towards Abigail, who still wouldn't look at him.

'Did you get our sweet little six-year-old girl shot?'

'Only a little bit!'

Abigail suddenly got up out of her seat and walked round to sit sideways in her mother's lap. The bottom lip was even more prominent when it reappeared and she made sure she was facing away from her big, slow dad. Joel couldn't stop himself from laughing.

His joy dropped away quickly.

Beyond his wife's wide grin and against the backdrop of constant movement and excitement, a police officer stood still. She wore a crisp-looking uniform: a white shirt tucked into pleated trousers over shiny shoes. A hat too, with a rim that shimmered as it reflected the pulsing Laser Quest sign behind where he now sat.

'What's the matter?' Michelle's voice cut through the noise.

'Nothing, hon. Did you want another tea? I'd better get this one a peace offering.' He forced a smile towards his daughter but was already moving away. The policewoman had folded her hands across her chest as if she was at ease. Now she opened them and let them fall by her sides as Joel got closer.

'Tell me you're not here for me on my daughter's birthday,' he growled.

'That's how you know it's important, Detective Inspector Norris.'

Joel gritted his teeth at the use of his work title. Today was about being a father and a husband. He wasn't due to be an Inspector again until Monday morning.

45

'More important than my family? We might disagree on that, *superintendent*.'

'We have an opportunity.' Superintendent Debbie Marsden always seemed to be filled with intensity, today even more so than usual.

Joel glanced at where Michelle still sat with her back to them, her shoulders rounded where she had their daughter wrapped in a hug.

'Is it an opportunity to destroy my marriage, ma'am? You've made a strong start. Would you mind?' He gestured for the conversation to continue somewhere they would be out of sight. Marsden followed as Joel led her behind where a kitchen area jutted out.

'How on earth did you find me here?'

'I'm a police officer. A resourceful one at that, Joel. I can still find people.'

'Someone squealed me up!'

'Your neighbour – the one who was out cleaning his car in the freezing cold. Apparently your daughter told him how you were taking her "shooting lasers". Is that appropriate for a little girl's birthday?'

The superintendent was naturally a stern woman, tall and broad and built for strength. She wasn't assigned a specific department or area manager; instead she was tasked with finding efficiency improvements across the whole force. It was a tough job – stripped to its basics, her role was to travel round the county challenging the norm and upsetting those working under it. Debbie Marsden certainly had the right skillset. Now, somehow, he found himself at the centre of her latest project but was still some way from being convinced that it was a good place to be.

'Appropriate? She's brilliant at it!' Joel waved the score sheet that was still in his hand. 'Top scorer for the yellow team! And damned near the top player in the whole thing. She scares me a little bit, if I'm honest.'

46

'Impressive.'

'It is. And I should get back to her.'

'We need to bring this project forward, Joel. As I said, we have an opportunity.'

'Project!' Joel said. The word tickled him, like it softened what they were doing. The project in question was messing with the current setup within Major Crime for Kent. Currently each division had its own Major Crime department covering investigations on their patch. Ma'am Marsden's latest efficiency proposal was a centralised team based out of Headquarters who could travel where they were needed. Part of her proposal had included a description of Major Crime departments as finding themselves 'sitting idle waiting for death'. Detectives working in that area of the business would be well used to focusing on the details and Joel could only imagine their reaction to the word 'Idle'.

'We have a body washed up on a beach down in Dover. Sus circs.'

'Sus how?' Joel asked. 'We get a fair few suicides down there, don't we?'

'We do. Not too many with the head missing.'

That caught Joel out a little. 'And do we have any reported missing? Lost property is recorded separate, sometimes it can be overlooked . . .'

'I thought you wanted to get back to your wife and daughter, Joel. Now's hardly the time to be cracking funnies.'

'I do. Only I'm getting this feeling that I'm about to be sent to the beach and not in a family-outing-with-an-ice-cream kinda way, more poking a dead thing with a stick.'

'The local CID are already in attendance; their DS spoke to me from the scene. They called it sus and were looking to hand it over. The east division Major Crime would have to take it on but they weren't exactly champing at the bit so I got in there and told them not to bother.'

'Major Crime didn't want it?'

47

'Whether they wanted it or not wouldn't have mattered; it was coming their way. It's just not a sexy murder, you know what I mean?'

'I reckon I do.' Joel did, in the way only a police officer can possibly understand how a murder can be described as 'sexy'.

'Well, it's not some pretty teenage girl with trophies hacked off and a crucifix burnt into her chest, there's no media outcry or bawling parents and certainly no commendation or book deal at the end of it. This is why I think it will be perfect for us. By all accounts it's some sad loser with no real friends and a million potential enemies. The DS will give you a far more detailed brief, of course.'

'Perfect for *me*, you mean?'

Marsden seemed to hesitate for the first time. 'That is what I mean, but if you don't think you're up to it . . .' She faded out. She wasn't very good at this. Joel had been off for just under a month for something he had been forced to categorise as *stress*. It was the first time he could recall taking more than a day off for anything and it had caught everyone by surprise – no one more than him.

'I'm fine. I'm raring to get back.'

'Of course you are. And this way you get to experience leading a murder investigation without the scrutiny. This is just the sort of thing I was waiting for to kick this whole thing off.'

Joel was rubbing at his face, and the superintendent picked up on it. 'What's the matter?' she said.

'I mean, I agree with you, Ma'am, this is the sort of thing that will be ideal for me and my team . . . but I don't have a team. Our last conversation was about how I was going to be shadowing the next murder investigation. Is this not it?'

'Well, yes, it is. But there's been a change of plan.'

'With respect, Ma'am, the old plan made sense.'

'Now it isn't possible. My colleague on the SLT who has

48

overall responsibility for Major Crime is not supportive of you tagging along. Seems we either take the job or not. I did tell you this would be a political animal.'

It seemed to Joel that everything was political when it came to the Senior Leadership Team. 'You know how resource-intensive an investigation like this can be. Who are my foot soldiers?'

'The sergeant who is on scene now has a list of fast-track actions. He also has a team of DCs at his disposal to be getting through them. I have made it clear that they are to continue to be at your disposal moving forward.'

'CID are busy, bursting at the seams even.'

'They are. But having spoken to the DS down there now I can tell you another thing: they're bursting to be given the opportunity to work on something like this. What would you rather do, a shitty domestic, a no-hope burglary report, or getting your teeth into a murder investigation led by a char-ismatic and committed new DI?'

'You missed out gullible.'

'Did I? I won't do that again.' She smiled. Joel couldn't quite muster the same. 'Look, I'm on hand for what you need and when you need it. I've already tipped off the Force Resource Unit that we might need to pull detectives or uniform coppers onto this so they can start setting something aside. I can secure an overtime budget if it's needed but for now you just need to see what we have. Is there anything else you think you need right now?'

The superintendent was still smiling.

'You want me to go now? On my daughter's birthday?'

'No! Goodness no. All the actions you would expect are in hand. CSI haven't even attended yet; the scene's being held by uniform . . . This is handled until at least tomorrow morning.'

'Tomorrow morning?'

'Absolutely! You could even take the weekend, get the offi-cial handover on Monday. The CID team who have been

49

running the investigation are on until Tuesday. Now then . . .' The superintendent brought her phone out to fiddle with it. 'I've just sent you the contact details for the DS on scene so you can make contact with him tonight if you want to.'

'Tonight?' Joel was aware he was now smiling.

'I know what you're like, Joel. I thought you might want the option. But for now you should get back to your thing.'

'My daughter's birthday,' Joel reminded her.

'Exactly that. Anything else you need right now?'

'Joel?' Joel heard his wife call. She was standing among the throng with her hands on her hips, seemingly taking in the superintendent from head to toe before fixing back on him. 'Are you coming back? We're doing the cake. Now.' She didn't wait for an answer. Joel sighed towards his boss.

'Maybe a marriage counsellor,' he said.

50

Chapter 7

'Hey! Good to see you!' Danny said, managing to muster the strength to greet his wife. It was 10 a.m. and he was back holding Callie's hand at her bedside. Sharon was usually at the hospital at this time and his slot was either first thing or later in the day. It had somehow become an acceptable routine for them both. But today Danny had found himself yearning for a friendly face – his wife's specifically.

'You look tired, Danny,' Sharon said, skipping the niceties. He still hadn't slept. He had hoped the cold shower and coffee had removed the exhaustion from his face. 'You're not normally here at this time either.'

'And that's ridiculous, isn't it? We're her parents, we should be here together. You made sure of it yesterday, I'm making sure of it today.' Danny tried even harder to sound bright and alert.

'I don't think she's too aware who's here or when at the moment,' Sharon said.

'We don't know that for sure, and I meant for us. Constantly coming here separately makes no sense to me. We're both struggling, we should at least have each other.'

'Have each other?'

Danny tutted, coffee always makes him talk fast. He still

51

wasn't thinking straight either. It was a bad combination. 'I don't mean . . . just that we still need to be there for each other, even if it's just a day a week. I know I need it sometimes, you must too?' He stopped, waiting for her reply, knowing that he was starting to sound desperate and out of character.

'Are you OK? You seem a little . . . amped. You're not on anything, are you . . .?'

'NO! No . . . sorry, no. Coffee, that's all. I've not been sleeping. I know I've not been dealing with this very well. I know that's made it worse for you, for Jamie. I know that. But we're a family and families do better when they go through shit like this together. That's all I mean.'

'They should do, sure.' Sharon pulled the bag that had been held tight to her side off her shoulder, like she had finally decided she was staying. Her expression turned to surprise when a tear dripped from Danny's eye. He had hastily sniffed to try and stop it.

'Jesus, Danny! It's OK! Hey, come on . . .' She stepped up to him, her arms out for an embrace. He jerked away with an involuntary hiss when she pressed against the bruising on his lower chest where the butt of a shotgun had kicked back at him a matter of hours earlier.

'What? What did I do?' Sharon still had her arms out as her eyes hunted down his body.

'Nothing! Sorry, I got another ingrowing toenail is all. It catches against my shoe sometimes.' She stepped back in. This time he was prepared and able to twist to be slightly side-on. There was no pain. His chin rested on her shoulder, her hair smelt familiar, it was all familiar. 'I miss you,' he said, his voice breaking.

'I miss you too. This would put pressure on anyone. It's just about what you let that pressure do.' She pushed him away gently but kept hold of his arms like she was sizing him up.

'Are you eating OK? I swear there's less to hug!'

The look of concern on her face was genuine and suddenly

52

Danny wanted to tell her everything. About last night, about what he had done, about what was starting to eat him up inside. He had killed a man. But he dismissed it. He couldn't tell her. Despite what Marcus Olsen was and what he had done, Danny knew his wife, he knew that she would never agree with his actions. Danny wasn't sure that he did himself anymore.

'Hotel food. You know, it's all a bit beige. I pick at it.' Danny said.

'You fancy something home-cooked? With Jamie?' she asked.

Danny nodded and had to seal his mouth tightly shut to hold back another sob. Right now he couldn't think of anything he wanted to do more. 'That would be great.'

'Tonight?'

'Okay then.' His words were rushed, he couldn't leave any room for his emotion to spill out.

'No beer. Not before, not during,' Sharon said. The warmth was still present but there was steel to her words.

'Or after. I'm off that, OK. I don't need it anymore!'

'One step at a time, Danny. Just be on your best behaviour tonight. Jamie will be delighted to see you but you can't let him down like last time, not again.'

'I know that.' Danny held his breath to quell the emotion this time. 'Maybe we can get back to being a family, Sharon, maybe we can get back to that.'

'One step at a time, like I said. Nothing's changed, OK. I just don't like to see you upset.'

Danny nodded. He wiped his face, suddenly embarrassed. 'I think something has changed – for me, I mean.'

Sharon's smile was the first genuine one she had given him for months. 'I hope you're right, I really do.'

53

Chapter 8

Joel stepped out into his garden and instantly wished he had added another layer to his jumper and jeans. He glanced back, still unable to shake the feeling that he was sneaking out for an illicit phone call even though his wife had okayed it. She'd listened to his summary of the conversation with his superintendent and recognised that it would require some action on his part.

Michelle was being supportive – just like she always was – but that wasn't something Joel wanted to be testing. She knew him better than anyone, knew how passionate he could be about his job, but she had also seen first-hand how destructive that could be. He knew she was worried about him, about his return to work, and it had been made worse by his inability to assure her that he wasn't worried too.

Even now, standing out in the cold, he knew he was hesitating, putting off making the call that would suck him back into the world of policing. He had never considered it could be a world that would overwhelm him – not like that – leaving him shaken to the core, his confidence lost, his mind a thick fog of confusion. The Job had rallied around him, the bosses, his team too, but he had eyed every one of those initial contacts with suspicion. He knew that people love a

54

drama, they love it when someone else falls apart, especially someone like him – the Tactical Support Group Sergeant with 'ten years of breaking doors and busting heads' as stated on the card his team had got him, to mark his decade leading them.

Joel's application for the Inspector's exam had been the very next day. Ma'am Marsden was on the final interview panel that had later ratified his promotion and, unknown to him, was already sizing him up for a brand-new role. He had agreed almost offhand, without any consideration for the size of the task of moving from the sergeant of the TSG to an investigative DI, and why would he? At that time, he genuinely thought he could do anything.

It was just a few days later when everything he thought he knew about himself was to be tipped upside down. Now, when he lifted the phone to his ear, he was riddled with something that had become a new familiar: doubt.

'Hello?' The phone was answered almost straightaway.

'DS Andrews?' Joel said.

'Yes. You must be Inspector Norris. Ma'am Marsden warned me you would be calling.'

'Good to hear. Did she say what for?'

'An update, as best as I have at least.'

'What do you have?'

'A body. And for once I can say that quite literally. It would appear something's removed the head.'

'Something?'

'CSI say a "jagged instrument". I took that to mean a saw rather than the edge of a piano.'

'I think you're probably right.'

'And boss, it doesn't look like it was mechanical, that is, not a chainsaw or a disc cutter. It's a real mess . . . Someone did it by hand and it took a while. That's significant, isn't it?'

Joel took a moment. 'I think it must be.'

'CSI explained in great detail how difficult that is, how

55

determined you would need to be to saw a man's head off . . . It takes a certain sort of person to work CSI, doesn't it?' There was nervous laughter.

'It certainly does. So, someone was very upset with our victim, upset enough to go to a lot of unnecessary effort.'

'Unnecessary?'

Joel used his free hand to rub at his face. He turned back towards his house to look through the large glass doors and straight into his kitchen, to where his youngest daughter had appeared, spinning and dancing with a balloon trailing from her hand. Even from here he could see the joy on her face. The colours were vivid under bright lights and she stood out on a gloomy day. He was very much back in this world now – back in with both feet.

'If you're sawing up a body it's normally for practical reasons. To hide it, transport it, make it easier to get rid of. This sounds more symbolic,' Joel said.

'They certainly didn't do a good job at hiding it. Our offender must have pushed the body into the sea when the tide was coming in. It might have taken it along the coast a little but it's always going to end up washing back up on the beach. It wasn't in the water for long.'

'The mistake of an amateur or he was meant to be found?' Joel was thinking out loud, and the DS must have recognised this as he ignored the question.

'CSI put his prints through the lantern and they came straight back. He's known to us.'

'Go on?'

'Marcus Olsen. Convicted paedophile.'

'That gives us a possible motive. What were his convictions?'

'Possession of images only, but he was convicted on two separate occasions.'

'Contact offences?'

'None.'

'Any named victims?'

56

'Not that I can find, but that's not unusual for indecent images.'

'It's not.'

'But his conviction would have been public knowledge. We found a piece in the archives of a local newspaper. The article was also shared on social media and there are any number of comments suggesting various parts of him that should be removed. Maybe someone took that literally.'

'Maybe. But if you're looking for a child abuser to hack to pieces there are plenty more in the public domain with far worse offending. Marcus Olsen must have been chosen for a more personal reason.'

'And there lies the key.' DS Andrews sighed as he spoke. Joel detected exhaustion in it.

'Do you have much more to do today?'

'A fair bit. I'm still at the scene, just waiting for CSI to finish with the body so one of my guys can accompany it to the morgue. Then I've got some writing to do. I've had my team doing some work on the victim back at the office and from the last update they haven't been able to find an obvious next of kin. The intelligence around him is pretty typical for a sex offender: looks like a bit of a loner, moved away from West Kent when he received some low-level threats, not known to the police for any other reasons. I'm waiting for Child Protection to come back to me with anything more but he's still being managed by West Kent. I'll chase that up tomorrow.'

'Threats? What was that about?'

'Two separate intel reports, both around the time he was doing the rounds on social media three years ago. Graffiti on the door of his flat and shouted insults on the street. No offenders. We'll go through his list of associates. I want to talk to as many as I can to find out if anyone has spoken to him recently. Maybe he talked about a more serious threat.'

'Maybe. Sounds like a good idea.'

'Ma'am Marsden . . . she said you're not back 'til Monday. She wants me to run this until then . . .'

57

'Monday officially. I'm hoping to come in over the weekend and I'm on the end of the phone for you and your team. I know it's not ideal.'

'It's fine, really. The boss . . . she told me you were just coming back, so . . .'

Joel could tell just from his tone that she had added a few more details in than that. 'Like I said, I'll be in over the weekend. It would be useful if there was something for me to read through.'

'I'll update the log with everything we have so far when I get back in. Anything more that comes in will be on there. I'll make sure you have access. Is there anything you want done that I haven't mentioned?'

'Not at all, sounds like you have it all under control.'

'Do I?' DS Andrews now emitted a nervous laugh. 'Not bad for my first murder investigation then.'

Joel didn't think this was the right time to announce it was his too. He opted for 'I'm on the phone if you need me' instead.

'I'll try not to.'

Joel ended the call and started back towards his house and the family he could see within it. The first call was done but still he couldn't shake a nagging feeling.

Maybe he wasn't ready.

DS Andrews was glad to finish the call; cold gusts of wind were sweeping in unabashed off the English Channel and had been biting at his exposed hands. Now he pushed them into the warmth of his coat pocket.

'That the SIO?' a woman's voice asked, sternly enough to cut through the wind rather than be carried. Sandra Allum – Kent's most senior CSI officer and a familiar face at the more serious crimes.

'So it would seem.'

'Is he coming out? Only we're just about ready to go here.' She stood straighter from where she had been stooped over

58

the headless corpse of Marcus Olsen. He had been watching her wrap the hands and feet in clear plastic ready for transportation when his phone had rung, even managing to smile at her quip about how their victim had been kind enough to save her the job of wrapping up the head too. She had laid out a white body bag, using the smooth pebbles of St Margaret's beach to hold it down. The backdrop was Dover's famous white cliffs, the dramatic chunk of white even more brilliant due to a recent chalk slip that had taken any stains or patches of moss with it. Huge chalk boulders were now gathered at the bottom of the cliff to be constantly prodded and probed by the movement of a curious sea. There was a pub too: the aptly named Coastguard, the landlord of which had been kind enough to offer a temporary injection of warmth via a coffee cup in exchange for an opportunity to pump him for information on what the tide had brought in. The initial find had drawn a clump of people who had gathered in the car park, but only a few hardy souls now remained. The crowd had thinned noticeably when the landlord was sent away with nothing new to report.

On another day this was a beautiful place. Today, DS Andrews was waiting for the inevitable request to help with lifting a soaked and bloody corpse into the zip-up body bag. And in the freezing cold.

'He's not coming out, no. He doesn't start back until Monday officially. Seems I'll be running it until then.'

'Stitch-up?' He could still detect Sandra's grin, despite the mask and hood covering most of her face.

DS Andrews shrugged. 'Beats reviewing crime reports, I suppose.'

'Why choose an SIO on leave?' she said.

'He's not on leave. Stress apparently . . . Bad reaction to a job and that was that.'

Sandra was squatting back down to fidget with the body bag, the wind was still arriving in unpredictable gusts that

59

looked capable of unsettling the pebbles. The last thing anyone wanted was to give the car park spectators the image of a foot chase with a body bag. Already she had taken down the tent, confident that the incline of the beach was shielding them enough for this last part. She stopped what she was doing to look up now.

'And he's coming back to this?' she said.

'He is. He's a TSG skipper too, I don't think he's an investigator by trade. Just promoted.'

'And he's coming back to this!' Sandra said again. 'What genius made that call?' DS Andrews shrugged again. 'Talking of genius, I've met a few of the TSG skippers on searches, rarely a clever one.'

'They are generally a type.'

'What's his name?'

'Norris. Joel Norris.'

Sandra shook her head. 'The name does ring a bell. No doubt we've crossed paths but I can't say I have an opinion.'

'Bit of an unknown entity then. He was saying all the right things on the phone.'

'So, not an idiot?'

'I never said that. He could still be an idiot, just one that's read the *Murder Investigation Manual*. He won't be getting much help either. The impression I got from Major Crime was that they're letting him fall on his sword.'

Sandra shifted her weight, clearly struggling to get a firm base on the shifting pebbles. She took hold of the bagged-up feet. 'In my experience that tends to happen very quickly. This is big-boy stuff.' She flicked her head towards the torso. 'Cop hold of the other end, would you? Let's get this bagged up. And get your gloves and mask back on first. Just 'cause an amateur's taking over, doesn't mean we don't do our bit right.'

Chapter 9

Jamie was getting big. It had only been a couple of weeks since Danny had seen him last but it was enough for the change to be noticeable.

'You need a new shirt, I reckon. That's a bit tight on you now.'

His son was wearing an old football shirt. A replica of the last Gillingham shirt Danny had played in, two seasons ago, just before he had come back to Dover Athletic like some sort of returning hero. The first season back he had done OK, but the second season was a frustration of niggling injuries and he'd spent a lot of time on the sidelines. Danny had never dealt well with not playing. It made him feel useless and this time it was mixed up with the realisation that, at nearly thirty-seven, his playing days could soon be coming to an end. He was moody, unapproachable and distant. Even towards his children. He had spent the last few months before Callie's suicide attempt facing inwards at his own problems without even considering that anyone else might be suffering. Callie had been desperate for someone to talk to, for someone to take notice of her life and what she was going through. He knew that now; the material in that folder had made that clear.

61

'Know anyone who can get me one?' Jamie grinned. His voice snapped Danny's mind back to the present and he mirrored the grin while ruffling his son's hair because he knew he hated it.

They sat to eat. Danny in the seat that faced out into the garden, Sharon to his left, Jamie right in front and the family dog Zinedine in his usual position staring directly at Danny from a few paces away on the floor. His look was willing every morsel of food to be diverted. Zinedine was Jamie's dog really. A French Bulldog, hence he had chosen to name it after a true great of French football. A squat little thing, ears and appetite far too big for the rest of him but with a lovely temperament. Danny wouldn't admit it, but he missed 'Zee' almost as much as he missed his wife and kids.

Danny did his best to ignore the dog as they talked about school and work and laughed about grandparents. There was pudding too, then a black coffee just when Danny could feel his body starting to crash. Maybe Sharon had picked up on the yawns he had fought to conceal. Jamie stayed up the whole time. It wasn't so long ago that he would have slunk back to his bedroom at the earliest opportunity. They talked about his studies at school, Danny teased him about girls and being the man of the house and then, inevitably, conversation moved to football. Jamie was now captain of the Under 14s and he was visibly bursting to tell his dad. Danny did nothing to hide his delight, sweeping his son up in a big hug that turned into a headlock where he took another opportunity to mess up his hair – *getting a bit above your station now you're captain, are we?* Father and son soon ended up a crumpled, laughing heap on the floor with Zee licking at any exposed skin he could reach. Even Sharon was beaming when they finally made it back to their seats, both breathing heavily. Everything was almost like when it was good.

Except for the empty place at the table.

They didn't talk about Callie. Not about where she was, not about what had happened, no hollow talk about the first thing they would do as a family when she woke up. She came up in conversation only when Jamie referenced her – 'remember when me and Callie . . .' But that was all. Maybe this was what it was like to move on. Maybe this was what a normal mealtime could look like moving forward. Maybe Danny had made *normal* possible. For himself at least.

But he had *killed* a man.

This was the realisation that cut short his laughter when Jamie was goofing around near the end of the evening, refusing to go to bed. It had taken a fireman's carry in the end, and another reminder of his son's size. With Jamie dumped on his bed they resurrected a handshake that had once been a night-time ritual taken for granted but now made Danny ache to stay even more. Instead he bade his son goodnight and put his shoes on by the front door while Sharon and Zee watched in silence. She stood with her arms crossed but gave a good-humoured smile when Danny hopped to keep his balance with one shoe on. When he was done she stepped in to kiss him – a quick peck on the cheek – then a promise to see him soon and the beginnings of a twinkle in her smile.

'Maybe I could stay?' The moment Danny said the words the twinkle evaporated and he wished he could gather them back up again, like they had never happened.

'I . . . you know . . . we need to be careful what we're telling Jamie.'

'I wasn't going to tell him anything. His dad slept on the sofa, he'll see that for himself, and I just thought . . . I just thought we could have breakfast.'

'I know but . . . the message that sends. It's just not the right time, not now.'

'You're right. I've had a nice night. I guess I didn't want it to end.'

'Good night, Danny.' Sharon held the door open.

63

'I meant on the sofa, you know that, right?'

'I do and I am sorry, OK.'

'Don't be. You're right.'

Danny was back out into a night that had turned cold. The walk away from his house felt more alien than ever. Dinner had been so natural he had almost forgotten the weeks of being anywhere but here.

He pulled his car door open and the light was sudden and bright to illuminate the yellow steering wheel lock wrapped tight round his steering wheel.

'What the hell?' The lock had been a present from his dad who had seen a news item on the ease of stealing new cars, then demanded an unimpressed Danny put the key on his fob. Danny lifted the fob now. The key was still there. Danny had thrown the lock in the boot the moment his dad had left, never to be used again. And yet here it was, gripped tightly round his steering wheel.

Danny looked around. Lydden was a quiet village between Dover and Canterbury and no one was around. No one was ever around. He moved to lift the boot. There were no signs of any damage to any of the locks. The boot was empty. He moved back to the driver's seat and tried the key he had. The lock fell open. A piece of white paper came away to fall into the footwell. Danny opened it.

LAST ORDERS?

The words were handwritten and in the same scratchy style as the note that had tempted him to the paper mill.

Danny took the lock to the boot and lingered for a last glance at his house. His future was here. The last thing he wanted to do was drive away, to leave any of it behind.

'I just want to be back here . . .' he muttered. He didn't want to go back to his hotel and he sure as hell didn't want 'last orders' either.

64

But he could check that last night had gone OK, that it was all done. It would put paid to any anxiety he had.

And then he could focus everything on getting his family back.

Chapter 10

The lank-haired barman looked up when Danny pushed through the door. He stood wiping the bar under a darkened television screen – his routine for closure already well underway.

'Hey!' He stopped his work to call out like he had seen an old friend. 'I wondered what had happened to you! Usual?'

'Just a Coke. Lots of ice,' Danny replied. He paused at the door to take in the drinkers. A man and a woman sat together at the other end of the bar, behind them a partition that marked the start of the area laid out as tables for diners. Part of the closing ritual meant the lights above this area were dimmed to convey the message that the kitchen was shut. You could still sit at the tables though, as demonstrated by a figure seated facing away from where Danny stood at the bar. The seated man had wide shoulders wrapped in a fitted suit. Danny knew that he was supposed to go over and take the seat opposite. Lank hair said something when he placed the glass down on the bar, but Danny ignored him to scoop up the drink and move away.

'Last orders?' Danny said. He stood by the chair opposite the man rather than pulling it out to sit. 'Goes with the image, all this. Sitting in a dark booth and facing away all mysterious. Very *private detective*.'

'Not the choice I expected from you.' The man gestured at Danny's glass of Coke. 'Guess that means I'm drinking alone.'

'Did you break into my car?'

'Is it broken?'

'Did you break into my car?' Danny said again.

'I'm sorry, OK. I needed to get your attention.'

'That's beginning to get boring. You could have just come and spoken to me here. You know where I drink, you know my room.'

'And you might have ignored me. Tonight, at least.'

'I could have ignored the note in my car too.'

'You didn't though. That's what I meant by getting your attention. Over the years I've found the best way to get someone sat down in front of me is actually to piss them off. That doesn't mean I can't be apologetic about my tactics.'

'Who are you?' Danny leaned in and the chair creaked under his palms.

'I said "sat down in front of me". Would you mind? Only you're drawing attention.'

Danny sniffed. He hesitated for just a moment then put his Coke down and pulled the chair out. The man pursed his lips, waiting until Danny was still.

'Thank you. You know who I am. You know I'm a private investigator.'

'That's what you are, not who you are.'

'For some jobs that's the same thing. A bit like being a footballer, I would imagine.'

'You're police then, ex-police at least. That's how you get to be a private investigator, right?'

'I see you've been watching the movies, Mr Evans! It's always some ex-cop who ends up the PI, right? Usually disgraced and with a chip on their shoulder and a talent for martial arts. I've seen those movies too. The real world isn't quite like that. Finance is my background actually. I made a

67

good career out of detecting fraud for a private firm. Turns out there's nothing you can't find out about someone if you can see what they spend their money on.'

'And that's how you found . . .'

'Mr Olsen?' the man cut in enthusiastically and Danny twisted to look around, suddenly very self-aware. 'Yes, that's exactly how I found him. While his actions were almost certainly driven by his own desire he was also making good money out of it. He sold images and videos and he seemed to have the knack of providing what was in demand. I don't think I need to explain any more.' Danny clamped his jaw tightly shut. 'That's difficult to hear, I'm sure. Fortunately, karma, in this instance, was called Danny Evans.'

'Why did you do that?'

'Do what?'

'Set that up like I found it. For me?'

The man seemed to take a moment to consider his answer. 'There were a number of victims, a number of families left in pieces due to the actions of that man and I am sure that any one of them would have appreciated walking into that room and having that . . . opportunity. But when we had all of the information together it was your story that stood out. We saw a young woman lying in a hospital bed having been coerced into taking a fistful of tablets. And then we saw what was left of her family tearing themselves apart as a result. It was an easy decision as to who would be the first in line.'

'We?'

'Yes. I told you I was hired by the family of another victim to find this man. This was a while ago – years – and like you, they were unhappy when the police investigation reached a conclusion without closure, without someone to answer for their suffering. Fortunately, they had the means to ensure it didn't end there. The answers for that family led me to realise he was still very active.'

'So why didn't they walk into that room last night? Why

68

spend money, time and effort looking for vengeance and then serve it up for someone else?'

'You don't think they have their vengeance? The last time I saw Mr Olsen the back of his head was missing. And he sat in that building for a considerable amount of time with the barrel of a shotgun in his mouth. Waiting for you. He knew you were coming. He knew who you were and what that folder would tell you. All he could do was wait. That is a very specific sort of torture, would you not agree?'

'They were pretty certain I was going to do it then? What I did,' Danny said with bitterness in his tone.

The man lowered his glass to reveal a smile. 'We're all fathers, Mr Evans. And if you hadn't, that opportunity would have gone to someone else and he would have waited another day. That outcome was inevitable. I'm glad it was you.'

'That information, the stuff in that folder, where did that all come from? The police had practically nothing at all.'

'They didn't because all they had were the victims. Marcus Olsen was clever, aware of forensic interrogation of electronic devices, and he countered that. But I was able to find him. The source is always a lot more difficult to clean but in truth he wasn't trying anyway. Why would he? He never considered anyone was going to turn up at his door – and when I did I was able to be a lot more . . . persuasive than the police ever can.'

'Persuasive?'

'The shotgun, Mr Evans. The police don't point them in people's faces when they question them, which is a real shame, you can take that from me. People talk more.'

Danny took a moment. The man was making sense; the police had their hands tied by their codes of practice, by what they could and couldn't do. This guy didn't. There was still something nagging him about the whole setup however.

'So, this is nothing about me being some fall guy? This other dude not wanting to get his hands dirty?'

69

'A fair question from a man with twenty-four hours to go over and over what he did. I understand, of course I do. But what you must consider is that it would have been far less risky if the same man who had hired me had also been the one to pull that trigger. The key to staying under the radar in such matters is to control the episode and that means limiting the variables as much as is humanly possible.'

'Variables?'

'I was hired with a very specific intent: locate Mr Olsen in such a way that he could be removed without suspicion. I did as I was asked and I always understood that it would mean I would be complicit in a serious crime. The client and I were locked together in this venture for quite some time. Your involvement was late in the process and up until the moment you pulled that trigger you had neither committed nor instigated any crime. You could have reacted in a number of different ways. You were a variable.'

'How did your client know you wouldn't rat him out? You could have shopped him the moment he asked you.'

'I could. But people use private investigators in this country for a number of reasons. The classic is the suspicious husband who would have me track his wife in order to capture photos of her infidelity, like some voyeur-for-hire. Then there are the commercial enterprises who are losing money to fraudsters or thieves and suspect an inside involvement but have no desire for the damage to a reputation that comes with a police investigation. That was where I started out. Now I work as someone who finds people that either the authorities cannot or, more often these days, where the person hiring me wishes to find the person instead of the police.'

'Instead of the police? Why would you want to do that?'

'You're not a naïve man, Mr Evans. I think you know what I mean. There are plenty of examples of a person wronged by another where the judicial system cannot offer suitable satisfaction. The people that hire me are often looking

70

to find their own form of closure. Something more befitting the crime.'

'Befitting?'

'Take our Mr Olsen. He committed a number of offences and a good police investigation and conviction would have seen a sentence of between twelve to fifteen years in prison. The last time he was convicted on such charges he pled guilty, he was given credit for that and his sentence was reduced. The likelihood is that he would serve less than ten years. Mr Olsen was prolific and determined and he would be released to offend again. The only way to make the world a safer and better place in regards to that man was to take the action you did.'

'And murder him.' *Murder.* The word caught in Danny's throat. He took a hurried swig of his drink, suddenly wishing he had opted for something stronger.

'I don't clear up after murderers.' The man's smile was gone; now there was a determination to his expression and an edge to his voice.

'You did then? Clear up, I mean.' Danny said.

'I'm good at it. You don't need to have any concerns. The layout would have looked rather dramatic, I can imagine, certainly on seeing it for the first time. But much of that was for forensic reasons. The plastic sheeting, the material of the ropes, the positioning of the shotgun; even the shot was more wadding than shot as it's so much easier to collect. It was all designed to allow me a quick exit once you had made yours.'

'But there was so much . . . mess.'

'There was. The client insisted on the shotgun. I tried to talk him into something a little more clinical, a different method entirely in fact, but he wanted terror. He wanted a man to sit in silence and wait for his fate. To wait for you and to know what that fate was going to look like the whole time. What you saw is what I came up with.'

'Where is he? Olsen, I mean?'

71

'You're not a fan of the local news, I see. They have already reported a washed-up body.'

'News? What do you mean?' Danny suddenly sat straighter. The man opposite him reacted by showing his palms.

'Calm down, Mr Evans! It's all exactly as was meant. Again, the client was rather insistent. He wanted him dumped in the sea like a piece of rubbish. Again, I might have had a different idea but it's not a terrible option. It allows for the limitation of forensic opportunities and—'

'The sea! And it's on the news!' Danny spun to look around, to make sure he was still out of earshot. He leaned in anyway, his words now contained within a hiss. 'Don't you take him right out and weigh him down?'

'Back to the movie references?' The man grinned now, wide and smug, and Danny had to resist lashing out at it. His smile was quick to drop away. 'Don't always believe what you see. That means getting hold of a boat, launching it from somewhere, leaving a paper trail, prompting questions . . . and that's before you've found a way to get your cargo on board. Better a quiet stretch of beach and let nature take its course.'

'So there's nothing to link any of this to me?'

'No. Don't forget our fates are now very much tied together. If someone were to look at you they would be one step closer to looking at me and that's the last thing I would want.'

Danny was finally able to relax enough to sit back in his chair. The man opposite him oozed confidence. He gave the impression this wasn't his first time either.

'So, it's over.' Danny let out a long sigh. 'I appreciate you meeting me, putting my mind at rest, letting me in on the bigger picture. I had questions. Last night was just emotions, you know? I got there, I read what there was and I didn't even think. But when that shotgun went off it was like flicking a switch. I knew what I had done and I just needed to get away. I don't want to be worrying about him, he's a piece of

72

shit, he doesn't deserve for anyone to be thinking about him. I just wish he was still rotting on the seabed.'

'I understand.'

Danny patted his thighs and took a final, long swig of his drink. Now the tension was gone he could feel the exhaustion creeping back in. Maybe tonight he would actually be able to get some sleep without needing half a bottle of rum. He had a meeting about his new job in the morning. He could be in good shape for it. For a moment, he flushed with good feelings, like this could be the start of the rest of his life.

'Well then, have a nice life.' Danny stood up.

'There is a little more to this story.' The man stayed seated. The half-smile was back. He rubbed at his facial hair then his arms fell open by his side.

'Is there anything more I need to know?' Danny said, his good feeling leaking away for anxiety to creep back in

'There's a little more you need to do.'

'Do? I would say I was done, wouldn't you? The man . . .' Danny was suddenly aware that he was standing up and talking louder. He surveyed the bar again. There was only one punter left that he could see: an elderly gent who looked to be struggling with rolling a cigarette at the bar. Lank-hair was out of sight completely. 'The man's gone,' Danny hissed.

'He didn't work alone. There's one other who was significant. She was key to a lot of his offending.'

'She? A woman?'

'Happens more than you think. People find people. Think about it, your passion is football, how many of the mates you have now did you meet through that passion? Sex offenders are no different.'

'What, they join clubs, do they? All meet up on a Wednesday night under the floodlights to fiddle with kids?'

'Almost. The internet, Danny, it's changed the world and mostly for the worse. Swap a kickabout then a pint for an online chatroom and an exchange of images, videos or worse.

73

And if your penchant is underage girls or curious boys there's no better ally than a woman. And this woman will definitely not be concerning herself with the loss of contact with Mr Olsen. She will move on quickly and she will be in high demand.'

'Then find her. Do what you do. What do you need me for?'

'I have found her. And now we intend to give you the same opportunity as we did last night.'

Danny actually laughed, but it came out as a snort forced through his nose. 'You want me to . . . again? I appreciate the thought but I think I will pass. I'm done. I got what I needed. Marcus Olsen was it.' Danny turned to move away.

'This was part of the deal, Mr Evans.'

Danny spun on his heels, his voice back to a hiss. 'I never made no deal. I don't even know who you are.'

'You entered into a deal the moment you pulled that trigger.' The seated man no longer seemed so concerned about keeping his voice low. Danny looked to the old man who had finished prepping his cigarette and now stumbled off his stool with it hanging between his lips. Lank-hair was back in sight too, placing towels over the top of the beer pumps, the final part of his routine. He saw Danny looking over and smiled.

'For the road?' the barman called out.

'No. Thanks. I'm just leaving.' Danny replied.

'I'll be in touch, Danny. We need to finish this. You need to finish this.' The seated man hadn't moved his gaze from Danny, whose only response was to continue for the door. He had no intention of looking back. Any response he gave now would only show up the anxiety that had returned to fog his mind and twist into a tight ball in his stomach. He didn't want to show any weakness, he wanted to be resolute. He had given his answer.

This *was* finished.

74

Chapter 11

Friday

The next morning Danny stumbled away from his meeting with the Dover Athletic hierarchy feeling nothing but relieved to be away. This should have been a big moment, a time for celebration even. Danny had just signed a new contract as a coach at Dover Athletic and received a commitment from the club that they would support him with all the qualifications he needed to move into football management. Football was all he knew. This meant an extension to his career indefinitely. It should mean everything to him but he just felt empty. He had taken the long way back from the office to walk part of the stands at Crabble, to take in the lush green of the football pitch. This was a sight that always stoked something deep inside him. But not today; today there was nothing.

His agent seemed to be in a rush too. In the carpark, Marty headed for his own car, calling out that he would send the papers over and they could speak on the phone about the contract. Then he said, 'Don't worry though, it's a good one!' before slamming the door shut. His BMW spun its wheels in the gravel car park in his haste to get away, and a thumbs-up appeared out of the window.

Danny got into his own car. He let the dust settle then

dropped his window to get some air in. He had struggled to breathe in there at times. He couldn't focus. The events of the last few days turned over and over in his mind and made him as angry as they did anxious. He didn't deserve to be haunted – not by that man – not by the vivid memory of his wide eyes and the moment they were snuffed out, or the sound of his last breath that came with a twitch of his restrained limbs while clumps of blood and something thick and white ran down the freshly painted walls behind. Marcus Olsen should at least have the decency to disappear now he was dead.

A phone was ringing. It wasn't his. There were other cars in the car park but they were empty. He stepped out. The ringing was muffled but it sounded like it was coming from behind him. He walked to the rear of his car where the noise was coming from.

Lifting the boot he saw the screen on a cheap-looking phone showing *no caller ID*. It was laid out next to where Danny had discarded the steering lock the night before. He took one last look around, waiting to see who was playing the joke on him. There was no movement at all. The phone rang out. Its screen had a green glow that faded away as he watched. It rang again almost instantly. Danny picked it up this time.

'Hello?'

'You found it then.' The voice was instantly familiar. The suited man.

'You're still breaking into my car then. Would you mind stopping that.'

'I wouldn't need to, only we left unfinished business last night.'

The man's tone sounded gruffer today, more businesslike.

'I don't agree. I told you I was done.'

'Listen, Mr Evans, perhaps what I said last night sounded like you have a choice in all this but that's not really the case. I thought you would be keen once you knew that this woman had a big part in what happened to your daughter. She's just

76

as guilty as our other friend was. We will set it up, you will finish it off.'

'What do you mean, I don't have a choice?' Danny felt his anger building. 'Of course I have a choice.' He ducked into the driver's seat of his car, pulling the door shut and closing the window.

'I was really hoping you would just agree. I would much rather that was the case. Now the police have Marcus Olsen's body it can quickly get rather out of control. There are no links to you at this stage but that is very easily rectified.'

'Links? What do you mean? You told me this was sorted, and a link to me puts you at risk too when I tell them what I know. You said that was the last thing you wanted.'

'And what do you know, Mr Evans? Ask yourself that. And then think how it might all sound under questioning, when you talk about how you met a man in a bar while you were intoxicated who set this whole thing up. How do you think that sounds? What checkable facts do you have about me that back up that suggestion?'

'The police have ways, they can do things, find things out. They'll still come looking for you. I know you have something to do with a girl that was abused by Olsen, or at least you were hired by someone who does. I'll tell them that and they can start there.'

'Which girl? Was it even one who reported herself to be a victim, or did I tell you that I work for people who don't necessarily go to the police first – or at all? You need to listen more, Mr Evans. And you need to understand your position better too. If you want to bail out on this now then you will stop receiving my assistance. My client is quite insistent. He wants his vengeance and so far you've done half a job. Without me you'll just be a plain old murderer. And I don't clean up after murderers.'

'Hang on just a fucking second—'

'Two p.m. Drive to the Cliffe Hotel on Dover's seafront.

77

There is a bench on the promenade opposite in loving memory of Henry Reachman. Be sitting in it at 2 p.m. I will have clear instructions. It will be very easy.'

'And if I don't?'

'The police will be a step closer to finding a murderer.'

Chapter 12

Danny didn't go to Dover's seafront. He went to see his daughter instead. He wasn't a man who appreciated being backed into a corner, not when he was sure he was being bluffed. Nothing good could come from putting Danny in the spotlight for the murder of Marcus Olsen; not for anyone.

Danny was by Callie's side when the hands on his watch shifted to 2 p.m. The passing of the appointment seemed to calm him even more. He had made himself clear and his no-show would reinforce that. He was done. He squeezed Callie's hand a little firmer. It was cool to the touch, just like always. Her eyes moved behind the eyelids. It happened a lot and Danny had convinced himself that it was how she showed she was listening.

'I know what happened, Call.' His voice sounded rough, standing out even in the white noise of a hospital ward. He looked around to make sure no one was paying him any attention. A young girl in the next bed over was the only person close enough to be of concern and she was in a similar state to Callie. Danny cleared his throat to continue.

'*All* of it. I know about the messages, I know that some piece of . . . that a bad man tricked you. I don't want you to feel bad about that, I don't want you to feel bad about anything.

79

This isn't the first time he's done it, OK, you're not the first person he's tricked. When you reached out, when you thought you had found someone you could trust, that was him too. I know that now. He made you do what you did. But he didn't get away with it.' Danny gently brought her other hand over to make a warm pile. 'He's dead, Call . . .' He paused, like he might get some reaction, like this was the news Callie had been waiting for to wake from her slumber. 'I killed him.'

A tear dropped from his eye and tumbled onto her arm before he could stop it. 'And I'm so sorry. That it got to this, that it got this far. I wish . . . I wish I had known earlier. I wish I had been interested in anything other than myself.' The tears came faster now. He didn't want to let go of his daughter to catch them so they blurred his view and tickled his chin. There was nothing else he could say. He had been looking forward to coming here today, for the first time in a long time, seeing her face, telling her what he had done. He had almost been convinced that he had changed something, that he had made a difference. But he hadn't at all. Callie was still asleep; her future was still uncertain. And the emptiness he felt seemed almost bigger.

He had changed nothing.

80

Chapter 13

Danny peered across at the entrance to the hotel bar from the driver's seat of his Mercedes. The engine was still running and he considered pulling away, going for a drive, anything to stop him going in there for a drink. He was angry, and he knew what that might mean if he mixed it with alcohol. But he turned the engine off.

'You're stronger than that,' Danny said out loud. He would just go to his room, turn on the news, have a shower. Do what normal people do.

The corridor that led to his room was dark and there was a delay in the lights clunking on above him like they had been shaken awake. His footsteps felt heavy as he walked, like his body had held off his fatigue for as long as it could but was now sensing his proximity to his bed. Maybe he would even turn in for an early night, get some good sleep and wake up fresh enough to be able to talk to Sharon. Damage limitation.

He slowed up as he got to his door, even double-checking the room number was right. 'Do Not Disturb!' hung over the handle and Danny knew he hadn't left it there. The cleaner perhaps? He left it swinging, running his card over the lock to gain access. It flashed green and buzzed. The door pushed in.

The smell was the first suggestion that something might be

81

wrong. A scent reached round the door to stick in his throat: metallic and earthy. It was different to the now familiar smell of a turned-down room. He pushed the door wider. The window at the back was covered by closed curtains and a blackout blind. He pushed the card into the slot on the wall and the main light clunked on to illuminate the source.

His recoil was so strong he was forced backwards.

It looked like a dead animal had been dumped on the middle of his bed. A lump of dark hair held together by something damp enough to reflect the light. He could see a clump of white flesh the size of a fist jutting out from the hair; it finished with what looked like an untidy roll of black skin. The white bed linen was badly stained, a smudge of something dark, almost black, but he knew it was blood. Loud laughter suddenly erupted along the corridor and he panicked, stepping in as far as he dared; not quite enough, as the spring had the door nudge him in the back. He shuffled another inch and the door clicked shut. The smell seemed instantly worse. Danny took a step closer. He managed to break away to peer into the bathroom then around the room. Nothing else seemed out of place. He was soon fixed back on the lump of fur that was heavy enough to make a dint in the bed. He stepped round the foot of the bed. The first detail he made out was a pale ear lobe pushing out from between dark hair. Danny's hand shot to his mouth, but his steps continued. He was unable to take his eyes off it, unable to even blink. As terrified as he felt he needed to know for sure what it was.

It was a human head. What was left of Marcus Olsen. It looked different from when he'd seen it before, like a wax version – or a movie prop. But the smell, the flies that lifted and fell back to disturb the long hair – he could be in no doubt. This was real. When he stopped he was on the other side of the bed, which now acted like a barrier to his way out. The covered window was directly behind him. The head was laid out on its side, now facing him, the eyes part bloodshot,

82

part yellowed and the mouth open to reveal teeth stained with blackened blood. A black fly lifted from a separate patch of lighter red that was further up the bed. He watched as it dropped straight back down again.

A phone rang.

The ringtone was familiar – the same as the cheap phone he had found in the boot of his car. He spun away – away from the sight on his bed, away from the sound of the ringing phone – and clumsily clawed at the blind covering the window, pulling it from its housing in his desperation to get to the window latch. It would only open a few inches. He leaned forward, sucking air that he thought would be fresher, trying to stave off a panic attack. He shut his eyes and tried to focus on the booming sound of passing cars – something that was steady, reliable. A reminder that there was a world carrying on as normal outside this room. He pushed his forehead against the cold glass and lingered there. Finally, he stepped back and held his breath to turn round. He was calmer now. He told himself that this was all silly – a joke. Maybe even something that his mind had conjured as part of his exhaustion.

But it was still there, and the phone was still ringing. It had been cutting out and starting up again. The sound was muffled, coming from down to his left. The top drawer of a bedside cabinet revealed a bible and nothing else. He shut the drawer firmly and moved his search to the bed, where he lifted the pillow to reveal the phone underneath. The handset was spotted with something brown and another substance that looked stringy to the touch. He kept hold of the pillow, stripping the pillowcase to push his hand through and pick up the phone. It cut out again but the silence that followed only lasted a few seconds. The smell was suddenly overpowering. He walked the ringing phone into the bathroom, dropping it into the sink and running the tap to wet the pillowcase that he then wiped over the phone. It had fallen silent again. When the inevitable ring returned he was able to pick it up in his bare hands.

'Yes?' Danny's voice was meek.

'Mr Evans!' The suited man. The familiar voice seemed more jovial than usual. 'I trust you found a rather significant piece of the puzzle?'

'Puzzle? What the fuck is going on!' Danny shouted, his fear and panic bubbling out as rage.

'There is now a puzzle and the police have made a start on putting it together. You really don't listen to the local news, do you? They've issued an update on the body they found. Seems it was missing a significant part and they are now asking if anyone has any information. They're putting out a phone number if you think you might know something.'

'Why is it here?'

'That is exactly what the police will be asking, Danny. They won't really need you to answer, however. That item rather tells its own story.'

'You set me up!'

'You set yourself up. I gave you the option, I told you what would happen.'

'I'll tell them what happened, *exactly* what happened.'

'And what did happen *exactly*? You drove to a remote location on the request of a man you don't know to find Marcus Olsen trussed up with a shotgun in his mouth. Do you then tell them the bit about you pulling the trigger or would you scrub over that to get to the bit where the same man's head magically appeared in your hotel room?'

'If I go down they'll be looking for you too.'

'For how long, Danny, and how hard, really? What do you think happened to the shotgun that killed that man? Do you think I wiped it down properly, removed all traces of you and then destroyed it or do you think I'm staring at it right now, prints an' all? They'll know you fired the gun. They'll find his severed head in your hotel room and they'll find a

84

printed document that tells a very clear story of Marcus Olsen's involvement with your daughter. How much effort do you think they'll put into finding some mystery man who might have helped you set it all up? Not much, Danny. I don't think they'll care at all.'

'This has all been a stitch-up from the start. You've been playing me the whole time,' Danny said, his anger fading back to fear.

'The term "stitch-up" suggests you didn't get something you wanted out of all this and that isn't true, is it? And besides, this can still go away. All of it. That stinking head on your bed, the bloodstains on the wall, the stains you can't see on the carpet, the blood traces trapped in the U-bend of the sink in your bathroom where I washed my hands . . . all traces of what you did, Danny, traces you're barely capable of finding, let alone dealing with. But this is what I am good at. I clean up after people.'

'You said you don't clean up after murderers. You said that to me. Now you've made me a murderer.'

'A murderer is a man who kills for anything other than justice. I had high hopes for you, I thought we wanted the same thing.'

'I have my justice.'

'We do not have justice until a woman is dead too. She will start again, she may have already made contact with the next Callie. You have to finish this. That is how you justify that you did this for the right reasons: not to me, to yourself.'

Danny shifted. The light in the bathroom had cut out at his lack of movement. He moved instinctively to switch it back on. His movement turned him so he was facing the mirror. The bright light seemed focused on his face and he was forced to take in his own reflection. His skin had a washed-out pallor with a pattern of red veins. The bags under his eyes hung heavier and darker than ever over skin that had developed a rash from his first shave in a while that morning.

85

His hair was roughed up where he had been constantly pushing it around in his stress. He was still wearing a tie from his meeting; the knot was tight and low where he had pulled it away from his neck. He barely recognised the man staring back at him. He just wanted this to be over.

'I can't.' His voice was weak, barely a croak, and he watched his grimace in the mirror. He wanted to sound strong, to have conviction, to not sound like he felt: empty, beaten. Like he had nothing left. 'The other night was different. I didn't know where I was going, I got there and there was a lot of stuff that just swept me up, got me all riled. I did what I did in the heat of the moment. But this . . . this feels like cold blood. Like driving somewhere knowing I'm going there to kill someone. That ain't me,' Danny said.

'Then don't. But take a moment to think about what you are, what you want to be. A husband to Sharon, a father to Jamie and Callie. That means being there for them, being there when Jamie captains his football team to follow in his dad's footsteps, being there when Callie wakes up; she is never going to need you more. And being there for Sharon. She's a strong woman but she can't do this on her own. Not this time.'

'You don't know what you're talking about!' But he did, Danny could see that now; of course he had taken his time to find out what he could about his family. That could only be for one reason.

'I'm a private investigator. You know that. It's my job to know people. I know you too, I know you would give anything to have that family back, to be Danny Evans again. You can have that. Or you can go to prison while your kids grow old enough to resent you.' The man paused like he was waiting for a response. Danny didn't have one. His lips bumped together, and his eyes searched the mirror like he was imploring his reflection to have the answer. It didn't. The voice on the phone continued. 'The bench we discussed. This evening, 10 p.m. A final opportunity to make this right. Fail

86

to show and the police will have all they need by the morning. Leave your room as it is. I will deal with the clean-up and removal. Or do it yourself . . . if you think you're smarter than the forensics experts.'

'Please—' Danny was too late. The phone was dead. He threw it down hard enough for it to break up. He leaned against the sink, his gaze falling to rest on the plughole. Even from here he could see spots of red on the stainless steel. There was no way he could clean this place to pass a forensic exam and that thing in there . . . just the thought to having to move it made him want to vomit.

The voice on the phone had spoken of a choice. But Danny didn't have a choice at all.

Chapter 14

Stepping out of the heated interior of his car put Danny into a wind that rolled in off the sea under the cover of darkness to launch an assault. It came in gusts that stung his face like they were laden with ice. Dover's seafront felt like the bleakest place on earth.

It also felt like the loneliest. He took a moment with his hands plunged in his pockets and his chin dug into his collar to look out and scan the wide promenade in both directions. There was no movement at all, save for the white pockets of street lighting that shuffled and flickered on the slick surface where the gusts toyed with their housing. He had parked right outside the Cliffe Hotel. The ground floor was a popular restaurant, the frontage of which had bay windows big enough to house tables with cosy-looking orange lamps. They were all empty. All the sensible people were safely in their homes.

The benches were hidden, tucked into a wall that had a sweeping wave design to mimic the sea it faced. A neat stretch of lawn finished level with the top of the wall to further obstruct the view. Danny had to walk right out onto the promenade to be able to see them. He didn't need to be looking for plaques; one bench was already occupied.

88

'I have to say, I'm glad you came. I think you made the right decision.' The man spoke instantly, still facing forward, and his words came out as tight balls of mist. He rubbed gloved hands together. A quilted jacket was tight round his shoulders but the knot of a tie was still visible. The buttons on his sleeves flapped open with the movement where his forearms were too thick for them to fasten. Danny wasn't sure if he was wearing layers against the elements or if he was a larger build than Danny had remembered. Danny hadn't really taken much notice of him before. The first time they had met he had dismissed him as a crackpot trying to get a rise out of him. The second time he had been more concerned with the other people around them. Now there was no one else to worry about and Danny understood this man better. He understood him to be a threat to him – to everything.

'I don't really have a choice. You made sure of that.'

'I suppose you could say that.'

'What do you want from me?'

'For what it's worth, this isn't me. I'm a mouthpiece. I'm sorry I had to be so . . . persuasive in our phone conversation earlier. I don't have the time to make you see the advantages, to make you understand how this is in your best interests, in the best interests of everyone, in fact. I had to be a little direct and I apologise if that has damaged our relationship in any way.'

'You mean by threatening me with prison unless I do as you ask?'

'Not me, Mr Evans. Again, this is not me asking. I may agree with the thinking behind what is being asked here but my method would be quite different.'

'But you will still make sure I go to prison?'

'Of course. And I will make sure I don't. I'm very good at what I do. But this can be over for you soon. You just need to do the right thing.'

'I'm not sure I know what that is anymore.'

89

'Yes, you do. There's a bag under the bench. I'm going to get up and walk away in a moment. You will need to stay here long enough for me to get clear and then take the bag. Do not inspect the contents here. Drive out of the town.'

'What's in the bag?'

'Instructions. And the means to get the job done. A pistol. It's loaded so don't go having a look down the wrong end. Simple operation: point and squeeze.'

'Jesus . . .' Danny said, 'just like that.'

'She's every bit as guilty as Olsen was. Her crimes were worse, even: she builds trust with the sole purpose of destroying young women, removing their fight. Callie's a strong, intelligent young woman. I don't think for a moment she would have been fooled by Olsen on his own. He needed someone else. So when you aim that thing, just remember that she was that someone else.'

'Nothing in that folder mentioned anyone else. Not a woman, that's for sure.'

The man sighed. 'They even met a few times. Callie and this woman. They had contact via other means too. That report didn't contain half of what we found out. I just had to put enough in there that you would understand the man sitting in front of you. I didn't want to muddy the waters in that moment.'

'What do you mean, they met?'

'Like I said, you have a bright daughter. She didn't just go along with Olsen, even after she had sent him a few images and he had the leverage that had been enough for all the others. She even called his bluff at one point, told him if he was going to share her photos then just get it over with. That was when Olsen put this woman onto her. She made contact, played the role of a survivor who had also called him out. He's used her like that before. And it works. You get a girl who's struggling, who might be refusing to play along or considering speaking to their parents or to the

90

authorities, and then a woman makes contact claiming to have been through the same thing. She talked to Callie about what happened to her and how she survived it. She went heavy on how she kept the secret, did as she was told and it all went away like magic. It's an easy sell: she basically told Callie that taking the easy way out works. It's what she would have wanted to hear.'

'And a lie.'

'Absolutely a lie. This woman is a big part of the control element – the biggest even. They come from a position of trust and they allow the offender to escalate his demands.'

'It's a lot of effort. Just so they can get their rocks off looking at pictures of naked kids. What the hell is wrong with these people?'

'This woman isn't interested in any of that!' The man scoffed like it was obvious. 'This is just about money.'

'Money?' Danny rounded on him.

'Yes, money! Of course money. Olsen might have been a twisted pervert but I told you he was making a lot of money servicing other twisted perverts. Which meant he could pay people to help him, pay them well. The fact that this woman's motivation was only financial makes her the worst of the lot of them in my eyes. These other men were working off a compulsion at least.'

'My daughter's life is ruined . . . She could be dead. One of the doctors said she should be dead, like it was some miracle we still have her. We've been warned that Callie might not come back like we remember. She might never be the same again. A couple of times I've found myself wondering if she could have been better off dying. How can I think like that?' Danny was voicing his thoughts, trying to put all the pieces in place in his mind.

'Because you might be right. No matter what happens from here on in, none of your lives will be the same again; not your wife, not your son and certainly not Callie. She didn't deserve

91

this; your family didn't deserve this. This woman has ruined your family, ruined your *life*. This may feel like you're being forced into doing something you don't want to do today but if you don't, if you walk away from this, ten years from now this meeting will still be playing heavy on your heart. You will regret not taking this chance.'

'Because I'll be in prison! You'll make sure of that.'

'I will. But even if you were at home with your family, entirely back to normal – if there is such a thing – it would make no difference. You'll always have this niggle in the back of your mind, you'll always wonder what this woman is doing, what other families are going through because of her.'

'You're good at this.' Danny sniffed. He fixed on a distant bright light. A cargo ship – and a long way out to sea. From this distance it just looked like a long grey slab balanced tentatively on the horizon.

'At what?'

'Making murder seem like a good idea.'

The man chuckled, and Danny clenched his jaw at his carefree attitude.

'This job will do that to you. I made good money when I was legit. I found a lot of fraudsters, retrieved a lot of money and I was paid a good percentage for doing it. But I rarely felt anything. It was always just a job. What I do now, the money's sporadic, never as good, but it makes a difference. It's good work; important. I never considered I might find something important enough to make murder a good idea.'

Danny could feel tension in the whole of his upper body. He'd been sitting bolt upright, his whole body rigid. He sat back, pulling his shoulders down as he did to try and breath deeper.

'Money . . . This woman, she does this for money,' Danny muttered.

'It still surprises me what people will do for financial gain.'

'Not you then?' Danny said. His side flared like his muscles

92

had fused as he turned to the man, who was still looking out to sea.

'Me?'

'You make your money out of finding people for the rich, people who want them taken out, like this woman. How come you don't do a more complete service? Surely that would improve your take?'

'You mean pulling the trigger myself?' The man chuckled again. 'I've certainly been asked enough.'

'And then there would be no need for people like me. What was it you called me? A variable, right?'

The man held his smile. 'It would certainly be a lot easier. But that would make me a killer for money, no better than the people I find. The only right way to take another life is for justice and that can't be found with a cold death at the hands of a stranger. Justice can only be delivered by the wronged, by the victim. By the people and the families torn apart.'

'Have you ever killed anyone? For any reason?'

'No.' He stood up now, tugging at his jacket to straighten it, shifting his trousers so they fell over the same smart shoes. He started to walk away but cast a last glance towards Danny. 'I'm not sure I have it in me.'

93

Chapter 15

Danny left the car's radio off to drive away from Dover in silence. He had been listening to the local station for the short journey to the seafront in the hope that he could call the man's bluff, that there would be no mention of a 'body found' or of a 'murder investigation'. But both phrases had been mentioned numerous times by DJs and newsreaders who could barely believe something so newsworthy had happened in their sleepy town. *A headless corpse!* The newsreader had almost sung the words, her excitement increasing with every word until she had handed back to an equally thrilled DJ. He'd even referenced the story as he had set up the next song: 'The next track I'm going to play you was already in the can so please don't think it's a reference to that horrific story from St Margaret's beach! This is The Verve and "Lucky Man" . . .'

That was the point Danny had turned it off. Now the only sound in the cabin was the drone of the tyres as he sat at 60mph on the inside lane of a quiet A2. He had his instructions. His directions too. He shifted his gaze from his cold, white headlights to glance at his sat nav. He was seventeen minutes away.

He didn't know Sittingbourne well. Football stadiums and pubs were generally how he negotiated towns, but Sittingbourne

94

was not a place in which he had visited either recently. He was thankful for his sat nav. A postcode had been left for him by the suited man and it took him directly to the street. The instructions found with it told him this was just where he was to leave the car. It was residential, tightly packed and crammed with parked cars. Most of the houses had lit windows. It was gone 11 p.m. and the occupants would be settled for the night, most already in bed.

He found a space. He had needed to drift some way past the alleyway that the instructions told him to use. The appearance of interior lights when he silenced the car made him self-conscious and hasty. He caught his foot on the seatbelt and stumbled into the middle of the road.

'Take it easy!' he muttered to himself. He needed to slow down, to be more deliberate. He could feel his heart pulsing in his chest. His breathing was shallow and even that felt rushed. He opened the boot of his car. The bag under the bench had also contained a solid lump wrapped in towelling. The pistol. It had to be. He'd left it wrapped up and hid it under the floor with the space saver wheel. He hadn't wanted it in the cabin with him.

He leaned in to unwrap it. The streetlighting leaked past him to catch on the matt black barrel. The handle was plastic. He wasn't expecting that. He didn't know what to expect. His idea of a pistol was largely based on cowboy movies.

It was lighter than he had expected too and ergonomically pleasing to the point of being comfortable in his grip: a well-designed murder weapon. Danny felt a shiver that wasn't caused by the freezing mist that hung beneath the streetlights.

The alleyway held a thicker darkness and Danny was glad of it. His right hand trailed by his side with the pistol gripped tight. As much as he wanted to conceal it, the suppressor screwed to the end made it an awkward length and he didn't trust it not to go off in his pocket or his waistband. He didn't trust himself.

95

The alleyway ended by taking him out into a road that looked identical to the one he had just left. He turned right to walk the pavement. More tightly packed houses had him surrounded, but he knew he must head for where it opened up into a new-build block of flats at the end. His left hand fiddled with a black, circular lump of plastic that should grant him access to the building. It worked. He wafted it at a panel beside a sturdy door, a light flashed and a clacking sound made him flinch.

He hesitated for just a moment to remind himself of the details. Two flights up. Door number eleven was always unlocked. Two shots to the central mass of the pictured female. Then leave.

Simple.

It was bright as he stepped into the building, the light thrown by large circles that clung to the wall and flickered with the shadows of doomed moths. He strode past them, then past the doors of the flats on the ground floor, turning back on himself to move up the internal stairs. He could hear noises as he went: televisions, music, human interaction – normal life. There was no time to stop and consider his place in it, to consider what he was about to do. He had slipped into matchday mode. He was there to win at all costs.

Second floor. The door numbers increased as he moved past them. Nine was the first on this floor, then ten swept past. He didn't even pause as he reached eleven. The door handle dipped in his hand as promised and the door pushed into darkness. He stepped forward. There was noise from straight ahead, canned laughter to accompany a flickering silver light from the end of a long hallway with closed doors either side. He walked towards it, lingering at the end of the hall to take in a television playing to a figure laid out on the sofa. He pressed the light switch. It came on a dirty yellow to illuminate a young woman who didn't move. She was facing out. It wasn't her.

96

There wasn't supposed to be anyone else here!

The woman made no movement; her eyes were shut. He turned away, back the way he had come. He opened the first door he came to: bathroom. He was too hasty and the door bumped against the wall. Empty. He pressed another switch, and light flooded the hall, this time a much brighter white. Then a noise, something scraping the floor on the other side of a closed door. Danny stopped still. It was involuntary, like he was frozen to the spot. He had to force movement. His hand reached out to push the door open and reveal a block of darkness. A woman appeared from it, her eyes narrowed against the light, her arms out like she was reaching for him. She was wearing jeans and a light-coloured jumper, and her foot dragged like she might trip.

They locked eyes. Her hair was pulled back in a ponytail: just like her picture. Her mouth contorted, parting her lips like she was going to speak. Danny lifted and fired as one. The sound was like a violent hiss delivered right to his ear and louder than he had expected, to bounce around the hall. He had shut his eyes. When he opened them again the woman was gone.

Danny moved forward. A door-shaped block of light framed the woman on the floor. She was leaning back onto the foot of a bed, her left arm pushing out at the mattress like she was struggling to get back up. She groaned like she was clawing for breath. There was blood. A clump on the bed that showed up against the white, he couldn't see where it was coming from. Her top had soaked so much and so quickly it was like her whole front was erupting. Danny lifted the pistol to squint down it. The iron sights on the top of the barrel met with the centre of her mass and he pulled the trigger for the second time. He was ready for the sound but it still filled the room around him. The hiss threatened to unbalance him as he jerked away from it.

He took a moment to remember the way out. The front

97

door had fallen back shut, his clammy hand slid off the smooth metal of the handle in his haste and he had to focus to get it open. The soles of his shoes squeaked as he turned sharply on the tiles of the communal hall and made for the stairs. He passed the same front doors to hear the same sounds as on the way in, the same by-products of normal human life. He felt numb to it now, like he wasn't part of it.

He didn't look back.

Chapter 16

Saturday

The sun was barely up, its rays so timid they hadn't made a start on the heavy frost that coated the grass. It coated the grave too, giving the black headstone a white dusting on its top and shoulders. Richard Maddox sat facing it, still enough that he could be made out of stone himself. He only moved when a stranger's voice punctured the scene.

'There's a beautiful view over there. You can see the whole of West Hythe, right down to the sea. It almost feels like you can see the whole world!' The stranger sat down on the same bench and Richard shuffled enough to edge away from him. He didn't reply. He wasn't here to talk or make new friends. 'Angela Maddox,' the voice continued, and a man's pointing finger loomed into his periphery. 'Your wife?'

Richard turned to the man now. 'Do you have someone here you wish to see?'

'No. Just the view.'

'The view isn't here, is it?' Richard's gaze lingered on him. He didn't think he had seen him here before. The man was younger than him – twenty years younger, he reckoned – which would put him in his late forties, but Richard was finding it more and more difficult to get ages right. The man was well dressed. A smart overcoat and trousers, leather gloves and

99

two-tone shoes that were mostly brown and classic in style. That would be the word he would use to describe him overall – classic. You don't get many younger men dressing well these days. He had a beard that was mostly consumed by patches of grey, the edges shaved so sharp it almost looked fake. His facial hair matched his hairstyle: short, neat and grey. He was tanned too, maybe from a bottle or a salon; he certainly looked like the sort of person who might waste his time on a sunbed.

'No. I didn't mean any offence. I'm sorry, you looked sad. I mean, I know we're in a graveyard, this is where people come to be sad after all but . . . I'm sorry, OK. I'm an idiot sometimes, I guess I just thought I could cheer you up maybe. There's this "pay it forward" thing about at the moment. Have you heard of it?'

'No.' Richard was back facing out. He was doing his best to look like he wasn't interested in engaging.

'No, well, basically you try and do a good deed when you can. For no reason, for no reward, just to help the world become a better place one good deed at a time.' He fell silent then snorted a laugh. 'Stupid idea really. I suppose it could be an excuse for some people to put their nose where it isn't wanted. I didn't mean to upset you.'

Richard felt the seat flex as the man lifted his weight to stand. Richard sighed. 'It's fine, OK. I don't mean to snap. I like the sentiment. My wife would have liked it even more. She was into all that . . . do-gooding crap.'

The man laughed. It left his face as a whirl of mist. 'None taken.'

'I don't need cheering up, thank you. I'm not sure you have the ability to improve this situation anyway.' He gestured at Angela.

'So, she *was* your wife?'

'Still is, you could say.'

'You could.'

100

'I'm not sure you would be any good at cheering up mourners anyway, friend. You don't seem to have the nuance of language.' Richard laughed this time. He wasn't sure where it came from but it was genuine. The man sat back down; he was laughing too.

'You're right. Subtlety isn't one of my strengths,' he said. Richard was just about to admit that it wasn't his either, especially when he was here, especially when he just wanted to be left alone. But the man's next words stole his ability to speak at all.

'I know who killed your wife, Richard. There might be a subtle way of saying that but I've always been the same when it comes to important things: just say what you need to say.'

'What are you talking about?' Richard managed when his breath came back.

'The hit-and-run with the stolen car. She was just out for a walk with your dog. Well, her dog really; Missy, right? That's what your wife named her, it was the first thing she said when one of the dogs ran out of the litter and right to her feet.'

'How could you . . .?'

'The police found the car burned out. They had a few suspects at one time. A group of mates, but they all had their stories straight, didn't they? It wasn't going anywhere. They didn't even get it to a courtroom. In a couple of weeks it will be a year to the day since she took that walk and never came back. I think you deserve to know.'

'Who are you?' Richard's voice shook with anger. The man was sitting differently now, no longer cross-legged with his limbs pulled in tight to combat the cold. Now the man was leaning back against the frozen slats, his legs apart, his hands by his side. He looked bigger suddenly, broader. He bit his bottom lip like he was considering his reply.

'I'm an investigator by trade, Richard, and I shouldn't be here.'

'What do you mean you shouldn't be here?'

101

'Three years ago I worked for an insurance company. My job was to make sure they weren't paying out for fraudulent claims, but it very soon became a role of making sure they weren't paying out at all. It got worse and worse, until I'd finally had enough and walked. None of that matters to you, I know that, but I'm trying to make amends for some of what went on. That's really what I meant by a good deed. I want my conscience to be clear.'

'Your conscience? Why didn't you just hand what you have to the police at the time?'

The man shook his head. 'We did. They weren't interested. They said it wasn't proof of anything. We got hold of some phone records that were the key to our whole investigation. The car that hit your wife was stolen, but you know that. The man who owned that car is a bit of a hardman, not someone you would choose to steal from. Anyway, he had some contacts in telecommunications and he got us some good information. Then he leaned on some local lads who knew a bit of this and that, got a bit punchy and *voila!* The truth.'

'You come to me, here, with "a bit of this and that"! What the hell does that even mean? I had some sicko crackpots call my phone at home when the story was in the papers. I wasn't stupid enough to be riled up then and I won't give you the satisfac—'

'Woah! Richard . . . I'm sorry, OK. I'm not explaining myself well. I'm not a sicko or a crackpot! I know what I saw. But the police couldn't use any of it. Can you imagine going to court when the only evidence was from some dodgy fella who had his car nicked and then kicked the hell out of a few lads to find out who did it? And this after his mate got some illegal phone information! None of it was admissible evidence in the eyes of the law . . . but you're not the law, Richard. You're the poor bastard left behind. And Angela—'

'Don't you say her name, please! You don't say her name.' Richard felt his heart suddenly hammer in his chest. The shake

102

in his voice was increasingly obvious. He had never been good at hiding his anger. Or controlling it. The man held his hands up. There were a few moments of silence. Richard focused back on her grave, his eyes tripping over her name as they blurred with every pulse of his heart. Both men fell silent. It was long enough for Richard to recover a little. When the man spoke again it was to read his wife's epitaph in a deep voice.

'To live in the hearts we leave behind is not to die.'

Richard's anger turned to sadness. He had picked those words out from a list the funeral home had presented him with. He hadn't been prepared for their questions: Did he want flowers? What sort of service? Who should go? What two lines of words did he want to sum up her life? It had all been too much. He had ended up pointing numbly, nodding his head at the right moments then typing his pin number to pay for it all. He didn't want choices. He just wanted her back. A few months later he had been sat on this very bench and he had read those words out to realise that they were for him. He had been trying to comfort himself. They didn't seem to offer him any comfort now.

'It's not true though, is it, Richard? She doesn't live anywhere and all that you got left with is a *pain* in your heart that you don't know what to do with. I can help.'

'I don't want your *fucking* HELP!' Richard's feet slammed against the ground and he stood up straight. His heart beat so hard in his chest it felt like it was trying to get out. His vision blurred, worse this time, enough to remove all sense of detail. His whole view was just a whirl of blue merging into grey and green. He felt himself stumble forward. A black object appeared in front of him and took hold of him by the shoulder. He grabbed it back, steadying himself before he had one of his falls.

'It's OK! I've got you.' The same voice. The same man. Richard didn't reply. He was still unsteady. He took a step

103

back, feeling for the wood of the bench. The man helped him back into it. Richard flashed angry again, more at himself this time, at the fact that he had become so old and weak. And useless. 'I didn't mean to upset you, OK. Take it easy . . . I'm sorry, this was a bad idea.' The voice again.

Richard hung his head, waiting for his vision to clear. By the time it had, the man was gone.

Chapter 17

Inspector Joel Norris scrolled down his computer screen, high-lighting a good chunk of his emails as he went. Joel had spent a month away from this inbox and had no intention of spending the next month going through them. Instead he worked on the logic that anything important would be sent again. When he pressed the *delete* key only three were left standing and they were all from Detective Sergeant Ian Andrews of CID.

It made him feel better.

The three emails from DS Andrews contained a detailed list of everything that had been completed so far. It was extensive, a good example of how quickly you can progress fast-track actions when you have a team of detectives to call upon. Joel knew he couldn't rely on CID to continue their support – DS Andrews' last email made it very clear that this was him handing over. Joel would need to raise the issue of recruitment again. Although it might make sense to secure some office space to put them in first. Joel had missed a call from Superintendent Marsden earlier that morning that he was still to return. Maybe now was the time he could get some time-scales. He took his phone out. The missed calls from Marsden had now increased to three.

105

'Joel, you do know the whole idea of a phone is to make you contactable.' The irritation in her voice was enough to stop Joel reminding her that it was a Saturday and he wasn't technically due back at work until Monday. This didn't seem like the time for technicalities.

'Is there something you need?' he said instead.

'Where are you?'

'Nackington. I thought I would set up at the closest place until you get me—'

'You need to go up to Sittingbourne. There's been a shooting.'

'A shooting?' Joel said. 'Linked to my headless man in Dover?'

'No. I've seen the same handover you have about Marcus Olsen. CID have done you proud. That's now a slow-time investigation for you to come back to. There was a shooting overnight. This is what your team was meant for, Joel . . .'

'What team?'

'You have a sergeant.'

'I do?' Joel said. 'The last I heard I didn't even have an applicant.'

'Someone called me this morning to ask for the job personally.'

'Someone, who?'

'Lucy Rose. She's a DS in CID on the West. She's worked Child Protection, has a lot of experience.'

'And she called you this morning, just like that, just as another job is coming in?'

'Fine, she called me *because* of this job, Joel. She knows the victim.'

'What?' Joel couldn't stop a groan. 'Then she definitely can't be part of the investigation team. Of course she can't.'

'It's not like that. A lot of people are going to know her. The victim is Hannah Ribbons. She's a source handler.'

106

'A source handler . . .' Joel couldn't help but exhale in surprise.

'Only for a couple of weeks. She was a detective before that. Joel, I need you to get up there. Someone's killed a police officer.'

Chapter 18

Joel's sat nav didn't need to announce that he had reached his destination. Numerous marked police cars with their high-visibility occupants, a CSI marked van and a middle-aged man with a professional-looking camera jutting from his chest had already made that clear. The photographer reacted like he had been jabbed in the side when Joel stepped out of the car. He jerked his camera to his face and paced forward. The clicking shutter could be heard over an officer's remonstrations as he stepped away from the communal entrance to meet the photographer head on.

'I told you already, residents only!'

A second officer had stayed by the door. Joel showed him his badge, lingering long enough for him to note the details on the scene log. He read his name out loud as he did so. Behind him a young woman was leaning against a brick wall close to the block's entrance. She looked mid-twenties. She was slim with light brown hair that was pulled back in a ponytail that trailed halfway down her back. She had slender fingers that moved a takeaway coffee cup to thick lips, and wore a blouse and trousers down to sensible shoes, with a suit jacket hung over her arm.

'Do you know where you're going, boss?' the officer said to get his attention.

'I'll take him up,' the woman said. 'DS Lucy Rose.' She handed her coffee cup to the officer, who already had a collection in a sack at his feet. Joel shook her hand.

'Joel Norris. I understand we might be working together.'

'That's right.'

'Have you been here long?'

'A little while now.'

'Long enough to know what the hell's going on?'

'I've found out what I can. I went up but not in. The CSI said she didn't want to be repeating herself and that I should come back when I've got you.' DS Rose started moving away, her pace instantly brisk, and Joel watched her go through the door.

'Shall we then?' Joel muttered towards the door, which was already swinging back shut.

There was activity at most of the flats. Everyone loved a cop show. Some of the doors were just ajar for the occupants to listen out for anything interesting, others were hurriedly pushed shut when Joel and the DS walked past. At least two were wide open with people sitting on chairs that had been dragged into the doorway so they could greet any officers that passed in the hope of a snippet of something juicy, maybe even something they could sell to the man with a camera downstairs.

'You CID?' one particularly large lady said. She was wedged into a deckchair in the last doorway of the first floor. The smile that followed her question lifted her cheeks to the point where her eyes looked closed. 'Or Murder Squad maybe?' She clapped her hands in her excitement.

'Neither of them,' Joel said.

'What about the pretty girl? She need to take my details down?'

109

DS Rose responded by stopping directly in front of the woman. She looked her up and down before replying: 'Hell no.'

Joel watched as DS Rose moved away. He was left to lock eyes with the woman who was now flushing from her chest, her eyes wide where her smile had tumbled away. Joel shrugged.

The whole of the second floor was taped off. Another officer in uniform moved away from the filthy window he had been leaning against to meet them on the corridor at the top of the stone steps. There was another log to sign, this one for the inner cordon, plus a whole new layer of clothes to wear. The officer gestured to where the forensic suits, gloves and overshoes were individually sealed in a box pushed against the wall.

Joel was the first ready and he stepped through the door of Flat 11. He paused on the threshold, looking ahead to get an idea of the layout. The front door opened on a long hall that led to the back of the flat, where he could see a side view of a sofa. The layout already looked familiar. In his previous role he had led a million search warrants, enough to know that blocks of flats were often built to a standard template. If he was right, the living room at the back would also run into a kitchen area while the doors coming off the hall to the left and right would be the bedroom and bathroom. His first impression was of a place that was run down but not untidy. He had hurriedly skimmed the CAD on the way up. This started with the typed notes from the initial answer of the 999 call but also included basic intelligence on any persons or places mentioned. The 'CAD' system, or Computer Aided Dispatch, doesn't print in a clear or logical way and Joel never felt that the computer was much of an 'aid' at all. He had been able to pick out a few details, including that the scene was suspected to be the home address of a drug user. The threadbare carpet, scuffed walls and absence of anything remotely homely matched that lifestyle. People in the tightest grip of addiction could reach the point where they didn't have enough personal belongings to make a place untidy.

There was movement at the end of the corridor. A white suit appeared with hood up and a mask covering a good portion of her face. He could still make out a middle-aged woman. Dark hair was just visible under her hood, pulled back to reveal a shine on her forehead. Her suit was different in colour from the one Joel was wearing and labelled 'CSI'. She held a biro that jiggled as she noted something in her pocket book.

'The first door on your right. She's still in there. I haven't done much in the room, not until after ballistics have been.' Despite being slightly muffled the woman's voice was deep, matter-of-fact and instantly confident.

'Hannah's here!' It was DS Rose who breathed a reply, heavy with shock, like it had only just sunk in what she was about to see. The woman labelled as CSI stopped her writing to take in the sergeant.

'You the one that knew her well?' the CSI officer said.

'I did.'

'Two shots to the chest and stomach. Close range. It would have been quick.' DS Rose nodded like she didn't know what to say to that. 'You can't go in the room, I'm still processing it. You don't need to anyway,' their CSI colleague continued. 'You can see what you need to from the door.'

'Understood,' Joel replied while his new DS seemed to hesitate and it was he that took the few paces to the door and braced himself to look in.

The room was lit in stark white by a CSI lamp in the left corner. It was needed; the ceiling light was missing a bulb and the curtains were pulled shut. The bed dominated the room. Even more so than the corpse laid out in its shadow. The bedding was off-white, making the bloodstains vivid – although there wasn't much blood. Two shots to the centre of her mass would have done catastrophic damage but it was probably contained mostly inside Hannah. Joel had seen the result of

111

gunshot wounds before; in that instance a man had taken a bullet in the hip. The bone had fragmented into tiny pieces of shrapnel that had shredded his major organs in an instant but from the outside there had been very little clue. At the post-mortem the pathologist had tried to help Joel's understanding: *You know Brick Breaker, the computer game? You bounce your ball off the face of a brick and you'll break that one but if you get the ball in behind the front layer of bricks you can rip out the guts with just one shot and the outer wall doesn't change a bit. You'd never know!* The analogy had stuck with him, as had the pathologist's apparent delight.

For now, Hannah could almost be mistaken for someone sleeping. She was on her side, her back to the bed. She looked small – almost childlike – bunched up like she was cowering from a storm at the window. She was wearing a jumper that had cream-coloured arms but the front was largely a thick blood stain left to dry. Hannah's brown hair was pulled back to reveal the shocking white pallor of her forehead.

'Okay then.' Joel had to clear his throat to get some authority in his voice. 'What do we know? And I'm sorry . . . I didn't get your name?' Joel directed his question at the woman with CSI stamped on her suit.

'Sandra. And at this stage, like I always say, we don't *know* anything. All I do is gather up exactly what is here and th—'

'I know the process, I know it takes time for definite answers, but you must have some early opinions – nothing I'll hold you to.' Joel tried to give a reassuring smile.

'I don't normally like giving opinions. Forensics is a science. We work with facts. We can start with those. She was shot twice. Judging by where she is positioned and where she has leaked she was probably standing in the doorway when she the first one hit. She was on her back when I found her, and the first attending officers are sure they didn't move her when they tried CPR. They didn't try for long. She's on her side from

112

where I rolled her. She has two entry wounds and one exit. She also has part of a finger missing which could be consistent with a defensive wound. There's a shell to be recovered from the floor. It's a 9mm, which is a little unusual.'

'Unusual?'

'That it's out of the body. I'm no ballistics expert, that's why I haven't done much with her until one gets here, but a 9mm round doesn't usually go through. You get an entry wound and then a whole lot of mess inside. We often don't find a 9mm round until the post-mortem.'

'Brick Breaker'. The phrase fell from Joel's lips but just quietly enough for it to be ignored. Sandra continued.

'The fact one of them went through means, to me at least, that it was fired from very close range. Would you excuse me?' Joel stepped back for Sandra to move past him through the doorway and into the room. He was aware of DS Rose moving in closer behind him. There were stepping plates laid out and Sandra was careful to use them. She stopped on the plate closest to Hannah, crouching down so her knee was positioned just above Hannah's head.

'If you really want my *opinion,* the through-shot was the second one. First one takes her off her feet, the second one the shooter stood over her. Close range.' Sandra stood back up and twisted so her back was to Joel, then took on the posture of someone who might be pointing a pistol downwards. It made Joel shudder. He didn't need a clearer image of what had happened here. He only hoped that the first shot had taken her out, that there wasn't enough life left to stare up at her killer.

'The second shot was to make sure. She never stood a chance,' Joel said, still thinking out loud.

'That's much truer than you might realise,' Sandra said. She moved to another stepping plate on the right side of the body that allowed her to kneel near to Hannah's feet. Her gloved hand gently lifted her jean leg.

113

'What the hell is that?' Joel moved into the room, onto the nearest stepping plate.

'A shackle,' Sandra said. 'I think that's what you would call it. Heavy duty, the sort you might clamp round a bear's ankle, looking at how thick it is. No way she was getting out of it. The chain wraps around the bed post and is then secured to the radiator.'

'Shackled?' Joel gasped and turned back to DS Rose. He could only see her eyes and a little of the skin around them but her shock was tangible. She finally met Joel's gaze. 'The boss told me she'd been source handling for a few weeks at best. How the hell does she end up chained by the ankle and shot twice in some shithole flat?' Joel demanded. DS Rose shrugged. It looked like it was all she could manage. 'How well do you know her? Did she talk to you about what she was doing?'

'We worked together . . .' DS Rose took a half-step back, her gloved hand pushing at the door surround like she might be steadying herself. 'Child Protection, but different teams for most of it. She stayed in touch but you know what it's like when you're handling . . . She didn't really talk details.'

'Do you know why she was here? Have we been told that, at least?' Joel could feel frustration rising through him; he needed to keep it in check. He wasn't frustrated with his new DS, it was the situation – Debbie Marsden perhaps. You can't just be directed to a job where a police officer has been shot dead without any background. It wasn't fair. He had worked with source teams before and had a good understanding. Source handlers were on the cusp of being undercover police officers. The basic of a handler's role was to meet with informants, people who had information for sale that could assist the police, but it was so much more than that. A handler and their source needed to spend time together, the officer needed to understand the motivation for sharing information, the provenance, who else knew and how. It wasn't a job you could

114

get wrong. Most informants were criminals themselves, even involved in the very enterprise they were sharing information about. No one liked a grass; no one liked the system that made grassing a possibility either. Source handling was a dangerous occupation and the rules were strict, the processes tight, tried and tested. Joel knew two of the most basic rules: you *never* work alone and you *never* attend a residential address. From what Joel could see in front of him, Hannah Ribbons had broken both those rules. And paid a heavy price.

'The girl who lives here, she's on the books, she's given intel before, but no one's told me any more than that. Maybe someone found out and came here to catch her in the act.' DS Rose's voice carried her emotion.

Joel shook his head. 'I don't think so. I've known of handlers blown out before but they get fronted up, a bit of a slap at worst. The shits like to gloat that they know what they are. But they don't do this. Criminals know we want information, they know we go out asking for it, and source handling is all part of the game. But no one wants the scrutiny that comes with murdering a police officer, it's an incredible act of self-harm.'

'So whatever information was being shared, it had to be something that makes all this worthwhile.'

'Yes, it does,' Joel said and turned back to take in Hannah's form. 'This feels more than murder to me, more like an assassination . . .'

'Professional, you mean?'

'Maybe. But someone took the time to chain her up. You wouldn't do that if you were just here to kill her.'

'So the shooter was asking her what she knew?' DS Rose spoke again.

'Could be.' Joel cast his eye back over the blood on the bed. It was concentrated as a circular patch on the bottom right of the duvet – the part of the bed closest to the door. 'But they left the shackle.'

'And you think that means something?'

'We have to assume the whole point of that was to stop her escaping, to have control over her so once you shoot someone that need is gone. Why would you leave it?'

'Why not?'

'Because it tells us a story. It tells us that this wasn't some burglary that escalated, it tells us that this was something a lot more serious. That helps us. Why would you do that?'

'Because they wanted us to know?' DS Rose said and plunged them both into silence. It was Sandra who spoke next.

'I'm not one for getting hopes up but it does give us a forensic opportunity. Metal chains and clasps are good for traces, no matter how careful you are, lots of moving, pinchy bits. I've got lucky before.'

Joel took in the scene again. 'I know that. I think the killer might know that too. If it were me, I'd have her shackle herself. If I'm the one with the gun, I'm the one with all the power, why risk doing it?'

'It's been brought here though. This isn't something they've found lying around in the flat,' Sandra retorted.

'Which means it was premeditated. All of it. We know the occupant here is an informant, but nothing about what information she was giving, who she was talking about, what sort of offences even.' Joel turned towards his DS, but her only reply was to give her shoulders a slight lift, her eyes still pulled to where her friend was laid out in front of her.

'Ah, back to things we know. Somewhere I'm a lot more comfortable.' Sandra's stern exterior seemed to relax, there might even have been a smile behind her mask, and it eased some of the tension in the room. 'We know the occupant is dead too. She was found—'

'She's dead?' Joel cut her off, the surprise in his voice unavoidable, and he suddenly wished he had had the time to read the whole CAD.

116

'No one tells you anything, do they?' Sandra replied.

'It would appear not.'

'She was found at the same time and is still in the living room. Toxicology will give you the facts on that one but in normal circumstances my *opinion* would be a clear overdose. She's surrounded by paraphernalia, she's a clear user, track marks – everything you would expect,' Sandra said.

'You knew this was a double murder?' Joel spoke to his DS now.

'I did.'

Joel was quick to turn back to Sandra. 'So these aren't normal circumstances.'

'Far from it,' Sandra replied.

'We can't rule out that our drug user killed Hannah and then killed herself,' DS Rose said. 'Maybe she called her here with that intention?'

'Maybe,' Sandra answered.

'You don't think so?' Joel said and Sandra licked her lips before replying.

'I dunno, that doesn't feel right to me. Does it to you?'

'Feel right!' Joel couldn't help but chuckle. 'You were scolding me for asking for an opinion earlier. Now you want to talk about feelings!'

'You're right. I should know my place.' Her stern exterior was further eroded – her smile now unmistakable.

'I agree with you, I think we can rule her out. There's a story here and we're missing a lot of it. The weapon for a start. Someone took it with them, which means someone's missing from the scene,' Joel said, then turned to DS Rose: 'Who found her and called it in?'

'One of the occupant's mates. Came up to get a tenner she was owed, found the door insecure and called us when she saw what was in here. Uniform took a statement but she was off her face apparently.'

'And no one reported a gunshot?' Joel said.

'There are no other CADs, no.'

'We all just walked that hall, even our footsteps were bouncing around out there. A gunshot would have had every flat calling it in.'

'So, our killer found a way to make it quiet?'

'A suppressor. It's the only way.'

'What about wrapping it in something?' DS Rose looked to be actively searching the room for something that might back her up.

Joel looked at Sandra. 'I went to a scene before, someone fired through a pillow. It was a right mess. The pillow pretty much exploded.'

'It would. And it's not much quieter either. That's what happens when people believe what they see on the movies.'

'A suppressor is a specialist piece of kit,' Joel said.

'So maybe your assassination theory's right?' DS Rose said.

'Maybe,' Joel said, then he noticed Sandra's eyes lingering on him, the visible bits of her face bunched up like she was smiling again. 'What?'

'Nothing . . .'

'You need to say something? Come on, we're all friends now.'

She shrugged. 'You came up in conversation at another job. Word is that you're some TSG sergeant with barely a day detecting murders under your belt. Then you turn up here built like a rugby prop in a shirt a little too tight around your biceps and I was expecting an idiot.'

'Normally I try not to disappoint,' Joel said.

'You're not. Take that as you will.'

'So, what happens now?' Joel was keen to move the subject on. 'I assume you have a busy afternoon ahead of you?'

'I do. Ballistics are aware but no telling when they'll actually get here. I can't do much until they're finished. So far all I've done is a quick search but I will need full swabs, pictures and fibre mapping, then—'

118

'Fibre mapping?' Joel cut in, then in response to Sandra's disapproving look added: 'Just assume I'm some idiot with a shirt collar tight enough to restrict the blood to my brain . . .' he said and Sandra grinned.

'It's not as technical as it sounds, just lots of small, sticky squares. I cover the victim head to toe and number each one. Then they are photographed, removed and seized one-by-one. I'll then review each one for trace evidence and, if I find anything I can tell exactly where it came from on her body.'

'Sounds time-consuming.'

'It's utterly tedious is what it is. But necessary. We've had some good results from it. Then I'll do nail scraping, hair combing and swab her hands before I get her ready for transport to the morgue. That is, wrapping her feet, hands and head in plastic bags and then into a body bag. She won't be moved until tomorrow at the earliest.'

'You said you've searched her already. Anything?'

'Loose search for obvious wounds, to make sure she's not lying on the murder weapon, and I patted the pockets. I'll do a much more thorough search before she's bagged up. The first patrol on scene found her wallet with just a bank card in it; it was how she was ID'd. No mobile phone though.'

Joel rubbed at his face, his gaze back on the crumpled corpse that Sandra would soon be *bagging up*. It barely looked like a person. The colour of dried blood always reminded Joel of autumn leaves raked together and turning to mush. He would take that image over the reality right now.

DS Rose must have been looking at her too, because she turned to Sandra and said, 'Be gentle with her.'

Sandra's exterior softened. 'There's nothing a good CSI officer respects more than the dead. They have all the answers, see.'

'Let's hope so,' Joel said. 'We should have a look at the rest. Then I need to get up to speed as best I can. It seems I have a lot of catching up to do.'

119

'Body number two is through in the living room. That's not nearly as interesting,' Sandra said.

'Body number two,' Joel said. He couldn't help but sound incredulous.

'That's not what some TSG skipper wants to hear on their first day as an SIO investigating murder, is it?' Sandra's eyes twinkled again.

'No. And that will be why my superintendent missed that part out.'

There wasn't much else. The second victim was also still in situ in the living room amid a very familiar scene of a wasted life. A stick-thin young woman with numerous signs of drug use on various parts of her body was laid out with trousers pulled down to expose where she had injected the fatal dose into her groin. She was surrounded by paraphernalia as promised. It didn't help with any theories. It could well be that the woman happened to overdose at the same time as Hannah Ribbons was being murdered by gunshot in the only bedroom, but Joel couldn't quite see in his mind the order of events in that flat. Whatever had gone on, he was sure the key to putting it all together was understanding Hannah rather than the dead drug user.

Joel needed to get away. He swapped contact details with Sandra and smiled when she made him promise that he wouldn't go on to be a disappointment after all.

'I'm not sure I can promise much right now,' he said.

'You do have the look of a man thrown in at the deep end.' She beamed. 'One thing at a time, that's all you can do.'

'I agree and the first thing to do is to meet my new sergeant.'

'Oh,' Sandra said. She was loitering by the front door to the flat while Joel was stripping away his forensic layer. DS Rose was a little further away, looking out of the filthy window at the end of the corridor and out of earshot. 'I assumed Lucy was it?'

120

'She is, as of twenty-five minutes ago.'

This time Sandra's laugh was loud enough to bounce around the space. 'Someone really is setting you up to fail here, aren't they?' she said. Joel managed just a smirk.

'That's certainly what it feels like.'

Chapter 19

Google Maps guided them to a coffee-shop chain in an industrial estate nearby. DS Rose took a seat, choosing a corner booth a little distance away from anyone else while Joel waited at the counter for their drinks. She positioned herself with her back to him, her head turning occasionally like she might be looking out of the window.

'Are you OK?' Joel put the drinks down and stepped past to sit opposite.

'Not really. She was a friend of mine . . . Seeing her like that.'

'I can imagine. Not ideal for this to be the first case . . .'

'It's why I'm here. The only reason,' DS Rose snapped then pushed herself back in her chair, her head turning to the side again, her attention back out the window. She bit her bottom lip like she might have been hasty.

'I figured a coffee was a good idea for a couple of reasons. I need to get up to speed with this investigation, with what you know, but we also need to get to know each other a bit. Maybe that's where we should start,' Joel said. 'So, let's make this informal. You've just seen your mate laid out on the floor, you're angry and upset. This is a free pass to say what you're thinking. About me, about this investigation . . . about what it is you really want to say.'

'What I'm thinking?' DS Rose whipped round to face Joel. 'You want to be part of finding the person that did this to your mate, I get that, so you phoned my superintendent to be put on the investigation. But now you seem angry to be here.'

'I phoned Major Crime first' – DS Rose leaned forward now, her expression angry – 'and they told me it was nothing to do with them, told me some superintendent had thrown her weight around, saw this as a juicy way of launching some new team that would get her to the next rank and taken it off them. Major Crime, with their core of twelve experienced detectives and all the other experts they can call on. Two detective sergeants, a guvnor, a Detective Chief Inspector who's an experienced SIO, all ready and waiting to start finding out who shot and killed one of our own back there. But not now. Now they're all sitting on their hands and they're just waiting. See, when this investigation fails, Major Crime can use it to show that they can't be replaced after all and everything goes back to the way it was. But what about Hannah? The people that did this to her? She deserves better than being abandoned as some political pawn. She's dead, she was murdered.'

'When it fails?' Joel said.

'Sandra was right about you, you're no SIO. You're not even a detective.'

'My badge says different.'

'When was your last investigation, the last time you formally interviewed someone even?'

Joel sat back now. He sugared his drink, deliberately taking his time. 'Ten years would be about right for a formal interview. But questioning people – criminals, witnesses, people standing out on a ledge with every intention of jumping – every day since. We're police officers, we question everything, we investigate everything. You don't need to be on a specific unit to do that.'

'Roles on this new team have been advertised for a while. I saw them, I was even encouraged to apply. When I looked

123

into it I dismissed it, I dismissed you. You skippered a Tactical Support Group for a decade, that's smashing people's doors, fighting outside nightclubs, and farting competitions in a van with your mates. And now you think you can play at detective to secure your promotion. Maybe that was fine when it wasn't my mate laid out dead, her killer out there somewhere. But now it is.'

'So here you are to save the investigation,' Joel said.

'Here I am. Your superintendent knows I'm not staying, that I'm off after this. She agreed this was a secondment. Did she tell you that?'

'No one's told me anything, but it's OK, I'm getting used to it. On that note I'm going to head into a police station to catch up with what I missed and to start a policy log. At least then, when this fails, the Major Crime lot can have a good laugh at my amateur investigation.' Joel stood up. 'I suggest you stay here and finish your coffee, use it as time to think, because once you leave here we're back to ranks, we're back to me being the inspector and you the sergeant, that means you respecting me until I do something that means you don't. You don't rate me right now, based on a reputation, on what you think I've been doing for the last ten years, and that's down to you; if you don't rate me based on what you see going forward then that's down to me. I don't intend to let anyone down. Not you, not your mate back there either. You know nothing about me, you just proved that. Take your time.'

Joel left his coffee. DS Rose stayed where she was; her head didn't even turn as he passed. Joel was desperate for team members, never more so than now with a headless corpse in Dover and now two more bodies on the other side of the county. But he wasn't sure DS Rose was going to be much help at all.

124

Chapter 20

'Blimey, Rich, maybe you should ease up on the coffee!' Glenn Morris slid into the seat opposite. He looked hassled. His cheeks were a mottled red as he yanked at a black scarf that looked like it was winning. 'You look like shit, I have to say it. True friends are always the ones who will say it! How have you been getting on?' Glenn leaned forward, his expression, his body language, everything about him carrying an intensity.

'I'm OK,' Richard said.

'Are you?'

'Yes!'

'So you call me for an emergency catch-up because you're fine? You could at least make something up. Incontinence maybe, or, I tell you what would make my day, erectile dysfunction! Did you want to talk about that?' Glenn grinned to make Richard regret his tone.

'That will be the last thing to die, let me tell you that for nothing.' Richard even managed to laugh, and he felt a little more relaxed for it. His old friend laughed too. Glenn was bigger than Richard, in every way, and his laughter seemed to emphasise it. He leaned his head back so his wide neck and belly could shake with each guffaw. Even the noise was

125

big. Glenn had always been loud. It had helped during their army days and had become a standing joke: if Richard ever needed to know where he should be going he could always follow Glenn. It had helped him a number of times during Operation Banner, when both men had been part of a British army operating in the streets of Northern Ireland. This was where they had first met as young men, not realising that they were from the same area of the country. A lifelong friendship was quickly cemented – along with a commitment to meeting up at least once a week to talk about when life was better.

When the laughter settled down, the look Glenn gave Richard was one of genuine concern.

'Are you still struggling to sleep?' Glenn said and Richard waved him away. It wasn't even a consideration anymore. He barely slept, but he was used to it by now. 'What's the matter then?'

'Are you not staying?' Richard said, referencing the fact that Glenn was still wearing his coat. Glenn tutted, his face a grimace as he wrestled with his jacket. 'My back. Honestly, if I had known that one day just taking a coat off would be agony I think I might have taken more risks in the army days!' He finished the job then showed his contempt as he threw it onto the seat next to him. 'I don't take my coat off for everyone, you know.' Glenn clicked his fingers, 'I should write that down! What a chat-up line!' There was more laughter. It was weaker when it came and quicker to leave. Glenn settled on an expression that carried a clear message: it was time to talk about the reason they were here. Suddenly it felt to Richard like a bad idea. But it was too late now.

'I went to see Angela this morning,' Richard started.

'You go every morning, don't you?'

'Rain or shine.'

'Blueberry?' Glenn gestured to one of the muffins that still clogged the tray. Neither of them had touched their drinks.

126

'No!'

'Do you mind if I do? I figure if I'm going to wait all day for you to get to the point I might as well keep my strength up.'

'There was someone there, OK. Someone I hadn't seen before . . .'

'Who?' Glenn spoke with his mouth full. He dropped the rest of the muffin back onto the plate.

'I don't know.' Richard tutted, cursing his inability to speak clearly, to be succinct when he was stressed. 'The papers ran a few stories at the time, when it all happened. I got some calls. Some arseholes who thought they would see if they could get a rise.'

'Journalists? Those scu—'

'No!' Richard cut him off. 'They can't have been. They weren't asking me for my side of the story or anything like that, it was just like they were revelling in my misery. Like they wanted to make it worse. Sick bastards, is all.'

'Did you tell the police? Surely they—'

'No!' Richard snapped. Again. Glenn sat back. Richard seemed to take a deep breath. 'Sorry. This isn't about them. I'm not making any sense . . . I just wonder if I met someone with the same agenda as them sick bastards this morning is all. I guess I just wanted to talk about it.'

'So talk about it. What happened?'

'I was just sat with her. I forgot my gloves and flask, left them on the side together so I wasn't going to stay so long. I told her that, I know she would understand. A man sat down next to me.'

'What man?' Glenn's eyes narrowed.

'I don't know. A man. Forties probably, big build, smart. He said he was there for the view. I told him the view was on the other side of the grounds and I was almost rude. I don't like talking to people up there. But he didn't leave. Then he said he knew me. He used my name, he knew that Angela was my wife. He said he was some private investigator and

127

that at the time of the accident he was working with insurance fraud. He said he knew who had killed Angela.'

There was a silence. Glenn finally filled it with a sigh. 'Did he tell you? A name, I mean?'

'No.' Richard tutted again.

Glenn sighed again. 'I can imagine . . . I can imagine how difficult this has all been and I can imagine how much you want to believe that—'

'I didn't really give him a chance. I got angry. I just thought he was there for a windup . . .' Richard knew how this was sounding out loud.

'And you don't think he was? There to wind you up, I mean?'

'I don't know!' That feeling again, that feeling of being old and useless and doddery. Glenn was the last person in the world he wanted to show weakness too. He wasn't going to admit that he had struggled to even get off that bench this morning, that he had needed to sit for twenty minutes until his heart had settled and his vision was back. He had been so sure at first, so angry that someone would seek him out while he was sitting with Angela, that someone would choose that moment to make false promises. The cruelty. But the more he had gone back over what he had said, the more he was doubting himself and his convictions.

'Okay,' Glenn said. 'I would have got angry too. I don't see why someone would want to talk to anyone while they were at a graveside. That really isn't the time—'

'Missy . . .' Richard cut back in. 'When we went to see the litter, when we picked her out, there were eight dogs. A big litter. They'd wrapped bows round them all. Three pink and five blue. When we walked in I was talking to the breeder, but Angela, she went straight over. The pups were all together, bunched around their mum. But one puppy broke away. It had a little pink bow and it headed straight for Angela. I'll never forget. Angela went down to her knee and she held

128

out her hand and that little pup bundled right onto it to be picked up. And Angela . . .' Richard had to take a moment, the memory as clear as if he was there now. His wife's face was never more beautiful than when it was filled with a beaming smile. He had known straight away that it was love. 'Angela held that pup in her hand and she said, "Well, hello there, Missy!" First thing she said. And that was it. The puppy was ours and the name stuck. We never told anyone that.'

'Missy? Your dog . . .? You've lost me here, mate.'

'The name, Missy's name! It was one of those moments you have when you're a couple. Perfection. An in-joke that lasts the rest of your life. You didn't know that, did you? My closest friend. Friends of us both.'

'Know what, Richard?' Glenn's frustration was obvious now.

'Missy! How she got her name. That was it.'

'Oh, well no. Angela told me that she chose the name but I don't think you ever told me the full story.'

'But *he* knew it! Some random man on a bench almost a year after she . . . a year later. He knew that and no one else should. Then he said he knew who had been driving that car. What if he was telling the truth?'

'But the police . . .? How could he? It was investigated, they arrested people and did what they do. How could this man—'

'He said he had seen evidence that they couldn't use. Someone roughed someone else up for information so the police can't use it. I didn't listen, not to the full thing. My temper, since all this – I don't listen, I just bite.'

'It's OK, mate. That comes to us all. You just saw me lose my shit with a jacket!'

'I've just been feeling more and more . . . useless. I'm not washed up just yet, I know I'm not . . . but we're not what we were in our prime.'

129

'You speak for yourself, old man!' Glenn's guffaw was back. 'If this ain't my prime then I'm still on my way up!'

Richard smiled. His old friend always had a way of making him feel better. There was a longer silence. Glenn made the most of it, using the time to lift their drinks from the tray.

'Look, Rich, everything changed for you in an instant and I think you're still trying to catch up with it all. But you're getting there, I know you are. You talk about Angela a lot. Maybe you told someone about the Missy thing? That's possible, right? And some arsehole picked up on it and is throwing it back at you to mess with your mind.'

'You think people would do that?'

'Hundred per cent. You said yourself about those phone calls you had. People like to say things for a reaction – shitty things. You only have to go onto that Facebook thing and see what people say. I'm part of some veteran groups and sure as eggs are eggs, you'll get at least one a month come on there spouting some shit for a reaction. People can't help themselves. It's a cry for attention from someone who can't live without it. There are some sad little shits out there.'

'Are you talking about me or the Facebook thing now?'

'Both maybe!' Glenn chuckled.

'This wasn't some little oik. He was older, well dressed, well spoken. And when I got angry he apologised and left. If he was after a reaction why would he leave when I was just getting wound up?'

'Maybe he got what he wanted. Probably just enough to go home and rub one out. That's the sort of person you're talking about,' Glenn said. The smile on his face now had an edge of sympathy.

'You don't think he knows anything? You think it was just a windup?'

'Twelve months later. Why come to you now? And when you're chatting to your wife's headstone. That's an emotive

130

place, he could have bet on a reaction there. I think he might have got what he wanted.'

'I've been thinking about it ever since. I'm worried that I won't be able to stop thinking about it until I know for sure,' Richard said.

'Tell you what, did he leave a number or anything? I'll give him a call. I'll be happy to. I'll meet this arsehole in person. He won't get a reaction from me, then we'll see his agenda for what it is.' The smile was gone; Glenn's tone was full of anger and determination.

'He didn't leave me anything.'

Glenn's anger dropped away with a longer sigh this time. 'Of course he didn't! Think about that. If he was serious, of course he would have left you some way of getting back to him. Time-wasting arsehole. I wouldn't give him another thought. That's half the problem, I think – you've got plenty of time to sit and think.'

Richard sat back to slurp his tea. Glenn was right. He felt sure now. He did talk about Angela a lot, maybe he had told the story about Missy to someone. This man had spotted a weakness and got the reaction he was after. Richard wasn't angry anymore. He felt relieved.

'You're right. Thinking doesn't do anyone any good.'

'Did I tell you that? Sounds like the sort of thing I would say.' Glenn was smiling again. 'You were talking about getting back into work. I think that's a good idea. You liked it there.'

'I'm ready. I keep meaning to call up and make an appointment to go and see my manager.'

'Appointment? It's a shop, ain't it? Pop in there on the way back and see if you can talk to someone now. At least get the ball rolling.' Glenn was back to picking at the top of his blueberry cake.

'Maybe I will. Thanks, Glenn.'

'My pleasure. Have you talked to your boy recently? I've told you before that you should lean on him more. You're

131

always a better bloke to have a cup of tea with when you've spent some time with your grandson.'

'Colin's busy. He has his own life, his own family. The last thing he wants is his old man calling him up with silly problems.' Richard couldn't hide the melancholy in his own voice. He didn't want it to be true but he didn't think he was very welcome at his son's house.

'You're family. And this ain't some silly problem.'

'He has his hands full. It really doesn't matter, I just wanted to talk it out with someone. Cheers, this has been helpful.'

'Any time. Just as long as I know you're all right.' Pity was overriding the sympathy in his smile this time.

'I'm fine.'

'I know this is eating you up is all, and I don't like to see it. This has been an obsession for a long time – knowing who was driving that car – but it won't change anything. Even if you found out.'

'It might change how I feel.'

'It won't bring her back.'

'I'm not stupid, Glenn. I know that.' Glenn held his hands up like he was surrendering the point. 'Let me ask you, if it had been different for your Linda, if it wasn't an illness that took her, if she was run down by some coward who didn't stop, who kept going, who burnt out the car so he wouldn't have to answer for what he had done . . . and you found him. What would you do?'

'It wasn't though, was it? It was an illness and it was a long time ago. So I know it gets easier, not much, just enough that you can keep going.'

'I'm not trying to upset you, but if that was what happened, if you had the chance to find who did it . . .'

'Find them? Where is this going, Richard? You never said anything about finding them.'

'This guy, he told me he knew who he was but the police

132

weren't interested because of how he knew. Why else would I need to know a name if it wasn't to find him?'

'I suppose you have a point.'

'So what would you do?'

Glenn shrugged his big shoulders. 'I dunno. I mean, I would want some answers, I guess. I would want to know what happened. Why he didn't stop and do the decent thing. People can make mistakes.'

'He was saving his own arse.'

Glenn shrugged again. 'I'm sure you're right. I guess I'm playing devil's advocate.'

'You are. You can do that when it's not your wife. Think again, it's Linda lying out on a stone-cold pavement, dying because someone came from nowhere and ran her down and they're not stopping. And she's never coming home.'

'Jesus, Rich . . .'

'You can't get justice from the police. Not ever. But you find out who he is.' Richard held his friend's stare with an intensity that had been missing since they had both stepped away from the army. Glenn moved to sit straighter. He stared back, never looking to break the gaze, recognising that Richard was reading him.

'I'm not sure what you want me to say, Rich. Our days of sorting squabbles with a dance outside the pub are long g—'

'Squabbles!' Richard could feel his heart hammering. It started up so quick it took his breath away. 'This isn't some squabble with some lad who knocked your pint over, this is my wife, Glenn.' The last of his words were squeezed – it felt like his breath was running out at the same time as his throat was closing up. His vision blurred too, even quicker than normal, and a blackness seemed to close in from both sides. He thrust his hands out as his balance went and heard a clatter of crockery. A moment later his right hand was scalded.

'Okay, mate, take it easy!' Glenn's voice cut through his

133

blurred vision and the closing darkness. Another voice came from his left, a female voice, young-sounding.

'Is he OK?' she said.

'Of course I'm fucking OK!' Richard snapped towards it. He couldn't see her, all he could see was a dark red outline.

'He's fine, he's absolutely fine. Just chuck me a cloth, would you, and I'll clear this up.'

'I can clear it up!' Richard snapped again. He felt Glenn's big hand on his shoulder. He tried to jerk away, to push it off, but the grip was tight. 'I'm not totally fucking useless!' Richard said.

'Okay, mate, calm yourself down. There are kids an' that in here. Let's talk this out. My fault, I should be taking you more serious.' Glenn's voice was right in his ear, but when he heard it next it was directed away. 'Love, would you mind getting us a glass of water here, please? We're fine, love! It's OK. Just a glass of water and we'll be all good.' The voice came back into his ear. 'Okay, mate, we're good. She looks a bit pissed off, but I've got used to women looking at me like that.' Richard felt a bump on his hip where Glenn had slid into the seat beside him. 'You feeling OK, mate? You've gone a bit pale is all. Take a minute.'

Richard scrunched his eyes shut. He had made a scene. That was the last thing he wanted to do. He was there for a quiet chat with an old friend. To run the day's events past him for an opinion. He didn't know how it had got to this point. He couldn't control his emotions anymore. His vision cleared enough to make out details. Glenn got up to greet a young woman who was walking towards them with a large glass of water. He thanked her. She cast a filthy look over at him. When Glenn turned back the pity in his smile was far more brazen. Richard got to his feet.

'Woah! Where are you going there, mate? I reckon you need a little sit down for a while. Just until you get your breath back.'

He was weak. At least that was how Glenn saw him. Just what he wanted to avoid. Richard had to get out of there. He stepped away and his heel caught on the table leg and he stumbled a little. He could feel his heart beat again, back thumping in his chest, but his vision was still blurry. He kept moving, lifting his head to fix on the block of light down the end of the shop that he knew to be the exit.

'I'm not a washed-up old fool just yet,' he muttered.

Chapter 21

This hangover was the worst yet. Danny Evans massaged his puffy eyelids like it might work some life back into them. It was a few minutes before midday and he still hadn't even pulled back the curtains. He didn't want to. The eruption of light would no doubt agitate his state, but a bigger reason to keep the curtains shut was his refusal to embrace a new day. He didn't want to move on from last night, he didn't deserve to.

He had murdered someone.

It felt different. Marcus Olsen had come with a sense of detachment. Someone else had done all of the work. Someone else had got him to the building, someone else had tied him up to fill his mouth with the barrel of a shotgun. Danny could play that one down, strip it back to its basics. All he had done was pull on a strip of metal and even that he had been coerced into doing. He would challenge any father standing in that room, reading that material, to have done anything different.

But last night he had driven for an hour to walk into a building with a weapon in his hand. He had followed instructions and a woman was dead. He wasn't just a father seeking vengeance, he was a murderer.

He had made it back to his hotel in a daze, even forgetting the horror that he had left on the bed. But the suited man had been as good as his word. His bed looked fresh, there was a whiff of carpet cleaner and the sink was clear.

Still, he had needed to drink his petrol-station liquor to fend off the image of a young woman throwing her palms up at him like she was about to beg for her life. In fact, he had drunk well past that, to the point of slipping unconscious. His first wake-up had been on the floor of the bathroom and from there he had crawled to the foot of the bed to continue his slumber – even in an intoxicated state he still couldn't bring himself to clamber onto the sheets. Now he felt nausea with every movement. Even moving his eyes caused him discomfort, like he could actually feel the optic nerves working behind them.

Staggering to the bathroom, he filled his hands with water and slurped as much of it as he could. He had given up looking for the plastic beaker. He had given up looking for his phone too, but there was a buzzing now like it was ringing on silent. He stumbled back into the room and froze when the noise stopped, unsure if it hadn't just been a rhythm beating in his head. But it started again. He found it face down and pushed someway under his bed. Turning it the right way up made him grimace at the bright light. It was his wife. He felt panicked. What if she wanted to invite him round tonight? He couldn't go. Not feeling like this. Not after what he had just done. He couldn't think of an excuse either, not one that she wouldn't see straight through. She would know that it would take something catastrophic for him to stay away. Something like shooting a stranger twice in the chest.

The phone rang out and he sighed his relief. Maybe he would say he lost his phone. It wouldn't be the first time. He threw it onto the bed. He couldn't talk to her, not now. All he could think of was getting another drink, enough for it all to fade away again: the bloodied corpses, the mysterious private detectives. At least he was done with him now – there was something to drink to.

137

His gaze lifted to where he was standing in front of a small mirror. He hadn't got undressed from yesterday's clothes and now his shirt hung out and was creased, and his trousers had a dark stain from the knee down. He would shower first. Then he needed to get rid of these clothes. He would burn them like he had seen them do on the movies. The movies about murderers.

Sharon Evans swore then covered her mouth when her twelve-year-old son spoke behind her.

'What did Dad say? Is he coming?'

'I couldn't get hold of him. I'll keep trying.'

'He's not going to believe it!' Jamie beamed. He was more excited than Sharon could remember seeing him for a long time. She felt it too. For her it was still mixed up with doubt and worry, like it was all too good to be true. But she had heard it for herself. The doctors were encouraged, the pneumonia was gone and Callie's lung function was back, enough that they were going to start lowering her sedation and remove the antibiotics. Her daughter was going to wake naturally and it should be soon. Sharon had been warned that Callie would not be instantly as they remembered, she wouldn't be properly lucid for a good few days at least. But Sharon didn't care. It was a huge leap forwards and a moment she wanted to share with her husband. This was everything they had been praying for. Sharon had stepped away from the hospital bed, but even now she could see them changing Callie's position to make her more comfortable for when she was awake.

For when she was awake.

For the first time, Sharon could dare to believe it was going to happen and she suddenly felt anxious to get back to her. She typed out a quick message asking Danny to call her back.

138

Chapter 22

Just to be pulling into the car park, to watch the barrier lift as he swiped his fob to access the staff car park behind the large DIY store that had been his place of work for more than six years, it all felt so good to Richard. His entrance was accepted. He was somewhere he belonged, somewhere he had a purpose. Somewhere he wasn't just a dithering old fool. Glenn was usually right about most things and today he had been right about one for sure: it was time he did something about getting back to work.

The car park was busy. On a Saturday there were additional workers to cover the busier weekends. He took the last space then got out of the car, inhaling the familiar scent from the cardboard-crushing machine that was positioned next to the staff entrance, and feeling himself beaming as he made for the door. Elizabeth was so close on the other side she looked startled as he pushed the door. She was a heavy smoker, her cigarette already in her mouth like she couldn't wait.

'Oh! Hey, Richard!' She had a large build, her face was always blotched somewhat red, and she had health issues that were restricting her duties more and more. When Richard was last here she was being moved from the shop floor to a permanent seat at the tills. He'd overheard some of the other staff

139

complaining about it but Richard liked her. She lived on her own, craved a different life and found comfort in a bad lifestyle. It didn't make her a bad person.

'Elizabeth! Good to see you.'

'Now I know you're back! You're still the only person that calls me that!'

'Sorry . . . Lizzie,' he said, and the small talk ran out. Elizabeth's expression changed, her brow creased, her lips pursed and Richard recognised someone who was just about to offer their condolences. He had already come back to work once since losing Angela, but his return had been too early and a big reason he hadn't been able to cope was the reactions of his colleagues. For some reason, people felt the need to go straight into insincere attempts at sympathy or empty gestures of *anything I can do, you just let me know* while they pussyfooted around him like he was made of porcelain. He was quick to cut in before Elizabeth could speak again.

'Is Carole in?' he asked her.

'Oh, yeah! She was in the loading area last I see her. That's . . . that's why I'm here actually.' Lizzie suddenly looked embarrassed. 'I've snuck out for an extra break. I don't normally but it's just so busy . . .' Her words petered out. Richard had his hand raised.

'I understand, mum's the word.' He winked too.

Elizabeth's smile was genuine. Richard held the door for her and continued along the corridor. She heard Elizabeth call after him. 'It's so nice to see you back!'

The loading area was on the other side of the building. Richard walked past the offices and break room to go out onto the shop floor. Again, the smell was the thing that was instantly recognisable. It was a mix of freshly cut wood and forklift truck fumes: delicious. He made his way across the aisles, waving and nodding as co-workers did a double-take then broke out into a smile. Some started forming their sympathy faces but he swept past them all before they could

140

add words. The load area was instantly cooler. The big doors were open straight ahead. The lumbering shape of a lorry pulled away, filling the large space with noise and more fumes. It was all so familiar and Richard's desire to be back in amongst it all was getting stronger with every step. Carole was straight ahead and bent forward over a clipboard, her pen busy. Richard waited a few paces away until she finished. She still jumped.

'Oh! I didn't see you there! Wait . . . Do we have an appointment?'

'No! No, nothing like that. I just thought I would pop in and see you. Have you got a moment for a quick chat?'

'Chat? Yes, of course. I could do with a coffee anyway.'

'Sounds good!'

Carole led the way back to the break room. It was empty of people and almost empty of furniture. A few scattered chairs, a vending machine that had a loud buzz, and a drinks machine next to it that vended coffee for twenty-five pence a cup that tasted every bit like coffee that cost twenty-five pence a cup. Richard used to bring his own. He had complained about it so much that Angela had bought him a large flask that she would fill for him before every shift. Now it was the flask that accompanied him to her graveside.

'Coffee?' Carole had a shrill voice. It seemed to suit her. She was a shrill individual, short, stout and direct, but then she was management in a male-dominated industry and more than held her own. Richard had seen her tear lorry drivers, employees and mocking labourers to pieces when she needed to. She certainly didn't suffer fools.

'Thanks. Extra sugar from there please.'

'To hide the taste?' She grinned.

'Absolutely.'

'So, what can I do for you?' The machine clunked and whirred. Carole let it do its thing and pulled a seat so they were at the same table.

141

'Do for me? It's really what I can do for you, actually. I wanted to pop in and let you know that I am ready and raring to come back. Well, ready at least!' Richard snorted a laugh. He reeled it back into a half-smile as Carole's dropped away.

'Oh, I see.'

'You don't seem sure? It wasn't that long ago that we talked about my return. You've been wonderful, right from the off, *take as long as you need,* and that's been so good for me. I want to start repaying that faith. I'll work whatever you need. I know you had some ideas about how I could do a few days a week or shortened days, but I really think I can just come back and do what you need.'

'I did say that.' Carole's lips were pursed, her expression dangerously close to someone who was about to offer their sympathies.

'So here I am,' Richard added. 'I can just come back on the same terms, fulltime as it was, and then if I find there's an issue I can talk to you about it and maybe drop a day. What's the matter?' He stopped. Carole's body language had changed. She held one arm with the other, supporting it so she could rub at a mouth that now formed a slight scowl.

'Oh goodness, Richard! Nothing is the matter! Here we are, a hard worker back in the building and ready to pick up where they left off! I'm just concerned. Maybe your ears have been burning in fact – we've been talking, me, the senior management team and HR. We're all very worried about you.'

'You don't need to worry. That's very kind. The best thing for me is to get back to work. To be busy again.'

'Is it?'

'What do you mean? Of course it is. It's been nearly twelve months since . . . And I know I came back too early after, I know that now. But this time away has been just what I needed.'

142

'You didn't cope, Richard. I couldn't put you out the front, you couldn't talk to customers. Your job . . . That's really all it is. I need to be able to rely on my staff for that.'

'Like I said, it was too early. But that won't happen again, I'm actually looking forward to getting back out there and helping people out. I've missed that.'

'It's been three months since we've seen you. Some of your credentials have expired in that time, Richard. You'll need to requalify on a few of the health and safety bits to get back up to speed. We've got a new system at the tills too. A lot can happen in three months in the world of DIY!'

'So it seems. Nothing I can't catch up with. I'll do it in my own time if it's a problem.'

Carole pushed herself back now, her palms out like she was retreating. 'I'm sure there won't be any need for that! There's been some changes, way above me but they're filtering down. Previously the recruitment drive was very much towards . . . experienced employees—'

'Old people,' Richard cut in.

'I prefer experienced. It made a lot of sense too but the landscape of DIY stores is very much changing. We've tipped over on our online sales.'

'Tipped over?'

Carole tutted. Maybe the meaning was obvious. 'Tipped over fifty percent. Now online sales are the *majority* of sales and that's a very conscious effort. Some items we are now listing online only and if people come in here we're actually—'

'Does this matter to me?' Richard snapped. He could feel his heart racing again. He could tell Carole was building towards something and it didn't feel like it was good news.

'It matters. We're not taking on so many experienced staff members. We find they have difficulty with the speed the business is changing at, with the new direction.'

'I'm not asking to be taken on; I'm ready to come back.'

'And I'm telling you that won't be possible.' Carole leaned

143

on the table now, her fingers interlocked. She was waiting for a response. For a moment Richard didn't have one.

'But we talked. You said I was welcome. You said for me to take as long as I liked!'

'I did. This is all above me. Businesses change, they have to, to survive.'

'But I was good here, I was good for you. I had a setback is all but I'm feeling good about coming back here.'

'A setback . . . Richard, your wife died and—'

'I know she fucking died, Carole, I don't have my head permanently up my own arse like those management types you're talking about, I just meant . . .' Richard had to stop. His breath had run out. He took a moment, tried to fill the gap with tutting like he was too angry to speak, not fighting his own body.

'Look, Richard, we're not taking on a seventy-year-old. Not for the foreseeable future.'

'I'm sixty-eight.'

'Sixty-eight then. We have a new MD – Brett – and he's got big new ideas for us. He's taking us in a different direction. And if he doesn't then the whole business will fall behind our competitors and none of us will have jobs.'

'People don't want some teenager talking to them about how to fix or improve their homes,' Richard tried again.

'People work differently these days. There's not a single DIY job that doesn't have a step-by-step video online. They just want their materials, which means they just want someone who can work out how best to get it to them. Now come on, this is a good thing! I had the same conversation with Henry a month or so ago. He agreed and took retirement. He popped in the other day and he's glad he walked away while he's still young enough to enjoy life. He talked about how he might have dropped dead in the aisles rather than admit it was time to call it a day. Surely you've considered this?'

'No.'

144

'Enjoy your life. This is your chance.'

'ALONE!' Richard slammed his fist down at the same time. It was the second time he had made Carole jump, but this time she looked a lot less impressed. Richard stood up. His chest was beating harder now, and he had to lean on the back of the chair for a moment. He had a reply, he was going to tell Carole to tell *Brett* that he could be the one to drop dead. But he needed to get out of there. He couldn't speak, his breath was gone. Carole was still seated. She was looking up at him, that faux-sympathy now very much a fixture. But Richard could see right through it. She was looking at him like she thought he was pathetic.

He recovered enough to walk but not to talk at the same time. Carole didn't stop him. He heard Elizabeth call out as he walked back across the shop floor, but he didn't even acknowledge her. This wasn't how he wanted to leave this place. He had turned up full of the idea of roaring back into the workplace but had ended up leaving with a whimper.

He found his car parked in the last space and sobbed, letting the last few days consume him.

145

Chapter 23

Sunday

The frost was thicker even than the morning before and Richard was thankful that he had remembered his gloves this time. He had put them to use scraping the thick frost from one side of the bench so he could sit. He had his flask too, the one his wife had bought for him when he had got his new job at the DIY store. He had filled it right to the top, an amount that used to last him a whole day at work. He didn't know how long he was going to be here today but he fancied it would be a while. He had a lot to talk about.

'Morning, my love. A fresh one today!' Richard used to talk to his wife no matter what, but today checked he was alone first. He didn't want to be the sad, lonely old man sitting on the bench talking to the ghosts of his past. It was just gone 7 a.m. When he had stepped off the glistening path to walk the short stretch through the grass to his bench there had been no signs of any disturbance in the frost. No one else was about. Just him and his ghosts. Just how he liked it.

He pulled the lid from his flask. The centre popped up to steam instantly. The steam increased as he poured, enough to coat his glasses in moisture. He put the coffee down next to him to wipe the lenses.

'I hoped you would be here.' The voice came from behind

146

him. Richard spun to a wide outline, a figure dressed in dark clothing, of which Richard could make out a long, smart jacket. Richard went back to wiping his glasses. When he put them back on, the man hadn't moved and he could see better, enough to recognise the same man who had been a visitor the previous morning. The private investigator with no tact. He must have come back for another go.

'Can't say I was thinking the same about you. This is not the time or the place, sonny. You should have more respect for the dead.'

'The dead don't need or want anything. It's the living that I concern myself with.'

'You mean me!' Richard's laughter was a tight ball of mist that quickly dissipated. 'Who even are you?'

'I just wanted to apologise. That was all. Yesterday, when I came to see you, I really did want to do something right for once. I felt like I let you down before. I still feel like that. I saw a broken man whose life was ruined through no fault of his own. I thought if that were me, if I was that man, then I would want someone to come and tell me what they knew, especially if I was hurting at a graveside. It might not change anything but this information is not for me. It's no good to me. I never even met your wife but like I said yesterday I'm not so good at subtle. So I'm sorry. That's all I wanted to say. I won't bother you anymore.'

Richard had stayed facing his wife but he turned to look behind him now. He watched the back of the man as he moved away until his dark colours seemed to lighten where the freezing mist started to consume him.

'Do you have a card?' Richard called after him. 'Something . . . In case I want to talk to you later?' The man stopped and spun on the grass. He had his hands firmly pushed into his coat pockets. It made him look wider.

'No. I really shouldn't be here. I could get into trouble. I can't leave any details, anything that leads back to me.'

147

'Some good deed,' Richard said.

'I tried. That will be good enough for me. I wanted to try at least.' Now the mist swallowed him whole. Richard scooped up his coffee and shook it out of the lid. The burning hot remnants slopped on his exposed wrist and he barely noticed. He rose to his feet to search the mist to try to spot the man's direction. He could go after him. Maybe he *should* go after him. He shook his head. Maybe that was what the man wanted; once Richard went chasing him for information the tables had turned. Richard had enough life experience to know a sales technique when he saw it, and he didn't want anything of what the man was selling.

'Good deed!' Richard puffed his words out. 'No one does anything for nothing.' He poured another coffee.

The mist continued to drift over and around him while he talked it all out with Angela. He talked about how he and Glenn had argued for the first time in forever; how it wasn't Glenn's fault, it was just that he was starting to feel so useless. He was lashing out, he knew that. Angela had told him about it enough. He talked about his job too and how he was now officially retired. He laughed about the plans they had discussed for their retirement: holiday homes, camper vans and that crazy idea of repeating their honeymoon in that terrible little B&B in deepest Wales that had, by all accounts, become even more terrible in the forty-odd years that had followed. He felt better. He always did, but as with any high there was always the inevitability of coming down the other side. For Richard, this came when his coffee ran dry or when the frozen mist finally penetrated his layers – whichever came first.

It was soon time to go.

He took his hand out of his glove to kiss his fingertips, then to rest them gently on her headstone. His shiver was instant and violent. It wasn't a reaction to the cold but to a vivid memory – the sensation took him back to Angela, to the last time he had seen her. He had followed her ambulance to hospital and his memories of that place were disjointed and partial: vivid white walls and flashes of his wife's pale skin through the blur of movement that was all around her. Then she was taken away. The next time he saw the same medical staff they were slower, more deliberate and they were looking at him, building up to tell him it had all been for nothing. He didn't want his last image of her to be desperate attempts at revival, a fight for life. He wanted to see calmness, to see peace.

All he had got was stillness.

Her leg was crushed, her hips out of shape, her hair a clump of blood. They had cleaned her face for him but there was no peace, not to him. He had kissed his fingertips to place them gently on her cheek then and the shock of that sensation was what came back to him now. He ran his eyes over her headstone one last time, lingering on the inscription: *To live in the hearts we leave behind is not to die.*

'Then what?' he scoffed. 'Then we're just nothing, are we?'

When Richard returned to his car, his windscreen had collected a layer of the mist. He was in the driver's seat trying to work the heaters before he noticed the piece of paper tucked under the wiper on the outside. It was small, lined and with a jagged edge like it had been torn from a notepad. He climbed back out, looking around as he did. His car was parked tight against the perimeter wall of Lympne Castle. The mist was the only movement, a creak in his car door the only sound. He lifted the handwritten note, and read:

I still can't walk away from this. I've made you an appointment at my temporary office. Today – midday. All the answers will be there but they are for you and you only. Please, if I see you with someone else then we will not meet. Not today, not ever. I don't wish to sound dramatic but I have gone out on a limb here.

149

If you do not come then I will understand. I will know that I have done all that I can and I will be satisfied.

I require nothing in return. All I want is my own peace of mind. This is the only way.

CT15 4AN. Block B. Room 2.12.

Richard leaned on the roof of his car to keep himself steady. Again, he peered out into the mist. It was starting to thin, the sun now visible behind it as a white blur. Still there was no movement, no one around, certainly not a smartly dressed man that he could challenge, demand to know what the hell he wanted from him. He was tired. He wanted to be left alone, that was all. But he did want answers. He had always wanted answers. And what if this was his only chance?

He screwed the note up and discarded it on the passenger seat.

150

Chapter 24

'He's in his shed.'

Justine Maddox stood in the doorway and fixed Richard with an expectant look – the expectation being that Richard would go away and find his son. There was certainly no suggestion he was welcome inside the house, but Richard had got used to that now.

'I'll see if I can find him then.' Richard considered making small talk but the option went with the shutting of the front door. He paced across what would once have been a busy yard, bursting with life, the rough concrete covered in the debris that came with keeping a variety of farm animals. Now the main barn was converted into his son's house and underfoot was pristine block paving in neat swirls with sharp borders. The 'shed' was also a barn conversion, although much smaller and with the original façade largely hidden behind layers of darkened weatherboard to match the house. It formed a double garage with a carport reaching out from the side. His son worked out of the office above it. When he had built it he had boasted how it would save him commuting into the City every day, but Richard knew it hadn't quite panned out that way. His son worked in aviation insurance, an industry that seemed to be all about face-to-face meetings with clients, so

151

all the addition of a home office had done was to extend Colin's working day long into the evenings. When Richard had pointed this out it had turned into an argument. It was at a time when everything seemed to turn into an argument. Richard didn't tend to point things out any more.

'Colin!' he called out through one of the raised double doors. He heard his son before he saw him. Something solid bumped down onto a wooden surface, scuffing the floor, then his face leaned round.

'Oh, Dad. Hey.'

'How are you?' Richard said, his tone overcompensating for his son's lack of enthusiasm.

'Everything OK?' Colin replied immediately then stepped fully into view. He was wiping his hands with a rag.

'Fine! I can come and see you without there being something wrong, can't I?'

'You can. Of course you can. I would shake your hand, but' – he lifted greasy palms – 'just tinkering with the MG.' He stepped back in for Richard to follow. Behind the garage doors the whole of the bottom was opened up as a large room with the stairs boxed in against the back wall. His classic car was up on a stand, wheels off. The bodywork could easily pass for something brand new in a showroom. This car was the only thing his son seemed to be passionate about these days.

'Don't worry,' Richard said. 'She's looking nice.'

'Yeah, she's getting there. Should be as good as new when she's done.' Colin stopped to stare at it now, his eyes flashing with enthusiasm. Richard could tell he was in love. 'Coffee?' his son said, finally.

'Sure.'

Colin made for the stairs rather than out and back to the house. Richard followed. The moment he got to the top step there was a flurry of noise and movement.

'GRAAAAAAANDAAAAD!' Thomas Maddox hit him in

152

the midriff and for a moment threatened to topple him back down the stairs. It would have taken them both, so tight was the hold his grandson now had round him.

'Thomas! I didn't know you were here.'

The boy backed away. He was still small in frame and build, small for twelve years old anyway. His face was a grin surrounded by freckles that mirrored the colour of his untidy mop of red hair. He was holding a games controller and gestured to a large screen behind him where some colourful-looking action was paused. 'They sent us home for half term. The dorm's got a leak, they need to do some maintenance or something. You wanna play?' he said excitedly.

'In a minute perhaps. Your dad was just going to make me a coffee.' Thomas spun away to run and leap onto a long sofa. The game resumed with a roar of noise.

'Jesus . . . Turn that down,' Colin shouted over the noise and Thomas did as he was told.

The top floor was different from when Richard had seen it last. Then it had been a large office space, the sofa down the end to face a pull-down movie screen. The screen was still fixed to the wall but the sofa had moved and more soft furnishings had appeared. Now the right side contained a sofa bed that was extended with ruffled sheets and a stack of pillows. From the stairs they had emerged straight into a small fitted kitchen area that was new too. The coffee machine was on a breakfast bar with one high stool pushed up against it. Colin gestured for him to sit.

'It's changed up here,' Richard said.

'I guess it has. When was the last time you were here?'

'It must be six months.'

'Six months? That's flown by.'

'It has. I don't like to just pop round uninvited. I know you're busy.'

'Still take your coffee white with one?' Colin said quickly, preventing a silence that could only have been awkward.

153

'Yes, please.'

Richard spun on his stool to look back out over the room. 'So, this is pretty much a self-contained annexe in here. It's evolved from a home office, I see,' he said.

'It has. I had a kitchen and a bathroom put in. The toilet's just through there. I still use it as an office. I've got my laptop set up on the desk but it left a lot of space wasted.'

'Do you sleep up here?'

Colin flicked his attention away from his coffee machine for just a moment. He shrugged as he went back to the drinks. 'Sometimes. If I'm working late then I don't like to disturb Justine over at the house, you know, she'll be in bed and the last thing she wants is me waking her up.'

'You have three spare bedrooms over there, four if you include Thomas's room.'

'Thomas's room is still Thomas's room!' Colin snapped.

'It is, when he's not at boarding school, when the dorm doesn't have a leak. That must be inconvenient.'

Colin slopped a mug down on the counter. 'Is that why you came today, to pick up on an old argument? We've talked about this. I need to work and that school is one of the best in the country. Thomas is getting opportunities like never before. He's not long back from a trip: Austria, skiing. You don't get that at the local secondary.'

'You don't. You do get a family to go back to though,' Richard said and regretted it instantly. He held his hands up and was quick to speak again: 'That came out wrong. I'm sorry. I didn't come here to argue.'

'Makes a change.'

'I just wish . . . I didn't know Thomas was back. I could have planned something, taken him off your hands for a day. There are places we could go.'

'You still can.'

'When does he go back?'

'A few days. It was all a bit last minute, OK. I didn't even

154

have to time to sort anything with work so I could look after him.'

'Justine couldn't help with that?' Richard said, aware that he was again walking a fine line. 'I assume she's still not working?'

'She's looking for work actually. She has a friend who does event planning. She was talking to me the other night about getting involved with that.'

'Event planning? That's good work. And this friend will give her a job at her events?'

'She's talking about setting something up. Her own business.'

'So, competition for her friend?'

'Well, I suppose she would be. But there's plenty to go around. We have another barn on the land. It would need a total renovation but we could run weddings in there. Have you any idea how much money there is in weddings?'

'A lot, I would imagine. A lot of work too.'

'Justine isn't afraid of hard work,' Colin snapped. 'Besides, we would take on a staff.'

Richard bit his tongue. He'd bet she would take on staff too. He had never known his daughter-in-law to work, or display an appetite to do so, for that matter. But that was far from the first thing he disliked about her. She was materialistic; money was all that mattered and Richard was certain it was why she had got involved with his son. They fell pregnant quickly. Both Richard and Angela had hoped that this might wake Justine up, that she would see that material wealth wasn't so important now she could be a mother – part of a family. Nothing can ever be more important than that. But she was even shirking motherhood. She had been able to convince Colin to send Thomas away to boarding school the moment he was old enough. Before that had been a string of nannies and day care while she sat in their large house shopping on the internet. The fact that

155

Angela hadn't liked her daughter-in-law either was enough for Richard. Angela saw the good in everyone. But raising it with Colin meant that father and son had fallen out for the first time ever, to the point of not even speaking. It had been a long way back.

'How is Thomas getting on at school now?' Richard looked over to where his grandson had moved to headphones to fully immerse himself in his game.

'He seems to be getting on really well. Better at least.'

'Better?'

'We had some issues to start with. It's a big transition, isn't it? Moving to halls.'

'It is at his age.'

'Is that all you came for then? A bit of a catch-up?' Colin swept up his coffee and took a gulp like he was suddenly rushing.

'Yes. I went to see your mother this morning and I found myself driving round rather than going home. It's been a rough couple of days so I thought I would head your way, see if I can't bring you down to my level!' Richard said, forcing a laugh.

Colin mirrored his smile but it was fleeting. 'Rough, how so?'

'Ah, nothing major. Just the realisation that I am both old and useless. It seems to feel official all of a sudden. Yesteday I went into work to talk about how I might go back, in what capacity at least. Turns out they see me as going back retired.'

'Retirement! I never thought I would see the day.' Colin finally managed a genuine smile.

'Me neither.'

'So what now?'

'I really don't know.'

'You know, most people embrace it – retirement, I mean. Most people work their whole life looking forward to it.' Colin seemed to be studying Richard closer.

'I was doing just that when your mother was still around.'

156

Another silence. This time it was allowed to grow until it got awkward.

'You must miss her,' Colin said eventually. 'She always knew what to do. I wish she was here to talk to.'

'I miss her every minute of every day. Cherish what you have, Colin. I know I'm just some silly old fool and you can just give me lip service if you want but this family of yours, make the most of them.'

'I would love to. If only Justine would give it a chance.' Colin's expression flickered like it might change. He turned away, sloshing his cup out in the sink.

'Are you OK? You and Justine, I mean?'

Colin stayed facing away. His head was dipped like he was still looking down at his cup. He suddenly leaned forward to take his weight on hands that gripped the sink. His shoulders shook. It was subtle at first, then a sound that Richard thought might be laughter. It wasn't until Colin sniffed that Richard knew his son was sobbing.

'Jesus, Colin, what the hell is going on?'

'Nothing. It's nothing! I've just been under a lot of pressure. I've been working a lot.' His son lifted his hands to wipe his face before he turned back. His eyes were a little red, and his arms hung forward like he was suddenly carrying extra weight.

'Are you sure that's all it is?' Richard pressed him. 'That bed over there, are you sleeping in it rather than your own?' Colin took a moment then nodded. 'Every night?' He nodded again. 'Is there anything I can do?'

'No!' He sounded angry now, it was instant. 'Of course there isn't! All you can do is tell me *you told me so* and that's the last thing I want to hear right now. I know you've never liked Justine . . .' He paused like he was catching his breath.

'She's not made it easy, son. I have tried but—'

'Not for long! I barely knew the girl and you were warning me off her. You know, sometimes I think I only married her to spite you. Big mistake that was.'

157

'Now come on, you can't blame me for any issues with—'

'Oh no! Of course I can't blame you. You know everything about parenting, about women, about making a family. You tell me that all the time, you like to rub my face in it, make sure I know that I've messed up just like you said I would.'

'Colin, now hold on—'

'I'm right, aren't I? I saw your face when I told you we were getting married. Mum was always better at hiding it. At least she gave Justine a chance, but even she stopped coming round. You were working on her in the background, I know that. And now she's gone.'

'That isn't true at all! Where the hell is all this coming from?'

'I'm *miserable,* Dad! OK? Just like you said I would be. So now you can gloat all you want, now you can tell me that you saw it coming a mile off just like you did when we sent Thomas away. *My* boy. My only son and I barely get to see him. We don't talk about him either, me and Justine. We don't talk about much if the truth be known. Sometimes I wonder if she even remembers she has a son—'

'Then leave,' Richard cut in this time. He was stern, his voice raised and strong. It finally silenced Colin, whose expression was shocked, the words having the same visible impact as if Richard had slapped him.

'I can't. I can't just walk away.'

'Yes, you can. That boy over there won't be a boy for long. You should be spending every minute you can with him. Take him with you.'

'Then you really would be right!'

'I don't care about being right. I don't care about anything but you and your happiness. And Thomas, of course.'

'But without Justine . . .'

Richard shrugged. 'Other people do it.'

'There you go again! There you are, telling me to get rid of my wife!'

158

'You just said you were miserable. If a relationship makes you miserable then walk away from it.'

'Walk away? Just like that.'

'You have the means, you have money. All you need is a little place and you can start again—'

'I don't want to start again! And money . . . Honestly, you have no idea. Justine . . . she has . . . she spends money, a lot of money, and she doesn't let small things like the fact that isn't any there to spend bother her. Someone like her can always get credit.'

'All the more reason to get out while you can, while there's still half of something.'

'Half of something! There's nothing left. What's half of nothing, you tell me that? In fact, it's worse. What's half of thousands of debt? Tens of thousands maybe. I've stopped looking.'

Colin fell silent. Richard did too. His son wasn't good at emotions; he was a closed book, had been all his life. Now Richard didn't know what to say. 'I can help. I have some savings, I can—'

'No,' Colin cut him off.

'Colin, come on, you're my son. I can help.'

'You can't though. That's just the thing. I know you think you can but you have no idea. You had this perfect thing with Mum and me and all you ever wanted. And you made me want that too. I got close. You tried to warn me and now you want to bail me out when it's all gone just the way you predicted it would. I don't want to be in your debt as well. At least the banks won't constantly remind me that they were right all along.'

'Is that what you think of me?'

Colin sighed. It was long and his body slumped with it. 'No . . . not really. I'm under a lot of pressure. I have a lot going on. I didn't mean . . . That wasn't fair. But this is something I need to sort out myself. You're here talking about

159

your retirement. You need to have something behind you for that.'

'I don't need much. I'm hardly travelling the world or lining up luxury cars.'

'You don't know what you need. Once you get past Mum, who knows, you might realise there's this whole world out there.'

'What do you mean?' Richard asked.

'I mean you've been mooching ever since she died. It happens. You need to get past it, you need to get on with your own life. Maybe meet someone else.'

Richard suppressed his first reaction. He could feel the anger building, his heart knocking in his chest. 'That sounds like good advice. Maybe for you too?'

'My wife isn't dead, OK. This is totally different.'

'No, she isn't. My wife is dead though, son, and I will take my time getting past that. And right now, I'm not even sure what "getting past it" means.'

Colin was shaking his head and tutting. 'I could talk to Mum. She understood me. I can't talk to you, I can't make you see.'

'Make me see? You're the one living in your garage. How about you get your own life sorted before you start concerning yourself with mine? My wife might be dead but she gave me forty happy years – blissful. You'll forgive me if I can't just let go of that.'

'Jesus! She's gone, you know that, right? And there you go again, reminding me of how you got it right.'

Richard stood up from the stool. 'I'll go. Dropping in uninvited was obviously a mistake. I had something I wanted to talk to you about but I should know I need to wait for the invite. How long will that take? A year, eighteen months?'

Colin didn't reply. Richard made for his grandson and Thomas threw his headphones off to grip him tight in a hug.

'You're leaving already?' Thomas whined.

160

'Yes, but I'm going to try and sort something, a day out before you go back. How does that sound?'

'Sounds mega, thanks, Grandad. You sure I can't give you a game on here before you go?' Richard looked back over to where his son stood with arms firmly crossed. He needed to go. He would try again, pick up Thomas for a day out, take some of the pressure off his son and maybe even be appreciated for doing it.

'Not today. But I'll sort something, OK?' Richard tightened his squeeze, lingering for as long as he could. Thomas was quick to put his headphones back on and sit down in front of his game. Richard moved straight for the way out, stopping briefly to take a last look at the ruffled bed sheets. 'Look, I didn't come here to fall out with you. You're all I've got left. That means I'm here for you, whatever you need, whatever I can do.'

'I'll bear that in mind.'

Richard ground his teeth. He needed to go away, to be calm.

'No, you won't,' he growled. He shook his head and started down the stairs. Colin called after him.

'No, I probably won't. What was it you said you were? Old and useless, wasn't it?'

Richard hurried back out into the fresh air. By the time he was pacing back across the yard his eyes had blurred to the point where he was just making for the silver block that he knew to be his car. He leaned on it, trying to catch his breath, waiting for the rage and stress to dissipate.

It took a couple of minutes. Then Richard got back into his car and cast a glance over to the main house, to where a curtain fell back shut.

'Just making sure I leave, are you? Don't you worry, my love, I know when I'm not wanted.'

161

Chapter 25

Sharon Evans had been trying to be strong for so long now it was part of her daily routine. Any time she stood by Callie's bed she refused to cry, to even look sad. She liked to talk to her, to update her with what was going on, and always with a song in her voice and a smile on her face. Even if it was generally forced and her updates felt totally pointless. Sharon's world now had a new perspective and so talking through an article on *Love Island* contestants to her sleeping daughter took every ounce of her energy.

But Callie had loved that show and, somehow, it had become their thing. Sharon and Callie had been watching it together for a while. Not because Sharon liked the programme – she detested the format entirely – but because it was something they could talk about, something they shared. Danny couldn't even be in the same room while the show was on, and Jamie would generally spend his evenings at the park with his mates and a football or in his room on his games console, so that hour of trash television became about mother and daughter laughing and scowling together. It was one of the few times when Callie seemed to really listen to her mother's opinions, when they really talked. It had never mattered that it was just about loose morals or bitchy strangers. Sometimes they would move onto other things and Callie would even open up a little. Sharon talked to friends who had daughters of a similar age and they professed their jealousy, about how they wished they still had something in common. They'd all agreed that when you have a teenage daughter you have to take any opportunity you get.

Sharon certainly knew that now.

Callie had been shifted to sit up straighter. She still had the tubes and machinery assisting her breathing but the nurses were expecting a reaction to them soon. The sedation was slowly being removed. Soon she would return to the world, her hands snatching and pulling at the obstructions in her throat. She was going to be scared and confused. Sharon wanted so much to be there when it happened. Jamie did too. He played football on a Sunday morning and today his game was on the outskirts of Ashford, giving Sharon the perfect opportunity to visit. When she had told him her plans it had been the first time she had ever seen him reluctant to play. He had wanted to come here, to be with his sister, to talk to her and tell her how much he had missed her. She had needed to promise that they would keep to their usual Sunday schedule and visit again later in the day – and of course she would – she never minded coming back.

'How's it going?' a voice came from behind her.

Sharon had been staring down, her whole world contained on that bed, but her head snapped up to the sound of the mother of another patient. The bed next to them held the delicate frame of a girl who was a similar age to Callie. She suffered with epilepsy and her mother had previously explained that her daughter had suffered with it all her life but her latest seizure had been so severe that she had been left further from consciousness even than Callie was.

Sharon had taken some comfort from comparing notes on their respective kids, and in knowing that she wasn't the only mother going through something like this. But the conversation

163

did come with guilt. The woman had talked candidly, to the point of breaking down, about how she sometimes felt like she wasn't scared while her little girl was asleep, it was the waking up that terrified her. Her daughter's seizures could come on without warning. They could be anywhere, doing anything, and she would suddenly start. The idea that all epileptics had a known trigger seemed to be a fallacy, or at least if her daughter had one then they hadn't worked it out yet. Even before the incident that hospitalised her she didn't want her daughter to go out, or even to be out of her sight. Instead she talked about how it had become normal for the family to stay at home, her daughter wrapped in metaphorical cotton wool. It sounded miserable. Sharon's guilt at stating that all she yearned for was a return to their normal life still hung heavy on her and she tried to avoid too much conversation. The two girls were the same age, they even looked similar at a glance. The same slight build and a similar colour to their hair and pattern in their freckles. Something Sharon has almost forgotten about since her daughter had discovered makeup.

Today the woman was holding a bunch of bright flowers tightly wrapped in glittery paper, which instantly gave Sharon a subject for small talk.

'It's going OK, thank you,' she said. 'Those are beautiful.'

'Oh, aren't they just! I stopped for a coffee on the way in. I like to stop for a couple of minutes when I get in this place . . .' She seemed to run out of words, like she felt bad about admitting a delay in coming up to see her daughter.

'I know what you mean.'

The woman visibly relaxed instantly. 'It's a mindset isn't it? Being here, I mean.'

'It is.'

'Anyway, where was I?' She tutted at herself. 'The flowers! I was just sat down there and I must have been looking a bit down because someone bought me these flowers from the florist right there in the foyer! We talked, only a few minutes,

164

but he said he wanted to give me these to remind me that these places are just as much about hope as sadness. What a lovely thing to do!' Her voice was breaking with the last few words.

'Ah, that is lovely.'

'You get creeps, you know, it wasn't like that. You know when something's genuine, don't you? His mother's here. I didn't ask why.'

'I think these places can bring that out in people. None of us want to be here. Certainly not our girls,' Sharon said.

'She's doing better.' The woman gesturing with her flowers at Callie. 'I'm so pleased for you.'

They had never exchanged names. Sharon had steered away from it. She didn't want a 'hospital buddy' – like this was somewhere she should get used to, somewhere she belonged.

'She is. It's strange how it's all changed. No one was promising anything and now they want to talk to me about aftercare, about what happens when we get her home.' Sharon's eyes dropped to where she smoothed her daughter's fringe.

'That's so wonderful.'

Sharon stopped herself asking after the girl in the next bed. Despite the woman's cheery grin, there still seemed to be a lot more sadness than hope, and Sharon went back to feeling awkward. The woman might have sensed it, and busied herself with unwrapping the flowers. There was a collection of vases on a trolley under the window. Flowers must be a regular thing. The woman walked over to it and Sharon waited until she was far enough away to speak to her daughter.

'Where were we, Callie?' It was so much easier to sound brighter now. Sharon took back hold of a hand; she was sure that Callie's hands felt warmer. She seemed more settled too. Her breathing and little movements were now like when Sharon and Danny had watched her sleep when she was a child. Sharon gently rubbed the back of her hand too. Callie's

165

eyelids flickered like there was movement behind, and her mouth twitched. Then she gagged. Callie's hands flailed; she was trying to lift them, and all the time the choking sound was getting worse. Sharon turned to shout but a nurse was already moving towards her.

'It's OK, my love, just let me . . .' The nurse pulled away the tape, then gently guided the tubes out of her throat. Callie's head was moving from side to side. The nurse continued to coo at her, telling her everything was OK. She seemed to listen, she seemed to understand. Once the obstruction was clear the nurse placed an oxygen mask over her face and stayed close, waiting for it to steam up. She checked the vitals before turning a beaming smile towards where Sharon was frozen still.

'Callie!' Sharon's eyes filled with tears. She moved back close, taking her daughter's hand in hers again. Then her baby girl murmured something. *She still had a voice!* 'Can you hear me, honey?' Callie's pupils were wide, the movement of her eyes laboured and slow but she was trying, she was reacting to her mother's voice. Sharon even thought she detected a faint smile; no, she *knew* it was a smile. It took Sharon's breath away. 'Oh Callie! It's so good to have you back!'

Her daughter's eyelids looked heavy. They blinked a couple of times and then slid back closed. There was a little more movement behind them but it faded away like she had fallen back asleep.

'She will sleep a lot. At first.' The nurse was still beaming. Sharon didn't look away from Callie, and ran her hand over Callie's fringe. 'You take all the time you need, little one!'

Sharon reacted to her phone vibrating in her pocket like she had been stung. It was just a banal update notification for her phone, but it served as a reminder. She was still waiting for Danny to get back to her – to hear anything at all. She had considered driving round local hotels to see if she could spot his car before coming to the hospital but there was no

166

time and no certainty that he was even staying in or around Dover. It hadn't been unusual for him to ignore his phone for a few days in the past; she'd known him to lose it or even leave it plugged in at work for three days before now. But since Callie's admission to hospital he'd been better. He hadn't always been in a state to make conversation but he had always answered. Still, she wasn't worried. Danny had a self-destruct button that he liked to press every now and then. He would be laid out on his bed or a mate's sofa somewhere – or in a ditch – and either way he would soon sleep off whatever chemicals he had used to rid himself of the real world.

'Let's try your dad again, shall we?' Sharon worked the phone one-handed so she didn't have to let her daughter's hand go. The nurse nodded and said she would be back. The phone rang and rang. Sharon could feel the desperation grow in her chest with every tone. *Hey, this is Danny Evans, leave me a message if you have to and I'll get right back to you.*

'Jesus, Danny!' The phone's beep was a starting pistol for Sharon to bark into her phone. 'This really isn't how I wanted to do this. Callie, she's coming round! Your daughter is breathing on her own, it's a matter of time . . . She's going to want to see you. We all want to see you! Where the hell are you? Call me back the moment you get this, OK?'

She hoped this would be the message that would finally puncture his bubble of self-pity. That's what it would be too – he was somewhere right now feeling sorry for himself. She knew him well enough. So far she had only left messages asking him to ring her back urgently, thinking that would be enough, that he would panic and think it was bad news about Callie. The whole time, they had both been so resigned that any news would be bad news. She didn't want to leave a message like that on his answerphone. She wanted him here, she wanted him to see for himself, she wanted to see his face

167

when he realised that their daughter was coming back to them.

He was going to be so happy.

The sudden vibration to Danny Evans's mobile phone caused it to slide down the smooth surface of the seat. The phone was still face down, how it had landed after it had been discarded. It had been ringing at the time and the distraction had been unwelcome.

Now the name *Sharon* was projected on to the black plastic. The angry vibration filled the empty interior for just a few seconds more and then the phone listed it with all the other missed calls.

The screen flashed again, a beep accompanying it to warn of a critical level in the battery. Then the screen went dark.

168

Chapter 26

The building was L-shaped and the entrance was tucked away where one stretch of windows formed an angle with another. Richard was out on foot and stopped five metres from the double doors to check for signs of life. There were none. Then he looked back over to where his car was silent in the car park. It was the only one. The weather had turned. It was still cold but now it teemed with light rain to give the site a darker coat of grey.

The office block was on the outskirts of an industrial estate in a small village called Tilmanstone. Richard's home of Dover was probably still the closest town but it was six miles or more away. The scenery on his approach was rural, then the trees and fields had given way to reveal the building and its grounds. He had checked the postcode was correct twice and turned away once. But curiosity had brought him back. He had accessed the car park through a farm-style steel gate that was already pushed open to leave a swooping scar on the tarmac. The tarmac itself was spotted with weeds that had found a weakness and pushed for the light.

The site and the building were dilapidated and disused. The lettering for a previous occupant had been removed but the brickwork still bore its stain: 'Fennell Engineering'. This

169

company name had also appeared on a plaque atop a lopsided post that announced the parking bay he had used as *Reserved – Managing Director.*

Richard couldn't know where the MD was or what might have become of them, just that they were not here now. It looked to him like no one was. He lifted the piece of paper to read out the words that were now damp enough to start to run.

'Block B. Room 2.12.' He looked up. It was still cold enough for his words to be visible as they drifted towards a set of double doors that were also labelled: 'Entrance BLOCK B'. He made for it.

The right door pushed open, scraping against a perished rubber floor that was peeling away. The sound was loud, made louder by the sparse interior beyond. The door clattered shut behind him. The echoes reinforced the impression of an empty building. He dropped the hood of his jacket and paused for any other signs of life. Still nothing.

A stairwell was directly in front of him, a desk to his right and a brick wall to his left. The steps looked to be made of solid concrete but there were gaps between them, enough that he could see lift doors that hung open. Room 2.12 was surely going to be on the second floor but there was no way he was taking the lift.

Walking up the stairs gave him a view out over his car and the sopping car park in its entirety. The chilly wind whipped and harassed the tallest of weeds to add to the overall impression of a place long abandoned.

'Temporary office?' Richard's nerves had him speaking out loud. Those were the words the man had used to describe this place. Surely there was no one based here legitimately? Richard came to a full stop on the stairs, even half-turned to go back. But he didn't. The man had been nervous about giving Richard any information, even met him at a silent spot in the early morning so as not to be seen with him. This seemed like a drastic length to go to for privacy but maybe it added a little more to what he was claiming. Maybe he did have information that would get him into trouble for sharing. He couldn't think of another reason to bring him here. When Richard started up again his pace was quicker.

The second-floor layout mirrored the ground. A couple of corporate-looking sofas were stacked on top of each other in the space where the front desk had been situated below. The lift doors, shut on this floor, faced an internal door with a long glass window, through which Richard could see a dark expanse of corridor. He moved into it. The first door on his right was labelled 'Room 2.1'. The doors went up sequentially. Down the far end of the corridor a weak light caused a slit window above a door to pulse a dirty white. There was power at least.

He moved forward, counting up as he did, glancing into each room. There was still some office furniture left: a few desks, some chairs with broken backs and a couple of steel filing cabinets with drawers out like tongues. Some of the ceiling tiles were missing too and short lengths of wire hung from the shadow that was left. The corridor itself was mainly shadow, the only source of light whatever bled out from the rooms.

Room 2.12.

It was on the right side. He peered in. The blinds were down to give just a hint of daylight etched around the squared edges. He could make out a circular white table in the centre of the room with a flat black piece of paper in the middle. There was nothing else. He pushed the door open.

'Hello?' His voice echoed in an empty room. 'HELLO! IT'S RICHARD? YOU LEFT ME AN APPOINTMENT.'

He shook his head. What the hell was he thinking? This was some joker taking advantage of a vulnerable old man. 'If something seems too good to be true, it generally is,' he muttered out loud. It was an old mantra, one that he had lived much

171

of his life by. It had never done him any harm either.

He took one last look in, still holding the door, ready to pull it shut, and as his eyes moved to the floor he spotted a white piece of paper that was taped down by his feet, close enough for him to miss on his first sweep. It was a typed note, addressing him personally.

RICHARD. YOU WILL NEED TO BE CALM AND YOU WILL NEED TO READ.

The right side of the paper was taken up by an arrow that looked to be hand drawn and pointed directly at the table. It led him back to the black piece of paper. Now he could see it wasn't paper at all. It was a folder.

'HELLO! IS THIS SOMEONE TRYING TO BE FUNNY?' he called out again. There was no answer. He opened the folder to the first page. It was just three typed words on ice-blue paper. They were enough to take his breath away.

ANGELA MADDOX – DECEASED.

His heart raced faster. Suddenly he needed the table, and splayed the fingertips of his free hand against the wood to steady himself. He could feel his heart rate picking up. He knew it was anger – rage, in fact. It would spread, it could rob him of his vision if he couldn't control it. This was a windup, someone taking delight in tormenting him, he was sure of it. He didn't want to give them the satisfaction. He flicked his gaze up to the corners of the room, expecting to see cameras. There was nothing there.

He was still gripping the folder. He turned the page. The next sheet was laid out like a report, on paper headed 'Watson Insurance Fraud Investigators', and next to that it said, 'Page 3 of 5'. This page was a subtle blue too.

Page 3 started like there was a chunk missing. It made no

172

sense at first, increasing his frustration, worsening the thumping in his chest. His eyes raced ahead to pick out thick blocks of black ink where words had been crossed out. He took a breath and forced himself to start from the first word:

CA was the owner of the vehicle. He is well connected and well known locally and was able to apply pressure to persons in a manner that the police would not be able to do. Specifically, he obtained information from . . .

Here was the first black strip, and another followed shortly after

who was the landlord of . . .

Another thick black strip.

'What the hell is this?' Richard flicked another look around the interior. But there were no answers there. He continued to read.

We always believed that the identity of the driver was well known in local circles. What was unclear was why his name was so well protected. It was initially suggested that he was a rival for CA and his car was targeted specifically. This has been found not to be the case.

The driver of the vehicle that caused the death of Angela Maddox is now known to be . . .

Richard took a sharp intake of breath when he saw the name, and the thump in his chest was at its worse yet. He needed to breathe, to relax. But relaxing was now the furthest thing from his mind. He had a name: the man who had killed his wife, the man who had taken his life away from him at

173

the same time. When he said that name again it was forced through a jaw locked tightly shut.

'Daniel Evans.'

Chapter 27

A few hours earlier

The first thing Danny was aware of was the pulsing light. There was no pattern to it, no reason for it. He was angry, confusion made him angry, furious even that he didn't know what the light was. Every pulse came with a high-pitched ticking sound so that even when he closed his eyes to the pain of the glare he couldn't get away from it. The fog in his mind was slow to clear but he was becoming more aware.

There was a taste in his mouth. It was artificial, strong enough to be overpowering and nothing like the normal taste when he woke up after a heavy session.

Aniseed perhaps? He tried to swallow. He couldn't close his mouth. *Why couldn't he close his mouth?*

Instead his teeth ground against something solid. He tried to move his head back, away from the light, away from the ticking noise and away from the obstruction in his mouth. He couldn't move. *Why couldn't he MOVE?*

His whole body tensed and he wanted to lash out, but every part of him met with resistance. He was held fast. Tied by a million ropes that felt like they were pressed against him everywhere. He breathed heavily to try to control the panic. He could hear his breath whistle as it moved past the obstruction

175

in his mouth. He forced his eyes open in a squint, trying to make out his surroundings, trying to remember how the hell he had got here. Details revealed themselves slowly. The pinging light was a flat panel, a mottled grey square that was surrounded by more mottled grey squares. Another few moments and he had recognition: ceiling tiles. The light was a ceiling lamp. He could make out the shape of the bulb now, a scorched 'C' flickering white hot behind translucent plastic. One of the tiles was missing and ropes stretched above him, twisting out of sight into the void. He fidgeted again. His feet were planted and he pushed them as hard as he could into the floor in an attempt to get up. He had powerful legs but still his body moved only slightly. Whatever he was seated on moved too and clunked under him as his thighs burned, and he had to abandon his attempt.

'Come now, Danny!' A familiar voice stopped Danny instantly. He tried to speak, to shout, to demand what the hell was going on but it only came out as a sound from the back of his throat. His teeth chomped down on the solid object again. Danny quickly moved to fight mode, tried to lash out with his hands, to lead with his right, always his strongest. But it was numb. So numb that for a panicked second he wondered if it was missing altogether. He concentrated and was sure there was some movement, enough to prompt blood-flow, so it felt like it was being pricked with tiny little needles. His left hand was by his side; he could feel it but it wouldn't move either, because it was restrained down there, tied to something solid.

Danny tried to speak again, his anger replaced by desperation. Now he wasn't trying to demand to know what was going on, now he was trying to plead, to beg to be set free. The bright white rope, the sounds that echoed around him like he was in an empty room, the sparse ceiling. The solid metal in his mouth. He suddenly knew exactly what this was. He had seen something just like it. He heard the gurgle his

176

throat was making too. It turned high-pitched, as close to a scream as he could get. He had heard that before too.

'You need to preserve your energy, Danny. You may have a long wait. But then' – Danny heard a snap of fingers – 'I have a good feeling it will be over just like that!' Danny gurgled again, lower, deeper, a real attempt to form words. He was still trying to beg. 'Because, you see, you killed a man's wife. Forty years of marriage' – another snap – 'gone! You were driving a stolen car, you mounted a pavement and you took her out, Danny. And to add insult to injury you even killed the poor man's beloved dog! You left him nothing. A life ruined and with nothing more to do than to spend every waking moment since then seeking vengeance. See, it's all in here.'

The light was suddenly gone, blocked by a jet-black folder held above his eyes. It looked identical to the folder Danny had held a few days before, the one he had flicked through to read about the man who had been seated in front of him, the one that had contained the words that had convinced him to blow the back of the man's head off. Only now he was swamped with doubt that anything he had read had been true. He gargled again then forced a moan. His teeth bit the solid object so hard it hurt.

'Everything is in here. About how you stole a car, drove it drunk while showing off to the people you were with – you're a local legend, after all – and then you saw this poor man's wife walking her dog along the pavement. So you aimed for her, knocking her down and leaving her to die.'

Now the sounds from Danny's throat were fuelled by rage. It shook him in his seat and the ropes flexed a little on one side but there was no real give. He was wasting his time. He fell still, only his chest rising and falling with the exertion. He could feel his pulse beating in his head and he shut his eyes as the light still flickered above to dazzle him. The light jogged a memory, the last one he had. He was in the hotel

177

bar, drinking in the afternoon, trying to wash away the memory of what he had done. The man in the suit had turned up. Danny had taken the gun with him when he had left and it was still in the boot of his car. The man wanted it; it was part of cleaning up. Danny had been glad to give him the keys but the man had stayed. Danny didn't know why, it was all so hazy. He remembered a bright light. White, just like the one that flickered at him now. Only this one hadn't flickered, this had been a block: *a doorway!* He remembered walking out the door, into sunlight, the suited man supporting him because he couldn't walk on his own. There was nothing after that.

'I bet I know what you're saying!' The man's voice had a chuckle as he spoke, tearing Danny away from his memories. 'You're trying to tell me that this isn't true at all, aren't you? I *know* that, Danny! You didn't run some old woman down or kill her dog. You didn't steal a car either, well, that I know of! But what does that matter? Just think how you'll be doing your bit for this poor old man who was facing going to his grave without his moment of vengeance. It's eating him alive, too. But now he can have it. The fact that he is shooting the wrong man in the roof of the mouth won't matter because he'll never know. But he will know freedom. Freedom from what holds him back every day of his life. You know what that's called, Danny? Pay it forward. A good deed for your fellow man. A sacrifice. There are worse ways to go.'

The light's flicker seemed quicker than ever, the pinging sound that accompanied it louder. But Danny was still able to make out the sound of footsteps moving away. He tried to call after them, but all he got was a pain in his jaw.

'Oh, and I bet you're also wondering about Marcus Olsen, you know, seeing as there's not a shred of truth in that black folder there.' Even from a distance the man's words were still clear. 'Marcus Olsen had nothing to do with your daughter,

178

Danny. I want you to know that. And as for the woman you killed, she was a police officer. Your daughter met her. She liked her too by all accounts. I think it's only right you know what you did before you die. Lies, Danny – that's what this is all about. Do you see where they can lead? Do you see what lies can do? There's an important lesson here, one you need to understand. Call it *my* good deed.'

Danny hardly noticed the pain in his jaw now as his voice came back with a higher pitch still, as close to a scream as he could manage. The sounds of the footsteps became more and more distant, and when Danny paused to suck in another lungful of air, they were gone completely.

Chapter 28

Richard's vision blurred to the point where he couldn't read any more of the printed words. He had to focus on his breathing, wait for his heart to stop hammering, take his time. Only when he got himself under control was he able to start reading again.

Information suggests that EVANS was at a house party near to the address where the vehicle was stolen. He was heavily intoxicated while also high on cocaine. A member of his party gained entry to the car and committed the theft by taking it back to the party but we now know it was EVANS who drove the vehicle from this point. The incident occurred within the first two miles of the journey. EVANS was described as 'showing off', or at least playing up to his persona. He was swerving the vehicle and using rapid acceleration and deceleration to scare or thrill the passengers.

On entering Green Lane, Dover, EVANS spotted a lone dog walker. The dog was on a lead by the (road) side of MADDOX. EVANS is reported to have made a bet with other occupants of the vehicle that he could run the dog down while avoiding the female. The account

180

states that, while the idea was EVANS'S, other occupants of the car may have encouraged him.

We know that EVANS then mounted the pavement on purpose. At this point his intention is said to be to run down the dog and not MADDOX. As intent is impossible to prove in this matter, we will continue with this theory, however, you will note that at least two other accounts (both of which could be described as hearsay) allege that EVANS'S intention quickly changed to also run down MADDOX and he announced this intention just prior to impact.

While we concede that his intention (and therefore the offence of premeditated murder) will be difficult to prove without EVANS himself making an admission, there is clear evidence of causing death by dangerous driving and further possible charges around his use of class A drugs, driving while unfit through drink or drugs, theft of vehicle, animal cruelty, criminal damage and other miscellaneous driving offences.

Death by Dangerous Driving now carries a maximum sentence of life. Witness accounts will be sufficient to prove this but these will need to be obtained by police in statement form to be submitted for court proceedings.

Kind regards . . .

Another black line. Another name omitted. It didn't matter. Richard now needed both hands to keep him steady. His fingers bleached white with the strain. He took a moment until he could stand straight again. There were more pages. He turned to the next. This time it was laid out like an email. The sender and receiver's details were all blacked out. Just the body of the email was left:

Just to confirm that in regards the MADDOX case, the police have confirmed that they will no longer be pursuing

181

this matter. We have provided all our material but they feel the methods utilised to obtain this evidence would lead them to be disregarded at any court proceeding. They are concerned specifically that 'torture' was used by CA, as well as numerous breaches of data protection. I think 'torture' is a little strong but when the police approached the witnesses they refused to provide witness testimony and/or attend court.

Of note, the police do not contest that the information is correct and in fact confirm that they are able to corroborate much of the information provided – such as EVANS'S presence at a house party, his leaving with the named persons, and the theft of the vehicle taking place nearby and at the material time.

In a phone conversation, the investigating officer confirmed that he also believed EVANS to be the offender in light of the information provided, but without evidence, and taking into account EVANS'S status in the local area, it was deemed not in the public interest to pursue the matter in court.

Regards,

'Not in the public interest.' Richard could barely hear his own voice over the thumping in his chest. He turned the page to where he instantly recognised screenshots of text messages, exactly the same formatting as his own phone. It was a conversation that ran down the page. The first message was from Danny E.

Did anyone talk to you yet? About the car?

The reply was labelled 'Tiny Tim'.

Nah, I told you they wouldn't mate. I was at that party like 10 minutes when u dragged me out for adventures! Dont think any1 even saw me!

182

Danny E: What about your mate? He sweet?'
Tiny Tim: As a nut! He knows who u r. Hes got ur back,
we both got ur back!
Danny E: Appreciated. I owe you a beer for this.
Tiny Tim: A beer, is that it! You mow down some little
old lady and I get a beer out of it!
Danny E: Not on here. You gotta delete that. This aint
a laughing matter.
Tiny Tim: Shit man, I'm only playing!
Danny E: I know that. Like I say, this aint funny. The
dog's face was tho! Them nine lives didn't last long did
they!
Tiny Tim: That's cats you prick! LMAO

The text messages ran out. A sentence in bold type was at the bottom of the page: **Inadmissible due to method to obtain.**

Richard turned the page and let out his breath as he did. The next page was a photocopied newspaper article from the local paper. It was dated around two years earlier. The headline was bold, looking like it would have been the lead for the back page: **Club Captain Danny 'The Beast' Evans in drink drive rap.**

There was a picture. A tall man, broad shoulders, neat brown hair pushed over to one side. He looked like he had been captured walking down a set of steps, doing up the buttons on his blazer. The photographer was side-on. The caption read: *Danny Evans leaving court after pleading guilty to drink drive charge.*

The story underneath gave much more detail but Richard skimmed it to pick out a summary: A Mercedes car had been stopped for driving erratically – swerving from side to side. Danny Evans was the only occupant. He was captain of the town's football team and had played at a higher level earlier in his career. He failed a breath test and was found to be twice

183

the legal limit. The court banned him from driving for a year. His sentence could have been two years but was more lenient after he pleaded guilty and the use of his vehicle for his employment and charity work was also taken into account. The article ended with Danny Evans wishing to thank his wife for standing by him while he sought the help he needed.

Standard. The sort of report Richard had seen a thousand times about people in the public eye when they were caught out. 'The help I need.' Divert it away. Make it sound like an addiction, like something you couldn't help. Richard had scoffed at his television a thousand times at excuses like that but he wouldn't scoff now. This was different. This was the man who had killed his wife.

He brought the folder closer. The image of Evans wasn't good, and he couldn't really make out the features of the man. He noted the report was over two years old. He turned the page to where a far better image peered out at him. This one was taken straight on. Almost like a mugshot the police might take. The man looked sullen, his thick lips only slightly curled up at the edges. The broad shoulders were there, as was the brown hair swept neatly to one side. He could see piercing green eyes below the fringe and a ragged nick on his left ear, like a piece had been torn off.

There were more pages. Richard could barely work his hands to turn them. He could feel his body being overcome with hate. It stood him straight, locked his jaw rigid and sucked the air from his lungs. His cheeks and brow ached where his face was held in a permanent scowl. The next page was another text message. This one was out on its own, out of any context, sent by 'Danny E'. But Richard didn't need any context. The words had everything he needed to understand:

Danny E: Too right, why should I go down for some dopey old bint. Ain't like anyone's gonna miss her anyway!

184

Reckon I did her a favour. Quick and easy. Maybe I could offer a service!

There were more typed words under the message. He couldn't read them, not straightaway. His vision was gone, his heartbeat now a jack hammer. and for a moment he thought his breath wasn't going to come back. He was back leaning on the table but he still felt dizzy. He took his time. He put the folder down flat and traced the words of the single typed sentence underneath with his finger. He had to do it twice before they sunk in:

The box on the chair. Then Room 2.13. Pay it forward.

He jerked away like the table was suddenly covered in snakes and stumbled two steps backwards. There were two chairs, both pushed in tight against the other side of the table. He couldn't bend, his knees wouldn't let him, instead he walked round and pulled the first chair out. The box was there: wooden, ornate with a tree trunk carved into the left side and twisting branches jutting out along the top. It was hinged on the side like a book. He opened it with shaky fingers to reveal a Browning 9mm pistol embedded in shaped padding. It was a weapon he knew well. It had been standard issue for the British army as a secondary weapon – standard issue for him. It had been a few years since he had seen one. He reached down for it. The weight, the feel, the distinctive smell of the oil – it was like he had never put it down. The pistol had been concealing another blue piece of paper. Another typed note, the font the same but larger:

THE ONLY JUSTICE LEFT.

His head lifted to face the door. Adrenalin fuelled him now. He strode back round the table, scooping up the folder on his

185

way out into the darkened corridor. He turned right. There was only a short stretch left and only one door. It faced him, marking the end of the corridor. This door was solid but it had the window above that still pulsed its dirty white. He reached out to work the handle.

Chapter 29

The door was heavier than the others and Richard had to adjust his stance to push it open. He lingered on the threshold. The gun in his grip had him back thinking like a soldier – *reveal a room, assess for threats, enter to neutralise.* The room beyond was large; the centre had been cleared, save for a man seated under the flickering light, facing him directly. Now Richard was in the room the flicker of the light was accompanied by a pinging noise. The chair was typical of an office but with bare metal where wheels might have been. The man was bound tight in white rope. His right arm was bent at the elbow like he was reaching up for his face but his fist was wrapped in tape. Something was taped to the hand to extend his reach and push firmly into his mouth, forcing his head back so he had no choice but to face the ceiling. Richard could see his eyes moving like he was struggling to get a view of who had entered the room. He made a noise that came out like a gurgle, like he was trying to say something.

Richard assessed the rest of the room and noticed a piece of paper on the floor. The man's legs twitched and writhed against the ropes as Richard bent close to them to pick it up. It contained more typed words:

Richard,
Danny Evans will never face criminal justice.
But now he has to face you.
The police will believe he came here to end his own life. There will be no questions.
His right arm has been raised for long enough that he will have no feeling and no control. Place the pistol in his hand and assist with pulling the trigger then leave the building the same way you came in.
I will ensure everything else is arranged.
This is my good deed in full.
Your friend.

Richard read to the end and let the paper fall to the floor. He moved in closer, close enough to almost be touching knees with Danny Evans, with the man who had killed his wife, who had taken everything from him. Richard had spent the months that followed obsessing over the details of what had happened that night. The police had been able to piece much of it together, enough for Richard to know that the driver hadn't stopped and that his wife wasn't killed instantly. His Angela had been lying on that cold pavement for nine minutes before she was spotted by a passing car and rushed to hospital. It was a painful and panicked end and Richard hadn't even made it in time to hold her hand. He had gone looking for her on the night, when she hadn't returned home. The feeling when he turned onto Green Lane, when he saw those blue lights slicing up a filthy black evening and he knew in his heart that it was all for Angela; it was something he would never forget.

She died alone and in pain. But over time the anger in Richard had subsided a little, enough that he could function day to day. He told himself that it was a terrible accident and the driver must have panicked. He pictured him as a young man who had made a mistake, inexperienced at driving

188

and inexperienced in life too, and in that instant he hadn't known what to do. And once he had made the decision to flee he couldn't go back, he couldn't make it good. So he had burned out the car and buried his head in the sand, hoping it would pass him by, but every day he was tortured with what he had done. Richard could have lived with that – just about – and he had almost convinced himself.

But now he knew the truth. He knew a name, Danny Evans, and he knew the man behind that name was a swaggering, arrogant, evil piece of shit who hadn't had a moment of remorse and who had carried on with his life of being adored. Angela was nothing to him, her death just a source of amusement. And it had been no accident, Danny Evans was a cold-blooded killer.

But so was Richard once.

His rage was out of control now. It was consuming him, it moved him forward to place one leg either side of Danny Evans's bound thighs like he was straddling him. He lifted the pistol to push it into the stricken man's pale palm and held Evans's finger firmly against the trigger. It was also rage that lifted him up onto his toes so he could see right into those piercing green eyes that were now wide with fear, while his throat gurgled. He could now see what was jutting out of his fist to push into his mouth; it looked like the metal extension from a vacuum cleaner but cut into a long U shape. It had coarse edges like it had been cut with a hacksaw. It was taped firmly to his hand at one end and the other pushed between those thick lips that had been shaped into a leering pose for his photo. The brown hair was present too – although not so neat and slightly longer to partly conceal the ear with the missing chunk. The green eyes that had been nonchalant in the picture now jiggled around in his skull, trying to see what was going on, and flared wide with fear.

Good.

The man's throat twitched and moved as he moaned. It was

189

panicked, desperate. The sound started low, building to a high-pitched shriek. Richard savoured it. Even waiting until Danny Evans ran out of air and his nostrils flared to power the next one.

'You should fucking scream. Quick and easy, that's what you said, right? Maybe *I'm* the one who should offer it as a service. This is for my wife!'

The pistol roared. He was so close that the rear of the weapon recoiled to catch Richard like a backhanded slap across the mouth. He didn't care.

It did nothing to wipe the big smile off his face.

Chapter 30

'You're calmer then!' Glenn smiled. 'I can tell that by the fact that you bought the coffees this time!' It was their regular coffee-shop meeting place. Glenn had refused meeting somewhere more private like at one of their houses, saying that he was already in the town and complaining that it was Richard's turn to buy. Richard didn't want to push it over the phone. It didn't matter anyway; no one was going to be taking notice of two old men in the corner.

Richard was aware he was still shaking. It had been a couple of hours since he had pulled that trigger but the adrenalin was still flooding back at a moment's notice. He took a second to peer around, to make sure there was no one near enough to overhear them, before he replied. 'I killed a man.' Richard leaned in, watching Glenn intently. He was lifting his cup to his lips. He didn't stop, the delay while he took his swig was maddening.

'We both did,' Glenn replied. 'It was a long time ago.'

'I don't mean then. I mean now. The man who killed my wife. I wanted you to know, I wanted to tell *someone*. There's no one else I trust.'

'What? What are you talking about?'

'I told you what happened, I told you someone came to

191

see me, someone who knew what happened that night with Angela. He came back.'

'Who? Who came back?'

'This same man. Same place. He knew I would be there. He came back and he gave me the opportunity to kill the man who murdered my wife. And I took it.'

Glenn's cup was still suspended in mid-air.

'And this isn't some sort of a windup? A joke? Or you testing me out, seeing how I react?'

'I wouldn't joke. Not about this. I shot him.'

Glenn was clumsy finding the saucer with his cup; he didn't look away, like he was waiting for Richard's expression to break into a smile. Richard stared back. He was just as keen to see Glenn's reaction when it sunk in, when he realised that his old mate wasn't just some doddery old fool long past his best.

'You're serious!' Glenn managed, finally.

Richard leaned back in his seat as he remembered the moment. 'I was braced for it. It was a Browning, familiar like an old friend. Something we've fired a thousand times before, at targets, at people. But this time was nothing like I remember. I still felt it everywhere, but . . . it wasn't like before. I used to recoil before it did, they told me that on the ranges. But not this time. It still had that same roar but it was like it was coming from me. You see this?' Richard touched the corner of his mouth where the solid stock had split his lip. 'I was so close to him when I did it that it caught me. I know better, but I wanted to look right at him.'

'Have you lost your fucking mind?' Glenn hissed. It barely registered. Richard wasn't looking at him anymore, he wasn't looking at anything. His eyes had glazed over, the memory of that moment still consuming him.

'It was so beautiful, Glenn, you should have been there. All in a moment, it was vengeance and it was power . . . It was a release from everything! From mourning, from the feeling

192

of utter, utter helplessness. I've had a problem, I thought it was stress. My heart thumps, I get short of breath, my eyes blur and I feel so weak. Like a proper old man. But today . . . there was none of that.' Richard's eyes snapped back to focus on his friend, 'It wasn't stress at all. It was fear. And I'm not scared of anything anymore.'

'What about prison for the rest of your life? Are you scared of that? I mean, are you serious?'

'I won't go to prison. It was a suicide. He was sat on a chair, his hand had been in position so long he was completely numb, he didn't even know I was pushing his finger on the trigger. No one will ever know it was me who finished the job.'

'Finished the job! Can you hear what you are saying right now? You *have* lost your mind!' Glenn hissed.

'I think I might have just got it back.' Richard couldn't stop smiling. He could feel it pulling at the cut on his lip. 'I've had some kicks in the teeth recently, life's way of telling me I'm washed up and useless. Maybe I'm not quite so useless after all.'

'Is that what this is about? Because you didn't get your job back? When you texted me about that you said you were fine with it . . .'

'I couldn't care less about my job. This was about Angela. I got all the answers, I know what happened. He was gloating about it, Glenn. I saw some messages he sent. My Angela was nothing to him, he was only worried about saving his own skin. He got what he deserved and you know what, I am *delighted* I got to be the one to do it.'

'What messages? What the hell happened?'

'It was all there. All the evidence this guy had found out, everything he knew.'

'Who is this guy that was there?'

Richard tutted. 'He wasn't there, but all the paperwork was, printouts of text messages this piece of shit sent after he had run her down. There was a group of them in the car, they all

193

knew about it, they were all talking about it after. They had to get their story straight.'

'Rich . . . Jesus! If you had something like that why didn't you just take it to the police?'

'Just hand it over and wait for them to do nothing? I did that before, remember? I spent months chasing them. I went knocking on doors where it happened, to find a witness, and every one of those people I spoke to said they hadn't seen a police officer. That's a basic, isn't it? They didn't care then and they certainly don't care now. And besides, they were offered the information, they were told everything I was shown. There was an email, it explained how the police turned the information down. Some officers came out to my house and told me to my face that they didn't have a clue who killed my wife. But they knew all along! They had it right in front of them but it was just too difficult to bother. They did nothing so I did something.'

'You shot him? You killed a man?'

'Yes.'

'Jesus, Rich . . . you're not a soldier anymore! You don't just get away with that, not people like us, not in the civvi world.'

'I'm not stupid, Glenn.'

'This isn't about stupid. I wouldn't have the first idea how to get away with something like that. You've seen the telly, the forensics they do, the resources they have!'

'It was suicide. He was tied to a chair. I just turned up and pulled the trigger and then I left. Some abandoned building. No one else was there, no one's been there for a long time.'

'And you just left him there?'

'There were instructions. It said I should just leave and this man was going to take it from there, leave it so it looked like a suicide.'

'This *man*? What man? Who is this man that you're suddenly trusting with your life? What's his name?'

194

Richard hesitated. His mind flashed with doubt for the first time since he had pulled that trigger. 'I don't know his name. I get the impression that you don't necessarily swap contact details for this sort of thing.'

'So a stranger just comes out of nowhere and tells you he's solved a mystery that the police couldn't solve in eighteen months, then he offers you the chance to shoot a man in a chair. And you take it, just like that. No questions?'

'They could have solved it, just not in a way that would work in the legal system. This was the only thing left, it was all there, I didn't have any questions left, trust me. It was all very clear. This man ran my Angela down in cold blood. And when she lay dying on the floor he drove off to save his own skin.' Richard leaned back, his mind turning to memories, but this time the images in his mind weren't so pleasant. 'She was lying on a damp pavement with her arm wrapped round Missy. Angela . . .' Richard took a moment; his flush of anger had turned to upset. 'I know she was conscious when someone finally saw her and stopped. She was even speaking. They had to pull our dead dog out from her grip. Can you imagine what the last minutes of her life were like for her? For my wife?'

'No,' Glenn said, his tone resigned, his head shaking.

'Well, let me tell you, I can, because I've been over it a thousand times in my mind. I go over it every time I close my eyes to try and sleep or just sit in a place like this with a cup of tea. But since I pulled that trigger I feel different – better. That bastard finally got what he deserved. He knew who I was too. You should have seen his eyes. *Fear*, Glenn! He was terrified of me. Why would he be so scared? I tell you why: he knew who I was and he knew what he had done to me, and he knew that there would be no more saving his own skin.'

Glenn was still shaking his head. 'I don't know what you want me to say, mate. I don't know why you would tell me either.'

195

'Because I wanted to tell someone. I can't tell Colin, he wouldn't understand. If I kept it to myself then the police will write off another suicide and this man just disappears for ever, like it never happened, like I never did what I did. Like I never took care of it. But I did. Telling you means I did.' Richard waited until Glenn met his gaze. 'And there's no one else in the world I trust more than you.'

196

Chapter 31

Joel sat at his own dining-room table. The look and smell were familiar, as was the sound of his youngest daughter bundling past him to put her favourite television show on, asking his wife for a biscuit only to be told that dinner wasn't far away.

He sat in the standard bustle. But it felt different, almost like he was sitting in someone else's place entirely. In his daze he looked around to pick out the little homely touches they had gradually added since they extended the back of the house last year.

The sight of Hannah Ribbons, his fallen colleague, still weighed heavy on his mind, as did the conversation that had followed with DS Rose. Joel needed an ally, someone he could work with, be honest with and talk to about feeling the pressure, like he had been thrown in at the deep end. Instead DS Rose had made it quite clear that she was there to be sure the pressure only increased.

It wasn't just his new colleague who was proving to be difficult either. The source unit had totally closed shop. Even Debbie Marsden wasn't expecting to get any information out of there until Monday at the earliest. It seemed so ridiculous to him: here was the man tasked with finding who had

197

murdered one of their own and they were withholding key information.

His wife put a cup of tea down in front of him to shake him from his musing.

'Thanks, love,' he muttered. She didn't acknowledge him. If the tea was a peace offering it seemed to fall short. They had had words. Michelle had seized on his obvious frustration when he had come home the previous day and took it as an opportunity to lecture him further about how he had returned to work too early and in the wrong department. She was worried about him. He knew that but he had reacted by getting angry, angry that she now saw him as someone who was fragile, someone who needed to talk about their fragility at the end of every shift. Once Joel had told her that she *didn't understand*, an escalation was inevitable. It had sounded patronising. That was the last thing Joel wanted to be, especially now, when they were past the time when he had assured Michelle she would be able to start putting her own career back together.

Michelle worked in marketing. She was good at it too – like a whirlwind, to use the words of her boss. She quickly pushed her way upwards to run her own department but then she had fallen pregnant and the change in attitude towards her seemed to be overnight. Redundancy came just a few months later and Joel had never seen her so lost. Of course, she had bounced back but only as far as she could on part-time hours. Michelle was being held back, and Joel could sense her frustration; she was capable of so much more. The girls were older now and they had talked about Michelle returning to full-time work, something that would be possible around the shifts of a detective working regular hours. But Joel had known from the start that the hours for any policing role were a guideline at best and investigating murder was never going to fit into a regular shift pattern. Michelle had agreed to 'see how it goes', but the elephant in the room was already telling

198

them both that Michelle was going to need to work round Joel more than ever.

When his phone rang it made him jump violently and he instantly looked over to where his wife had stopped what she was doing to stare back.

'I just need . . .' he muttered before sweeping the phone up. He paced through to the living room to get away from that stare. 'DI Norris.'

'Boss, sorry to call you up on a Sunday but I was given your name and told you would want to know.' Joel didn't recognise the voice but he did recognise a police officer demonstrating the ability to apologise while sounding unapologetic.

'Don't worry, how can I help?'

'I'm Sergeant Taylor, the patrol sergeant covering Dover and Deal. We have a dead person, sir. A suicide, but there's something out here that might be of interest to you. It might link to some job in Sittingbourne, a source handler shot dead? Does that mean something to you?'

'What have you got?'

'It's . . . would you normally come out to something like this?' The woman's voice was now full of doubt, like she was talking herself out of it.

'Turning out to dead bodies seems to be very normal, as it happens. This will be my third in a week.'

'Oh . . . I called my inspector and they said they would only come out if you didn't . . .'

'And they don't want to come.'

The woman laughed. 'I did get that impression. He said that he would get all the way out here and then you would want to come out anyway. He talked about missing out the middleman. I guess he thinks he is the middleman.'

'Sounds like you're right . . .' Joel hesitated, then turned back to where sounds were coming from the kitchen, of ovens being pulled open and baking trays sliding out. It was Michelle

199

checking the roast dinner. A Norris family Sunday tradition. And it would be ready soon.

'I can explain over the phone but my boss . . . he said you'd want to see it, said it looks like it might be really important?' The uncertainty was back in the sergeant's voice. Joel had hesitated too long.

'Send me details for my sat nav and I'll head out for a look.'

'That's great, sorry again. No one likes a call on a Sunday!' She sounded a little more genuine this time.

'I don't mind,' Joel lied. 'My wife on the other hand . . .'

'Your wife let you out!'

A young woman in a uniform sporting Sergeant chevrons on each shoulder stepped out of her patrol car to approach Joel the moment he pulled up. Her smile dropped away and she leaned into his window to make it obvious she was studying his face. 'And no black eyes. It went well then?'

'I took the coward's way out. I told her I was popping out for some milk.' Joel tried to stay deadpan but a smile forced its way through to give him away.

'Oh, I see! Do you normally put on a shirt and tie to go out for milk?'

'You don't?' Joel said.

'Fair point. We'd better speed this up then!' The sergeant had a giggle that was immediately infectious.

She got herself together to brief him, introducing herself again as Sergeant Taylor, then explaining that two of her team had responded to a call from a security guard doing his rounds. All were still inside. Joel could see another marked police car and a small white van marked *Security – Dog Handler*. They were the only cars in an otherwise empty car park. There was a general feeling of desolation. An even smattering of weeds surrounded a squat office block like they were planning an assault. The only clue to the building's

200

previous use was the name of an engineering firm that appeared as a stain on the brick frontage and seemed to stand out more in the damp. Joel started for the building, aware that in another hour or so the light would be gone completely.

The sergeant led the way towards the only entrance he could see. The door scraped loudly and the sergeant had to use some of her body weight to force it. He followed her up concrete steps and down a long, poorly lit corridor. Everything was uniform – the style and colour of the doors, the font used to identify individual rooms, even the redundant strip lighting overhead that passed like a cheap cartoon where the background repeated itself. The only thing to stand out was the flickering of a light high up at the end of a long corridor on the second floor. The sergeant made straight for it. This door was open. The first thing Joel saw was a uniform officer directly in front of him who quickly stepped out of the way to reveal the reason why there was a Sunday roast going begging at his home.

'Well . . . he made a right mess in here,' Joel said, voicing his instant reaction as he took in the seated corpse in the centre of the room. Some office furniture was scattered untidily around the outside, like it had been hastily dragged out of the way to clear the space. This was the corner office so there was a row of windows and blinds on two sides. The blinds on the east side looked to have been ripped away from the windows in a fit of violence. They were still attached at the bottom and dripped down to bunch up on the floor. On the north side the blinds had been left in place to shiver as a breeze rushed through an opening.

'He did. He left us a note too. Thoughtful.' The sergeant gestured at one of her officers who held up a clear evidence bag. The note inside was typed out in block capitals, the words grouped together in the middle of the page. Joel took it to read.

201

I DON'T KNOW WHAT TO SAY. THIS IS NOT SOMETHING I EVER WANTED TO WRITE BUT THIS IS NOT SOMETHING I EVER WANTED TO HAPPEN. CALLIE ... I CAN'T COPE WITH IT, ANY OF IT. I FEEL LIKE I'M IN PAIN EVERY MINUTE OF EVERY DAY AND NOTHING TOUCHES IT.

I HURT SOMEONE. IT WOULD NEVER HAVE HAPPENED IF SHE HAD DONE WHAT SHE WAS SUPPOSED TO. FOR US. FOR CALLIE.

WHEN I FOUND HER SHE WAS SOME-WHERE ELSE IN SITTINGBOURNE, WORKING SOMETHING ELSE. OUR DAUGHTER HAS BEEN FORGOTTEN.

I ONLY WENT THERE FOR SOME ANSWERS. I'M SO SORRY. I CAN'T CONTROL ANYTHING ANYMORE, THE DRINK, MY FAMILY LIFE, MY ANGER. I DON'T EVEN RECOGNISE MYSELF SOMETIMES.

I DIDN'T MEAN TO HURT HER.

I KNOW YOU'LL UNDERSTAND ONE DAY. WHATEVER THEY ALL SAY ABOUT ME, REMEMBER THAT YOU KNOW ME AND YOU KNOW THE PRESSURE I'VE BEEN UNDER. IT JUST GOT TOO MUCH.

I DON'T KNOW WHAT TO SAY TO JAMIE. I'M SORRY, TELL HIM THAT. TELL HIM TO BE GOOD! JUST TALK TO HIM, YOU'VE ALWAYS BEEN BETTER AT THAT THAN ME ANYWAY.

HE DESERVES BETTER. YOU ALL DO.

EVERYTHING I DID, IT WAS ALL FOR YOU. I LOVE YOU ALL MORE THAN YOU'LL EVER UNDERSTAND.

DANNY XXX

202

'Danny?' Joel said.

'Danny Evans,' the lad who'd handed him the note said.

'You know him?'

'A lot of people do, sir. He's a bit of a local celeb. Was captain for Dover Athletic for a long time. Played for the Gills too for a couple of seasons.'

'I see.'

'You OK?' the sergeant asked now. Joel was rubbing at his face, his eyes desperately hunting round the room.

'I can't make up my mind if I'm fantastic or fucked. Does that answer your question?' Joel took in the shock on the sergeant's face and was quick to apologise.

'Sorry. Barely a day into a murder investigation and this might be the resolution dropping into my lap . . .'

'Or . . .' the sergeant prompted.

'Or it just got a lot more complicated.' Joel didn't know how to feel; his lack of experience felt like it was on show for the first time. 'We just need to process the scene like normal. I'll worry about the links to my other job later.' He was talking out loud but he was coaching himself.

'Understood.'

'Where did he leave the note?' Joel said.

One of the PCs in uniform pointed to a chair that had been spun out to face them from under the window. 'On the chair. I got a picture of it in situ. His mobile phone was on the chair too. It was switched off. I've bagged that up too . . .' Joel paced over to the chair. He laid the note back where it was. 'Should I not have done that?'

'I wouldn't. Not at a scene like this. If you don't need to move something, don't. Have we made the call to CSI?'

'I called. He had a forty-minute journey time.' The sergeant checked her watch. 'Which will be around twenty minutes by now.'

'OK, good.' Joel fixed back on the body. He was looking from a different angle now, side-on, the man's head forward.

203

The back of the neck and head had taken on a freakish shape where it would have been distorted by the force of the shot. There was a clear splatter pattern behind too, the spray taking in the ceiling and blinds. The victim was wearing a shirt and what looked like chino trousers. His left hand was balanced in his lap, his right hung by his side. Now Joel saw the black object on his lap.

'Did anyone move that weapon?' Joel said.

'No. I do know better than that!' The same PC was now indignant.

Joel stepped a little closer, but not too close, stopping before he could disturb the blood that had pooled on the floor like a shadow, and leaned forward. The weapon was a pistol: a Browning 9mm, black with a raised grip held on by visible screws. The handle was towards him, the barrel part buried in the victim's shirt to point at his midriff.

'This is how you found him?' Joel directed his question towards the man in a white shirt with *Security* written in black over his breast pocket.

'Of course it is. I ain't touching that!' He wore a shocked expression, like he was still seeing the seated corpse for the first time. His wide eyes seemed wider behind thick-lensed glasses. He had the rasping voice and stained fingers of a heavy smoker.

'Any CCTV on this site?'

'No.' The accompanying headshake moved the man's glasses down his nose and his finger left a smear when he pushed them back. 'There are cameras that the company used to monitor down in the foyer. I guess they turned them off the day they left.'

'You guess?'

'I know they're off. I just meant that was probably what happened. No need to be monitoring an empty site.'

'But there is need for a security guard?' Joel said and the man's eyes flared even wider at the challenge.

'Once a week, that's all. Part of my Sunday round. Just to check the place ain't been screwed. There's still cables an' that, lots of copper if you know where to look. Or for squatters, in empty places in the town you do get 'em.'

'Do you check it's locked?'

'Yeah, every week.'

'And last Sunday?'

'It was. I have to do a tick-sheet. I wrote it down and everything.'

'And today?'

'Like it is. I could tell it was busted open straightaway.' His rasp now held an excited edge.

'I only saw one door?' Joel said.

'There's a few. The busted door is the main entrance.' He gestured to where the limp blinds hung to reveal the row of windows. Joel stepped to them to find the view out was directly over the car park and the entrance in question.

'So it was forced?' Joel said.

'Looks to me like the door's been popped,' the sergeant answered. 'The bolt's still locked out and the housing has a dent and some tool marks that look fresh.'

'OK then . . .' Joel took a moment, his attention back on the victim. He moved closer, stooping a little to get a look at the man's face. The head was forward to rest on his chest, the eyes open as wide as they could go and the pupils turned out slightly to give an unnatural expression that Joel had seen before with brain injuries. All that was left of his mouth was a mess of black coloured flesh and exposed bone.

'That's quite some damage to his mouth.' Joel was thinking out loud but he heard the sergeant shuffle a little closer to him.

'He shot himself in the mouth, boss. That's going to cause some damage, surely?'

Joel straightened up. 'He's shot himself in the face actually, that's not so easy to do. People use the mouth because you

205

can hold the barrel between your teeth and take out what you need instantly. It takes away the need to aim, probably because that's just about impossible when it's turned on yourself. It pulls off target and there's no guarantee you'll do the job. But Danny Evans seems to have been rather good at it.'

'What does that mean?'

'It could mean a few things. Right now it just doesn't look right . . .' Joel ran out of words; his attention had moved away from the face and he had to lean in closer still.

'But?' the sergeant said, prompting him.

'Gloves?' Joel snapped, his eyes still fixed on the seated man. He heard the sound of a Velcro pocket ripped open and a pair of forensic gloves were pushed into his periphery. He only needed to slip one on. He lit the torch function on his phone and pulled the top of the man's shirt away from his chest. 'Red marks. Do they look like restraint marks to you?' Joel had to lean away so the sergeant could see. She had to lean in quite close. The marks were slim and long to form a broken line, as if someone had been held in the same place for a length of time by something and had struggled against it.

'Restraints?' The sergeant shrugged as she moved away. 'Could be, I suppose.'

'How far did you say CSI are?'

'Any minute now, really.'

'Good.' Joel stepped back. His glove snapped at his fingers as he tugged it off. 'We need to treat this as sus until we know better. We'll need a wide cordon and no one else enters without full PPE. Have you got people you can spare for some instant enquiries?'

'How many do you need?' The sergeant suddenly seemed enthused. Joel took a moment to consider the size of the site, the limited access, the fact it was pretty much in the middle of nowhere – he didn't think he would need many more. But his experience of murder scenes to date was turning up to

206

lead the search for further evidence once CSI had done their bit. By that time the SIO had already made these sorts of decisions and the scene was already under control.

'How many have you got?' Joel said, stalling as the sergeant stared at him for some direction.

'The two that are already here, and me. I can get another double-crewed car out. Maybe a few more later but we're not exactly flush . . . Don't you have people you can call in for something like this?'

'Not on a Sunday. We just need to hold it for now. Let CSI work and then see where we are. These two fine officers can hold the scene if that's OK. I'd like a preliminary walkthrough of the whole building too.' Joel looked over to the security guard who was still staring at the body. When Joel spoke to him, he jerked his head away so violently it looked close to doing him some damage. 'Do you know the layout of the building?' Joel said.

'The layout . . . yeah . . . We had the contract when Fennell were here and the time before that. I worked the desk for a bit. I still come in most times now too. I got some stuff I keep here see, a kettle and a few other tea bits . . . I leave the tick sheet with them.' He seemed delighted to be helping.

Joel turned back to the sergeant, who readied herself for further instruction, but the words stuck in his throat and he looked back over at the security guard. 'You keep the tick sheet here?'

'Yeah, in a folder downstairs. Do you wanna see it?'

'What does it show?'

'Show? I mean, nothing really. It's just days of the week an' that. Laid out like a month planner. I write the time I'm here in the right day, give it my initials and job done. They never ask for it. I keep it here so I don't get my buildings mixed up.'

'Is it locked away?'

'Normally the door's locked so I don't need to worry. It's in a folder under the front desk. I said about the kettle and

207

there's a plug there. This is a tea stop 'cause someone's still paying the 'leccy bill. You don't get that in other places.'

'So someone could find it easy enough.'

'My kettle?'

'Your tick sheet that shows when you come here.'

'Oh . . . well, yeah.'

'What's the matter?' said the sergeant, her question aimed at Joel.

'Maybe nothing.' Joel stared back at the shadow of blood on the floor. It looked fresh to him, within the last twenty-four hours. 'Maybe it's just coincidence that Danny Evans died a day at most before someone checked the building.'

'Or maybe he knew when that was due,' the sergeant replied.

'Somebody might have,' Joel said. 'The door has tool marks, you said. Did we find what was used?'

'Not yet. We haven't really looked though.'

'Can you spare two more? That should be enough for the time being. They can do the walkthrough with our security friend here.' Joel didn't think for a minute that anyone involved in what had happened here would have stuck around, but it was belt and braces for his first job. Suddenly the idea of more officers here brought comfort.

'Is it a search? We've only got one search trained—'

'It's just a sweep to be sure no one else is here and for anything obvious. If we're going to have CSI working we should make sure they're alone.'

The sergeant nodded. 'OK, understood,' she said then seemed to stiffen. 'Do you think there might be someone else here?'

'No. If I thought that I would have firearms do it. It just needs to be done.'

'The note . . .' The young officer in uniform pointed back over at his neatly bagged exhibit. He suddenly looked a little terrified, like he wished he had stayed quiet. Joel stared at him until he spoke again. 'The note says he killed himself. So

208

are we not thinking that now?' he asked, seeming to brace himself for the reply.

'The *typed* note says suicide but there's not enough here for that to be conclusive.'

'What are you thinking?' the sergeant prompted, looking round again like she had just walked in.

'I'm thinking I've been to a lot of suicides in my time and this is the first one in a disused office. This place doesn't make sense to me.'

'It's the middle of nowhere, no one about, you would have privacy.' The sergeant shrugged.

'Which makes it the perfect place to commit murder. If Danny Evans wanted to take his own life and leave a note for his family to find, why do that here? And why choose the room furthest away from the entrance?'

'Unless he did know there was a security visit scheduled, like you said. The damage to the door was obvious, Kenneth here was always going to check.'

'The body's still a long way from that busted door. And what else might give Kenneth here an idea that something was wrong?'

'You've got me.'

'Where's Mr Evans's car? I didn't see one out in the car park and this is hardly on a bus route.'

'I didn't think of that.'

'I think if you want someone to know you're here you leave your car outside. Or leave your phone switched on.'

'Maybe his car's nearby, but he just didn't want anyone to come checking until he did what he needed to? I'll see if there are any cars registered to him on the Police National Computer and get a search going. That's the sort of thing a Police Community Support Officer can do for us.'

'That would be great.' Joel was still looking around the room. 'How many identical rooms did we pass to get here? Did you notice we were following the signs for the fire escape?

209

That tells me there must be access to another set of stairs this end of the building, close to here. The fact that I couldn't see them when I pulled in means they come out at the back of the building.'

'You mean for an escape!' The enthusiasm was evident in the sergeant's voice now.

Joel was still looking around the room. 'And the blinds, there are marks in the dust like they've been disturbed recently. Why pull the blinds from the window if it's privacy you want?' Then he pointed at the blinds still intact on the north side, which glowed white. 'The sun's over there if you wanted that on your face for the end. But if you had tied a man to a chair and you wanted to know if someone was coming – which window would you want revealed?'

'The one out to the car park.'

'And the main entrance. While giving yourself access to the fire escape that can't be seen from the main approach.'

'I reckon I can see why you're a detective!' The sergeant clapped her hands in excitement.

Joel couldn't help but smile. 'You might be the only one,' he said. He was pacing now, his confidence boosted, his attention back on the seated victim. 'The weapon looks wrong too.' Now Joel was thinking out loud but he had a captive audience.

'Wrong?' the sergeant replied.

'Just wrong . . . I can't imagine how it gets left on his lap like that.' Joel tried to run a simulation through his mind of Daniel Evans's arrival. The state of mind he must have been in to come here to end his own life. Yet he had cleared a space and dragged a chair out into the middle, and had pulled the blinds down to reveal a window that he then hadn't faced, preferring instead to face the door and whoever was to discover him from the hallway beyond. He had then turned the gun on himself at an awkward angle when he could have easily jammed it under his chin or in his teeth. Death would have

210

been quick, his loss of cognitive ability would have been instant, and yet the weapon had untangled itself from his trigger finger – or thumb as was more likely – to end up on his lap.

'Let's get a better grip on the outer cordon before anyone else gets here. We'll put it on from the main vehicle gate. The cars that are here will need to stay here for now; CSI will want tyre prints for elimination. And can you find out if we've got a Police Search Adviser on today? I doubt they'll have a team until tomorrow but they'll appreciate an early heads-up.'

'No problem.' Sergeant Taylor instantly stepped away, her phone already in her hand.

'Once the walkthrough's done I'll need to speak with you.' Joel was staring back over at the wide-eyed security guard.

'With me What for?' he breathed.

'Standard. Whoever finds the body has to tell us all about it. It should be a pretty simple statement, nothing to worry about.'

'OK . . .' he said, though he still seemed unsure.

'Where's your dog? Do you need to check on it, or . . .'

'My . . . Oh, I don't have a dog. The budget ran out.'

'Your van says—'

'I know, it says dog. We leave it on there as a bit of a warning, you know . . .'

'I see. I feel safer already.'

The sergeant walked back into view as she was ending a call. 'Right then. You've got four coming to help out. I'll stick around until I'm needed elsewhere. I spoke to the FRU who have the list of on-call PolSAs. They have your number to pass over once they get someone.'

'Excellent, thank you.'

'Anything else you need?'

'I don't think so. I'll speak with CSI and then I'm going to have a drive round the area to see what we've got in the way of CCTV or Automatic Number Plate Recognition. Even a

211

neighbour with a pair of eyes would do. I'm not holding out much hope seeing as we're in the middle of nowhere and it's a Sunday.'

'Some of the other units on the estate might have some activity, even on a Sunday.'

'They might. I'm just not sure any of them will be looking outwards. We'll see what we have.'

'I assume your team will be out here to take some of the strain?'

'My team?'

'Oh . . . do Major Crime not work Sundays?'

'Major Crime . . .' Joel smiled. 'They do, of course they do. My team is . . . well, it's me really. And a DS on a day off.'

'So it's just you?'

Joel shrugged, trying to play it down. 'There's not much that can't wait until tomorrow, on our side of the business anyway. Today it's CSI and starting a scene log and me seeing what I can find out about our victim. The one thing I will need to do is talk to the next of kin. Has anyone done that yet?'

'No,' the sergeant said. 'That's been assigned to me. The Force Control Room have put the details on a separate CAD. There's record of his wife, Sharon Evans. She lives out in Lydden so not that far from here.'

'OK, don't worry about that. I'll deliver the message. I'll need to talk to her anyway.'

'Can't say I'm disappointed,' the sergeant said, and Joel could certainly understand her relief. Delivering a death message was always the worst part of the job.

Movement down in the car park dragged Joel's attention. A small van pushed its way through the barrier. The livery announced it as his CSI support.

'Here come the cavalry. That trip out for a pint of milk is already looking pretty epic,' the sergeant said, her face now carrying more than a hint of mischief.

212

Joel checked his watch. 'Yeah, I might have to have a rethink on that.'

The sergeant's mischief spilled over into a broad grin. 'Up it to flowers, that would work for me.'

'I played the flowers card a long time ago.'

Chapter 32

Joel had reviewed the CAD to see what was known about Sharon Evans. The FCR had included details of the home address and brief information of two children, both shown as residing there. Part of his visit would be to get more details. It could be an essential part of his investigation, but before clarifying the setup at that family home he was going to have to destroy it.

The house sat back from the road at the end of a long drive. Joel had a sinking feeling as he noted the windows and porch were still in darkness, despite the gathering gloom, and the drive was empty of cars. He still swore when there was no response to his knock.

'She'll be out. Help you?'

Joel turned to a man just visible between two tall bushes on a neighbouring path.

'I was hoping to speak to Sharon Evans. Does she live here?'

'Who's asking?'

Joel didn't like flashing his warrant card at random neighbours, it could only fuel gossip, but the man's tone carried a warning that he wouldn't be giving out any information cheaply. 'I'm a police officer. She might be able to help me with my enquiries is all.'

'Police? I thought you lot had given up. If she's not in she'll be at the hospital.'

'Hospital?'

'With her daughter. Still in intensive care. She usually goes later on a Sunday after the boy plays football. You find him yet?'

'Find him?'

'The bastard that put her there. I wouldn't bother speaking to the family if you don't have good news, I think they're a bit upset with you lot.'

'I'll bear that in mind. Do you happen to have an up-to-date phone number for her? The number I have doesn't seem to connect.'

'I did say intensive care, didn't I?' The tone was laden with sarcasm now. 'She'll have it switched off, genius.'

'Thanks for your help.'

'I look forward to being able to say the same to you, officer. The whole community needs justice for those girls.'

'Noted.' Joel was moving away now, since continuing the conversation was only going to make it clear that he had no idea what this man was talking about. He felt his phone vibrating in his pocket, providing the ideal excuse to ignore the neighbour, who was calling something after him. His display showed DS ROSE. Joel had left a message on her phone with the briefest of updates. He had finished by telling her not to worry about coming in, that he could update her tomorrow.

'Hey.'

'Why didn't you call?' DS Rose was instantly on the offensive.

'I did. I assume this is a response to that.'

'Before. Before you went out to a murder scene. Why didn't you call?'

'I didn't know it was a murder scene. It still might not be. I didn't know what I had and I didn't see the point of ruining your Sunday as well as mine.'

'You should have called.'

215

Joel took a moment to make sure his response wasn't a barked reminder of the rank structure. He didn't let anyone talk to him the way she was. But over the phone with a lurking civilian wasn't the way to get that point across.

By the time he spoke again he was sealed back in his car.

'There wasn't much you could have done any—'

'You have a lead on who killed Hannah. You should have called me.'

'I may have, we don't know that for sure. There's a possible link but I need to get onto the system and—'

'Hannah Ribbons was the OIC for a blackmail case. Callie Evans was one of the victims, along with four or five other girls around the same age. Callie is Danny Evans's daughter. The families of those girls, they're all pissed off at the police, there's no offender. You should have called me.'

'How do you know—'

'I told you I worked with Hannah when she was child protection. I didn't work this case but I knew about it and I knew how obsessed she was with it. The fact we didn't get anyone in for it isn't down to Hannah, she couldn't have done more. Source handling was her dream job, but it came at the wrong time, she said as much. She didn't want to leave the Callie Evans job. So Danny Evans must have been angry at her for what happened to his daughter.'

'What did happen? I'm on my way to the wife now. It seems she's with her daughter.'

'At the hospital.'

'Yes.'

'I'll meet you there. Don't talk to her without me. They're upset enough as it is without you turning up and knowing nothing about that whole investigation.'

Joel took a breath. 'I'm not as stupid as you think I am. And we've had this conversation, the one where you respect my rank even if you don't respect my ability.' Joel waited. The reply followed a short silence.

216

'You're right, I don't mean to snap at you. But Hannah . . . she did everything she could . . .'

'Sharon Evans is at the William Harvey. I'll meet you in the lobby,' Joel said, then added: 'We need to do everything we can too. Think about whether you're helping or hindering that right now.'

Chapter 33

Sharon Evans nodded to thank the nurse who had just left a cup of tea by Callie's bedside. Sharon had stepped out from a room that was just off the main ward and labelled 'Relatives Room', having finished a tense phone call with her boss about when he could expect her to return. Sharon had explained that Callie was changing all the time – improving – and if she could just have another few days the picture might be entirely different. She worked for a haulage company, part of a busy team. There were enough workers to cover someone taking the odd day off or an irregular hour or two to pick up kids from school, but she was well beyond that. Her team had been great, the company overall had been great, everyone telling her how much they understood that she needed to be somewhere else – but the tone was changing. That phone call was the first time she sensed that the phrase 'of course we understand' was about to be followed by the word 'but'. It didn't quite happen, but it was coming.

Sharon needed to get back to being somewhere near to reliable and the only way she could see that happening started with Danny picking up his damned phone. She would need to try him again but it could wait until after that tea. The nurse who had left it for her now reappeared. She was east

Asian in appearance, petite and timid with a strong accent. Sharon hadn't seen her before but beyond the core of nurses looking after Callie, changes were common. Jamie sat on a chair on the other side of the bed, lost in a game on his mobile phone. Callie was still sleeping. Sharon was disappointed; she wanted Jamie to see something of his sister.

'Is everything OK?' Sharon said.

'There are some people here to see you,' the nurse replied.

'People? What people?'

The nurse looked embarrassed. 'They say they are police?' The nurse had lowered her voice so Jamie couldn't hear.

'OK . . . Did they say what they wanted?'

'Not to me. I'll get them.' The nurse moved out of sight for just a few seconds then came back pointing for the benefit of a man and woman. Even if the nurse hadn't told her, Sharon might have known they were police officers. The man was mid to late thirties. He had a thick neck and a broad chest visible through an open jacket with a tie running down the gap. The woman was younger, probably pretty if she smiled. Her hair was tied back like it got in the way of her day job and she held her arms tight across her front to trap a blue book with a pen hooked over the top. Both of them had the same stern, professional expression that must be part of the training for all police officers.

'Mrs Evans?' The man spoke. His voice was both warm and authoritative, like he had spent some time practising his introduction. She had talked to a lot of police officers in her recent past, but she didn't recognise this one.

'Sharon Evans, yes,' she said. She could feel the hackles rise on the back of her neck. An ancient instinct was kicking in. Something was wrong, she just knew it.

'I'm sorry to bother you here. I need to speak to you. The nurse says there's a room we can use . . .' He faded out to half-turn back the way he had walked.

'Can we not talk here?'

219

'We can . . . Your daughter, I understand?' He glanced beyond her for a moment.

'Callie. She could wake any moment. I don't like leaving her.'

'Of course. It's just—'

'Here's fine.' Sharon snapped. The woman police officer gave a slight reaction but the man's smile didn't even shift. Sharon spun away to where Jamie was still staring over. 'Jamie, you were going to the vending machine. I need to talk to the police.'

'The police! What about?' He blinked away from his phone and looked like he was taking in the officers for the first time.

'Your sister. I'll talk to you about it later.' Jamie huffed and took his time. The man waited for him to leave, exchanging glances with his colleague before speaking again.

'My name is Detective Inspector Joel Norris, this is DS Lucy Rose. I don't have an easy message for you this evening, Sharon. Would you at least sit down?'

'Tell me,' Sharon said, instinctively reaching out for the bed, just to make sure she was holding something.

'Danny Evans, your husband.' The officer paused for a moment, like that was her opportunity to deny it, to tell him he had the wrong person. All she did was tighten her grip on the bed. 'A male we believe to be Danny Evans has been found deceased earlier today, Sharon, I'm so sorry. There was nothing that could be done to help him . . .' He paused again. She could feel both of their eyes on her and knew they were waiting for a reaction – confirmation it had sunk in, perhaps. It hadn't. The words rolled around in her mind.

'Today?' she managed finally. Like that mattered.

'Yes. Although I can't confirm for sure when he died right now.'

'Died . . .' She looked for the chair now. She didn't sit in it but used the arm to take her weight. She looked over at

220

their sleeping daughter then turned away. Suddenly she couldn't look at her. What was she going to tell Callie now? And what about Jamie? She stood back up, her body suddenly flushing with panic, her breaths shorter and faster. The officer stepped towards her. She felt him take hold of her shoulders, his grip firm enough to puncture the sudden dizziness.

'Let's get you into that chair. You look a little unsteady there!' She felt the grip lead her. She went with it, the plastic seat cushion squeaked under her and she felt the coldness against her back. Next her tea was held out for her to take.

'Died . . .' she said again.

The police officer squatted down to her level. 'The way he was found suggests he might have taken his own life, Sharon.' Another pause for her reaction. Another gap for his words to mean something to her. She pushed out towards his voice, her body shifting forward at the same time, her momentum taking her onto her feet. She felt the back of her hand connect with him like a karate chop and he rolled away so she could step past. She heard crockery smash on the floor too and sudden heat against her ankle. She wanted him to stop talking, just for a moment. Every time he talked it was worse. The news was worse. She stepped away and moved into the corner where the long curtain was bunched up. She pushed up against it, close enough for it to fill her vision.

'Danny killed himself?' Her voice was barely a whisper but it was her voice, no longer that of a stranger, and instantly it seemed more real. Like it could even be true. She shook her head, gently at first but soon more vigorously. 'No . . . no, NO!' She found power from somewhere and spun on the balls of her feet. 'He wouldn't do that! He wouldn't do that, not Danny! He wouldn't be such a fucking coward!' She was flailing her arms, her vision now impaired by tears so the figure moving towards her was just a dark shape against the white of the wall behind. She felt her arms grabbed so they couldn't flail anymore, then wrapped up tight against her body like she

221

was hugging herself. She could sense the officer's strength; he was so close she could feel his body heat, scented with aftershave. When he let her arms go she reached out instinctively, grabbing him to sob into his front. She felt his arms hold her tight. She couldn't speak, there was nothing she could say. No one spoke until her sobbing ceased.

'I'm sorry,' she managed eventually and she pushed the officer away – a little too firmly – suddenly appalled at herself. It got worse when she saw the dark smudge on his shirt where her mascara had run.

'Don't be silly,' he replied. 'There's still that room available, I'm not here to make a show of you and your son . . .' Sharon suddenly flushed with panic. *Jamie!* She couldn't let him see her, not like this.

'My son . . . He'll wonder where I am.'

'We can ask the nurse to let him know you'll be back in a minute or two. He'll be fine out here.'

Sharon found herself being led back to the Relatives Room. There were more seats with thick plastic cushions that squeaked and shifted as they sat. The chairs were against a wall to face a low table with magazines scattered across it. The man pulled the furthest two seats out a little to face where Sharon had sat in the chair closest to the door. It was a good place if she needed to bolt. The moment the woman police officer pulled the door shut her anxiety was heightened enough for her to consider it.

'How?' All the strength in her voice was gone now. She felt empty, sobbed out and exhausted.

'A security guard doing his rounds noticed a forced door in a disused office block out in Tilmanstone. He found Danny seated with a pistol in his lap. It was already too late for him. It would appear he used the pistol to take his own life.'

Sharon's hand to her mouth was instinctive, and firm enough to make a slapping sound. 'What? He shot himself? Where the hell would he get a gun?'

222

'One of our questions is about the weapon, Sharon. Does he have any access to firearms that you know of?'

'Guns? No! He's not that sort of person. He plays football, what would he need with a gun?'

'Has he ever talked about them? Any fascination, any trips to a range or anything that would suggest he knew how to use one?'

'No. He did clay pigeon shooting, I remember that. It was in Dublin, a stag do for one of his mates. That's literally the only time he's ever mentioned anything like it and that was years ago.'

'Okay. What about Tilmanstone – the place – do you know it?'

'The Dover Youth played at a place called Tilmanstone. My son . . . Jamie . . . he played out there a few times.'

'So Danny would know it too.'

'He would know the pitch, he knows every football pitch in Kent I reckon, but an *office block*? I don't think Danny's ever set foot in an office block in his life.'

'Does he have anyone he knows out that way? Any reason to go there or even nearby?'

'No. What the hell was he doing out there?' She was racking her brains; none of this made sense.

'I don't know. But we're doing everything we can to find out.' Sharon couldn't stop a snort. She turned away, back to eyeing up the door. The urge to get out of there returned all at once.

'We've heard that before! My daughter was being abused. My daughter is *here* because she was being abused. Do you know how many of your lot told us that they were "doing everything they can"?'

'I don't. I'm not the officer investigating that case but I do have some knowledge of it. I couldn't possibly understand the upset, what you and Callie have been through—'

'Still are!'

223

'Of course. I can see that. And I know the police haven't got you any answers yet and I'm sorry about that. We don't ever close cases, not really. If something more—'

'Don't give me that! They're not even looking. I only found one of you who even pretended to care. She gave me her card, told me to call any time I wanted. She answered to start with but then someone else was picking up her phone to take messages. They told me she'd moved on. Other cases, easier ones maybe. *Moved on!* I wish we could just do that. Forget about all this and just move on like *DC Ribbons* did. I haven't taken your lot seriously since.'

'I know Hannah was the officer in the case—' The woman police officer spoke now but Sharon cut right across her.

'That's her. Hannah *fucking* Ribbons. The woman who promised me the world and delivered us nothing.' Sharon forced a snort. 'She was involved for the first few weeks or so, and those were the best weeks, I'll give her that. I actually thought we were going to get somewhere. Everyone since has just given us lip service, no one's promising anything anymore. Callie was one of the victims but there was a group of them, all friends, did you know that?'

'I do know—' the woman started only for Sharon to cut her off again.

'A group of friends forced to realise what a shithole of a world this really is. Our job, the parents, is to keep that away from our kids, to let them be kids for as long as they possibly can. I could hardly have failed worse. And the scum that did this to my daughter, to my family, to all those families, he's still out there. There's another family in his sights by now.' Sharon took another deep breath. She needed a moment. The woman sensed her opportunity.

'DC Ribbons . . . I assume you met her? Face to face, I mean,' she said, her tone soft.

'Met her? Of course I met with her! She came out, took statements, told us how sorry she was, what she was going

224

to do about it, how determined she was!' Sharon snorted again. 'That determination didn't last long, did it? She even came to one of the groups. The parents of all the girls get together, it was a support group at first but it was just a lot of bitching and moaning by the end. I don't go anymore.'

'And DC Ribbons went to this group?' the woman persisted.

'Why don't you know this? What is this? Why are you talking about her?' Sharon's surge of anger was so sudden it brought tears with it. 'Talk to her, ask her what she did and didn't do!'

'Did Danny go? To the support group I mean?' the woman officer said.

Sharon sighed. She took a moment to wipe her face. She suddenly felt weary. She was just about done talking, it was too much effort. 'No. That's not his thing. He sits and stews on his own, always has. Things eat him up quietly.' She suddenly realised what she might have implied. 'But not to the point where he would . . . Danny gets wound up and lashes out at the world but never at himself.'

'Did Danny ever meet DC Ribbons?'

This was the man's voice again and Sharon detected something in it that drew her to him; he was staring at her, and there was intensity in that too. She sat straighter where she had slumped back in the chair.

'I don't think he did. He spoke to a couple of your lot before . . . before Callie did what she did, but I don't think it was DC Ribbons. She did come to the house but . . . he couldn't cope with it, to be honest. Those first few days when it all came out were hell, I mean, it's all been a nightmare but one of the other girls reported it, it wasn't our Callie. So Danny was angry about that, angry that she was just going to let it go, not tell anyone. There was so much pressure on her, enough to put her on that park bench . . . Your lot were finding out bits of what had been going on and he just couldn't listen to it. God knows I found it hard enough. He couldn't

225

even look at Callie. It wasn't that he was angry at *her*, he's just so angry. I think Callie thought he blamed her and she went into her shell – they're similar like that, Callie and her dad. In the end he had to go. He'll tell you I kicked him out of the family home but I could see that being there was destroying him.' Sharon could feel emotion coming back now, and it threatened to consume her.

'Then Callie tried to end her life,' the officer said. 'Sounds like you're quite the incredible woman, Sharon. To even be talking to me about it. That's some strength.'

'Didn't do us any good though, did it?'

'You said that Danny moved out?' the woman officer cut back in.

Sharon took a moment to recover. 'He booked himself into some hotel, I hear.'

'What hotel, Sharon? Where is he staying?' The man spoke, his tone suddenly losing the warmth and patience.

Sharon laughed; it came from somewhere and petered out the moment it started. 'I don't even know! Sums up that man at the moment, his state of mind.'

'Do you know where his car is?' he said.

'No. Don't you? Wasn't it there with him?'

'It wasn't. We have a silver Mercedes C Class registered to him, is that still the one he uses?'

'I . . . I mean yeah, it must be. It's leased for another year but I don't know how he can be affording it. It must be at his hotel then.'

'How would he be paying for a room? Is there anything on your bank statement to give us a clue where he—'

'He thought of that. He has his own account. He never really used it but he's been transferring the money from our joint account to pay for his hotel room. It's a small fortune, to be honest. He told me that was why he was doing it that way. He said he didn't want me just turning up unannounced, but what he really meant is he didn't want me to see him in a state.'

226

'A state?' the woman officer said while her colleague sat back like he knew exactly what she meant. She said it anyway.

'Pissed. He's always liked a drink but socially. In the last couple of years I've seen a different man when the pressure's on, a man who has started using alcohol as a way to escape. It doesn't work, of course it doesn't – if it did I might do the same. That would be easy, wouldn't it? You let something like that happen to your daughter but it's OK, you can just forget it for the evening!' Her anger rose up but it was quickly replaced by exhaustion.

'Again, Sharon, I can't imagine.' His tone was softer too now. It annoyed her.

'Do you have children?' Sharon snapped.

'Two girls. Younger than Callie.'

'Then you *can* imagine. Those two girls when they're fifteen, someone getting hold of them without you knowing, manipulating them to send photos of themselves, to be indecent, to lose their innocence, to be thrust into the world of sick adults, for them to be so damaged that they just close down. I had no idea of the pain that girl was in until the phone call telling me she was being resuscitated on the ground in the park. Maybe you *can* imagine!' Sharon's voice was now just a hiss.

She got a reaction; the officer's jaw flexed. It was slight but she could tell a man struggling with a mental image.

'There was hope, you know,' Sharon continued. 'Callie's going to wake up on her own, we're going to get her back. Just this morning she reacted to me being here . . . I was so happy! But now . . . I've been thinking this last day or two about how we recover from this, how we limit the damage to her and to her younger brother when she does come back to us. How we might get some of that time back where they can just be kids. Danny and I . . . This whole thing has ripped us apart. These last few days when I couldn't get hold of him I realised how much I need him. We all do. The only way back from this is if we're all together. Danny has to be here. We

227

have to try and be as close to when it was good as we can. And now you come here and tell me . . .' Sharon couldn't speak. She couldn't cry either. She felt like her jaw had seized up, pressure building behind it. She rubbed her hands over her face. When she dropped them back into her lap she felt the officer take hold of them. His tone was at its softest yet.

'I need to show you something. It's not pleasant, I know none of this is. He left a note.'

Sharon sucked in a shallow breath and held onto it. Her free hand was back to cover her mouth. She watched as the inspector took a piece of paper out of his pocket and unfolded it to lay it in her hand. She hesitated. Finally she moved it close enough to read. She could see typed words but her eyes had blurred with tears. She didn't look at it, not straightaway, just held it in her hand for a moment until she could breathe again. When she did run her eyes over it nothing was going in. She had to read it twice, then a third time for it to start to mean anything.

'What is this? This isn't Danny, it doesn't even sound like Danny! Who typed this?'

'It's a copy of what was left for us to find. I brought it with me because I needed to know what your reaction would be.'

'This isn't him. Simple. What's this about him hurting someone? Danny doesn't hurt people.'

'I had a little look at his history. There was an assault back in—'

'He punched a guy who got up in his face! When he was out on the beer and a long time ago. He's had it his whole career – some guy sees a local footballer out relaxing and they see a target. Especially Danny. That nickname he was given was just about the worst thing that coulda happened. There's kudos in starting on The Beast. Blokes are idiots. They fight. Danny's never been the sort to go out looking but he won't back down. Not ever.'

'Has he ever mentioned Sittingbourne before? In any context?'

228

'No. Not to me.'

Sharon still had the note, and she fixed back on it to pick out more detail. 'And it says *her*? No way he hurts a woman. No way. Did you find her? Do that, find who he's talking about, speak to her and she'll tell you what happened. But my Danny, he wouldn't hurt a woman. I know him.'

'We think we have found her, Sharon. The woman he mentions is Hannah Ribbons and she was shot dead in a flat in Sittingbourne.'

'Hannah . . .' Sharon looked up to meet the officer's eyes. 'Shot dead . . .' Her words rushed out at the same time as her breath and she couldn't get any more back in. It was like she had taken a punch to the gut. 'No.' All that was left was a squeak. She stood up, seeing if that would help with the breathing. She discarded the note, pushing it off her lap. She didn't want to look at it, never mind have it touching her.

'Danny took his life a short time after. The gun he used . . . Part of the enquiries will be to check if it was the same one as the gun that killed DC Ribbons, but I think it will be . . .' His words hung like they had given a thickness to the air, enough to hold held her still. 'Your husband had clear motive. We know he was angry, the police who did get to speak to him have all included in their notes that he was angry, that he was anti-police, that he—'

'STOP!' Sharon's energy returned all at once. Her voice bounced off the door she was facing. 'Danny *was* angry, he was angry that his daughter nearly DIED, that she'll never be the same again, that none of us will! He's angry at all the pain, his pain, mine, our children, and what have you lot done? Nothing! He's angry about the drink drive charge. He held his hands up from the moment those lights come on behind him and you lot still took great pride in parading him in front of the press for photos when he was at his lowest point. Even putting out your own post on *fucking* Twitter, hanging him out to dry as an example to all that no one's

229

above the law, how even the captain of the town's football team gets arrested. Bully for you! He never pretended to be above it. He made a mistake and he held his hands up and you lot made a massive song and dance out of it. So yeah, he was angry. But shooting a young woman? Copper or not, my Danny . . . No!' She thrust her hand at the note that was still on the floor and now a blur behind thick tears. 'That isn't him!'

Sharon was close enough to wrench the door. She was through it before she heard it smack against the wall behind her. She marched back over to her daughter's bed, relieved to see that Jamie wasn't back yet. She hurriedly pulled all three curtains round the bed to make a cocoon, to make it just her and Callie with the rest of the world blocked out. She swept up her daughter's hand.

'It's going to be all right, honey. I promise you that.' But her words felt empty. She glanced round the three walls of curtain, already dreading that at some point she was going to have to open them to the world again.

Chapter 34

'Dammit.' Joel had stayed silent the whole walk back to the police parking bays, but now he thumped the steering wheel to express his frustration.

'What's the matter?' DS Rose leaned in through the driver's window. Her own car was parked just behind.

'I need a team. Some people I can point at a simple job.'

'Like?'

'Like calling round the local hotels. We need to find where Danny was staying so we can search that room. A team could do it within the hour.'

'Assuming he's booked in under his own name. It sounds like he was pretty determined to hide from his wife,' DS Rose said.

'Maybe. But people seem to know who he is round here.'

'So maybe he isn't staying round here. Or he's at some bed and breakfast in the arse end of nowhere. There's plenty of them in the Dover area.'

'There are. The CID sergeant did offer me help from his team. I'll see if that offer still stands in the morning.' Joel peered out into a darkness given an extra layer of thickness by cloud cover. It was drizzling too, the rain concealed in a breeze that was at least a little warmer. 'We're not finding that room tonight,' he muttered.

'Nothing changes by the morning anyway,' DS Rose said. 'Tomorrow we can put in the request with Danny Evans's bank to find who he's been paying. SOCU have their own financial investigators, they owe me a favour, they might even be able to get something over the phone.'

Joel considered this. She was right. A big part of life for the Serious and Organised Crime Unit was tracing money. They were good at it, they would be quick. Just not quick enough. 'I want to avoid room service going in there and cleaning up. We'll need a search, forensics too if we're thinking gunshot residue on his clothing from when . . .' Joel peered up at his colleague.

'From when he shot Hannah,' DS Rose said, finishing his sentence. Joel used the silence that followed to check the time. Joel had been out of the house long enough to wonder whether he should call his wife. She hadn't called him, which meant one of two things: she had fully anticipated that a callout to work could mean that he would be very late back – or she was furious. It was time to head home and see which option she had taken.

'We start again in the morning then,' Joel said but DS Rose still leaned against his car door. It was obvious she had more to say, although the rain was now running over her forehead.

'I know I've been . . . difficult,' she said finally. 'I just . . . Hannah deserves the best. Any copper killed on duty, they deserve the best, they don't deserve to be part of some political manoeuvrings by a senior officer trying to become more senior.'

'I agree with you.'

'I know you do. This isn't your fault.'

'For the record, the superintendent would agree too. She can lose sight of the big picture sometimes when she's excited but she sees us as just stepping in and leading whatever Major Crime team is in the area. I think she forgets that we don't

232

have her rank, people don't just do as we ask. And she believes in us.'

'She believes in you,' DS Rose said. 'She was positively glowing. I thought she was just talking like that because I was angry you were in charge, but she meant it. She says you're smart, rates you above most of the career detectives out there. Talked about how you "think different".'

'Is that meant to be a compliment?'

'I think it was. I don't know if that's true . . . not yet, at least.'

'And why would you? You're a good detective too by all accounts and a good detective doesn't believe anything they haven't seen for themselves.'

'They don't. But I liked you at the scene and you handled Sharon well. I wouldn't want to be the one breaking that news to her, not with everything that's gone on.'

'She's really been through it,' Joel said.

'She was one of the reasons Hannah was so desperate to make it right. The last time I talked to Hannah, she . . . I may have a theory on why we're not getting anything out of the source unit, why she was there in the first place.'

'Do you want to sit out of the rain at least?' Joel said. DS Rose moved round and the interior light that accompanied the door opening revealed just how wet she was. She kept the door open.

'First you need to understand that she got involved in cases, that she would do anything to get a result, but this case . . . Even for Hannah she was obsessed.'

'OK.'

'So, if she broke any rules it was always with the best of intentions. I don't want her being blamed for this, for what happened to her.'

'I'm not bothered if she made mistakes. I just want to know what happened.'

'Hannah talked to me about that case with those girls. She

233

had been working on it for two weeks or so and then Callie tried to kill herself. When a fifteen-year-old girl does that as part of a case you're investigating it hits you hard. But she couldn't turn down the source handler job when it came up. Someone got injured, bad enough to have to leave the team. Not how you would choose to get a job but she had to take it.'

'I can see that.'

'Hannah also saw it as an opportunity for Callie's case.'

'Go on?'

'She said she could come at it from a different angle. She talked to her new skipper about the job. He told her how they have sources that have given information about sex offenders before. Apparently it's the only information people will share for free, especially if you're talking about kid victims. Her skipper found someone who might be able to help so Hannah put herself forward to meet with them as soon as possible.'

'Do we know who?'

'No. She didn't tell me that. But it was blocked anyway. All handler meetings are run through a controller – a senior officer basically who has to authorise every meeting – and they wouldn't authorise this one. Hannah had only been on the team a couple of weeks and didn't have an existing relationship with this informant and it failed the risk assessment. Someone else on the team was going to be tasked with it, but it wouldn't be any time soon. Hannah said that the whole team were wrapped up in some big drugs job. She was frustrated.'

'So you think she did something off her own back?'

'I don't know that for sure, but I've never seen her so consumed . . . That was the last time I saw her.'

'So that could explain why she was at an informant's house, why she was on her own.'

'It could.'

'And now the source team have shut up shop because one

234

of their officers stepped out of their processes and got herself killed.'

'She didn't get herself killed. Someone shackled her to that bed and shot her twice,' DS Rose said.

'You're right, poor turn of phrase. We need to speak to the source team,' Joel said, 'more than ever.'

'We're getting nothing.'

Joel lit up his phone but changed his mind. 'First thing in the morning I'll speak to our superintendent again and see what she can do. We need to be a lot more difficult to ignore.'

Chapter 35

Monday

The graveyard at Lympne Church was never more beautiful than when it was in the throes of spring. The last twenty-four hours had felt like the flick of a switch to Richard – the signs of a harsh and barren winter nearing its end had suddenly arrived. The hedgerow that chased the perimeter of the church grounds had looked like it was drawn from charcoal in the bleakness of winter but it was now littered with shoots. Colour was emerging, too, on the taller trees; their thick roots might have been some way down in the steep valley but the thickening branches were peeking above the low stone wall. Directly behind the headstone of Angela Maddox, a cherry blossom tree had also started to wake and would soon dazzle as a bright pink backdrop. The blossom only lasted a week – less if there was a strong wind – but when it did shed its colour it only served to sprinkle petals like the most beautiful confetti over his wife's resting place. Last year the petals had started falling almost immediately after Angela had been laid to rest, like the gardens were welcoming her with colour – a ticker-tape parade for a returning hero. Angela was from Lympne originally, and one of her ancestors had even been the presiding vicar at this very church – that was how he had been able to bury her here. She had been a regular at their local church

236

but Richard had taken real comfort from the fact that her long sleep would be among old friends and family.

There was no freezing mist today and the rain from the previous night had cleared to leave a sun that was bright enough for him to feel its warmth. He actually undid his jacket before he undid the flask.

'Morning, my love!' He felt bright and inhaled the fresh morning air as he poured out his first coffee. Movement dragged his eye. A sheep emerged from the bushes as a blur, another one erupting from behind it. They both skipped away, the second clumsy where its foot dragged in the vegetation. Richard laughed. 'They're out again, keeping you company, I see!'

Angela loved nature and he loved the idea that animals felt safe enough to roam here. He leaned back, his arm along the top of the bench to open his whole body to the sun. He even closed his eyes – his face drenched enough that he could see the glow against his eyelids. For the first time in a long time, Richard felt good, invigorated even. He could remember endless occasions where he had sat on this bench with no real sense of anything else, like he was just waiting to join his wife in the ground. But not today.

'Who did you bring, Richard?' The voice was instantly recognisable and Richard's eyes opened to the strong sunlight. He was forced to look down, where he took in a pair of smart tan shoes with contrasting blue streak.

'Bring? What do you mean?' Richard said.

'Someone followed you here. He's watching. What did you tell him, Richard? Why did you bring him here?'

'Tell him?'

'About this. About me . . . What did you tell him?' The man was different – his voice was laden with emotion that seemed to be more sadness than anger.

Richard tried to look at him, but the man was just a silhouette, the sunshine directly above his shoulder and Richard had

237

to turn away. He did a sweep of the whole of the grounds, lingering on the wrought-iron entrance gate. He couldn't see anyone else. But Glenn hadn't taken well to being told he wasn't to come up here. Richard had been clear – he didn't need him – but he wouldn't be surprised if his friend had still followed him up here.

'Look, we're basically brothers. And I don't know you, I don't know who you are or why you did what you did.'

'I told you why. I told you I was doing a good deed. I know you've been suffering and I just wanted to give you the chance to make it right. But this was between us, between me and you. I told you that. This wasn't for other people. The moment you start involving other people it becomes . . . messy.'

'Messy? Not at all. I told you, I trust him like no one else left in the world. If he's here it's only to watch my back, just like he's always done. We're both suspicious of good deeds. I guess we were trained to believe that the world's just not like that.' Richard again tried to make eye contact with the man but he still wore the sun on his shoulder.

'Sometimes it is. Surely that's not so hard to see. And you trust this man?'

'With my life,' Richard said.

'And he knows what you did?'

'That's how much I trust him,' Richard confirmed.

The man sighed, and his stance changed a little – less tension perhaps. 'Look, spend some time with your wife, I shouldn't keep interrupting you here. But you have to understand that you cannot talk about what happened, about what I did for you, OK?'

'Do you think I want people to know? Glenn is different . . . He understands. We were in the army together, brothers-in-arms, we always had each other's back then and we always will.'

'Spend some time with your wife, Richard. These times are so special.'

'What about all this? Will I hear from you again?'

238

'You have your answers.'

'I do. Thank you . . . I can't tell you what this means to me. I feel . . . different. I can't explain it. I felt like the world was passing me by, like I was invisible. Useless even. But I don't feel like that now, I know I still have a place.'

'Just a good deed. Nothing else.' The man turned to step out of the sun and Richard watched him until he was out of sight. He never once looked back. Richard shook out the coffee that he had poured earlier. He would take a fresh one from the flask. But first he took out his phone to type out a message to Glenn. It was just like he had told him. He didn't need to be here, he should go home and they could meet later. He even promised to buy the coffee again. He finished the message by saying that they could both get on with their lives now and that he was sorry with how he had been acting recently. It would all be different now.

When Richard pushed the phone back into his pocket he was able to sit back and enjoy the sensation of warmth on his face again. He closed his eyes to it once more, listening for the gentle hiss of leaves catching in a breeze.

'Ah, Angela . . . I feel alive again! We're going to be OK now, me and you. I promise!'

239

Chapter 36

Richard had stayed with his wife for the whole flask of coffee and then stayed some more. Long enough for the pleasant sun to shorten the shadows – and still he felt reluctant to leave.

It was the thought of the meetup with Glenn that finally dragged him away. Richard was not surprised that there had been no reply to his message, Glenn was awful at checking his phone, but Richard still wanted to show his gratitude, to acknowledge that even after all this time, Glenn was still the only one watching his back. He had made a brief stop for a packet of Glenn's favourite biscuits – that should do it.

The moment he stepped out of his car, biscuits in hand, and took in his friend's home he knew something was different. It took another moment or so to pass for him to realise that it was the front door. It was slightly ajar, while the low gate at the start of his garden path was pulled shut. He checked his phone again – still no reply.

The gate pushed back against Richard's thigh on strong springs. A miniature windmill spun in the breeze, its bright colours blurring into each other as he walked past on a path that split a well-tended lawn. Glenn's house was the last one in a row and the front door stuck out of the side in the form of a small porch.

'Glenn?' he called out. The house was old council stock but from an era when they made them large enough for an actual family. Glenn's three children had long since moved out but even when his wife had passed he had dismissed any notion that he might move on.

There was no answer. Richard was at the door now. He placed the flat of his hand on it and leaned forward enough to see into the few inches of gap. The sun might have been brighter today, but its focus was on the front of the row, leaving little to penetrate the shadow behind the door round the side. He pushed it wider. The light changed for the better, enough for him to see the stairs in front of him. Glenn's shoes were stowed neatly in a rack down to his right. His jacket was hanging above them on a peg and his gloves were between them, lying over the radiator with the fingers lined up like Glenn had used a ruler. Always the soldier.

'Glenn?' Richard called out again, this time projecting his voice directly into the house. If he was in there, he would hear him. There was nothing in reply. Richard knew the layout well. Beyond the stairs and down the hall there was a living room with a view out to the front on the right side and access to a kitchen on the left. Whenever he visited they would usually spend their time in the living room, where Glenn had the comfiest armchairs Richard had ever experienced. It had become a standing joke that they would end up sat next to each other in some old people's home having insisted that the chairs came with them.

'What's the matter, cat got your tongue? I know what you're doing!' Richard called, and he did too. Glenn had done it before. He would leave the front door unlocked and then sit silently when he knew Richard was due. Then, when Richard appeared in the living room Glenn would call out: *Nearest the kettle, are you? Go on then, we'll have a brew!* And a big laugh would shake the big belly that always bunched up when he sat.

241

Richard stepped in. He closed the front door behind him with a flick of his elbow. There was still no noise. He paced down the hall.

'Are you playing ga—' He pushed open the door to the living room and the sight stole away the rest of his sentence. His eyes were pulled to where the big window flared bright. In front was a silhouette of his best friend but he knew instantly something was wrong. Glenn sat in his armchair but he was slumped over to one side. His chest, which always had a visible rise and fall, was still. As Richard approached his friend, he could see that his eyes were also still and any signs of life behind them gone. It didn't look real, like someone had replaced his best mate with a dummy and dressed it in a vest soaked in blood.

'Jesus, Glenn!' Richard shot his hand out, his fingers already poised to search for a pulse. Nothing. His skin felt cold and the blood that was thick on his front was already drying. Richard knew a thing or two about blood, about what it looked like, and he knew what death looked like: here it was, seated in front of him. He spun on his heels. His reactions might have dulled over time but the training was still there. He took in the room, assessing for threats. The only movement was from a flickering television playing silently to itself. It took Richard a couple of moments to realise that the figure moving on the screen was familiar.

It was him.

It was CCTV footage. In it, he was walking down a long corridor towards a door. The screen changed and he was still watching himself but now the view was angled down to where he was entering a big office. The screen version of him was hesitating on the threshold, his face turned towards the ground. The angle didn't show what he was looking at but of course Richard knew – this happened just yesterday, after all. He had been looking at a typed note on the floor. It took just a few seconds for him to read it and for his face to look back up,

242

though Richard remembered it as being much longer. The black folder was clear in his hands.

Now, he realised, it was in this room. A black folder, directly below the television, leaning against the cabinet and just tall enough to encroach on the screen slightly. Richard was supposed to see it, he was supposed to read it too, just like he had been the day before. He dropped to his knees next to it, already terrified of the contents, the biscuits discarded. The television screen was now directly in front of him and still showed his image. As he watched the screen, the angle changed again to a wider shot. Now he could see Danny Evans in the middle of a cleared space. The white ropes flared on the camera and even from a distance he could see the fear on the man's face. His eyes bulged and his body twitched where he fought the restraints and, unable to tear himself away, Richard was still watching at the moment the screen flashed.

The moment he had taken Danny Evans's life.

Richard closed his eyes and held them shut, like this was all a nightmare and if he waited long enough he might open them to a new reality – to everything back to the way it was before he had pulled that trigger. It had felt so right at the time but the footage – seeing what he had done from outside his own mind – it was so different from how he remembered it. That man had been helpless, tied down, no chance to even speak for himself. Richard felt his head shaking. He wouldn't have listened anyway. He was well beyond that. Angela always said he was a hothead. She said it like it was a criticism but Richard had never seen it like that. Sometimes you needed to react, you needed to let anger or fear guide you, that was how you survived. But this time she had been right.

The first page of the folder had just two lines, both in block capitals to shout out at him from the page.

DANNY EVANS DIED BECAUSE OF YOU.
GLENN MORRIS DIED BECAUSE OF YOU.

243

Richard's hand had a visible shake as he struggled to grip the blue-tinged paper. The next page made him exhale in a panicked whine, the folder slipping to bounce off his thighs and he pushed away from it, falling backwards onto his buttocks, crushing the biscuit packet to find an uncomfortable seat. He scrabbled for the folder, flicking back to the second page, to read again the single sentence it contained:

THOMAS MADDOX WILL DIE BECAUSE OF YOU.

244

Chapter 37

Sharon Evans ignored the reaction as a grand-looking front door was pulled open to her knocking. The house reminded her of a style she had seen in movies, like it should be lording over plantations in the deep south of America. Instead it was in the hamlet of River on the outskirts of Dover and close enough to the shallow rapids on the west side of Kearsney Abbey for the sound of the gurgling water to travel across the road.

Julia Kerner was the woman standing on the threshold with the look of unabashed surprise. They had been friends once, in as much as their daughters were friends, so they had all spent time together in the grounds of the abbey when their kids were young enough to need entertaining. Julia's daughter was called Abbey – named after the view from her bedroom window. Callie and Abbey had stayed friends, even after their interests had moved on from wading through the low waters and chirruping at the movement of fish or being pushed on the swings.

'Sharon! I didn't think you were coming to these anymore.'

By 'these' she meant meetings of their support group. It was Julia's idea to bring the parents together, and it had seemed like a good one when first suggested. Five kids had been

245

targeted for their innocence, the same offender known to be responsible for wrenching it away, and the perceived lack of police action had left five sets of parents struggling to come to terms with it all. It was somewhere to meet, to be angry, bitter and understood at the same time. But Sharon had quickly developed a suspicion that the setup was all for Julia, that she just liked to be in charge while also being seen as a linchpin by her community.

'I know. I had a little time away . . .' Sharon managed. She knew it would seem odd that she was here. She was invited for every gathering via text message, daily at first, but it had dropped back to once a week on a Monday. She had read the latest invite last night, and it had been the only thing that had cut through her daze. When they had got back from the hospital she had readied Jamie's school uniform, made his lunch and shrugged off his questions about if she was all right. She wasn't all right. She was on auto-pilot, trying to work out how she was going to tell her twelve-year-old son that his dad was gone. His hero. It had made her feel physically sick every time she had tried to form the words and in the end she couldn't do it. She would give him just one more day of normality. A Monday back at school with his mates after half-term. One more day to talk excitedly in class about nothing and to be told off for his troubles, to play football at lunch and then try and hide that he had scuffed his new school shoes when he got home. One more day. But Sharon had been left waiting for him in a silent, empty house. Coming here had somehow made sense. These people were the closest she would find to anyone who might have an understanding of what she was going through, but, more than that, she just couldn't face being alone.

'Of course. I'm just so glad that you realise that this group is here for you whenever you need it.' Julia tilted her head to provide another reminder of why Sharon had stopped coming here. Julia's whole demeanour was condescending. She liked

246

to say things that she thought made her sound wise and caring but her faux sympathy achieved the opposite. It was too late now. Julia closed the door behind her. Sharon was in.

'The group will be delighted to see you!' Julia said. Sharon followed her down the hall, all the rooms they passed looking like they were set up for a glossy magazine shoot. Julia was an interior designer, her home a constantly changing showcase of what she was capable of, and, Sharon was convinced, another reason she had insisted on hosting these get-togethers.

The tour ended in a large curved conservatory at the back of the house that instantly felt warm. Tasteful wicker furniture surrounded a round table with a tray of cups and a large teapot wearing a brightly coloured cosy. Julia gestured towards it. 'Help yourself. Ooh, I need to get some more biscuits! They seem to have gone down well.' She chuckled like she was delighted with herself. Sharon watched her leave then picked out a seat against the far wall. She was aware that the hushed conversation between the six women in the room had died down the moment she had walked in. She looked up to a row of smiles, all of them laden with that same faux sympathy. Sharon didn't know any of them very well but had the impression they all worked for themselves or in very flexible jobs. She remembered a conversation right at the beginning where they had all agreed to 'clear their diaries for Mondays', which suggested a lot more flexibility than she had.

What had seemed like a bad idea at the door was already feeling worse. Some of the faces were different and Sharon couldn't even be sure which families were represented anymore. With only the women left, it felt more coffee morning than support group. Early meetings had been dominated by angry fathers demanding answers. By now they must have realised that they were wasting their time here.

Julia returned with a plate of cookies that looked baked rather than shop-bought. 'So, Sharon, what brings you back to the fold?'

247

Fold. That was genuinely how Julia saw this too. A protective group – where she could be head protector.

'Danny . . . He's dead.' It just fell out. It was like she needed to say it to someone and it even caught Sharon out. The sob that followed filled a room that had fallen into an instant silence. Then there was the faint scuffle of jeans against seat material as someone moved towards her and she was grabbed in a hug by bony arms.

'Jesus, Sharon. Anything you need . . .' was whispered in her ear.

'Thank you,' Sharon said. It was all she could manage. She knew it was a stock response from a shocked room but it still made her feel better. Maybe it hadn't been such a bad idea to come here after all. She didn't need to tell them any more; she didn't think she could anyway. It didn't matter, not in that moment. Danny was dead, that was all that mattered.

248

Chapter 38

'Thomas! Not my Thomas . . . little Thomas!' The shake in Richard's hand was so bad he struggled to get it into his pocket for his phone. Operating it was harder still.

'Come on, come on!' He spoke at the phone but lashed out at the television that was still showing the same footage on a loop in Glenn's living room. It was back to the point where it showed him lingering on the threshold, where he had first seen Danny Evans. He felt like screaming at the image, at himself: *Turn around! Don't!* But all he could do was turn it off. Now the television showed the live version of himself as a reflection. His eyes were wide and panicked, his mouth hanging open ready to shoot with words the moment the damned phone was answered. And, just over his shoulder, he could see his best mate slumped over in his favourite chair while his blood dripped a rhythm into the carpet.

'Dad?' Colin said as he answered the phone, instantly sounding a combination of hassled and bored.

'Colin! Thomas, where is he? Where's Thomas, Colin? I need you to check!'

'Jesus, Dad, what's the matter with you?'

249

'Where is he? You need to call his school! Call his school, do it now and make sure he's OK. I can wait.'

'Call the . . . Dad, he's here, OK! He's right here, helping me with the classic. His dorm's sorted but his term doesn't start again until the middle of the week so I thought, you know, after what you said, I thought maybe—'

'He's there! He's there with you now and he's safe?'

'What the hell is going on, Dad? You sound stressed out?'

'No . . . I'm OK . . . Sorry, Colin, bad dream . . .' Richard broke off to catch a sob before it could escape down the phone. 'Look after the boy, OK?' It was all he could manage before cutting the call. His whole body slumped, like the tension had been the only thing holding him upright. He had to catch himself on his elbows for fear of collapsing to the carpet. It took all his strength just to get back to sitting up. He picked up the black folder again, opening it back to the page where his grandson's name appeared. He held it on his lap, screwing the page to turn it with one hand. The next read:

LEAVE NOW. TOUCH NOTHING.

YOU COMMITTED MURDER. THE FOOTAGE YOU CAN SEE WILL PUT YOU IN PRISON FOR THE REST OF YOUR NATURAL LIFE. THAT LEAVES ME OUT HERE WITH ONLY THOMAS TO ANSWER FOR YOUR LOOSE TONGUE.

THIS IS HOW YOU STAY FREE. THIS IS HOW YOU KEEP THOMAS SAFE.

LEAVE AND NEVER SPEAK OF THIS TO ANYONE AGAIN.

There were no more pages. No more were needed. The instructions were clear. He pushed himself back to his knees.

250

He would need a moment before he tried to get to his feet. He could feel his heart hammering in his chest, each beat like a blow that left him weaker. His vision was starting to blur. He needed to focus on his breathing. He concentrated on deep breaths until his sight was clear. He fixed on Glenn. Only now did he notice the medal pinned to his chest. It looked odd against the backdrop of an old T-shirt.

'Oh, Glenn!' Richard muttered, the sadness close to overwhelming him. The medal was the General Service Medal he had earned from his tours in Northern Ireland, just like Richard. The fact it was pinned to his chest told a story: this hadn't been someone sneaking up on his old friend and taking him out before he knew what was happening. Glenn had always said that if he knew it was coming, he wanted to go wearing that medal: *You get old and no one gives a shit. I want people to know what I did, when I could. We can't all die a hero but I was something once. We both were! Some more than others though, obviously . . .!* Then he'd slapped Richard so hard on the arm it had stung. He never did know his strength. His laughter at Richard's face was typical, head back, belly shaking, and Richard hadn't been able to resist laughing with him.

'Look at you,' Richard said out into the room now, fighting himself to continue. 'You managed to die the hero, old friend.' The blurring of his vision was through tears this time. 'Not me though, mate. I don't know what happened to me. I messed this all up . . . all of it.'

It was time to go. He was half way down the hall when he noticed the blue-tinged piece of paper that was taped to the inside of the front door. It was a school report from Battle Abbey Prep School. The report was for Thomas Maddox. The paper was headed with the school's address and it looked like the summary page. The last few lines were highlighted:

251

Overall, Thomas is a bright young man with a very bright future if he applies himself in the way we know he can. We are delighted with his progress and look forward to watching him develop into a fine young man.

Richard lashed out to rip it down. He screwed the page up, shoved it in his back pocket and hurried for his car.

252

Chapter 39

The constant drone of traffic punctured the car's cabin the moment the engine was silenced. It was like a constant dull whisper against the windows and even in a few moments of stillness Joel knew he would find it oppressive.

'No way I would want to stay here for long.' He was peering out at the row of windows that marked the individual rooms of a hotel just off the Duke of York's roundabout on the outskirts of Dover. DS Rose sat next to him and it was just gone 8 a.m. Joel had been lying in bed with the case running through his mind when the idea had come to him to put 'Danny Evans Football Agent' into a google search on his phone. The name Marty Johnson had come up immediately with Danny showing among his list of clients. There was a contact number for enquiries and Joel had stared at a bedside clock showing 1.14 a.m. and contemplated calling straight-away. He had decided against it. He needed something from Marty Johnson and he figured he was far more likely to get it at a reasonable hour. He had made the call at 7 a.m. exactly and its reception suggested his idea of a reasonable hour was a little different from Marty Johnson's. The agent had still been good enough to provide the name of Danny's hotel with just a little persuasion necessary.

253

'Not sure Danny Evans wanted to be here either,' DS Rose said, already reaching for her door. The traffic noise increased tenfold the moment the seal was broken. Joel caught her up just as the doors to the reception parted.

'In a rush, are we?'

'Sooner we get in, sooner we can go again. I hate hotels. This job will do that to you.'

'What makes you hate hotels?'

They were into the foyer. 'The only time I ever come to these places now is for death or rape,' DS Rose explained, speaking far too loudly in the sudden silence where the doors had sealed behind them.

Joel made eye contact with a slim woman who instantly sat straighter behind the desk as she stared over at them.

'We're police officers!' Joel blurted, 'which might explain my colleague's rather dramatic entrance there . . .'

'I see,' the woman said. 'Can I help?'

'Yes, let's start again. My name is DI Norris, this is DS Rose. We're investigating an incident involving a man called Danny Evans and we understand he has been staying here for a period of time?' Joel held out his warrant card to back up his story.

'Mr Evans is here, yes. I have not seen him today.'

'That's OK. We need to have a look in his room. Can you help us with that?

'Can I ask what this is about? I'm supposed to call the number we have for Mr Evans and ask permission, unless this is a matter of life or death?' The woman stood up, her hand now hovering over a desk phone, and eyed both officers like she was suddenly suspicious.

'I can assure you he won't be answering any calls. Mr Evans has been found deceased at another location. We need access to his room and maybe a chat with any members of staff that had contact with him.'

'De . . . Oh my goodness! I mean, of course . . . I'll show

254

you.' The woman scrabbled on her desk and in drawers. Her movements were rushed now, hasty. She knocked over a pen pot and dropped the key she was trying to push into a cabinet and tutted. When the cabinet did open she took a plastic card out and was instantly striding away from the desk. 'It's this way. Room eighteen.' She gestured at a fire door to her left. A long, slim panel of glass showed only a darkened corridor behind. Both officers had to do a little jog to catch her up.

'Eighteen,' the woman repeated after marching the length of an aggressively patterned carpet.

'Wonderful. Would you mind . . .?' Joel said, leaving the question open for the woman to get the hint. It took a few moments; she clearly intended to come in for a look herself.

'Oh! Of course! Tell me, can I get you a tea or coffee?'

'No, thank you. Hopefully we won't be here long. Much to the relief of my colleague – she has a bit of a phobia about these sorts of places.' His grin widened at DS Rose's obvious embarrassment.

'Yes, well, they're not for everyone,' the woman said before making her way back towards reception.

'Oh, could I just ask . . .' Joel called out, waiting for the woman to stop and turn. 'I mentioned staff members. Is there anyone that had more contact than others with Danny Evans? Anyone that might have an insight?'

'The bar,' the woman replied without hesitation. 'I think he spent a lot of his time over there.'

'Thank you,' Joel said, but she had already spun away.

'She definitely thinks I'm weird now,' DS Rose said.

'We're here to look round a dead man's room,' Joel said. 'We do a weird job.' He lifted the card to rest against the sensor. He had to push a *Do Not Disturb* hanger out of the way to get to it. The sensor flashed red and hissed at him twice to deny him access, but the third time was a charm.

Joel's immediate action was not to step in. Instead, he turned to lock eyes with DS Rose. Opening the door had stoked up

255

an odour that he knew all too well: death. Usually it was an overwhelming smell that could roll out of an open door like an assault, but here it was a little more subtle. He trapped the door open to survey the room. The window was directly opposite. A blackout blind was doing its job with just the merest hint of daylight at the bottom. He reached in to flick a light switch. Nothing happened.

'The card,' DS Rose said, pointing at a slot on the wall. He pushed the card in and the light was instant. Joel moved in. The bed was at the far end, just far enough away from the window that one could walk around it. It was made. The bedside cabinets were empty of any clutter, and a dresser against the wall that faced the foot of the bed was tidy too. The only thing to suggest the room was even in use was a packed suitcase standing on its end by the far wall.

'And he's been in this room for two weeks, has he?'

'A little over,' DS Rose said.

'Keeps it tidy, doesn't he?'

'Shame about the smell.' DS Rose turned to the bathroom as she spoke – the only place left to search. Joel led the way. The door was next to where they had come into the room and was closed. He pushed it open to reveal more darkness. The light switch was on the outside. He pushed it and the noise of a fan squeaking to life was instant.

'Shit!' Joel hastily reached for the isolator switch that would turn the fan off. He'd learned that from experience. His CSI colleagues would not thank him for starting up something that was designed to suck traces out of a room.

'Boss . . .' DS Rose had stepped in ahead of him. Joel joined her. She had been blocking the view of the shower tray. She stepped aside. 'What the hell is that?'

256

Chapter 40

Julia Korner pushed the grand front door shut behind Sharon, who took a moment as she stepped back out into the bright sunshine. The sound of the gurgling stream in the grounds of the Abbey was still there to greet her, as was the warmth from weak sunshine on her face. She felt a little better than an hour earlier when the sun had been on her back to push her into the house. She hadn't said much more, it had mostly been crying into the shoulders of people she barely knew, who had, in turn, whispered in her ear about how she was *so strong*. She didn't feel it. Far from it. Just the thought of Jamie coming home from school was almost enough to floor her. She knew he would come straight in and ask after his sister, his expression one of hope that a normal family life was getting closer every day. She was going to have to be the one to snatch that hope away for ever.

She tried not to think about it now. She wanted to go home. She was ready to be alone again, to be somewhere she could close the door. Still she couldn't accept that Danny would take his own life, and the more she considered it, the less likely it seemed. But it was worse than that: the police had said he had taken the life of someone else. That wasn't possible. That wasn't Danny.

257

She checked her phone for the umpteenth time that day and got the same result. She hadn't missed a call from the police; they hadn't tried calling her to tell her it was all a big mistake. Danny hadn't called either, apologising that he had lost his phone while out on a bender. The silence was deafening. She only hoped that the group she was leaving behind would be as silent. She had begged them not to share, at least until she had spoken to her son.

When she pulled up outside her home four minutes later, her phone was ringing. She dropped it in the footwell in her haste to answer.

'Dammit!' The seatbelt caught her as she tried to jerk forward. She had to slow her movements down. The caller showed as *withheld*.

'Hello?'

'Sharon Evans?' A man's voice, deep and assured.

'Who is this?'

'One down, Sharon. You will lose everything you hold dear. No more lies. I told you that bef—' Sharon cut the call. Her hand shook as she held down the button to turn it off and instantly regretted it. Maybe she should use it to call the police? To tell them that the calls were happening again.

But she didn't. She left the phone off and pushed it into her pocket instead. What was the point? The last time they had said there was nothing they could do, that the calls were 'untraceable'. It had sounded like a fob-off at the time. The calls had started when the papers had run the story about Callie, her admission to hospital and how it was linked to a police investigation. They couldn't name her, supposedly for her own protection, but they could make it damned obvious who they were writing about. The stories in the press had been hard. They were unavoidable, as were the trolls that liked to add their poisonous comments. Social media seemed to have a knack of bringing out the worst in people. Sharon knew why: it was because they could hide behind their screens,

258

behind their fake names and fake profile pictures. These people were cowards looking for a reaction. She convinced herself that the calls were the same.

Sharon threw her phone straight onto the kitchen counter when she got inside but she didn't take her eyes off it. This felt different. The timing, for one. She ran the phone call back through her mind. It made her shiver: *One down, Sharon!*

Was that the voice of the man who had killed her husband? Maybe she should call the police.

She reached into her pocket for the card the nurse had given her before she had left her daughter's bedside, the one the 'nice police officer' had asked her to pass over.

'DI Joel Norris,' she read aloud. 'Let's see if you'll take me seriously.'

Chapter 41

'Just so happens I have a body missing one of these.' Joel rolled the tightly tied bag over with his pen. It came to a rest against the edge of the shower tray in the hotel room still booked in the name of Danny Evans. The movement worsened the smell and caused straw-coloured fluid to run down the inside of the clear plastic bag. The change of position also made it far clearer what the bag contained and Joel could now fix on a set of melancholic eyes that stared out above a jagged neck wound. The stark white of human bone stood out from the dark tones of clotted blood and black hair.

Joel looked up to where DS Rose had taken a step away too. He could hardly blame her. 'The job just down the road from here, the body on the beach. The superintendent said that was coming to us too.' She spoke with her hand hovering over her mouth.

'It already did. And there I was worrying that it might be taking a back seat indefinitely. Looks like I'll be working on that sooner than I thought, seeing as it appears to be linked.' Joel straightened up, sniffed at his pen and put it back in his pocket.

'How though?' DS Rose said, still speaking through her fingers.

260

'Well, the dead man who took the life of our colleague also has a severed head in his hotel room that is very likely to match up with a recently discovered body.'

'Very good. You know what I mean.'

'Marcus Olsen is a registered sex offender. Danny Evans had a reason to dislike sex offenders. We will need to do a little more work to strengthen the link but that sounds like a place to start.' Joel took a moment to run his eyes over the interior of the bathroom. Again, there was nothing to suggest recent use. The room had the feeling of being prepped for the next arrival.

'What sort of room service cleans up round a rotting head?' he said.

'There was a *Do Not Disturb* hanger outside. We need to check how long that's been adhered to. Someone *has* cleaned up.'

'They have. And it makes no sense for that someone to be Danny Evans.'

'Not if he planned to kill himself,' DS Rose said.

'Not if he planned to leave a severed head in the bathroom,' Joel replied, squatting back down to take in the bagged mess in front of him. 'Have you seen this?' He was round the other side from DS Rose and pointing with his little finger.

'The dead head? Yeah, I've seen it,' she said but didn't move any closer.

'I didn't have you down as the squeamish type, Lucy Rose,' Joel said with a grin.

'I just don't like dead heads. They stink so much worse than the living ones I've met.'

'Not always,' Joel mused. 'The back of the head, here . . .'

'What about it?'

'It's missing.' Joel brought his pen back out to shift the bag again. He tried to inspect the wound, but it wasn't going to be possible through the bag.

'Missing?'

261

'A large chunk of the back of the skull, near the base. You know what that makes me think?'

'That this is some sort of sick treasure hunt, and the back of the skull is in someone else's shower tray?' DS Rose's voice was muffled now, her fingers shut when Joel had stoked up the smell.

'That he was shot in the mouth,' Joel said. 'Does that sound familiar to you?'

'It might to Danny Evans.'

Joel's phone rang in his pocket and he stood up. The display showed a number he didn't recognise. 'DI Norris,' he said, taking a few steps back from their grim discovery.

'Oh . . . look, sorry to call you. It's Sharon Evans . . . You said I could call if there was anything I thought might be important. About Danny . . . my husband?'

'Mrs Evans, of course.' Joel made eye contact with his colleague.

'I was angry. I know we didn't get off to the best start but you have to understand that the police . . . We haven't had the best of times.'

'I know that. It's OK—'

'I told you Danny wouldn't kill himself,' Sharon cut in.

'You did.'

'I got a phone call . . .'

'Oh?'

'It's difficult to explain but it was someone threatening us. It might be nothing but he just said: *one down*. You know, like maybe Danny was the first and he was responsible. Maybe someone just heard what's happened and they . . . This sounds ridiculous, doesn't it? I've had calls before, a month ago. The police said it was nothing then. It'll be nothing now.' Joel heard a tut like Sharon Evans was now scolding herself for even calling.

'It doesn't sound like nothing to me. I could do with talking

262

to you again anyway. How about we meet up? Things are always easier face to face.'

'Talk to me, what about?'

'Some developments, Mrs Evans, some things you might be able to help us understand.'

'I don't know what more I can say. I have to pick Jamie up from school later, he's at the Grammar . . .' She paused for a moment. Joel heard a sniff like she was struggling to hold it all together. 'I haven't told him about his dad. I don't even know where to start. How do I do that?'

Joel was suddenly aware that he hadn't stopped to consider Jamie. 'That's not going to be easy, Mrs Evans. I can't even imagine. Maybe I can help. I can be there when you talk to him, for questions, or I could even be the one saying the words?'

'No, it needs to be me.' She made a sound like she was still battling with herself. 'I appreciate the offer.'

'No problem. Maybe we can meet before the school run. We can talk it out, what you might say to Jamie. I'm not far away from you.'

'You mean come to my house now? No, I don't think that's . . . I don't want the police here. Somewhere out maybe . . .'

'Wherever you're comfortable.'

'Comfortable . . .' She seemed to fade out. 'I don't think I can remember what that feels like.'

'Poor turn of phrase, Mrs Evans. There's a place on Folkestone Road, does a good coffee: Farthingloe. Do you know it?'

'I know it.'

'It should be quiet this time of day and it's close to the school. Can you be there in an hour?'

'I can. These "developments" you want to talk about – it's not more bad news, is it? Please, Inspector Norris, I don't think I can take it right now.'

263

Joel's gaze dropped to the bloody mass of hair and flesh wrapped in a bag and discarded in the shower tray of her husband's hotel room.

'I'll see you in an hour.'

Chapter 42

Joel eyed the coffee machine as he took a seat at the bar. DS Rose stayed standing. She was staring at a barman who had acknowledged them with a briefly raised hand but seemed determined to keep his head down and act busy. Finally he stood straighter to smile at Joel's colleague.

'You with the cops, I take it?' he said. 'I just saw your lot turn up.' He gestured at the window but remained fixed on DS Rose. Joel had summoned a marked patrol to come to their location and stand on the door to Danny Evans's hotel room. It was a crime scene now. Joel didn't know how long it might be for, since they were quickly running out of CSI resources.

'DI Norris, if I can drag you away from the prettier one,' Joel said and the barman looked back at him with colour filling his cheeks.

'I'm sure you're both pretty in your own way,' he said.

'I have been told that. What's your name?' Joel asked.

'Darryl.'

'Thank you, Darryl. Tell me what you do here.'

Darryl stepped back to open his arms out to the bar. 'I work the bar?'

'And I'm a detective, which means I never like to presume. How long have you been working here?'

265

'Couple of years. It was a Saturday job at first, bit of cash while I did college in the week, you know, so I could work somewhere better.' He suddenly grinned, like the death of his hopes and dreams was hilarious to him. 'Life, hey, never quite works out like you want.'

'Has a habit of doing that. Your coffee machine, does it work?'

'Sure. You want one?'

'Two maybe?' He looked over at DS Rose. She nodded.

'Black, extra sugar,' she said.

'Two of them.' Joel said.

'The bittersweet!' The barman chuckled towards DS Rose. He had longer hair than seemed to be the fashion and it wasn't like he looked after it either. It had a greasy sheen at the sides where it was pulled in tight to be wrapped up at the back. It was only just long enough to stay in place but a wisp had got free that he needed to constantly scoop behind his right ear. 'You know why they call it that?' He was still talking at DS Rose.

'Seems pretty obvious,' she said.

'Bitter coffee and sweet sugar, right? But that's not the only reason. People ask for that as a hangover cure. Works well, I'm told. You get the double kick of caffeine and sugar to get the blood pumping again, move the toxins around a bit. And a night out is sweet, right? So the next day is your bitter payoff.'

'Very clever,' DS Rose replied.

'So, is that it? Did you have a few last night, detective?'

'No,' DS Rose said, dryly.

'Do you get out for a drink much?'

'No.'

'Maybe that's because no one asks you, or . . .?'

'No.'

Joel managed to catch his laughter. The kid seemed to take his colleague's abruptness on the chin and turned to the coffee

266

machine to announce that he was 'firing her up'. Joel spoke to his back.

'There's a man staying at the hotel, has been for a couple of weeks. I understand he's been in here a few times?' Joel held out a picture on his phone. He'd had the force control room send through the mugshot they had taken of Evans when he was arrested for his drink-drive charge.

'Danny Evans. He's been in here, yeah.'

'You know him?'

'I do. Even if he had never been in here I would know who he is. Most people do round here. Is he OK?'

'Why would you ask that?'

Darryl turned back to reply. 'You're the cops! You don't come here unless something bad's happened.'

'Usually we get asked if someone's in trouble.'

'Is he?'

'Did he come in here a lot?'

'Every night! And not just the night, sometimes the afternoon too. I think he was verging on a problem with it. That's why I'm asking if he's all right. I did try and say something, you know, it's part of the job if you think you need to intervene . . . I care like that.' He smiled at DS Rose again.

'You still served him though?' she said and his smile dipped away.

'He's an adult. A grown man comes in here and orders a drink and I serve him. He comes in and orders drinks every night until he's steaming and it's not my business to stop him. I tried to find out a bit about him, to see if there's a place in there for me to maybe suggest he ease up on the sauce.'

'And did you? Find a place, I mean?' Joel took over again.

'Not with him. He didn't like the small talk. Any talk really. That's why I say he might be getting a problem. He just came in here for a drink, no other reason.'

'He ever come in here with anyone else?'

'I never saw anyone else.' Darryl finished the coffees and

267

put them on the bar and stood so both his palms rested on the counter top. His right hand trapped a cloth. He looked away from them both to wipe it over the counter.

'That's the second lie you've told,' DS Rose said. 'The first lie was when you said how you cared about him.'

Darryl shrugged and stopped his wiping for just a moment. When he started up again it suddenly seemed more fraught. 'I don't like to see anyone do themselves harm. He seemed all right. I think he was trying to sort his life out.'

''He's dead, Darryl.' Joel leaned in to up the pressure. 'So, who did he talk to in here? If you really do care.'

'Dead! But he was just in here like two days ago!' The lad's shock seemed genuine.

'On his own?'

Darryl's lips parted then slammed shut. Whatever his first reaction was going to be he had changed his mind. 'I don't take much notice, I—'

'Who, Darryl? Or do I need to bring you in on suspicion of involvement in his death? You don't know how serious this all is.'

'Involvement! I just served him his beer! A rum chaser, that was it. That was all I did.'

'Who?'

'Some bloke, OK. But he gave me like a hundred notes and the old "you ain't seen me" treatment, you know what I mean?'

'No. Tell me.'

'You ain't seen me. He was never here, you know!'

'What did he say, exactly?'

Darryl huffed. 'The last time I saw Danny he was sat at that table over there. It woulda been Saturday afternoon and he was stressed out, I could tell. I didn't ask him what it was about, none of my business! He was lining them up right from the start. At the bar. Then this bloke comes in and they go over to that table. This bloke gets him another couple of

268

beers in and Danny's like, out of it. As hammered as I've seen him. He can't have eaten anything all day, not the way he went. Then this guy comes over, says he's got to take him back to his room and slips me a roll of notes. Says how much he would appreciate it if I forgot that he was ever there. Or ever had been. Those were his words, pretty much spot on, I think!'

'Or what?'

'What do you mean?'

'He didn't make any threats? Tell you would what happen if you told anyone?'

'No. It wasn't like that. Like I said, he gave me money to mind my own business. I guess he thought that would do the job but I didn't know it would be the cops asking about it! A hundred don't cover that. I know you lot, you could just look at CCTV, ask about and show me up as a liar.'

'Now that you're offering.'

Darryl rolled his eyes. 'There's nothing in here. I think there's a camera outside, covers the door but I can't work the system.'

'Can you download it?'

'Reception over at the hotel run it. We don't have nothing to do with it over here.'

'And it was definitely Saturday afternoon?'

'Yeah.'

'What time?'

'Musta been like, half one, two maybe. He don't often get in here for the afternoon. I was on an overtime shift so I know it was Saturday.'

'What else can you tell me about the man he was with?'

Darryl shrugged. 'Old, white fella but tanned. Well-dressed.'

'Old? How old?'

'I dunno, older than you! What are you? Like thirty-five, tops! Ain't you proper young and proper hench to be a police inspector?'

269

Joel took a sip of his bittersweet and pulled his lips back over his teeth at the taste. 'What can I say, this was just a Saturday job to start with. So this man was older than me, was he?'

'Like fifty. In good shape though, not as big as you but still a gym rat I reckon. I thought he might have been . . . you know . . . like maybe he was interested in Danny. You see it all at these places, I tell you. Not that there's anything wrong with that . . .'

'You mean gay?'

'I dunno, I mean he was all tanned and dressed nice and buying up loads of drinks for Danny. Then he tells me he's taking him back to his room and slips me a wad to forget all about it.'

'You thought he was going to rape Danny Evans in his hotel room?' DS Rose cut in with what was quickly becoming her custom subtlety.

'Nah, not like rape! Shit, you go straight for the throat, don't ya! I was thinking that maybe he was trying to get Danny to do something he might not do when he was sober. I dunno. There was just something odd about the fella.'

'Odd?'

'Intense. The way he looked at Danny. And thinking back, he might have been loading him up with the drinks. He definitely wanted something from him. And Danny's reaction, seemed to me like he wasn't too pleased to see him but at the same time he didn't tell him to piss off, you know? It was all a bit odd.'

'What did you mean by well-dressed?' Joel interjected, taking over the questioning again.

'Suited. But a good suit, like when you get all measured up an' that. Then there were shoes and a nice coat over the lot. Flashy watch too. All in he looked like he weren't short of a few bob.'

270

'What do you remember about the watch?'

'Big, silver strap and face. Expensive-looking, that's about it.'

'Was he staying here?' Joel asked.

'I don't think so.'

'What about his car? Did you see him turn up?'

'Nope. Or leave. Saturdays are the busiest afternoons.'

'Does the CCTV cover the car park?'

'Not really, only a bit round the back. But, like I said, you'll have to go over to the hotel for all that.'

'Anything else you want to tell us? Anything else that might be relevant?'

'Not that I can think of.'

Joel took a moment. 'Was it just one time that this man was in here talking to Danny?'

'No. A couple of times at least. But all the last few days.'

'And you hadn't seen him before that?'

Darryl shrugged. 'A lot of people come and go. I only noticed him when he was talking to Danny. I ain't saying he hasn't been in here before but I don't remember him.'

'OK. I'll get someone up here who has the time to go through the CCTV over at reception.'

'Someone?'

'A detective.'

'You got somewhere to be?' Daryl was back to grinning. 'Maybe you could leave your colleague here? I can do her another bittersweet and make sure she gets all the help she needs?' Joel couldn't knock his persistence but it was DS Rose who reacted by pushing a ten-pound note onto the bar.

'For the drinks,' she said and gathered up her things to leave.

Daryl lifted his hands as far from the note as he could. 'No need for that, these are on me.'

'No, they're not. Keep the change,' she said and moved towards the door. Joel put his card down on the bar.

'In case you think of anything else relevant,' he said and followed DS Rose out.

'That's quite a tip!' Darryl called out after them.

'It is,' DS Rose replied without looking back. 'So either you're worth every penny or I can't wait to get out of here.'

Chapter 43

Farthingloe café was a converted barn at the end of a loose track on the outskirts of Dover. Joel parked the car next to a vintage tractor that might have been placed there in keeping with the atmosphere or had simply been left to rust where it had collapsed on its chassis.

Sharon Evans was already there. Inside was open plan with just a couple of tables occupied. Sharon was tucked in a corner, almost directly under the angry glow of a bar heater that was angled out from the wall. Joel could feel the heat from it as he took a seat opposite her at the table. DS Rose took the seat next to him.

'Mrs Evans, thanks for coming to meet us.'

'Not like I have anywhere else to be. Don't know what to do with myself, to be honest.'

'I can imagine.'

'I was rude. When you came to the hospital.'

Joel waved her away. 'We're certainly not judging you for that, if you're worried.'

'I'm not. But I'm not like that. I remember when it took a lot to wind me up. I barely remember that person now.'

'You've had a lot thrown at you in a short space of time. For the record I think you're handling it all as well as anyone

273

could. Tell us about this phone call. Maybe we can take something off your plate.'

'I doubt it. I've had calls like this before. You couldn't do anything then.'

'What was said exactly?'

'This time, some man called. He said, "One down." He must have been talking about Danny. I had similar calls six weeks or so ago, when there was stuff in the papers about us. Only the local rag. They were covering the story about Callie and the other girls with the indecent images. The law says they can't use the girls' names but they're perfectly fine to use Danny's name as part of it. It was obvious our Callie was involved. They didn't even try and make contact with us either to check their so-called facts.'

'I guess they thought you would tell them where to go.'

'I would have liked the opportunity.'

'And the voice, it was the same?'

'Yes, I'm certain of that.'

'Who got the calls?'

'Just me. Only ever me.'

'And what did you do when it happened last time? Did you block them or change your number or anything?'

'Both. The number's withheld but your lot went to the phone company to get it. They told me it was a burner. I don't really know what that means, but that was when you stopped looking.'

'And it was withheld today, too?'

'Yep. Another burner, no doubt, and on my new number.'

'Do many people have that?'

'I mean, I don't broadcast it, but I'll give it out to family and friends. You do, don't you? I don't know what they do with it after. I wouldn't say I was paranoid about giving it out.'

'And that was all he said? "One down"?'

'I hung up when I recognised the same voice. I didn't want

274

to give him any satisfaction. We had a lot of other stuff on social media when Danny was in the paper for his drink-driving thing. I thought this might even be the same person, some sicko trying to get a reaction. But I thought about that call, about what he said. How could he know about Danny unless he was involved somehow?'

'We haven't released any details but these things can have a way of getting out there. We just came from the hotel he's been staying in, so it will no doubt soon be public knowledge that he has passed away. The police will release an official statement to the press but we don't always do that straight-away. But Danny's a bit of a local celeb, I guess it's newsworthy. It only takes one person to stick it up on their social media and it's everywhere.'

'That was after this call though, surely?'

'Our hotel visit was but it's an example of how it can happen.'

'I did tell a group of women. I mentioned this support group when I spoke to you earlier, the one DC Ribbons came to. I didn't know where else to go. It's like a coffee morning now . . .'

Joel detected a little anger. 'And you think one of them might have leaked it?'

'A room full of bitchy gossips! The more I think about it, the more I think I might have caused this. I should have just stayed at home. The call was five minutes after I left, just shows how desperate they are with the gossip.'

'How long were you there?'

'An hour, just over. Some were on their phones at times but these days it's what people do. I asked them to keep it to them-selves but someone could have been posting it up while they were looking me in the face for all I know.'

'Did anyone stand out to you as asking questions? Someone who might have wanted more detail than seemed normal?'

'No, not really. They just let me talk. I just walked in and

275

blurted about Danny. I think they were all a bit shocked so I kinda talked to fill the silence. I didn't give details about what happened, but I mentioned how Danny had been finding it difficult and had moved out. I talked about Callie too, I said it looked like she's going to recover and how I'm just praying that she comes back fully recovered . . . It all just fell out. It felt good to have people listening – even those people.'

'Do you know everyone who was there by name?'

'I could name them all, I think; it's the same women as a month ago and a few new faces. Even Marilyn was there.'

'Marilyn?'

'Luckhurst. Her daughter was on the outskirts of the whole thing. Callie was convinced that she was a victim too. She told DC Ribbons, but I don't think Emma ever admitted it. I suppose with Marilyn being there today she must have by now. She's a bit strange . . .'

'Strange? Marilyn, you mean?'

'Yeah, just a little insular, you know. She's never really said much to me but today she was the first one to get hold of me for a hug! It felt a bit odd. Emma's her girl. Emma and Callie are mates.'

'From school?' DS Rose asked.

'No. They're at different schools. They used to go to the same dance class, then lost touch until Emma moved and started hanging out in the park with the group. Emma used to talk to Callie, but then she's that sort of girl, easy to talk to. Emma had some family issues earlier in the year, Callie even paused *Love Island* to tell me about it!' Sharon's eyes suddenly sparked like it was a pleasant memory. 'I think Emma's dad gives them both a hard time.'

'Who's that?'

Sharon shrugged. 'I don't know him. I've never even seen him about. He works for himself, Callie said, and he can go away weeks at a time. Like I said, your lot must have spoken

276

to her by now. Last I heard they had split up and moved out.'

DS Rose took a writing pad out. She pushed it onto the table. 'Would you be able to list everyone who was there? Maybe which of the victims they are linked to and how, if you know that too.'

Sharon blinked at the pen like she was considering it, but she eventually picked it up. Joel continued to talk while she wrote.

'Were there any men in this group?'

'No, and I've heard that voice on the phone enough to know it's not anyone I've met, if that's what you're getting at. That would be pretty stupid, wouldn't it? His voice wasn't even disguised.'

'You'd be surprised at the stupidity I've seen doing this job. Don't get me wrong, I'm all for it, the stupid ones are easier to catch.'

'I'm sure they are.'

'What happened with Callic? Did Danny have an opinion who was responsible?'

Sharon stopped writing to look up. 'Opinion? What do you mean?'

'Did he talk about wanting to find who was responsible, maybe when the police didn't come up with someone?'

'Of course he did. There only had to be a mention of something like it on the news and he was off. Danny was very angry – all the time, it seemed, and at everyone. But not angry enough . . . Not DC Ribbons.'

'Was he doing anything himself to try and find out who was responsible?'

'What do you mean?'

'Did he ever talk about names of anyone he thought could be involved, anything like that?'

'Not that I knew of, but recently, at the hospital, he said something about speaking to a private investigator. He said this

277

guy told him he had answers. I asked him where he had got the money to pay a private investigator, but he said there was no money involved, he said the bloke just came up to him in a bar.'

'What did you think of that?'

Sharon shrugged. 'It doesn't sound likely, does it? I said it would be someone trying to scam him. If he was in a bar he would be half-cut, maybe stupid enough to go on and pay someone for their bullshit.'

'Did he do that? Did he pay for information?' Joel asked.

'He said he didn't, said he told him to piss off, but who knows with Danny . . . Suddenly I feel like I hardly know him.'

'Did he give you a name or an agency, anything about this guy he is supposed to have met?'

'No. Just said he was an older fella. He talked about him wearing a suit too, like that meant he could be trusted. Danny was desperate to know who had targeted the girls – our girl – but he was a mess. No way he was thinking straight.'

'So he never mentioned any names? Anyone he suspected, maybe he even talked about looking for someone?'

'No. The only thing Danny was looking for was his next drink.'

Joel sat back. 'I think we should look at the security around you and your family. That would seem sensible.'

'I thought about that, but I think you're right, I think someone has leaked what's happened and the same sicko from before has phoned again to see if he can get a better reaction this time. I did call Jamie's school. No one can get to him there – schools are pretty shut down these days. And Callie . . . well, she's on a ward with constant supervision. I'll talk to them when I'm next there but . . .' She shrugged again. Joel recognised someone downplaying a threat. He'd seen it before. It would be making her feel better to find simple explanations.

'I'll do that if you like. They might take it more seriously if it comes from us,' Joel said.

'OK, thanks.'

'And you?' Joel asked.

'Me?' Sharon sat back as a waitress arrived with a tray of drinks. 'What can someone possibly do to me to make my life worse?'

Sharon left first. Joel and DS Rose remained silent as they watched her go. From the coffee shop, she was going straight to pick up her twelve-year-old son, and they both had a sense of what the next phase was going to be like for the Evans family.

'You can see why Hannah got so invested in all this. Families and their kids, it always seems to matter more.' DS Rose's words punctured the silence.

'It does,' Joel said. 'I need to understand that case better, or at least I need to understand what Hannah was doing with it.'

'All she could,' DS Rose said, her tone edging on anger.

'I don't mean like a case review, I mean I want to understand who she was talking to, what she'd been saying, who she was upsetting. That case got her killed.'

'By Danny Evans. And we understand his motivation to do that, don't we?'

'We do. It's everything else I don't understand, not yet. Where is the file?'

'It will have been uploaded – we can see it anywhere we can access Athena,' DS Rose said, referring to the local computer system used day-to-day, alongside other national databases such as PNC. The local system was more user-friendly and contained everything from convictions at court to anecdotal intelligence, making it far more useful as a research tool. Athena was also where case papers would be uploaded in preparation for sharing with the Crown Prosecution

279

Service if charge advice was being sought. Officers could upload every scrap of material they had on a case, including any handwritten notes, but only in specific circumstances when a case was going to court and a not-guilty plea had been entered. Hannah's case didn't meet these criteria and Athena might only reflect the official case papers. Joel wanted handwritten notes and scribbles, he wanted theories and abandoned lines of enquiry – the next best thing to talking to Hannah directly.

'Call me old-school, but I prefer to hold the actual file. Maybe we can find the daybook Hannah was working from too, or anything where she's written something down.'

'Everything would be in her daybook; Child Protection are hot on that. They're treated as sensitive too, so she would have needed to archive it when she left the department. Archived books are stored at Folkestone for two years, then moved to storage for the next five. The paper file will be there as well.'

'Folkestone it is then. Can you call the property store on the way? Save waiting around while they find it.'

'You in a rush to get away?' DS Rose asked.

'The source handling team Hannah was with finish at four at Nackington. We've still had nothing out of there, so I want to see if I can't up the pressure a little, maybe give them something that's harder to ignore.'

'You can't get anywhere near them, not if they don't want to let you in. I don't think there's anywhere more secure than the source unit.'

'I know that and I know you think my background isn't massively relevant for working investigations, but I did bring one useful skill over from my time on the TSG.'

'What's that?'

'Getting through a closed door.'

280

Chapter 44

Joel felt jaded. Maybe a month away from police work had made him soft and was the reason he felt so tired, or maybe it was the five minutes of non-stop beating on solid wood. He was on the ground floor at Nackington and the door now stinging his knuckles was barring access to the source unit for the Eastern Region: Hannah Ribbons's last place of work. Her direct supervisor was a Sergeant Alan Miles, someone Joel didn't know. The internal duties system told Joel that Alan Miles had been due off at 4 p.m. and it was now close to 5 p.m., but a lifetime of knocking on doors for wanted people had given him a sixth sense. There was someone in there. And Joel didn't like being ignored.

'ALAN! ALAN MILES!' Joel bellowed at the door, 'I SPOKE TO ONE OF YOUR TEAM, I KNOW YOU'RE IN THERE. I'M NOT LEAVING, SO IF YOU WANT TO YOU'RE GOING TO HAVE TO TALK TO ME.' Joel stopped to push his ear up against the solid wood to see if his lie had prompted a response and was just about to start his next assault when he heard a noise the other side. He stepped back as the handle dipped and the door pulled in just enough for a full and tired-looking face to appear, its cracked lips pouting their disdain through a full beard.

281

'You don't give up easy, I'll give you that,' the man croaked then sighed. He pulled the door wider then stepped away. Joel took his opportunity to move in behind him as the figure crossed an open-plan office to make for an individual office in the far corner. 'Do you know the best thing about working in the source unit and being based out here?' the man called out. Joel didn't answer until he had taken up the seat opposite without being invited.

'Go on,' Joel said.

'If you need to hide, no one can get to you.'

'And yet here I am!' Joel said.

'Here you are. DI Norris, I assume.'

'You got my messages then? And you can call me Joel. You can even call me the names you were muttering while I was hammering at your door for all I care.'

The man's tired features formed a smile. 'We need a thicker door.'

'You must be Alan Miles while we're assuming things?' Joel held out his hand for Miles to shake.

'Who squealed me up? Told you I was still here?' Miles said.

'No one actually. But it's the Monday after a weekend when you lost one of your officers out on active duty. I reckoned you'd be having one of those shifts that never ends.'

'You appear to be very happy about that,' he said, his own expression now slipping back to fatigue tinged with sadness.

'You made me wait. And seeing as I'm having a similar time of it I thought maybe we could feel sorry for ourselves together. There's every possibility that we're both having long days trying to answer the questions we should be asking each other.'

'Listen, I'm sorry, OK, I did get your messages, I know you want to speak to me but I have my orders. I've been told to keep my head down, not to talk to anyone. This whole thing . . . They're looking for someone to pin this all on and my arse is currently the one on show.'

'Sounds painful.'

282

'I don't think I've ever had a more painful weekend.'

'Hannah's weekend was worse.'

'You think I don't know that!' All of Alan Miles's pleasantries dropped away, his voice now a growl that sat him straighter and the hand that had been running over his beard now made a fist that rested on the table between them. 'My job is to look after my team.'

'So, what happened?'

'I don't know.' Miles relaxed enough to sit back a little.

'While we're talking about jobs, mine is to find the person responsible for murdering Hannah. I can't do that unless I'm involved in the fallout in here. I know how sensitive this work is but you have to appreciate that Hannah's role is top of my list of things that might have got her killed.'

'Hannah's role didn't get her killed so much as her interpretation of it,' Alan Miles said, his anger back.

'What does that mean?'

'Look, my bosses know who you are, they know you're SIO. They told me that they would talk to you and made it quite clear that I shouldn't. So that's where we are. You will still get all the answers you need, just not from me.'

'Did they tell you we have a suspect?' Joel instantly knew from Miles's reaction that they didn't.

'Who?'

'This has to be an exchange of information. I'm not just going to sit here and tell you what I know with nothing in return. Let's miss out the bosses and their bullshit, shall we?'

'Bullshit it might be, but they specifically told me not to.'

'I'll act surprised. I don't care about the politics in here, the finger pointing, none of it. We believe Hannah was shot by a man called Danny Evans. He has a fifteen-year-old daughter who was extorted for indecent images; she was one victim of five that we know of. Hannah Ribbons was the OIC assigned to that case while she was in Child Protection, but a little more than two weeks into that investigation she got

283

an opportunity to join you here, which she took. I've only skimmed through the casefile but it's obvious she crammed a lot into that two weeks. Hannah was obsessed, working similar hours to you and me right now, I would imagine. And it got her killed.'

'Jesus . . .' Miles muttered, his shoulders slumping further.

'So . . . your turn.'

'I told you . . .'

'You've told me nothing. How about I rough you up a bit?' Joel leaned forward to lick his lips, his head lolling to one side. 'Then you can tell whoever you're so terrified of that I beat it out of you?' Miles's eyes flared a little, like he believed him for a moment. 'You know that's a joke, right?' Joel said, but kept his expression neutral.

Alan Miles sighed again. 'The truth is, we don't know, OK. We don't know what's going on here and everyone's in a bit of a panic trying to work out what happened, who should have stopped it.'

Joel took a moment to take a breath and catch his temper. Suddenly the empty threat of roughing a colleague up for information wasn't such a flight of fancy. 'I went to the scene yesterday,' Joel started through gritted teeth, 'Hannah was still there. She was lying on her side and she looked small, like a child. She was shot twice from close range while her ankle was chained to a bed post. One of the shots took a piece of her finger off. You know what I think that means?'

'Means?' Miles spoke out from where he had taken to holding his head in his hands.

'It means she was begging.' Joel lifted his hands out at chest height towards Miles, his palms up so they pointed at him. 'The killer was pointing a gun at her and she was terrified and she was desperate. You're never going to stop a bullet with your hand, we all know that, but in that moment when desperation takes over you would throw your hands towards it, wouldn't you? Wouldn't *you?*'

284

Miles's gaze had drifted; his eyes had lost their focus. They snapped back now.

'Sure,' Miles said.

'So then why was she shackled to the bed of a known drug user in the middle of Sittingbourne in the first place?'

'I . . . we don't have the answers either; we don't know anything.'

'You know more than that. Even I know more than that. I'll tell you what I do know, shall I? I know Hannah talked to you about these five victims she was leaving behind and I know you gave her hope. You made her think that there might be another angle, that she didn't have to leave it behind after all. So you can imagine what I think of you right now.' Joel fixed his eyes on the man opposite. He didn't have to wait long for the reaction he wanted.

'You think I did this?' Miles said.

'Shot her twice at close range? Of course not. But maybe you provided the wild goose for her to chase.'

'It wasn't a wild . . .'

'What was it then?' Joel leaned in to keep the pressure up. Miles's reaction was to push away from him and stand. He took a few steps, stopping to face a wall like a naughty boy sent to think about what he had done.

'She shouldn't even have been there . . .'

'I know that. Source handlers don't go to private addresses, not ever. They don't go out alone either, do they?'

'No. The process in here is very strict, it's what . . . it's how we keep officers safe.'

'Tell me about it. What is the system?' Joel knew enough already but he needed to get Miles talking so he had something to pick apart.

'There's a system, it's the first thing we train, Hannah knew it. If an informant wants to talk to us they call a number that takes a recorded message. Then, whoever's on call at that time gets a text to say a message has been left and they call the

285

voicemail. It's pin-coded. I get the alert too. The handler listens to the recorded message and will call the informant back direct to arrange a meeting. The meeting happens during daytime hours and it will be two handlers at a public venue. The meeting and the venue are both authorised by the controller or they don't happen at all.'

'Controller?'

'Our guvnor. Your job if you were in here.'

'Did you get a message Friday night?'

'No. There was no call-in, no voicemail left and Hannah didn't have the phone anyway. We have two handsets in the team and one's with me all the time. Hannah . . .'

'Hannah called the informant to set it up,' Joel said. 'And she didn't tell you.'

'She didn't tell anyone.'

'We ID'd the other girl that was there, the one who was left to look like an overdose: Macie Sutton. She's on our systems as a drug user, shoplifter, some fraud offences and a spate of distraction burglaries. Nothing about her being an informant but she is, isn't she?'

'She is, but you wouldn't be able to see that. We keep all that on a different part of the system, it's hidden to most users.'

'But not to Hannah.'

'No.'

'How did she even know to look at Macie Sutton?'

'I did tell her, OK, about Sutton. But you have to understand the ball was rolling for an official approach and she knew that. But it can be a long process, a lot of risk assessments, a lot of planning. It was on the back burner, but I was doing what I could. We're no different here to anywhere else – a lot more work than cops.'

'And Hannah didn't want to wait.'

'I guess not.'

'Okay, so what don't I know about Macie Sutton?'

286

'She was an informant for us. She was cuckooed by county line drug dealers for a while. She gave us good information about them, also about some piece of shit who was basically pimping her out at one point. Hers was not a happy life.'

'Hannah wouldn't have risked her career to go and see her about out-of-town drug dealers.'

'She wouldn't. She didn't. How good are you at acting surprised?' Miles now had a smile of resignation, like he knew that Joel wasn't leaving until he had what he needed. Joel let him continue. 'Macie Sutton gave us some stuff a little while ago about a man who had a big collection of indecent images of kids. He was trading with them, making a reasonable living by all accounts, and Macie was upset about this. She called us up out of nowhere and said she'd talk to us for free. The intel was good – very detailed – but we struggled to parallel source what she was giving us.'

'No one else knew?' Joel said. He knew what this meant. A common issue with intelligence received from a source is the provenance. A circle of trust between criminals can be so small that acting on that information would immediately reveal who had come forward, something police needed to prevent at all costs. To do this, information only left the source unit when it was *parallel sourced*, that is, when it could be demonstrated that the information could have come from somewhere other than the person who had provided it.

'No one else could. Any child sex offender will have a very tight circle – they may not have a circle at all, not beyond a fake profile on the dark web at least.'

'But Macie Sutton was part of someone's circle?'

'She was. Her brother's a man called Marcus Olsen.'

'Marcus Olsen!' Joel sat straighter.

'I know . . . I know he's been found dead too.'

'In two different places. And you didn't think this was relevant until now?' Joel was back to considering roughing up a colleague.

287

Miles ran his hand through his hair. 'What I think doesn't really matter right now. We handle information in here that can get people killed – that's the whole purpose of this unit, to provide a place for that information to live, to make a difference, but in a way that no one gets hurt. Three people are dead.'

'Four,' Joel cut in. 'Not wanting to make your day any worse but Danny Evans killed himself with the same gun he used to shoot Hannah.'

'Killed himself?' Miles's repetition was born from shock not disbelief.

'Probably.'

'Probably?'

'I was called out to have a look at him. I've been back to work for three days and I've already had my fill of dead people. Now it might make more sense that he took his own life.'

'How so?'

'I don't know for sure, I need to put it all together, but we have a convicted paedophile, an informant who can provide access to him and the police officer investigating, all dead. Danny Evans might have a reason to want every one of those people dead. It wouldn't be the first time someone did something like that and then took their own life.'

'Job done then? Glad I could help.'

'Easy as that.' Joel managed a smile now. 'I need to get back to it. I have a DS who will need updating too; a fresh set of eyes might have a fresh set of questions. We're based upstairs. Are you here until late?'

Miles shrugged. 'I have a camper van and today I was sure to bring it in. Does that answer your question?'

'What information can you share officially?'

'Officially, nothing. I told you I shouldn't even be talking to you. Unofficially I'll go back over our systems and get you anything that stands out as relevant. I want answers for Hannah as much as anyone, you know that, right?'

288

'Of course.'

'Sounds like the bastard that shot her has already paid the same price. Shame really, would have been more fitting to put him through the same justice system.'

'Would have been nice to ask him a few questions about how she died too,' Joel said. He got to his feet to leave.

'You're really not convinced he killed himself?'

Joel shrugged. 'I should be: man loses his shit when his daughter is abused, tortures and kills the bastard responsible, then the people that might be able to link him to murder. Then realises what he's done and shoots himself . . .'

'That makes sense.'

'It does. And right now, little else does.'

289

Chapter 45

'At last, the dream team is complete!'

Joel hadn't expected a cheery greeting on return to his stolen office one storey above the source unit and he certainly hadn't expected it to be from Superintendent Debbie Marsden. She already had a coffee. She lifted it out like it was a toast. DS Rose was in the desk opposite, her face close enough to the monitor for it to light her up.

'Two of us, ma'am. Are we calling that a team now?' Joel's reply was instant.

'Very good. I see what you did there – subtle as a brick, Joel, that's exactly why I personally chose you to lead this *team*. And don't you worry. I have started going through the applications for DCs – or foot soldiers, as I believe you called them.'

'We have some then? Applications, I mean.'

'We have some. And the more you're out and about, spreading the good word, being visible at all the juicy jobs, the more I expect to have in to choose from. I reckon we'll have the cream of the crop. The finest detectives Kent has to offer!'

'The finest? Just one who can sit and do a CCTV review will do me. You should have seen the battle I had just to get a detective down to Dover to do that.'

'Battle with who?' Marsden's tone turned stern.

'It doesn't matter. It's getting done but I'm still pulling on our CID colleagues.'

'You need me to have a quiet word with someone?'

'I think that's the last thing we need to be doing right now. We're trying to make friends rather than tell on them. But thank you.'

'But I'm great at making friends! I just tell them that we're friends and we're friends!' The glee was back in the superintendent's voice. 'It's why I'm here actually. I thought I would come down and see the source unit, seeing as how they're not returning my calls. I'm starting to take it personally now.' Her expression blackened. 'And they would much rather be my friend, I can assure you of that.'

'I just came from there. The skipper talked to me. He's under the cosh at the moment but I think we have what we need.'

'Oh?' The superintendent took a seat in front of a whiteboard where DS Rose had previously started scribbling names and notes. 'What you need to close the case and dust your hands, you mean?'

'It might bring that closer,' Joel said.

'Go on.'

'We had a body washed up on a beach in Dover, the job that was supposed to be my gentle introduction to murder enquiries. Yesterday, DS Rose and I found a matching head in Danny Evans's hotel room. We know Marcus Olsen was convicted of child sex offences and a moment ago I found out that the woman suspected to have overdosed in the next room from Hannah Ribbons was Marcus Olsen's sister. She's called Macie Sutton. Sutton had previously been happy to talk to us about how her brother trades in indecent images. Hannah Ribbons found out about Sutton when she joined the source unit and the ball was rolling for an official approach. However, Hannah couldn't wait. Her visit was off the record.'

291

Joel looked over to DS Rose for this last bit of his update. Her only reaction was to fold her arms across her chest. But Joel knew she would be hurting.

'Hence the source team closing ranks,' the superintendent chimed in.

'I think so. Although I don't think they have anything to worry about. Hannah seems to have gone off-script on her own. She was obsessed, this is one that got under her skin and DS Rose will tell you she was just like that.' DS Rose didn't add anything; it was the superintendent that prompted for more.

'So what else do we know?'

'Well, we know that all of these people are dead. We're waiting on official confirmation that the head and body are a match but that's a formality. DS Rose here has email confirmation that Danny Evans's fingerprints were found on an internal door handle at Sutton's flat. We also have verbal confirmation that the weapon used to kill Hannah was the same that later made a good-sized hole in Danny Evans's head.' Joel paused for breath and to take in the reaction of his superintendent.

'Wow! You see, I knew you were the team to crack this.' The superintendent looked delighted with herself. 'Very neat and tidy too: we have Danny Evans as our man for the three murders and then he does the decent thing of saving us a lot of time and effort by removing his own ability to deny it.'

'We need to evidence the links between Danny and his victims. That shouldn't be difficult – there are still a number of loose ends, but on the surface it's starting to make sense.'

'On the surface?' The superintendent's tone carried warning now.

'His suicide. I didn't like it from the moment I walked into that scene. Some bits didn't ring true.'

'Which bits?'

'Hang on.' Joel had the high-definition pictures taken by

292

the attending CSI. They had captured Danny from just about every angle and every distance. He was laying them out on a dusty table when the superintendent spoke again.

'What did you think of the suicide, Lucy?'

'I didn't go out there, Ma'am.' DS Rose had to clear her throat first. It made the words sound harsher.

'That was my bad and I have been reprimanded for it,' Joel said. 'I have to get used to the fact that I can't do everything on my own.' He flickered a smile at DS Rose. The superintendent seemed to pick up on it; she pursed her lips and looked from one detective to the other.

'The longer you two work together the more effective you'll get, I'm sure of that.'

'That maybe true, Ma'am, but . . .' DS Rose cut in but then quickly stopped.

'Yes, yes, I haven't forgotten. I am holding your old position open, but I'm still convinced that you're going to fall in love with this role and never want to go back!' The superintendent snorted a laugh that no one else joined in with. Instead, Joel moved the room's attention back to the photos by pointing at the first.

'This is a close-up of Danny Evans's face,' he said. 'You can see the damage to the mouth – this here is what's left of his top lip and teeth and this is the first thing that raised questions. Danny Evans didn't shoot himself in the mouth, he shot himself in the face.'

'Personal preference? Either one gets the job done?' the superintendent said.

'It does, but people choose the mouth for a reason.' Joel searched the office until his eyes fell on a stapler. He wiped a layer of dust and pulled it open, holding the thicker end to turn it back on himself like Danny Evans might have with his gun. 'If this is a gun you put it in your mouth and clamp it in place with your jaw.' Joel did as he stated, then demonstrated how it was held in place. He took it back out to speak.

293

'Triggers on guns are not easy to pull, not when the gun isn't held firm, something that isn't possible with a pistol turned on itself. You definitely can't aim. Danny Evans shot himself in the roof of the mouth, he got it dead on, through his top lip and without being able to see it.'

'He couldn't see it?'

'Not judging by the trajectory. He had his head right back, his eyes to the ceiling. Why would you do that?'

'He didn't want to see it coming,' DS Rose offered.

'Then shut your eyes. Don't make it more difficult.'

'So you're saying he didn't shoot himself.' The caution was back in the superintendent's tone.

'It would be very neat and tidy if he did. No one outstanding for us to look for—'

'Except there is.' DS Rose spoke again. 'We know Danny Evans met with someone a couple of times at his hotel around the time of the murders and just before he killed himself. The barman at his hotel told us that.'

'Danny Evans's wife mentioned him too, or at least she said that Danny was speaking to a private investigator in a bar—'

'A private investigator would make sense, wouldn't it? The PI works out that Olsen abused his kid, maybe he supplies the address for him too. You just need to verify that with him and this is over, isn't it?'

'We have to find him first. Danny didn't tell Sharon anything about this guy. I spoke to his agent too and he had no idea what I was talking about, he just said Danny was cut up about his daughter, drinking too much to cope, but no suggestion Danny was doing anything about it. And do you know what else he told me?'

'Go on.'

'Danny signed a new contract a few days ago to take up a coaching role. A three-year contract, the next stage in his career. Does that sound like a man planning to murder three people and then himself?'

294

'It spiralled. Maybe he just wanted to find who put his daughter in hospital with evidence to give to the police and when his private investigator delivered it he lost the plot. You can see how that might happen.'

'I can,' Joel admitted. 'But Danny didn't look right. We found his car parked at his hotel too. I had our CID friends call round taxi firms for three towns – none of them dropped Danny anywhere near that site. The bus route out there is so complicated it's barely worth considering; not when I know Danny has a car. Why wouldn't he take it?'

'He clearly wasn't in a good state of mind.'

'It would make sense if someone else drove him,' Joel said. 'We did some phone work too. Danny Evans's phone was on a chair next to him. It was dead. There's a period when the phone went dark. It was turned off in the area where we now know he was staying and turned back on where his body was found. Why would he do that?'

'To help us find him?' Marsen said.

'So why not leave it on for the journey?' Joel said.

'The barman,' DS Rose said, suddenly sounding excited. 'He said Danny left with a man. He was drunk and he was taking him back to his room.'

'He did,' Joel said.

'Do we know he definitely took him back?'

'Not for certain. The CCTV I was talking about might help. CID are reviewing but the hotel staff said that coverage isn't good.'

The superintendent cut back in, her tone that of someone far from convinced. 'We need to look at the basics here, like a motive. Who else has a motive to kill those three people – four if we're saying Danny was foul play?'

'Maybe . . .' DS Rose started speaking and stood up from her desk. She moved to hover over the photos but her eyes looked glazed, like she was thinking something through. 'What if you're the man who was responsible for blackmailing

295

those girls, the man Hannah was after. Wouldn't you have a motive?'

'But we're saying that's Marcus Olsen, right?' the superintendent said.

'Are we? Hannah had another name, someone she was convinced with and I know it wasn't *Marcus Olsen*.' She tutted and reached for the file that contained all the material Hannah had gathered on those girls, scrabbling to open it up. 'She told me about it. Someone was arrested for possession of indecent images and among those images were some the five girls had sent. She wanted to nick him for the blackmail and interview him, but she wasn't allowed. The officer investigating the possession offence was asked to put it to him in interview, but it was a question thrown in at the end and of course he just went "no comment". They didn't pursue it from there.'

Joel came back with anger clear in his tone. 'Surely there were other lines of enquiry? The interview is a tiny part of an investigation.'

'He went guilty on the possession charge and they figured there was no point pursuing the blackmail. Between Hannah's bosses and CPS they didn't think it would make a difference to any conviction and it could only delay things. This was an opportunity to get him to court and dealt with on a guilty plea. If they started pursuing something he had gone not guilty on, it would have delayed the whole thing.' DS Rose looked resigned, like it was something she had seen many times.

'What does a delay matter? We should be throwing the book at these people,' Joel said.

When DS Rose spoke again it was like she was trying to choose her words carefully. 'Child Protection can be a unique place to work. Anywhere else and you try and stick them on with whatever offence you can find, but I know first-hand that it can be different in there . . . A blackmail offence committed online . . . You're talking a forensic search of his

296

computer, a further search of his house, and you'd still be left with an offence that might be very difficult to prove. A lot more work and probably no change to his sentence.'

'What was his sentence?'

'Suspended. For two years.'

'Suspended!' Joel huffed. 'So he didn't even go to prison. And five victims whose abuser never answers for what he did.'

'Hannah would agree with you, but that's how it goes in there. Just a few weeks ago I was on a child protection warrant after we received good intel that the occupant had images on his phone. The warrant got us in but there were strict instructions to only seize the phone and that's all we did. I saw a computer tower and any number of pen drives in the few minutes I was in there – who knows what other stuff was on them? But we didn't look. We're told to prove possession, to get them charged and convicted so they can be monitored. That's how it works with offenders on the lower end of the scale, and there is some logic there. The department is swamped and we had to prioritise contact offences.'

'Contact offences?' Joel said.

'Men making arrangements to meet up with children, those that aren't satisfied with pictures alone.'

'But surely one leads to the other?'

'It can. I was in a conversation with a DCI once about the very same thing and I still remember what she said: in a sinking ship, do you plug the holes or bail out the water?'

'Ma'am?' Joel turned his frustration towards the superintendent, who had fallen silent. She now erupted in a sigh.

'Lucy's right. There is no area of the business more stretched. Last I heard there's a four-month backlog to get the search warrants done in the first place so you can be damned sure there isn't the appetite to do more of a search than is required when you get there. You need one image to prove possession, Joel. There is an argument for stopping once you have it. The

297

only difference between proving possession of one image or the possession of a thousand images can be a lot of work for us, not the outcome for the offender.'

'What about identifying victims? Safeguarding children?' Joel looked at both women in turn. They looked as resigned as each other.

'I agree. There was a time when we would take everything, discover a million images and someone would sift through them, grading each one and trying to work out if there was a chance of identifying the poor little bastard in the pictures. That does still happen if there's any suggestion of a contact offence or if you have a father with kids around the age and sex of his chosen victims, then you would run through and make sure his kids don't feature . . .' The superintendent faded out, her frame slumped like she was beaten. 'The world of Child Protection is messed up and the last one you would want to get the better of us, but the sheer volume, the way these people operate . . . I can see how the decision could have been made in Hannah's case.'

'That was why she was so obsessed,' Joel said. 'Not because she didn't know who had blackmailed those girls – she knew exactly who it was, but her hands were tied by the organisation, she wasn't allowed to prove it.'

DS Rose sat straighter. 'Unless she could get some new information, something that could reopen the case, get the subject re-interviewed and another search done.'

'Like the sort of information a source handler could get?' Joel said. 'Alan Miles said something about sex offenders having a very tight circle. Marcus Olsen had those pictures on his computer so if he wasn't the person who blackmailed those girls to get hold of them . . .'

'Then he may well have known the man who did.'

Joel took a moment, his gaze falling back on the pictures of Danny Evans's broken face. 'Danny Evans wouldn't let it rest either. Between him and Hannah they were getting close to what they needed. And now they're dead. And so is Olsen and his sister. All the people who might have had knowledge.'

'So, we're saying the person that abused Callie Evans is now a suspect for shooting her dad?' The superintendent ruffled her hair as she spoke.

'Let's just say this may not be as neat and tidy as it appears,' Joel said.

Chapter 46

'Christopher Hennershaw'. The tip caught on the whiteboard to squeak with every movement as DS Rose wrote. She underlined it twice then stepped away. They both stared at it, just like they had been staring at it in Hannah's notes periodically for the last two hours. It was Joel who thought it might help move them forward if they wrote it up on a board. Joel huffed when it didn't have an instant effect.

Superintendent Marsden was gone. She had taken a call an hour and a half earlier that had seen her hurrying away, a last yell over her shoulder to be 'kept informed'.

'Hannah's legacy,' DS Rose said finally. 'This was her man.'

'That's good enough for me.'

'So where do we go from here? The superintendent said no to a search warrant, so we're not getting that. We don't have reasonable suspicion to arrest him and then search under Section 32 either.'

'We don't, we have a theory based on circumstantial evidence. Nothing solid.'

'So where do we go from here?'

Joel had a thought. 'Hang on, you said he got a suspended sentence so that means strict court conditions. Read them out.'

DS Rose bent back over her keyboard for a couple of taps

300

then straightened to read from her screen. 'Condition of residence . . . No unsupervised contact with a child under the age of eighteen . . . Not to be in possession of any devices that can connect to the internet—'

'That one!' Joel clapped his hands and DS Rose beamed a smile at the same time. 'This is your area, so this is where you tell me that a police officer can go round and check that condition at any time. It doesn't have to be scheduled. We're police officers!' he said excitedly.

'We can and we are.'

'So we go round and we search for anything that might connect to the internet. Only I bring my mates from the old search team and they might just happen to stumble over something that links him to the murders. We won't need much more for reasonable suspicion.'

'Hang on there, that's a Child Protection function and there's a lot of legislation around it. They won't be happy if we just—'

'Child Protection won't be happy if we ask their opinion, and I don't intend on doing that. Once we find evidence linking him to four murders no one will care that we didn't tip off the right department before we went. That condition gives us a search power, that's what we need. What other options do we have?'

DS Rose took a moment then she nodded. 'OK then.'

'OK then. I need to make some calls but I reckon I can get a proper search sorted for tomorrow morning. You can drive, I'll call them on the way.'

'On the way?' DS Rose said.

Joel grinned, and waited long enough for it to catch on. 'You don't have to come but I still remember your face the last time I left you out of all the fun.'

'Fun?'

'Actually it's probably nothing to do with our case, more that Hannah left a loose end, and it's in her notes. A woman

301

called Marilyn Luckhurst. Sharon mentioned her to us earlier. It looks like Hannah was helping her out with issues around domestic violence as an aside from this case. But it was all off-record so now Hannah's gone there's no one left to pick that up.'

'There's a whole domestic violence unit. You could hand it over to them.'

'I could . . . Hannah has three entries in her daybook, three different dates. That's three separate meetings she took with Marilyn Luckhurst. Hannah really wanted to help this woman.'

'Marilyn's daughter is suspected to have been blackmailed too,' DS Rose said.

'Emma Luckhurst, fourteen years old. But officially the family have denied she was a victim at all and the meetings don't seem to have been about Emma. Let's get going. I'll pick out the key bits on the way over and read them out. You'll see what I mean. We're probably just going to end up with a referral to the DV unit but . . .'

'But Hannah wanted to help this woman,' DS Rose said.

'She did. It's a quick conversation to make Marilyn Luckhurst aware that DC Ribbons can't help her anymore, but that doesn't mean she's alone.' Joel started to move out of the office but stopped when his sergeant actually appeared to be smiling. 'What?'

'Hannah . . . She would be delighted. Which means I am too.'

Joel looked beyond her at the board. 'It's no skin off our nose really. Tomorrow morning is what matters.' He fixed on the name written out and underlined. 'Christopher Hennershaw, you piece of shit, we're coming for you first thing. And Hannah Ribbons sent us.'

302

Chapter 47

Crabble Hill linked the town of Dover to the hamlet of River and was crammed tight in every sense of the word. From the houses that were firmly pushed together into a terraced row of sandy-brown to the parked cars that were a testament to the parking ability of the locals. Even the traffic that streamed past was bunched together, enough that it pushed them past the Luckhurst address and round a corner to be faced with a huge railway bridge looming large above them. It held Joel's attention but DS Rose slowed to make a tight left turn. Joel saw a faded sign labelled 'The Phoenix Railway Club' pass by his window. The drive was long and bumpy with stones that crunched and pinged out from under the tyres, seemingly leading them along the back of the houses they had just passed.

'Looks like my kinda place!' DS Rose quipped. Straight ahead a tired-looking skittle alley stole a good portion of the car park while the bridge still stood like a slab of passive aggression on their right. DS Rose nosed the car into the closest space and silenced the engine.

They needed to walk back the way they had come. Joel noted the double doors of the Phoenix Railway Club's entrance were covered in wooden boards and secured with a shiny metal clasp. The windows along the front were largely boarded now too. At the far end some of the boards had been pulled away and the glass behind either bore the scars of thrown stones or was missing completely.

'Doesn't look like it's been closed down too long. Any downturn takes these types of places out first,' DS Rose offered as Joel still studied it.

'It'll rise up from the ashes with a name like that.' Joel grinned at his joke and only got a shake of the head from his colleague.

Back on the pavements of Crabble Hill their pace quickened. Joel led as they walked up the slim garden path and he banged on the door.

'Yes?' The woman's appearance was quick, her chest heaving like she might have run.

'Marilyn Luckhurst?' Joel said, and the woman just stared back, the gap in the door decreasing slowly. Joel made introductions, and by the time he had finished there was just enough of a sliver for him to make out a single, glinting eye.

'Police?' she said, finally.

'Were you expecting someone else?' Joel replied.

'What do you want?'

'May we come in?'

'What about?' she asked through the remaining crack.

'It's a sensitive matter. I was hoping you might be able to help us out.'

'I can't help, what is it about?'

'Is your husband here?' Joel asked.

The eye got wider, then she said, 'No.'

'That's good to hear. I'm glad you took DC Ribbons's advice.' The woman's attention had moved to his colleague, but it snapped back to Joel now.

'What do you want?'

'DC Ribbons, you spoke to her a lot.'

'Who says I did?' Marilyn asked, and Joel waited her out. It was just a few seconds before she started up again. 'I never

304

said anything to her that was on record, she gave me her word.'

'And she kept her word. She took it to her grave, in fact.' Again Joel waited. This time for his meaning to sink in. It took a little longer but the door suddenly shifted open wider. It was enough for Joel to see that behind Marilyn was thick shadow. She turned to step into it and both detectives took it as an invitation to follow.

They found Marilyn in the first room off the hall. It was a small living room with exposed floorboards that creaked under her incessant pacing. Both detectives hung by the door to give her space. There was a long sofa pointing at a mantelpiece with a clock in its centre and a small television sat on the floor in the corner. Nothing else was in place. Instead there were stacks of cardboard boxes and two large plastic crates under the window. Thick curtains were drawn. Joel flicked a switch and an exposed bulb hanging down by its wire made Marilyn react like she preferred the gloom.

'Sorry,' Joel chuckled, 'poor eyesight and a clumsy nature! I wouldn't want to trip on one of the boxes and break anything. Are you moving?'

'No. I just never . . . Where did you park? Are you in one of those police cars?' She stopped her pacing to lock onto Joel, her face flushed with fear, her lips tightly pursed. She had tied-back mousy brown hair that frizzed at the edges, and grey roots that looked to be spreading out as Joel watched. She wore casual jeans and a long-sleeved top, both tight enough to show how thin she was. Frail even. And tired.

'We're in a plain car, it could belong to anyone. We're parked in a space behind the house, there's a closed-down club—'

'You can't stay there. Not long. You only get residents' cars down there now and he knows all of them.'

'He? Your husband?'

'What did you mean? Hannah and her grave?'

305

Joel took a moment. He needed the conversation to slow down for the woman to be able to focus on one thing at a time. 'Hannah Ribbons was caught up in an incident while she was on duty. She's dead, Mrs Luckhurst, and we're trying to find out why.'

'Dead . . .' Her voice was nothing more than a whisper now. Her eyes moved around in her head like she was looking for something to rest on. Finally she settled back on the inspector.

'I left her a message . . . I told her that I couldn't speak with her anymore. I thought that was why I hadn't heard back.' Marilyn started pacing again, her words mumbled towards the bare floorboards, her head shaking.

'Why could you not talk to her anymore?' DS Rose asked. The woman's answer was instant.

'She'd moved on! I shouldn't have been talking to her anyway.' Marilyn stopped at the closest point of her circuit to the officers, close enough for Joel to naturally want to step back, but he held his ground.

'Did she tell you that? Did she say that you couldn't talk to her anymore?' DS Rose said. This time the answer wasn't so quick. She took her time, still stood close to them both, looking like she was studying DS Rose closely.

'Never.' She spun on her heels quick enough to have Joel ducking away from her flicked hair. She resumed pacing.

'DC Ribbons was investigating a blackmail offence. Five teenage girls were victims, but she knew there was a sixth girl, didn't she? Your daughter, is it Emma?' Joel took back over.

'She's gone.' This time the pacing stopped at the furthest point and Marilyn was facing away, her head lifted like she might be staring at the pulled curtains. 'She's gone and she won't be coming back.'

'DC Ribbons was as good as her word. There's nothing in the casefile about Emma, but she wrote notes when she met with you. What was it, three times?'

306

'Three times. She didn't write anything.' Marilyn was still facing away.

'She would have written her notes after then, but she put in there what happened to Emma, what you told her.'

This was the longest pause yet, enough for Joel to fix on the sound of cars passing the front.

'My Emma . . .'

'DC Ribbons left her alone, didn't she? She didn't force the issue, she knew Emma's mental health was suffering enough already. But that wasn't the main reason, was it?' Joel said.

'You can't be here. It's been too long, it's been too long now.' Marilyn turned to set off, her pace quicker.

'Your husband – Nicholas – that's right, isn't it? He's a very controlling man but he struggled with Emma. She's a fourteen-year-old girl, after all, and teenage girls don't react well to being controlled, do they?'

'You need to leave, you need to take that car away.'

'You moved here to get away from him, to get you both away from him, but it didn't work, did it? It wasn't far enough. And Hannah was going to help you get away from him for good. That's why you haven't even unpacked, isn't it?'

Marilyn's voice was now little more than a whisper and it was directed downwards, like she was coaching herself. 'I can't do this, not again. Hannah was good to me, she was good to me . . . she was so good to me. I felt safe with her . . .'

'You had a deal, an agreement, Hannah wrote that down too.' Joel pushed on, despite the obvious increase in Marilyn's stress levels. He was near the end of what he knew, of what he had managed to decipher from Hannah's shorthand updates and what he could take from Marilyn's reactions. 'What were you going to tell her when she got you safe? Something about your husband, maybe the reason why you're so scared of him?' Marilyn still paced, her head still down, her headshakes almost constant, her lips moving with incoherent mumbles. Joel waited her out.

307

'No, no . . . nothing like that, you don't understand.' She shook her head, more mumbles, more thoughts tumbling out of her mouth. 'My Nicholas and my Emma . . . He loves her, he's always loved her, he would do anything for her.' She stepped in close again, her voice back to a murmur. 'You can't always keep the things you love, not so close, not like that. We couldn't tell him, not about what she did, what she was forced to do . . .'

'Nicholas doesn't know that Emma sent images of herself?' Joel said.

Marilyn suddenly looked up as if she had woken from a trance, fear in her eyes. 'He knows! I've never seen a man so angry. Emma thought . . . she thought he was angry at her, he thought this was all her fault. It was the last thing, the pressure of it all . . . My Emma – she couldn't cope. She's on a secure ward now . . .' She spun back into more pacing, her voice louder. 'They said she's had a full breakdown, that she presents like someone who's seen a terrible thing . . . But there's lots of colour there, that's what I thought the moment I went in there. Bright and lots of colour. I took her favourite teddy and she took it so tight like when she was five years old. They never stop being your baby, do they?'

'They don't,' Joel agreed. 'DC Ribbons was working hard, she'd started the ball rolling to get you moved—'

'It doesn't matter now! With Emma where she is we can't . . . we couldn't leave. Hannah knew that.'

'You look ready to leave to me.'

'Everything ready, everything boxed,' she muttered it twice with the cadence of a nursery rhyme.

'And you were going to talk to DC Ribbons, to tell her something about Nicholas. Maybe you were going to tell her why you're so scared. Does he beat you?'

'Nicholas loves us. He loves his family. The kids . . . they don't deserve . . . Our children are innocent.' She fixed on Joel, lingering for a moment, her utter desperation clear. 'And you have to go, you have to go now.'

308

'Did Hannah ever speak to him?' DS Rose cut in. She took a step forward like she wanted to increase the pressure.

'No. He didn't want the police, not ever.'

'His daughter was blackmailed by a paedophile and he didn't want the police involved?' DS Rose said.

'Please!' Marilyn said urgently. DS Rose was so close that Marilyn was able to reach out for her wrist, reinforcing her pleading. 'You need to leave, you need to leave now, right now!'

'Okay, Marilyn. We understand,' Joel said. 'But the man who blackmailed those girls, who blackmailed Emma, we're making progress on that. I want to be able to talk to you, to keep you informed. Can I do that?' Joel took his card out of his pocket and waved it, trying to break the spell between Marilyn and DS Rose. 'Maybe you can call me when you know it's safe to do so, save me turning back up here?'

Marilyn looked over at him, still holding DS Rose by the wrist. 'Please . . . please don't come here. He'll know!' The fear was so real it went against every instinct for Joel to walk away.

'Hannah gave you her word, didn't she? That she would keep you safe. She might be gone but I'm here and now it's my word, OK?' Joel suddenly didn't want to be handing this over to anyone else as a DV Referral. He felt invested. He wanted to help.

Marilyn fixed on him again, her lips trembled, her jaw creased and she huffed through her nose. She was fighting herself; there was something she needed to say. Finally she forced her words.

'You need to go.'

309

Chapter 48

The doors swooshing open seemed to be just the invitation an empty cigarette carton and crushed bottle of juice were waiting for. They made a dart for the public entrance to Folkestone Police Station behind a chilly breeze that swept in to fill the front counter in an instant. Hayley Mears tugged the zip up on her police-issue fleece top until it covered her chin.

'Good afternoon.' The man who stepped in from the thickening dusk had a deep voice, though it was muffled by a front counter that was higher than a standard reception might be – but then a standard reception didn't need to factor in someone coming off the street to leap over it and attack the persons behind. Hayley had manned this desk for over ten years – enough time to have just about seen it all. She stood up to greet her latest visitor. He didn't look like a man about to leap over. He looked old enough to know better and was dressed more like he was late for a wedding than up for a fight. He wore a tie that caught in the harsh ceiling lights and fell down a shirt that hinted at a straight crease across the front like it had been fresh out of a packet that morning. He had a sniff, suggesting the cold had got to him, and his nose glowed red to stand out more against a neat beard that was largely grey, its edges determined by a razor. She recognised him as one of the regulars.

'Good afternoon,' she said. 'I'll put a call in.' The man nodded and spun for the plastic seats that were bolted to the far wall. He perched on the edge of a seat, his feet apart, leaning forward to wring his hands.

'They'll be down in just a moment,' Hayley called out and received a terse 'Thanks' in reply. Hayley remained standing, pretending to be busy by moving bits around her desk. It was less than a minute before a male detective from Child Protection arrived. It wasn't the same person Hayley had spoken to on the phone. The seated man slapped his thighs as he stood up to shake the detective's outstretched hand. The detective was instantly cheery when he said, 'This shouldn't take long' and then they were both gone. Hayley's attention was now drawn to where the doors parted again as her colleague Gary arrived. A crisp packet led the charge this time, scraping across the concrete before being trampled under his foot. He was late back from an appointment, his face looking flushed and hassled.

'Ah, Gary! Could you do me a favour and just pick those few bits up? Every time that door opens the breeze drags something in. It's driving me crazy.' Gary looked unimpressed. He was much younger than her, young enough for this to be his first job. He reached out for the carrier bag that Hayley wafted at him. 'Thanks, love!'

He didn't take long. Hayley was glad when he finished so the doors could close to the chill.

'Getting cold again!' she said as he made his way across the front of the counter.

'Was all right earlier in the sun. Not that we get much being cooped up in here though.' Gary paced through to the back office where he stayed for a few minutes. By the time he reappeared he had shed his coat.

'I didn't realise the time, forty minutes and we'll be closing up. Much going on?' he said, then sniffed.

311

The internal door clacked and shook before she could answer. The man in his shiny tie and packet shirt reappeared. The same detective who had welcomed him in now hung at the internal door to speak. 'See you in a couple of weeks then.' They shook hands again, the metal case of the visitor's watch catching in the light. The detective turned to where Hayley had already opened the folder where she recorded the visits for registered sex offenders. She knew the process. Hayley watched the man out until the doors fell shut behind him.

'Does he work nearby? An office or something?' Hayley spoke to the detective who was still holding the internal door open.

'Nope. I reckon he puts a shirt and tie on just for you, Hayley!' His eyes sparkled with mischief. 'He's always dressed up.'

'I think I'll pass on that one, thanks,' she replied. 'More like he thinks you'll go easy on him if he looks smart.'

'Who knows what a man like that is thinking. Probably best we don't know. Have you got all the details you need?' Hayley nodded. The detectives did the easy part – a brief interview where they would check he hadn't moved house and that they had an up-to-date telephone number, and where they would ask if he was adhering to whatever conditions had been set for him. Hayley's part was then to make sure it was updated on PNC that he had attended. If she didn't, an arrest warrant was generated automatically.

'I have. I'll make sure he's updated. Unless you tell me someone will kick his door in at 3 a.m. if I don't! Then I might be tempted to let it slip my mind . . .'

The detective smiled. 'More like I would have a shitty email from someone very senior by the morning and a lot of paper-work to do. I'd much rather you saved me the trouble if it's all the same with you.'

'Fine. You win!'

A wink and he was gone. Hayley turned to where she could

312

still see the tall figure hurrying away from her police station. It was a long walk to the pavement. He made it now and turned left. He had his hands thrust in his pocket and his chin dug into his collar like he was feeling the cold. A street lamp spluttered to life like it had been waiting for him.

'He gives me the creeps,' she said.

'That's because you know what he's done. That's enough to give anyone the creeps,' Gary replied.

'Even if I didn't there's something about him. Someone like that shouldn't be allowed to walk the streets a free man.'

'He's monitored, don't forget,' Gary scoffed. 'That's how he gets to walk free. He comes in here, they ask him if he's behaving, he tells them what they want to hear and off he goes.'

'System's a joke,' Hayley agreed.

'You don't think he is then? Behaving, I mean?'

Hayley took a moment, watching across the lawns at the front of the police station as the man walked left to right, passing from one streetlight to the next.

'A man like that,' she mused, 'he's already ruined lives to take what he wants and he gets to just walk away from here. Why would he stop?'

313

Chapter 49

Joel pushed the file away like it might make him feel better. It didn't. Papers still spewed out of its side and others were scattered across his kitchen table. After their conversation with Marilyn Luckhurst, Joel had sent them both home, announcing that they had an early start and a long day expected the next day. There was nothing more they could achieve by going back over the same material again and again. But Joel had failed to heed his own advice, scooping up everything he needed to be able to do just that.

He looked up longingly towards the kettle.

'Is that your murderer?' Michelle appeared to sweep past him and hover over the table. She gestured at where he also had his laptop open. He had dared check his email, opening one from DS Andrews, who was sharing the findings of his two officers who had finished their review of the hotel CCTV. It was good work too, at least as good as it could be. The hotel had only one camera that was of any use, covering the main entrance, and they had gone through three days of movements so far. Joel had been sent a still image of the only man hotel staff couldn't identify in that time. It was last thing on the Tuesday night. The image was terrible. It was a *man* though, he was sure of that. His dark grey jacket hung on broad

314

shoulders, he had matching trousers and a blob of brown for shoes. His feet were captured mid-stride; the shoe at the back was the closest to the camera and might have a blur of blue too. To further add to his frustration, the face was completely obscured by the rim of a hat. Overall, it was as good as useless. He had still forwarded it to DS Rose. He didn't think she would see anything he couldn't but he was trying to ensure he shared everything.

'It could be anyone, if I'm honest,' Joel said and pushed his laptop shut.

'The kids are upstairs. They're waiting for their dad so they can read him a bedtime story,' Michelle explained.

'No, they're not.' He leaned back to grin at his wife.

'No, they're not,' his wife agreed, 'they're on their iPads. Abigail said she can already read every word ever so why does she have to keep doing it and Daisy will only read to you if it's the instructions on how to make slime.'

'How to make slime?'

'Your project for the weekend, she says. You promised apparently. Assuming you get a weekend.'

Joel sighed. 'I'll try and get something. Making slime can't take that long, can it?'

'Monday and you're already having to *try*.'

'Monday and I'm saying I don't break promises to my girls.'

Joel felt his wife's hands run over his shoulders, down his chest and over his tie. She kissed the top of his head and he could feel her lips move as she spoke. 'I'm worried about you. Straight back into long days and already bringing your work home. You need to look after yourself. You were supposed to go back to something a little more laid-back. At least for a while.'

'The one thing you don't do is ask for "laid-back". Welfare would have me doing an admin role tied to a desk. I can promise you that would stress me out more.'

'You would be shadowing, that's what you said. Following

315

someone else around while they did all the work and you learned the ropes. That sounded ideal.'

'I know. It didn't quite work out.'

'And now you're chasing murderers? Is that the right thing for you to be doing?'

'I think it is. I care about it, it feels important. And one of the victims . . . She was one of us. A copper. I want to be part of piecing this together, Michelle.'

His wife stepped away and walked to the other side of the kitchen table where she could watch him closely. 'And are you?'

'I think so, but I feel like I'm missing something and I've never wanted to get answers more. I guess I'm going to have to get used to that. Seems to go with the territory.'

'I'm sure it does.'

'Today I met a mother who's waiting for the right time to tell her young son that his dad is never coming home. I can't imagine the day they're having. I offered to help her out, even say the words for her. I was relieved when she said no.'

'You need to be looking after yourself, too, Joel. I know you, you suck up a little bit of what you see, you care too much. And it's not your job to make everything better for the rest of the world. No matter how much you would like to.'

'You'd just brush it off, would you? Like it doesn't matter?' Joel snapped and immediately wished he hadn't. 'Sorry, I know what you mean. I'm fine, I promise.'

'I'm still not sure you need this sort of pressure straightaway.'

'The pressure's good, it keeps me motivated. This is very different to . . . to what happened before. I've had time to understand it, to understand myself too. I'm better prepared. You get to the point where you think you're totally untouchable and then something catches you out. It's a reminder that I'm not, no one is. I'm stronger now, Michelle. Stronger and better prepared.' Joel stood up. 'Now, if you don't mind I need to go find out how slime is made and nothing is more important

316

than that right now.' He kissed his wife, on the lips this time, and when he pulled away he was careful to show off his best smile before heading for the stairs. However, his wife knew him better than anyone and it would only take her a moment to detect the doubt leaking out from behind that smile.

Sharon Evans stopped herself from knocking, opting to rest her knuckle against Jamie's bedroom door while she held her breath to listen. She couldn't hear anything. No movement, no music, no games console, not even Zinedine causing trouble. It was dark now too. She'd kept the hall light off so light should be leaking out from under Jamie's door. But there was nothing. It had been a couple of hours since she'd spoken to him and told him about his dad. She just wanted a response, some clue as to where his head was at. She was getting nothing.

She had been expecting a fight, and dreading it. She thought she knew Jamie well enough to know his reaction. She had expected angry, a refusal to believe it, for him to shout at her for lying and to be furious that she would do that. But it had been nothing like that. He had quietly listened, his face had changed, his skin ran pale. But that was it.

I need to be on my own. That was all he had said. She'd let him go, taking the time to consider why he had reacted like that. The answer when it came seemed so simple: Jamie wasn't surprised. Maybe he had even been expecting it. As much as she had tried to hide his father's downward spiral he must have seen right through it. She should have protected him better.

She was still leaning on her son's door when her phone rang in her back pocket. She moved away through the darkness and down the stairs to answer it.

'Mrs Evans?'

'Yes?' She said.

'Hello, sorry to bother you. It's Maggie . . . from the hospital?'

317

'Maggie, is everything OK with Callie?' Maggie's title was Nurse Watts, but Sharon had got to know her well enough to call her Maggie. She was posted to the ITU ward at William Harvey – and Callie specifically.

'Yes, everything's fine, I just wanted to let you know that Callie's a lot more lucid. She woke up very confused but she's calmer now, sitting up and having a drink. I know you wanted to be here, but it's sod's law isn't it! She's still very tired and she's got a very sore throat so she can't talk very well but she's been asking for you.'

'Oh God! Yes! We'll be straight there! Thank you, thank you . . . That's so wonderful!' Sharon felt a burst of elation. She turned back to the stairs, taking two at a time to reach the landing. Jamie's door was at the end and again her fist was raised to knock. Again she held it back. This time it was a tide of emotion that stopped her. This was good news, everything she had been waiting for – but now it meant something entirely different.

Now she was going to have to tell another of her children that their dad was gone.

Chapter 50

Richard Maddox sat in front of him. Just like Glenn Morris had. Richard was looking up, fear clear in his eyes, but defiance too, maybe even more than his friend. Not that it mattered. Fear was all he needed. Fear was control. And he was the one holding the gun.

Richard was holding his medal in his right hand. A piece of old metal to look at, but one thing he had learned from spending time with Glenn Morris was just how much significance these old men placed on their past.

'You're going to kill me now then? Just like you killed Glenn?' Richard's words sounded like they were forced from a tight chest that had a visible rise and fall. He was gripping the medal so tight his knuckles were flushed.

'I don't think you understand what I've been trying to do for you, Richard. I don't want to hurt you, I want to set you free,' he said.

'Set me free?'

'From your pain. From everything that was holding you back. And I did that, didn't I? And then you involved someone else when this was just for you, Richard, this was all just for you.'

'I told you . . . Glenn was like my brother . . . I trusted him.' Richard's tone carried his defiance too.

319

'I need something more from you. You need to make amends, you need to keep your grandson safe, you need to help me. One good deed deserves another, you've heard that, right?'

'My grandson? But I did everything you asked!'

'This was never supposed to be about me asking for anything. This was me giving you an opportunity. All I *asked* was for you to follow your sense of justice. You didn't have to pull that trigger, you could have walked away but you did what you needed to. Now you need to help me.'

'Help you? My best friend . . . stabbed like a piece of meat. Left to bleed out, a war hero . . .'

'Yes, he was, Richard. So you will see that your actions have consequences. You should also know that inaction has consequences for you now. The first thing you can do is drop that knife.' He gestured towards Richard's left hand now, his knuckles just as white, his grip just as tight. Richard hesitated, but only for a moment. The knife fell with a muted thud onto the carpeted floor of his own living room. The man had taken one of Richard's T-shirts from a drawer upstairs. He wrapped the knife in it now. It was a chef's knife, the handle heavy with a fake pearl effect that matched the rest in Glenn Morris's kitchen.

'I cleaned the blade after. I used the sink at your friend's house but it was just a rinse. You can't get all traces of blood off without a strong bleach. The police will find Glenn Morris's blood on this. Now they'll find your fingerprints and fibres from your clothing too. You and Glenn were friends but you argued and it got out of hand; you stabbed him to death. That's not a very hard sell, Richard, not when they see the way you despatched Danny Evans. Or you can assist me with another good deed, one that benefits the entire world, and the police will never know of any of it.'

'Good deed? What good deed?'

He stepped forward, the gun still gripped firmly by his side.

320

He had been battling his emotion, the rage that wouldn't go away, like it was now a permanent layer just under the skin. But it wasn't for Richard, at least it was never supposed to be. He managed to swallow it back down so he could speak.

'Danny Evans was just the start. Tomorrow morning we wipe the rest of that poisonous family from the face of the earth.'

Chapter 51

'It's OK, you don't need to talk.' But Callie was trying, between sips of water and gulps of air. Nurse Maggie Watkins had been at Callie's bedside when Sharon and Jamie had arrived, her face lighting up the moment they had come into sight. All Maggie had got back was a terse grimace from them both. The nurses might have seen something similar before with families arriving in this situation, barely able to believe that it was true, that they might be able to speak to their loved one again after so much time with nothing but hope. The truth for Sharon and her son was so much more.

Maggie was holding a plastic drinking bottle for Callie with a straw arching out of the top. Sharon took over. It looked like a struggle. Maggie was talking at Sharon, telling her how it was normal for a patient waking up like this to have a sore throat. They had sometimes needed to be aggressive getting tubes into her, which would cause damage that was unseen but inevitable. Maggie also explained that Callie was drowsy and would be confused for a while – no telling how long – and that this was all perfectly normal. Sharon was only half listening. She had hung on every word said to her in here for the last month or so, but in that moment she didn't care. Not about the prognosis, not about odds and chances, not about

322

anything anymore. Callie was awake, looking around, her lips even curling into the beginnings of a smile. Jamie was the other side of the bed, a smile spreading across his face when his sister twisted towards him but fading just as quickly when Callie turned back to search for her straw. Sharon helped her find it, all the time trying to ignore Jamie's desperate attempts to make eye contact with her. She knew that he was after assurance, a brief smile back, something to tell him that everything was going to be OK. She couldn't. She didn't have it in her. They had agreed on the way over that this was not the time to tell Callie anything about what was going on and of course it was the right decision. Sharon wasn't even sure if Callie knew where she was or what was going on around her.

Then Callie shrugged the straw out of her mouth and locked eyes with her mother. It took Sharon's breath away. Just to be looking in those eyes again, to be smiling, to be smiled back at. It was everything. Callie opened her mouth and a hacking sound came from her throat. She lifted a shaky hand to it, her face twisted in a grimace. When she opened her mouth again she made the same sound. This time the grimace was more clearly one of frustration, like she was trying to talk and angry she couldn't.

'It's OK, honey, don't talk, not until it's comfortable. You'll be fixed soon enough and we can have a right good chat!'

Callie made the same noise for a third time while still fixed on Sharon, then she was able to force a word. It was obscured by another cough but there could be no mistaking it.

'Dad!' she croaked.

And just like that, Sharon thought her heart was going to burst.

323

Chapter 52

Tuesday

Joel attacked the door to Christopher Hennershaw's house like he might be able to bounce it open with his fist. There were no pauses, just a barrage of blows, the sort of knock you couldn't ignore.

'Can I help you?' A man appeared. He was in his late forties, his eyes squinting like this was his first glimpse of the daylight. The voice coming from behind his beard was heavy with sleep. Joel recognised Hennershaw from his police mugshot. The man's eyes darted beyond the two detectives to the search team behind them.

'We need to come in, Mr Hennershaw.'

'Can I ask why?'

'This is your friendly check on your bail conditions.'

'All of you?' His voice was raised just enough to express his surprise.

'All of us.'

'I signed at the police station, just like I'm supposed to. Just yesterday.'

'Good for you,' Joel said.

'DC Smalling . . . she comes round regularly. Where is she?' Hennershaw looked to be searching each of the officers

324

standing on the drive for a friendly face. All he got was crossed arms and impatience.

'I have no idea,' Joel said and stepped forward. Hennershaw, wearing a tight white vest and boxer shorts, had the door trapped in his armpit. He seemed to get the hint and let go of the door to step back, his odd socks sliding on the wooden floor. Joel pushed through to the living room, where he swept a mess of DVD cases, television remotes and crumb-covered plates from the sofa to make a space. 'Sit,' he ordered and Hennershaw did as he was told.

'Is this really necessary? You'll disturb mother. She's eighty-two, this is why I ask that you call ahead.'

'Where's the console?' Joel demanded, his eyes scouring the television stand.

'I dunno what you're talking about!' the man stuttered, his indignation now gone.

'That controller just for show, is it?' Joel pointed at the Playstation controller lying on the sofa; the pillow that had been covering it was still in his other hand. 'Those officers out on the drive are a specialist search team, here to search for any evidence that you're breaching your bail. Seems they won't have to look too hard. You can help me out or I can have them tear this place apart. Where's the console?'

'I don't know . . . That's not mine!'

'Let me guess, your eighty-two-year-old mother's a big fan of *Grand Theft Auto*, is she?'

'No . . . Come on! This is so unfair!' The man rocked forward, his look now pleading. 'DC Smalling just comes in for a chat. She has a look round but there's a trust there. Ask her!'

'DC Smalling isn't here, I am. Where is it?' Joel growled.

The man slumped. His face suddenly creased, a sob escaping from somewhere in its centre. He dropped his hands to his sides like a child throwing a tantrum. 'Behind the television, all right! But I just use it for games. You can check it!'

325

The man lifted eyes that now flushed red and heavy and Joel threw the pillow down onto the sofa, his anger and frustration spilling over. He turned away from the weeping image of Christopher Hennershaw to fix on DS Rose and her expression mirrored his own.

'He's not right, is he?' Joel said.

'No,' she said, her head shaking, 'we got this wrong.'

Hennershaw brought his knees up onto the sofa to further give the impression of a snivelling, cowering heap. They had come here looking for a man capable of multiple murders, whose victims included Danny Evans, the man known locally as The Beast. Just a few moments in his home and nothing about Christopher Hennershaw suggested he was that man.

They were back to square one.

He thanked the elderly lady who had taken such care preparing his bunch of flowers. White lilies. She offered him a card to go with it.

'For your message,' she said with a chuckle that had a real warmth to it.

'No, thank you.'

The lady nodded like she understood entirely. 'Just being here is enough.' She leaned into him, her hand reaching out to rest on the arm that held the flowers. 'I must say, it's so nice to see a man making an effort. If it were me, lying in my sick bed, I would want a visit from a man in a suit and polished shoes. It says a lot about you!'

'I'm sure you're right,' he said and tried to step away. She still had a grip.

'Oh, trust me! My husband used to say the same. The shoes especially – he would always say you could tell a man's character by the shine of his shoes. I guess that makes you all right by me.'

His eyes followed hers to rest on the tanned leather of his

shoes, where they were criss-crossed with blue material and the instep of the right was starting to show a thread.

'They were a gift,' he said. 'I try to look after things other people took the time to pick out. They're starting to wear now though. That's what happens, isn't it? You can look after things as much as you want but they still get old. They get worn out. They die.'

The woman's smile faded away. She let go of his arm and took a step backwards. 'I suppose you're right about that,' she said.

'A florist must know better than most.' He held the flowers across his chest now to inhale their scent. 'These are perfect: fresh and beautiful. But soon they'll be dead, thrown out to rot in the ground.'

The woman took another step back. 'Enjoy them while you can, then!' Her laughter was nervous now, awkward. He revelled in her discomfort for another few moments before moving away. He didn't have time to linger. He knew Sharon Evans had never arrived at the start of visiting hours yet – her mornings were busy – but things change. She couldn't be sleeping well at the moment and any *normal* routine was surely long gone. He had made certain of that.

He reached up to shift his trilby a little as he stepped through the queue for the foyer coffee shop, emerging to pick his corridor. He was sure he had worked out the location of every CCTV camera on his route but that didn't stop him being careful. All the cameras were up high, which was why his eyes chased the floor, concealed under the brim of his hat.

He reached the stairs. There were two flights that twisted back on each other, then another walk down a long corridor. Still no one was taking any notice of him. He passed a man in overalls who looked to be clinging on to a floor polisher. Medical staff too, in various coloured scrubs, one of whom opened the secure door to the ITU ward as he approached. She was on her way out. She took a quick look at him, her

327

eyes flashing up from his smart shoes to his bunch of flowers, smart tie and subtle smile. She held the door for him.

'Thanks,' he said and watched as she continued on her way out. She didn't look back and he let his breath go.

He was inside.

The door fell slowly shut behind him under its own steam. A moment later and the locking system clacked loudly. This was the first time he had gone beyond that door and he needed to take a moment to assess. He had been able to walk the route right up to that door but he couldn't come in here. Not until now. He was only going to be able to come in here once.

Straight ahead he could see a curved desk against the left wall. The monitors and scattered paperwork identified it as the nurses' station. There was no one at it. He couldn't see anyone moving at all.

He took the syringe out of his pocket. It was fully extended, its belly blurred with a clear liquid. More than enough. It would be quick. Callie Evans's breathing was going to slow to a stop almost as soon as he injected her. The woman who also had a daughter in here had told him how Callie was improving – 'out of the woods', she had said, and she wasn't being as closely monitored as some of the others. Two cheap bunches of flowers and some words of support were all it had taken to get the woman talking, to get all the information he needed.

He liked the idea of Callie being monitored less. In his mind he had a perfect vision of Callie slipping away silently, lying undiscovered until her mother arrived to realise all at once that he was a man of his word.

He lined the syringe up so it was concealed against the tied stems of the flowers. Then he moved forwards.

He couldn't know if there were cameras in the ward. He had seen them covering doors in other parts of the hospital and didn't want to be taking chances now. He kept his head down, his eyes darting ahead from under the brim of his hat. He held the flowers up to obscure his right side as he walked.

328

The right side was where all the patients were arranged in rows. Only one bed had a visitor but it was someone sitting in a high-backed chair that was mainly angled away. No one was paying him any attention. The ward was five open areas. Callie was in the third, right next to the woman's daughter. He knew that they tried to keep the areas to one gender, to put children together too. It was why he had targeted a mother in the first place.

He slowed his pace, using the time to tell himself to stay calm. This was to be the first time he had ever set eyes on Callie Evans, and he didn't know how it was going to feel. Everything had been building to this, everything. He couldn't let his emotions spill out. Anger stood out, something he could ill afford. He could be emotional later.

The sun was bright at the window as he turned into the third area. Six beds. Three on the left, three on the right – laid out so their feet pointed at each other. He knew Callie was on the left side, he knew she was fifteen years old, and he was sure she would be clearly labelled for him by documentation at the end of the bed carrying her name.

He was right.

The clatter of the letterbox made Sharon jump. She had allowed her eyes to go out of focus while she was lost in her thoughts. She was anxious to get moving, to be anywhere but here, but the whole morning had been a battle to get Jamie to eat something. Finally he had made a start on breakfast and now he was giving Zinedine a lap round the block after insisting that he walked him every morning. Still they hadn't spoken about his dad. They needed that conversation but it was obvious he was doing all he could to be away from her. She planned on trying to talk to him while he was in the car, but he must have worked that out for himself and now he was trying his best to delay them leaving – even though it was to go and see his sister.

329

She was leaning on a kitchen unit, and the front door was at the opposite end of the house, but when her eyes snapped into focus she had a view of the postman moving away as a red smudge behind the frosted glass. She put her mug down and straightened up, trying to stretch off her fatigue as she went. Two bills were quickly discarded. The third envelope froze her to the spot:

To *the remaining Evans.*

She quickly glanced back up the hall to where the back door was still ajar, then tore at the envelope. Inside was a single folded sheet. The message was simple. A large image dominated the page: the four members of her family in photo-copied colour. She recognised the image as one that Dover Athletic had put up on their website previously. The club photographer had caught the whole Evans family watching from the stands when Danny was injured for a couple of games, and had decided it was worthy of a mention. This printed version of the photo was different – graffitied. Danny's face was crossed out by a black 'X' from the swipe of a thick pen. Sharon's hand jerked to cover her mouth.

So was Callie's.

So was Jamie's.

A single typed sentence stood below the image:

TIME'S UP.

330

Chapter 53

Joel was leaning in close enough for the full experience. Christopher Hennershaw stank of fear. Joel had opened there was a lot more to be found in his house and it hadn't taken long for the team to start bringing him finds.

'I need your unlock code.' Joel did nothing to conceal his delight as he now thrust a mobile phone towards the seated man. The phone had been found tucked behind a loose skirting board in the room Hennershaw still occupied, and his whole demeanour had changed the moment the find was called out. Hennershaw was no longer acting the petulant child; now he was terrified.

'I don't have to give you that,' he said.

'You're absolutely right.' Joel got even closer, close enough to feel his body heat. 'But let me tell you what happens now. You're already under arrest for breach of bail. Later you're going to be interviewed, where you will have every opportunity to lie in order to save your own skin. Do that and you might get bailed. But this little beauty here, the fact it was hidden, means I now suspect there are other offences on here and I bet I can get a custody sergeant to agree. The fact you're holding back your code gives me grounds for remand. After all, I don't know what those offences are – who those victims

331

might be – and I can't have you running free while I look into it. So, remand means prison and then I put sending-your-phone-off to the bottom of my to-do pile. I suggest you pack a little more than an overnight bag.'

Again Hennershaw looked beyond him, over at DS Rose. He would get no help from her either.

'There's nothing on it anyway,' he stuttered.

'Of course there isn't.'

'Two, seven, zero, eight. My mum's birthday,' he mumbled.

'She must be so proud.' Joel punched it in. It worked. 'Thanks. I'll hand this over to some people I know who can find everything that's ever been done on it. Including any deletions, scrambling, blackmail of fifteen-year-old girls. That sort of thing.'

Christopher reacted like he had been poked. 'Blackmail? So that's what this is all about. I got asked about that already. It was all dropped.'

Joel bent forward, his face as close to Hennershaw as he could manage so he wouldn't miss a single one of his hissed words. 'Hannah Ribbons never dropped it, not for a fucking moment. You understand? She knows what you are, she knows what you did. She's the reason we're here, she's the reason for the search team, she's the reason none us will rest until you answer for what you did.'

Hennershaw's lips twitched then bumped together. If he had a reply it was stuck somewhere inside him. Joel could feel his phone ringing in his pocket anyway. He straightened up, his eye still on Hennershaw, enjoying every moment of his suffering.

'DI Norris,' he said.

'He's gone! I don't know what to do!' A woman's voice, upset, barely able to speak through a sob that became a wail. Joel moved now, away from the piece of shit seated in front of him, out through the front door and into the freshness of the early morning.

'Who is this?' Joel said, 'who's gone?'

332

'It's Sharon, Sharon Evans . . .' Another sob, then a distorted voice like her head had fallen forward and her lips were pressed up against the mouthpiece. 'He's gone . . . Jamie . . . I can't find him!'

'Sharon, I need a bit more, OK. What's going on? Are you at home?'

'He's gone . . . I didn't listen, he was just going round the block, someone took him!'

'Sharon, where are you? You're not making any sense. I'll come to you. Tell me where you are.'

'At home. But I need to go, I need to go to Callie!' Her voice was back to a wail. Joel wasn't going to get anything more from her over the phone.

'I'll be right there.'

He turned back towards the house. DS Rose had already joined him outside. 'Everything OK?' she said.

'We need to go. Sharon Evans is at home but something's going on. She said her son's been taken.'

'OK. What about here?'

'The team are bringing Hennershaw in. Child Protection can take it from here. I think we're going to be needed elsewhere.'

333

Chapter 54

DS Rose had called ahead while Joel drove. Access to the Evans family home was already obstructed by two marked police cars parked untidily across the drive. Joel was happy the reaction had been so fast. If someone really had taken Jamie Evans, an immediate and resource-intensive reaction would give the best odds of finding him. He also knew how quickly those odds shrank after the first hour of searching.

Joel and DS Rose's arrival prompted the patrol sergeant to give an immediate briefing. He appeared to be the only officer in the house.

'We've searched the house but only for persons. Negative. The mother said her son walked out the gate at the back of the house to go round the block with the dog, something he does every day. My officers are out on foot in that area. I've got more patrols coming, I called up for anyone with a car and a pair of eyes and I'll be sending them out to bang on doors, search gardens, roam the streets . . . everything we'd normally do. We got a few numbers for friends that he hangs round with, and I was just calling them to see if he's there, but . . . well, I don't think he is, sir.'

'What makes you say that?' Joel could tell there was something more.

'We found the dog. He was dragging his lead behind him. The mother said she received a threat.' He broke off, ducking out of the hall where they had gathered, to retrieve something. It was a piece of paper already sealed in a police evidence bag. Joel flipped it over. He felt DS Rose push in close to him to see.

'Jesus!' Joel said at the image of the Evans family – three of the four crossed out – that stared back up at him. '"Time's up"? The daughter.'

The sergeant already had his hands raised like he was waiting for Joel's realisation. 'We already have someone at the hospital. They've sealed off the ward. The mother insisted on going too.'

'Sealed it off? What happened?' Joel asked.

'I'm waiting for an update. We do . . . we do have a death. A female patient, sus circs . . , I don't know any more but I can guess the same as you can.'

'We need to go, we need to be there. Sharon's the key to this.' Joel turned to DS Rose, who nodded her agreement. There was nothing more they could do here. The search was in hand, the surrounding streets would be flooded with uniform officers, the word out with the community if it wasn't already. If Jamie Evans was in the area he would be spotted very soon. But Joel had a terrible feeling in his gut that Jamie Evans wasn't anywhere near here at all. And the all-important 'golden hour' since Joel had received that panicked call from Sharon Evans was already gone.

Joel's shoes squeaked as he stopped at the door to the ITU ward, DS Rose beside him. Both of them stared at the officer there, who was writing in his pocket book. Joel held his warrant card out and spoke hurriedly.

'Is Sharon Evans in there?'

'A separate room. She wouldn't leave,' the officer said. 'Are you in charge, if I get asked by the nurses again? They want us out the way, I think.'

335

'I'm sure they do.' Joel moved past. The door behind him had a wedge holding it open. Initially the ward was just like the last time he had been here, but a few steps in and he could see more uniform officers standing at the foot of a bed in the third area up. It was where he had spoken to Sharon, where her daughter had been recovering behind her.

Another uniform police officer approached them. He was sombre as he pointed out the Relatives Room, where Sharon Evans was. Joel hesitated for just a moment on the threshold, the cold metal of the handle pressed into his palm. He could barely imagine the misery on the other side of this door.

Sharon Evans was alone. Despite the chairs lining the wall on the right side she sat on the floor, her back to the far wall so she was facing them as they entered. The door shut behind them. Sharon didn't react to the noise. She was sitting still, her knees pulled up so she could hug them, her eyes down so all Joel could see was the top of her head.

'Sharon. It's Joel Norris. I got here as quick as I could,' he said, and paused for a response. When nothing came, he spoke again: 'I went to your house first. Every available officer, uniform, plain-clothed, PCSO, even the civilian investigators, they're all out looking. We've put appeals out locally, direct to the people. Neighbourhood Watch groups are turning out on foot, I'm sure we will—'

'She's dead because of me.' Sharon lifted her head to reveal eyes obscured by her swollen cheeks. Her forehead had a red mark where it had been resting against her forearm.

Joel cleared his throat. 'This isn't your fault.'

'This is all because of me. I swapped those folders and a little girl died. I didn't take those threats seriously and my little boy . . . he's gone.' She fixed on Joel, her desperation clear. 'He's dead, isn't he? Someone came here to hurt my Callie and they came to my home to hurt my boy. I was right there!'

'Tell me what happened, Sharon.'

336

Sharon was shaking her head now, words tumbling from her with the movement. Joel and DS Rose had to step closer to be able to hear.

'The calls. I told you about the calls. Just after Danny . . . How he said we were "one down".'

'You told me about that one. Were there others?'

'No!' Sharon tutted, frustrated at herself, like she couldn't organise her thoughts to be clear. 'Before. I got calls before, I told you about them. Then there was the one that made me talk to you. Then the post came this morning and . . . it was everything all at once. I couldn't find Jamie and I thought that Callie was . . .' She broke off as emotion swept over her. Joel waited. 'I thought she was dead. I've had a bad feeling since that call, I've been trying to tell myself that it was nothing, just some sicko trying to get a reaction. We get it a lot, this family I mean, the same reaction to whatever bullshit social media has on us this week. But this time I just knew it was different. Last night . . . Callie has a folder that hooks on the end of her bed here. It's got her name on it and it's supposed to be all her notes. I complained. I was coming in every day and looking at it. The nurses are supposed to check on her at regular times, all through the night, and then write observations, how she looks, how she's doing, all her temperatures and fluids. I know it's not for me but I like to come in and see she's had a good night, to know that people are checking in on her. But they've been putting it all on a computer instead . . .'

'Callie's okay?' DS Rose spoke now, her voice just as hushed.

'Last night . . . I was here late,' Sharon continued. 'We got a call to say she was more awake so me and Jamie rushed here and it was true!' Sharon took another moment, fighting to continue talking. 'She was sat up and looking at me, trying to talk, asking for my help to get a drink. It was so wonderful!' Her smile was just a flicker. 'Then it was time to leave and I didn't want to. All this time waiting and then she was suddenly

337

looking right at me . . . She could even smile!' Sharon's puffy right eye suddenly spat a tear. 'But I had a bad feeling, I've had it a while but last night . . . it was so strong. I couldn't explain it, not to anyone here or to you, you would just think I was going crazy, but I had to do something. We're getting her back, my little girl . . . It was all I could think of. I swapped the folders. It was late and I was looking back at her and I saw this folder with her name written on it. When it gets out she's awake again she'll be back in the news, people will be interested. And I just want her left alone. I never really thought . . .' She broke into sobs again.

'What happened today, Sharon?' Joel said.

'That letter came this morning and I just felt so stupid. I haven't done *anything* to make my kids safer. I mean, that's a picture of us all, for Christ's sake, whoever sent that knows what she looks like. They know where we live too and they . . . I couldn't find Jamie. What do you do? Stay there, come here . . . I didn't know. I've never felt so alone. So desperate!' The tear this time was quickly followed by another.

'It's OK. Take your time.'

'The police turned up and people were out looking straight-away. They said I needed to be at home in case he came back but I couldn't stay there. The police brought me here and . . . the other girl . . . she has epilepsy . . . they do look similar. We said that, me and her mother . . . her poor mother!' Sharon had to surrender to her sobs again, and Joel sat patiently.

'What happened to the girl?'

'Her mother was screaming. She must have been just behind us when we got here. She might even have seen us running up here and wondered what the hell was going on. We got to the ward and one of the doctors was shouting at everyone, he wanted to know what the nurses had injected her with. They didn't know what he was talking about. He kept shouting that she had been injected with something, there was blood on her arm, a fresh bunch of flowers between her legs and

338

she was . . . she was gone. The doctor picked up the folder where all her observations were . . . It was Callie's folder! He was so angry. I just stood back and watched it all play out. I couldn't do anything, I couldn't even speak. That poor woman, her mother, she just collapsed in front of me. I couldn't even help her. I'm a monster!'

'It's OK, Sharon. You—'

'It's not OK! I didn't tell you everything. I didn't tell you, I didn't tell Danny either, and look what's happened. Look what's happened to my family!'

'What have you not told me, Sharon?'

'Find my Jamie . . . please!' Sharon had been lost, her eyes down and opaque. Now they met Joel's and the look of a beaten woman was starting to evaporate.

'We're doing all we can. If there's something I need to know that helps us find him, Sharon . . .'

She was back to shaking her head, and it seemed to force out more words. 'Callie. She was the first, OK . . . All her friends, she was the one who introduced them to that man. She didn't know what she was doing! He . . . he gave her things. A new phone, iPad. She went on a shopping trip for clothes with vouchers but it wasn't for nothing. She had to introduce this man into the lives of her friends, as an exchange. She didn't know what for at first, she didn't know what he was going to do!'

Joel was suddenly aware that they were both looming over her. He moved to one of the seats off to the right, the plastic squeaking under him. 'And you knew about this?'

'Not straightaway and when she did come to me it was too late. But she couldn't live with it. I know that's why she did what she did. She was hurting so bad and there was nothing I could do to make her feel any better. Then one of the mums called the police, Julia Kerner, she found out what was happening to her daughter and suddenly it was ten times worse. The pressure on my Callie. It was me, Inspector Norris. I told her not

339

to talk to the police, not to tell them her part. It was two weeks after Julia called that she went to that park bench . . .'

'What about her dad?'

'Danny? We couldn't tell Danny! She wanted to at first but I made her promise not to. I was just trying to limit the damage this was doing, to all of us. But look at us now . . . This is all my fault.'

'Did Callie know who it was? Did she ever give you a name?'

'No. That was why I didn't think there was any point telling you everything. I didn't want her getting into trouble. She was tricked, just like I told you lot, that's still true. She thought she was talking to some boy at first, a boy her age who was being friendly. But she was being groomed. She sent off some photos, a silly little girl who just wanted a boy to like her. But it wasn't a boy at all. If the others knew that she was the one who had shared the girls' details, if they knew she had introduced him, that she was the start of it all, it would be the end for her. She would be hounded.'

Joel took a moment to try and organise his thoughts. 'But the other girls must know, if she introduced them to someone who blackmailed them. How can you keep that secret?'

Sharon shifted now, finally struggling upright. Joel and DS Rose stayed seated as she paced to the door and for a moment Joel thought she was going to leave. Instead she stood facing it, gazing out of the slit of a window as she spoke again. 'It's not so simple. Whoever this man was, he's clever. He uses a few social media accounts. In one of them he was posing as a teenage girl – that was the account that Callie pushed. She had no choice. She knew it wasn't really a teenage girl by then but she still gave it her endorsement so the other girls linked with this account too. She had to. Then he would involve other accounts in their conversations . . . I don't even think Callie was sure what was real and what wasn't by the end.'

'And he used one of those accounts to blackmail them?'

340

'It took DC Ribbons a while to confirm that all of the girls were even being blackmailed by the same person. She said it was only the fact that the language was so similar that let her connect them all. Who knows how many accounts he has in total. Callie encouraged them to be friends with him, and she shared some information directly with him too, some stuff about the other girls, so he would know enough to be convincing, enough that he could pretend they had stuff in common. He even pretended to know gossip about boys they all knew and talked about. That came from Callie. But you have to believe me when I say that she didn't know he was going to do what he did . . . It all sounds so ridiculous now!'

'It doesn't. Not at all. I know this sort of thing goes on. These men, they're very clever with what they do and they'll go to any length to get what they want. If it hadn't been Callie it would have been someone else.'

'But it wasn't, was it?' Sharon spun back to face into the room. 'It was Callie, she was targeted because of who she is, because she's popular, because of who we are. I've been ignoring it, trying to get on with my life, but I should have talked to you earlier. Someone knows, don't they? That's what this is all about. Danny was talking about a private investigator, he said someone else hired him. I thought he was lying, but he wasn't, was he? Someone found out what Callie did, that's what this is all about. She didn't have a choice, inspector. He was blackmailing her too, right from the start. And it was me telling her not to talk about it and now I'm being punished. That photo –' she took a moment, fighting to keep herself together '– it's everything I love crossed out, Inspector!'

'Is there anything else, Sharon? We need to find your son, we need to keep you and Callie safe. Is there anything else you haven't told us?'

'No!' The tears fell thicker and faster now. 'Do you think I would keep something to myself now? After all that's happened? You need to find him, please find my Jamie!' Her

341

voice was back to a wail now, similar to how she had sounded on the phone.

Joel got to his feet. 'We'll do everything we can,' he said, as Sharon continued to fall apart in front of him.

'Please . . . please don't tell people what Callie did. They won't understand!'

'I think we're at that point now, Sharon. You're not going to be able to keep that secret anymore.'

'She didn't know what she was doing. She didn't mean for anyone to get hurt like they did. I can't tell you how much she struggled with what she did to her friends. When DC Ribbons came round to speak to us, that was when she realised what had happened to them all and she couldn't live with herself. It's been so long, I'm just getting her back . . . Please!'

Joel stepped closer and took her by the shoulders. 'This is going to come out. You can't keep this secret. The girls and their families deserve to know what happened, but we will tell them that you're helping us now. We've arrested someone today. Maybe that will take some of the attention off what you did. But Callie's part will come out in full. You need to be ready for that.'

'Ready . . .' Sharon looked exhausted. 'Ready to defend my daughter, you mean? How can I defend anyone now . . .? I just killed a girl.'

342

Chapter 55

Joel pressed the cup to his mouth and sucked the hot drink on autopilot, his gaze on the material laid out in front of him. He'd forgotten about the foul-tasting coffee dispensed by machines in police stations and it seemed Dover was no different.

'We need to get the coffee situation resolved,' he muttered, even as he forced the liquid down and went back for another sip.

'Add it to the list,' DS Rose replied. They had found a makeshift office in the depths of Dover Police Station that had the feeling of a meeting room and claimed it by spreading out material from Hannah Ribbons's casefile. Both their police radios were on. The patrol sergeant was still leading the search for Jamie Evans from the Evans's home address and one of the radios was monitoring its progress. The other radio was on the local channel in case anything significant was reported on there. Joel had laid out the case material in six rows, one for each of the families known to be victims of blackmail. Five of the six rows stretched out to fill the desks, stuffed with witness statements, phone downloads and seizures. After what Sharon had told them, he was more certain than ever that the answers were contained somewhere in this material.

343

The noise and confusion in the office were increased by the shrill ring of a mobile phone.

'Ma'am,' Joel said in answer. He had been expecting Superintendent Marsden to call; he was only surprised it had taken so long.

'Joel, a fine mess we have down there, I see.'

'It seems to be getting messier all the time,' Joel said.

'Then you may be relieved to hear that we're sending reinforcements.'

'Anyone you can spare. The FRU are already directing anyone they can this way for the search.'

'For the search, yes. The reinforcements are for you personally.'

'For me?'

'Yes. This is getting bigger all the time. Major Crime have agreed to assist. The DCI will be heading to Dover nick for an RV and a full briefing. He'll have troops in tow, they'll want to hit the ground running.'

'Major Crime? To lead the search, you mean?' That was a Major Crime function – a missing person with suspected foul play. But there was something in Marsden's tone.

'The search is under control. The sergeant down there is very experienced. The DCI is for more of a general overview.'

'General overview? That sounds more like a handover than a briefing?'

'It does, doesn't it . . . Is that such a bad thing, Joel? For your first job this is hardly fair now, is it? We have another scene at the hospital – a child no less. And now a twelve-year-old boy missing . . . I think we need to be seen to be doing what we can.'

'I am doing what I can.'

'I know that. The organisation, Joel, we need to be seen to be doing what *we* can. And that means a Major Crime DCI who might have led the way on something like this before. You'll still be key, he'll need to know everything you do and you'll be by his side going forward, but . . .'

'But you don't know that. And my lack of experience was okay all the while the victim was some piece of shit signing on the sex offenders' register. Now it's someone we care about I'm not good enough?'

The superintendent huffed. 'Come on, Joel, I know you want to find the boy as much as anyone does. And whoever is leading this trail of destruction too. No one's saying you're not doing a great job . . .'

'Then let me carry on doing it.'

'You are. Just with some help. Get yourself back to Dover Police Station and be ready to hand over. The DCI is coming from Chatham but he's already on his way. He may call ahead. You need to be ready, Joel, you need to show him what we've been doing down there. Get this done, then we can regroup, get you a team and a decent place to work from, and we're better prepared when the next job comes in. This is my fault, this was my mistake.'

'I was?'

'Don't be so precious. You know what I mean.' The tone change was instant. 'I'm getting another call. It will be about all this. You know what to do.'

When Joel dropped the phone, DS Rose looked expectant. Joel broke away from her to walk over to the window.

'Major Crime have made their point, have they?' DS Rose said. Joel stared out over an elevated view of the River Dour that ran alongside the station. On the other side of the river a concrete car park butted up against the historic old town gaol, with its tiny leaded windows in the basement that hinted at where the cells once were. Suddenly he found himself yearning for simpler times.

'Politics. All my career I've done all I can to avoid it. It gets in the way,' he said.

'I agree.'

'So we do that now. Here and now.'

'We do?' DS Rose didn't sound so sure.

345

'We don't have time for briefings, handovers or point-scoring among departments. We know enough, it's all in here.' Joel gestured at the mess of papers laid out on the desks. 'The Evans family, they've upset people, put their kids in danger . . . So who wants them hurt?'

'You just answered your own question there, surely? All the families have a reason.'

'OK, so who's most likely? We've got PNC prints for all of the parents and a few other extended family members that showed up as associated on the system. And what do we know from that?'

'None of them have any real history with the police. No convictions. A couple of domestic calls to one couple a few years back but not a single arrest among them. There's nothing in there that tells us where we should be looking.'

'I agree. So what we know doesn't help, but what don't we know?'

'Are you speaking in riddles to piss me off?' DS Rose crossed her arms.

Joel returned to gesture at the table. 'They all engaged. They all did everything they could to help Hannah Ribbons catch the bastard that groomed their daughters, of course they did. Yes, some got disenchanted a few weeks in, but they all gave statements, they all sat down with Hannah . . . Except?'

'The Luckhursts,' DS Rose said, her arms falling back to her side.

'More specific than that: Nicholas Luckhurst.'

'OK. His wife said he doesn't like the police. That's hardly unusual. I'm surprised he's the only one from the five families that gave us a pill, to be honest.'

'She did. She's terrified of him. There was something there, something I can't shake loose. She wanted to tell us something, she fought with herself not to.'

'About her husband. That's the impression I had. I think she's been the victim of abuse for a while at his hands and

346

she's building up to making those allegations. Hannah was building her trust. We've all seen cases like that before.'

'Marilyn Luckhurst is the person who knows Nicholas best. She's someone he supposedly loves. Why is she so scared of him? Maybe she knows what he's capable of.'

'Murder?' DS Rose said.

'If we had the time we would go and see them all again, every one of these families, and we would find out as much as we could. Everything there is to know about the lot of them. But we don't have that time, all we have is what's in front of us. Who would you focus on, where are the gaps?' Joel gestured again at the busy desks. He was winding himself up now.

DS Rose looked a lot more enthused. 'OK, so it has to be Nicholas Luckhurst. But there's nothing on the police systems, and his wife didn't want to talk about him – she doesn't want us back there at all. I don't think she'll talk if we just turn up.'

'I don't think we have any choice.'

'Aren't you supposed to be giving a briefing?'

'To the DCI. Marsden told me to meet him at Dover Police Station.'

'And you didn't tell her we're already here.'

'I didn't. And by the time he gets here I have every intention of being somewhere else. We need something more, we need something to go back there for . . .' Joel spun to the table where he had put Hannah Ribbons's day book. He had marked the three entries that covered her meetings with Marilyn Luckhurst, using Post-It notes. He turned to the first of them now, his eyes skimming over the scratchy writing. There were still parts he could barely decipher. The notes were detailed, and the first meeting had started with the standardised 'DASH questions' completed. This was the framework for determining risk used by all police officers discussing domestic violence. There were 25 questions, many of them yes/no

347

answers. Hannah had written out numbers 1–25 in the margin with an answer next to each of them. His eyes ran down the row of yes/no responses and stopped on question 17. Hannah had written: 'Yes. Selemo.'

'Selemo?' Joel muttered.

'What?'

'Have you got your DASH card?' Joel referenced an aide-memoire with all the required questions that was issued to every frontline officer. It was laminated and stiff, perfect for a TSG Team trying to open a locked door quietly. Joel had used his one too many times, however, and binned it as a tattered mess a long time before.

'Back of my book,' DS Rose said.

'What's question seventeen?'

DS Rose flicked her daybook to the back cover and read from her card. 'Is the partner in employment?'

'Employment . . . Employment!' Joel suddenly raced back over the notes, flicking to all three meetings. 'There's nothing here about that, we don't know what he does. Selemo . . . That's Hannah's writing. She must mean self-employed, it's shorthand, I can see it now. But doing what?'

'Hang on.' DS Rose disturbed a terminal and opened a web browser. 'Companies House. We can run a search. If he's self-employed he could be registered.'

'Surely Hannah did that?' Joel was still skimming the words.

'She might, doesn't mean she wrote down what she found.'

Joel wasn't convinced. Judging by her notes, Hannah wrote just about everything down. 'Read out his details,' DS Rose said, then typed them in as he did. Joel moved to stand behind her.

'There!' he said. A list of Luckhursts had come up, and Joel recognised one. Records gave the address the Luckhurst family had moved from recently, and showed Nathan William Luckhurst as registering a business there. The only other information was the sector it was concerned in. 'Finance,' Joel read

348

out. DS Rose clicked on the record. More details appeared. Joel skimmed them. DS Rose was a second ahead of Joel with her reaction, she got to her feet. Then he saw it too.

'He's registered in Fraud and Liability Detection,' Joel said.

DS Rose scooped up the car keys. 'He is.' She said. 'Nathan Luckhurst is a private investigator.'

349

Chapter 56

The traffic going back through Dover was so heavy that it brought them to a standstill. Joel had turned his phone right down and his police radio right up. They were continuing to monitor the search for Jamie Evans. It was still local, but the updates that had been energetic and hopeful at first were now flat and routine. Another patrol checking off another road of garden searches and door knocks: *Negative*.

Of course it was. These were the actions that would find someone suspected to have wandered off, like a confused and elderly person in their slippers at 3 a.m. But this was a young boy who had been abducted, a boy to whom real harm was intended, who might already be out of time.

Joel pressed his horn. The only reaction was a hand thrown up in the car in front and DS Rose spinning round to him like he had poked her in the side.

'What are you doing that for?'

Joel didn't reply. It was a reasonable question. The cause of the blockage ahead was plain: a large flatbed lorry was trying to manoeuvre through a gap on the left side of the road, its back laden with building materials and a crane to unload them with. Men in high-visibility clothing were making a hash of letting traffic through the thin gap that was left. It was all for the creation of new housing and he could see a sign giving the project a name and a strapline: *The Old Mill – A New Development. For the people of Dover.*

Finally they started moving. A break in the high wall on the left side revealed an open gate, through which the flatbed was still reversing, and Joel got a snapshot of a mini-digger bouncing from right to left across a row of brand-new houses. The next landmark to pass his window was a petrol station, which he knew signalled the start of Crabble Hill – and Marilyn Luckhurst's address.

'I still say we should call it in,' DS Rose said. 'This could be everything.'

'It could be nothing. We're just going to ask a question and if we call it in we'll have to say where we are. Then some DCI will order us back, only to send someone else out to make the same enquiry. And more time gets wasted.'

'What if he's there? Nicholas, I mean?'

'Then we get to ask him personally,' Joel said.

This time there was no immediate answer from an out-of-breath occupant as Joel beat on the door. This time there was no response at all. He stepped back to take in the frontage. He didn't think the roughly pulled curtains at the windows had moved since his last visit.

'I'll try the landline again,' DS Rose said and lifted her phone. There was no mobile phone number for Marilyn – Hannah's notes had specifically stated that her husband hadn't allowed her to have one. Joel moved so he was close to the living-room bay window. The curtain was bundled up at the bottom where someone had got the drop wrong. He could hear the house phone ringing. He gestured at DS Rose, using his finger along his neck for her to cut the call. She did as she was told. He moved back to her to whisper instructions.

'Walk back to the car. Make sure you close the gate hard.' Joel returned to the living-room window, but this time he stood

351

to one side, his back pressed against the brick of the house while he stared intently at the curtain, ready for the faintest movement. DS Rose did her part. The gate slammed. She even threw her hands in the air and stomped out of sight towards where they had parked the car a little further down the road. Joel stayed as still as he could, the dull roar of traffic constant in front of him, the window almost against his left shoulder.

Thirty seconds passed before the curtain moved. Joel's reaction was instant: he spun and slapped the glass right where he had seen the flash of scraggly dark hair with spreading grey. The curtains fell back instantly but it didn't matter, now she knew he wasn't going away.

His hammering on the door reinforced that. When DS Rose jogged back Joel was on his knees, his lips touching the bristles of the letterbox as he bellowed through.

'POLICE! I KNOW YOU'RE IN THERE! WE JUST NEED TO TALK TO YOU!' He got up again to commence another assault on the door. He didn't need to. It opened a familiar sliver.

'You can't be here!' Marilyn Luckhurst hissed out at them.

'We need to speak to you, please.'

'He'll know! He talks to the neighbours, you can't be here shouting like that.'

'Then let us in.'

'I can't, not again. You need to leave me alone . . . please.'

'Or what? What happens if Nicholas knows the police were here? What are you so scared of?'

'Please. This can't happen. You don't understand.'

'Then make me understand. Tell me why we can't come here.'

Marilyn wore her shocked expression like a mask. There was no movement, not for a few seconds. Then she said, 'Please don't come here again.' And the door was pushed shut. Joel was ready for it, and stuck his foot out for the door to bounce off it.

'When we were here last, you said that your husband loved you and your family. Then you said, "Our children are

352

innocent." What did you mean by that?' Marilyn stared down at his foot. Her slim fingers still gripped the door and she was still half a step behind it, using it to hide behind. She didn't reply so Joel continued. 'It seemed odd at the time but I couldn't think why. You weren't just talking about Emma, were you? You were talking about other children too. The Evans children perhaps?'

She was back looking at him now, just one eye visible, but it was enough for Joel to see the unease.

'I fear for the safety of all children, for all those other girls but—'

'A fourteen-year-old girl is dead.' Joel leaned forward, his foot squeaking against the bottom of the door. There was still no give. The one eye that was visible still fixed on him. 'It should have been Callie Evans but someone made a mistake and the poor girl lying next to her in hospital got it instead. Think about that for a moment. An innocent little girl, wrong place wrong time, attacked in her hospital bed. That could have been anyone. That could have been Emma.'

Marilyn's nostrils flared with a breath, the only outward sign of a reaction.

'Callie's dad is dead too, shot dead just a few days after he met with a private investigator in a hotel not far from here. Your husband registered his own company at your previous address. What is it he does?'

'He doesn't . . . he doesn't work so much anymore . . .' she muttered, then trapped her bottom lip in her teeth like she shouldn't say another word.

'And when he did?'

'He worked on fraud detection, people stealing from their own firms, that sort of thing . . .'

'He's a private investigator, Marilyn, isn't he?'

'I . . . No, he works—'

'He may call it something different when it suits him, but that's his background. Is he here?'

353

'No!'

'Where is he?'

'I . . . I don't know.'

'An innocent child is dead. Danny Evans is dead. Jamie Evans is missing and his mother is beside herself. A whole family decimated, Marilyn. You've had your own disasters, your own challenges as a family, if you know something that can help us . . . Put yourself in Sharon's shoes for just a moment. If it was Emma that was missing . . .'

'I . . . Lots of colour . . . on the ward, it's bright and she has her teddy now. Just like when she was a child. Emma's safe.' Marilyn's eyes slammed shut, the grip tightened and Joel felt the pressure increase on his foot. He was losing her, she was shutting them out. She was shutting everything out.

Joel felt a soft touch on his hip and he half-turned as DS Rose stepped in next to him. She was gentle as she covered Marilyn's fingers. Joel stepped back, his shoe squeaking again as he pulled it out of the gap. When DS Rose spoke, it was still to a woman with her eyes tightly shut while she repeated the same words about Emma's secure ward in a terrified murmur.

'Hannah was my friend. She was fearless and she was fierce when she needed to be. But she had a heart so big it was always going to be what brought her down. She cared about you, about Emma, obsessed over it even, and she is the reason we are here. You can't help Hannah now, I can't either, and that eats me up inside, but I can find answers and I think you can help me with that. Why is our friend dead, Marilyn? Because I think that's eating you up too.'

Marilyn's lips stopped first. Then her eyes opened to focus, her eyelids fluttering like a settling butterfly. A couple of times she looked like she was ready to speak but stopped herself. DS Rose was patient. Marilyn took a final look beyond her doorstep and out into the steady din of traffic behind them. She cleared her throat before croaking a single word.

'Inside.'

Chapter 57

The same shadow swallowed Marilyn Luckhurst up as she turned and hurried away. The same darkened living room greeted the two officers, the same floorboards squeaked their disdain as she took up her pacing. This time Joel hung back to stand in the doorway while his colleague stepped into the room. And waited. The silence in that small, sparse space grew until it must have felt like it was pushing out at the sides, threatening to crush Marilyn with its pressure. She looked even more fragile today, thinner somehow, her pacing that of someone approaching a finishing line and ready to fall the moment they passed. Joel was feeling the pressure too. Anxiety gnawed at him – they were running out of time. He covered his mouth with his hand to stop barking out demands for answers. DS Rose would surely be just as desperate but he felt he could trust her. She knew what she was doing.

DS Rose finally spoke. She had perched on an arm of the sofa.

'From the beginning' was all she said and Marilyn stopped her pacing just long enough to throw her a look. She crossed the room twice more before she replied.

'Our children . . . St Peter and St Paul's . . . That's my church. I go there a lot. We talk about the children, they're all *our children*. That's what I meant but that doesn't mean you were wrong. The church is where I met Angela Maddox . . .' She halted again for more eye contact, like this name should mean something to the two officers. It didn't. Not instantly. Joel had done his best to read and memorise the key points from Hannah's casefile, and he was good with names, but he was certain that was a new one.

'I don't think I've met Angela,' DS Rose said.

'You won't either. Angela was knocked down. By a car, a year ago now. She was a lovely woman. It was very sad. It was so sad . . .'

'She was your friend?' DS Rose said and Joel shifted his stance, his desperation to speed things up threatening to burst out of him.

'Church was the only place I could ever go without Nicholas, the only place he would let me go on my own. I used to take Emma when she was younger but she's not interested anymore. Angela was always nice, always just . . . happy. Great with Emma! And then she was just gone. It was in the papers, a joy-rider knocked her down when she was out walking her dog. The world is so terrifying.'

'It can be. Marilyn, I talked about Hannah, about finding the missing Evans boy, does that have anything to do with Angela?'

'Angela . . . yes! Nicholas . . . I told him all about her, how she died, when she died how it made me feel sad . . .' She faded out again. Joel was just about to butt in, to let his frustration take over, when she suddenly straightened and her fragility gave way to something like anger. 'He used every word against me. Just like he always does,' she said. 'Hannah told me that's what controlling people do – they take your words and they use them for themselves. He told me that Danny Evans was driving that car, that Danny Evans had run my friend down. But I looked him up. For once in my life I didn't just take him at his word, I didn't just believe what he

356

told me. Danny Evans played football. He was playing football the night Angela was run down. The internet had a newspaper article. It couldn't have been him. I'm not allowed on the internet but I have a mobile phone that Nicholas doesn't know about.' She tutted again. 'I need to show you something. Upstairs.'

Joel stepped out of the doorway for Marilyn to lead the way. DS Rose was next. The wooden stairs resonated loudly with no carpet to deaden the noise. Marilyn pushed into the first room at the top of the stairs. It was a boxroom, barely big enough for them all to stand in, and made smaller still by numerous boxes stacked against the walls, the same type as Joel had seen downstairs. There was a camp bed too. It was against the wall on the right side. A sleeping bag was laid out on top like it was made up to be used. A coffee cup next to it had an inch of brown liquid at the bottom that had developed a skin. Beside it was a carrier bag, the backs of a pair of shoes visible inside.

'He's been staying here, Nicholas has,' Joel said.

'Yes. I don't like him coming here. I told him that, I finally told him that!' She looked delighted for a moment, then it dropped away. 'But he doesn't listen to me.' She selected a box stacked close to the door. Inside was a laptop that looked well used. It was black originally but the lid was covered in stickers of pink hearts and glittery fairies. 'This is Emma's. She had to have one for school but the internet is all disabled. I don't know how to work them, Nicholas did all that.' She lifted the lid and the noise of a fan was the first sign of life. It took another few seconds for the screen to light up and even then it was just a spinning icon. There was a slim desk pushed against the wall opposite the bed. A simple, fold-out metal chair was pushed under it. Marilyn put the laptop down on the desk to plunge her hand into her pocket. She lifted something out between her thumb and finger like it was the most precious diamond the world had ever seen.

357

'The boxes, it wasn't for me to move away, it was for us. That was what Nicholas said. He said when this was all finished we would move away and be a family again. I can't do that, I won't do that!' That muttering, terrified fragility of Marilyn Luckhurst was still falling away and steel was revealed behind it. The item in her hand was a pen drive. Marilyn pushed it into the side of the laptop. 'This is what I was going to give to Hannah. This was going to set us free from him.'

Chapter 58

Richard Maddox just needed to take a moment to sit in the stillness. He was in the driver's seat, and the dust he had disturbed drifted over the bonnet, catching in the last of the sunlight. It was only just peeking above the houses that were across the clearing in front of him. Soon it would be dark. And that might give him a whole new problem. He took a few deep breaths before turning to peer into the back.

Jamie Evans was big for his age. Richard had used that to his advantage: the boy's larger size had made it a tighter fit in the footwell behind the passenger seat. The restraints were tied round both his wrists and pulled tight to the mounting of the seat itself to force the boy forward with his head between his splayed knees and against the seatback. This meant he was out of sight of anyone driving alongside him and, if he decided to shout for help, it would largely be absorbed by the thick seat material. It was a fine line between an effective restraint and restrictive to his breathing, but this wasn't the first time Richard had needed to transport a prisoner in a car with just a cut-up seatbelt to work with. It was the first time it had been a twelve-year-old boy, though.

The man had been very clear – this boy, or his grandson. He had been clear with his instructions; he knew the boy's movements, that he walked the dog every morning, and where. The man was still demonstrating his ability to plan, to control every element. But he had made a mistake sending Richard to get something he wanted. He had made a mistake giving him time to think. And now Richard might be able to take some of that control back.

His palm was slippery with moisture against the butt of the shotgun that was on the passenger seat. It was a beautiful piece too, with dark, polished wood seamlessly merging into dark grey steel like it was all milled from the same piece. It was a Browning, of course. Glenn had been sure to point that out when he had first taken it from where it was concealed in a locked case in his kitchen cupboard to show his old friend. Richard could still remember his feeling of surprise. Since leaving the army, Richard had shied away from firearms – he had seen enough of guns and more significantly what they could do. He couldn't understand why anyone would want to use one as part of their leisure time. As ever, Glenn had made a joke to explain himself: *Yeah, but what about all the clay pigeons just left alone to breed how they want? Someone's got to keep their numbers down or we'll be riddled with them!*

Then he'd laughed that big laugh with his head back and his belly shaking. And Richard had been as powerless as always to stop himself from joining in.

But now laughter was the furthest thing from his mind.

He pulled the weapon across his lap. The hunting knife he had used to abduct Jamie was still on the passenger seat. He considered taking it too, but it was overkill. It had served its purpose: the best way to take a man off the street with the least amount of fuss was to press a blade against the back of the neck and to make very clear what damage it will do if instructions are not followed instantly and quietly. Of course it worked on a child too.

But Richard was done with being quiet. He was done

360

with making the least amount of fuss, with being concerned about being seen walking the streets with a double-barrelled shotgun.

He was here to make a noise.

Chapter 59

The first image silenced the room, tightened the ball of anxiety in the pit of Joel's stomach and forced him to reach for the back of the chair to steady himself.

It was Marcus Olsen. He was alive. He was sitting in a chair, bare-chested, with his hands behind his back in a position that suggested they were tied. He was staring his terror right into the lens of the camera. The next image had Joel holding his breath.

The after picture.

But the job wasn't quite finished. The head was still attached. A jagged saw was slick with a layer of red and black and slightly blurred where it hung down in a loose grip. Marcus Olsen, though, was entirely in focus. He was still sitting up. A rope was looped around his head, the two ends bunched up in the other fist of a solidly built man who stood behind him, also bare-chested; the hair on his chest that wasn't covered in blood and gore was grey to match his beard and head hair. The rope was keeping the head up. The moment captured looked to be the man taking a break from sawing at the neck.

'Jesus fuck!' Joel said.

'I'm sorry, I should have warned you. I should have said

that this is not pleasant. But I wanted to show you, I wanted you to know.'

'That is Nicholas? The man holding the saw is your husband?' Joel already knew the answer.

'Yes. But the man with him abuses children.' That steel in her seemed to be here to stay. The two police officers had both taken a step back but Marilyn had stayed straight-backed in her chair. Joel reflected that this wasn't the first time she had seen this image. She closed it to bring up the next.

It was Danny Evans.

Again there was a before and after. The before picture showed him restrained by any number of ropes. They held him tight while a half-pipe was taped to jut out of his fist and into his mouth to give Joel his answer as to why Danny Evans had been shot in the face. Another click of the mouse and more questions were quickly answered.

This time it was video footage that filled the screen. It looked like it was from a CCTV camera. Colour but grainy. Good enough. A different man again appeared on the left side. He looked older than Nicholas, scrawnier for sure. Danny was restrained on the right of the screen. The scrawny man walked from left to right, checked something he was holding in his hands then almost got onto the man's lap. Both the officers leaned away from the screen at the moment it flared white and Danny's head changed shape. Marilyn remained straight-backed and unflinching.

'That is Richard Maddox.' She stood up, her long finger still pointing at the man who had pulled the trigger. Then she backed away, again turning her attention to the boxes. She selected one, discarding the lid to bring out a black A4 folder. 'This is what Richard Maddox was given. This contains all the details about how Danny Evans ran his wife down.'

Joel took it from her. The first page was a real attention grabber:

'It is all a lie,' Marilyn continued. 'He made it all on this computer. I saw them. Richard was angry about his wife, angry that the police never got anyone for it. That was in the paper too.'

'Where is his computer?'

'He will have it with him. He always has it with him. I had to copy them when he was here. In the shower, or asleep. He wasn't careful, he would never think for one minute . . .' She clamped her mouth shut, her nose twitching her defiance. 'It was why I agreed to let him stay. I said he had to stay in here. He always left it on the floor under his bed . . . I didn't even feel scared. I knew that I had to give this to Hannah and then he would be gone for ever. And if I didn't, if he caught me, he would kill me too and this would all be over. But I didn't know . . . I didn't know it was already too late, that Hannah was . . .' The steel slipped and for a moment Joel thought she was about to be overwhelmed with emotion. Instead she snapped back straight. 'You have to promise me. You have to give me your word too, just like she did. He cannot come back here. Not ever.'

'Where is he, Marilyn?' Joel said.

Marilyn continued like she hadn't heard the question. 'I didn't know about the children either. What he was going to do to Callie. I know how angry he was but you have to believe me! There are other things in the box, another folder for Danny Evans, more lies. But this time . . . These are the lies that killed Hannah.'

'Where is he, Marilyn?' Joel said again.

'He can never come back here. Emma is where she is because of him . . . but he will kill me.'

'Tell us where he is.'

'Promise me.'

'You have my word. Your husband never comes back here. Please, Marilyn, where is he?'

'Close. He knew you were here looking for him. He came back to change his shoes. He said he didn't want to get them messed up. I asked him what he meant and he wouldn't answer.' She gestured at the carrier bag under the bed. 'He says they're all he has left of our Emma. He talks about her a lot like that, like she's dead. He hasn't visited her once. She bought him some shoes, before she got ill. Before any of this. I don't think he's taken them off since.'

Joel paced over to them, sliding them out to get a better look. He spun to show DS Rose the tan brown leather with a contrasting blue streak over the top.

'I recognise these,' Joel said.

'The hotel,' DS Rose replied. 'How close? Please . . .' She spoke to Marilyn now, taking her hands in hers.

'There's a club. It's closed down, has been for a while. He hides there. I think he'll be there now. He can see the cars that come and go too.'

'He won't have seen ours.' Joel dropped the shoes back into the bag and scrunched up the handles. 'He won't know we're coming.'

365

Chapter 60

The shotgun was weighty but well balanced. Richard had grabbed a box of ammunition too, ripping the top of the box off for ease of access in his jacket pocket. Glenn's shotgun took two cartridges, which would be more than enough, but he liked to be over-prepared – another throwback from his army days. The gun broke in its middle to expose the breech where the cartridges had a snug fit. When snapped closed the weapon formed a sleek line with the two barrels arranged on top of each other. Richard was now making sure that both barrels pointed at Nicholas Luckhurst's chest. He'd caught him by surprise. But it hadn't stopped him talking.

'What do you think you can achieve here, Richard? If you were going to shoot me you would have done it already.' The man leered. He seemed calm, which stoked Richard's anger even more, enough to rob him of his ability to reply. He knew he needed to control his emotions, that his own rage could floor him if it got out of hand. He'd made his captive pull his own chair out into the middle of the room to sit on. Now Richard grabbed another and positioned it so the back was almost against the knees of his target. The gun was suddenly feeling heavier, his chest thumping harder. He was starting to feel dizzy. He needed to ease the pressure. He needed to be strong, to be in control. He used the back of the chair as a rest for the barrel. Now he didn't need to worry about fatigue.

'Answers,' Richard said. 'You owe me that.'

'Owe you?' Nicholas grinned.

'Answers. You lied to me. Danny Evans didn't kill my wife, did he?'

Nicholas smiled. *He fucking smiled!* Richard felt his finger tighten on the trigger as the man changed his seating position, lifting his right leg to rest it over his left like he was sitting outside some Parisian coffee shop. Richard wanted to take that smiling head right off but he needed to wait. He wanted answers first. Nicholas parted his hands, which had been gripping his knee, and gave a sort of shrug. 'So, you got me. Very impressive, how did you work that one out?'

'When you forced me to abduct a boy off the street I needed tools. I don't have weapons at my house, I don't have the need for them anymore, but I knew Glenn did. I went round to his house. What do you think I found?'

Nicholas still held his smile as he shrugged again. 'Glenn's still where I left him,' Richard continued. 'Still sitting in his chair, still watching the footage of his best friend murdering Danny Evans. And the knife you used to murder him was there too. The one with the pearl handle that you forced me to hold. It was lying on top when I opened the bin. You're fitting me up. Danny Evans has nothing to do with me. You wanted him, you wanted his whole family, but you needed to make sure there was someone else in the frame. That someone else was me. And today I was supposed to take the Evans lad to my house. Why might that be? You were going to blame me for him too, weren't you?'

'I have your laptop too,' Nicholas said, resting his hands on his shin that was lying across his lap. 'It shows a lot of interesting internet searches and saved documents. Seems you've been very interested in the Evans family, but you're

367

also very interested in the layout of William Harvey Hospital too. And your car's pretty reasonable as a rental, did you know that? I took the same make and model out for a spin. I hope you don't mind that I used your plates to go through the ANPR barrier around the time Callie Evans was callously attacked in her hospital bed. I didn't pay either. You might be getting an angry letter about that.'

Richard felt a surge of anger and the underside of the shotgun scraped the chairback as he thrust it forward. He knelt on the seat of the chair and leaned right in, his teeth gritted. The ends of the barrels were finished in a polished metal that contrasted with the dark grey. The polished part now pushed into the man's lips.

'You don't know who killed my wife and you don't care!' Richard growled.

The man's right foot dropped to the ground. 'You're right. I just needed some stupid old fool to do my dirty work. You fitted the bill rather well, Richard.'

'Stupid old fool? Is that right?' Richard spat. He could feel his chest thumping, his vision blurring slightly with every beat. 'But who's on the wrong end of a shotgun now? You underestimated me, just like everyone else did. Open your *fucking* mouth!' Richard jabbed the shotgun firmer into the man's cheekbone. It was all he could manage, all his breath seemed to leave his lungs with it and he had to fight to take a big lungful back in. He needed to be calmer. The man's face flashed a grimace of pain. He turned his head for Richard to push the barrel against his lips. 'I said—'

'There's still a way out of this, for all us.' Nicholas cut him off, his words now hurried. 'You killed a man already. Kill me and you'll never see the outside of a prison cell. You'll never see your grandson again!' Richard pushed the barrel further forward, enjoying the change in the man. Nicholas's head was forced back, the barrel now resting under his nose.

'You told me the only way out was to kidnap the Evans

368

boy. Then you would leave my grandson alone. You were going to kill me too. At my home. No way you could leave me alive.'

'We can work this out still.'

'You don't have to open your mouth. It doesn't matter,' Richard hissed. 'I just thought it would be fitting. But this still works.' The man's eyes shifted to try and lock onto Richard, his lips parted like he was going to speak again. 'DON'T!' Richard's shout seemed to blur his vision more. His chest suddenly burned, like someone had thinned the oxygen in the room and he had to gasp to get enough to keep him upright. He shifted his feet to catch his balance, and as he did so his knee slid off the chair. He stumbled, his left hand reaching out for the seat of the chair. But suddenly it was whipped away and with it his last chance to stay upright.

He felt the shotgun snatched from his right hand, twisting him as he fell. The impact with the floor came an instant later through his right shoulder, then his side where the box of ammunition dug into his hip. He had dragged the chair over with him, and the clatter of its fall seemed to be all around him. His ear flashed with pain where it hit something firm, and the top layer of dust on the floor lifted to fill his nostrils and cling to the back of his throat. He moaned, still panting for breath. He couldn't see around him. He was only aware of someone pacing from the sound of footsteps on the wooden flooring. He felt a push against his chest, the force enough to roll him flat on his back, he flailed his arms but could do nothing to stop the box of ammunition from being dragged out of his pocket.

'You shouldn't have come here. You shouldn't have come for me. How did you find me?' The voice came to Richard out of a fog above him, where a dark shape was moving, pacing back and forth. The words were thick with venom.

Richard chuckled. It came from somewhere, the ridiculousness of the situation perhaps, all that had happened in the last few days and the hopelessness he now found himself in. 'You underestimated my old mate. You might have had me worked out, a silly old man blinded by my own anger, but you didn't reckon on Glenn. Always the soldier, that boy. He tagged you. A GPS Tracker on your car. Sent me an email with the details while you were still lying to me on that bench, when you were telling me that Glenn wouldn't matter, that it would be the last time I saw you.' Richard had regained enough strength to cough up what was lining his throat. He hacked it up and spat it onto the floor. His vision had returned enough that he could see his spit gleam in the weak light. Anything further away was still blurred at the edges. He could make out the shape of the man as he stopped pacing to stand over him. Richard raised himself off his painful ear to look up. The light now reflected off another surface close enough for him to see: the polished end of a shotgun barrel. He stared directly at it as he continued: 'That's how I found where your car was coming to and from. So I knocked on a few doors, yours eventually. But I wouldn't have known you were hiding out in here had I not got to speak to your wife. Do you know what she said to me? She made me promise to shoot you dead. What sort of a wife would say that, *Nicholas*?'

'You're lying!' The confidence seemed to slip for just a moment.

'I think you know I'm not. She hates you, no way you don't know it.'

'We'll see. You first, Richard, then we'll see just how much she hates me. I'll be sure to tell her you sent me.' The voice was still controlled but there was a rage that was increasing with every word.

Richard rolled a little more onto his back, shifting to stare straight up and fix on the ceiling. The clamour in his chest had gone. All that was left was a calmness and suddenly he wasn't staring at the ceiling, he was staring beyond it at a star-spotted sky, the way he'd done so many times in the last year when he had laid out, fixing on a distant light, convincing

370

himself it was Angela smiling down. She would be smiling now, he was sure of that. Because he was coming to join her.

Joel grabbed the large padlock on the main doors of the Phoenix Railway Club but there was no give. DS Rose appeared from where she had run round the left side of the building.

'Side entrance, insecure,' she hissed then turned back the way she'd come. Joel followed her. It was a short jog down the side of the building, following a path of flattened grass. DS Rose stopped at a door with a similar-looking padlock and sheets of wood screwed shut. He watched as she dropped to her knee and carefully pulled at a bottom piece that leaned against the door. When it came away the bottom panel of the UPVC door was missing, revealing a shadow behind. Joel pushed the carrier bag through first, then followed it on all fours. DS Rose came in behind him. They both stopped to take in their surroundings.

They had entered the kitchen. Here, the smell of cooking fat mingled with thick dust, and the lighting was poor where all the windows were boarded. Joel could see a short, dingy corridor that led into a large main function area. He could make out circular tables supporting upturned chairs. A shuttered bar was down the far end, lit by a bolt of sunshine where the boarding had been pulled from the window.

'Do it then! Come ON!' a shouted voice came from down the hall. Both officers reacted by squatting lower and holding their breath. There was a thud, then a sound that accompanied the chair skittering across Joel's view. The chair ended its journey with a loud crash, seemingly knocking others down. Joel felt a grip on his wrist: DS Rose pulling him back where he had started to move forwards. He turned to see her mouth a word he recognised instantly: *firearms*.

There was no time. DS Rose had updated their location as they had sprinted out the back of the Luckhurst house and Joel's phone had then burst into life to add another missed call to the growing list. If the Evans boy was still alive he was

371

in here, and with a man that they now knew was capable of extreme acts of violence.

Joel shook his head then pointed at the door they had just crawled through, willing DS Rose to go back outside. She didn't move and her stance made it clear she wasn't about to either. He turned back to the hall.

'NICHOLAS LUCKHURST,' Joel called, hoping there was authority in his raised voice. DS Rose backed away to the other side of the kitchen, stopping when she was pressed against stainless steel kitchen units. They faced each other, the entrance to the hall between them. Joel, on his hands and knees, leaned out as far as he dared. It wasn't far enough to see past the end of the hall. There was only silence now. 'Nicholas, I am Detective Inspector Joel Norris. I'm a firearms commander for Kent Police. I am armed and I have a team surrounding the building. There's no way out of here, you need to—'

'THE POLICE!' The voice that roared back sounded almost strangled, a furious shriek that echoed and roared – but it was nothing compared to the sound that followed: the sound of a fired shotgun.

Joel threw himself back against a solid cooker while DS Rose reacted by trying to make herself smaller. A second shot was quick to follow, then the sound of chunks of debris scattering over the floor. Joel froze, holding his breath, waiting for footfalls moving closer, for a gunman to erupt into the room. Instead he heard the distinctive sound of a barrel breaking open, of two spent shotgun cartridges ejecting to hit the floor while two new rounds dropped into a breech almost instantaneously. A snapping sound was confirmation of a shotgun readied to fire again. 'LOOK WHAT YOU DID! YOU BROUGHT THE POLICE HERE, LOOK WHAT YOU DID!' Another shot. This time the air between the two officers whistled and shots thudded into the back wall of the kitchen. An old pan spun then clanged to the ground.

Then came the sound of the gun breaking, more spent shells, new cartridges dropped then the gun snapping shut. Back up to its two-shot maximum. They didn't last long. Two more shots rang out. The hall ceiling threw its debris into the kitchen, the second shot causing a clock to leap from the wall. The sounds mingled into a blur, the low boom of the gunfire dominating, the damage all around them shrill in contrast. Glass seemed to be falling from everywhere.

Break, drop, snap! Another reload. Another two booms into the kitchen. DS Rose was wide-eyed, her hands over her head as she stared across at Joel. She was still trying to push herself backwards. More shrill glass.

Break, drop, snap! Now there were footsteps. Cautious. Moving closer. Joel reckoned they were at the beginning of the hall now. Glass crunched underfoot.

Boom! This was so close both officers jerked their hands to their ears. It would make no difference. The wooden board covering the top half of the door thudded with the impact, and a chunk of it fell away.

Break, drop, snap!

'I know what you've done! There's no walking away!' Joel called out, his mind rushing with alternatives, his ears whistling like they might be damaged, desperate to stop the onslaught. The footsteps stopped. Everything stopped. 'I know you did it for your daughter, because we couldn't get you answers.' Joel locked eyes with DS Rose, who was still bunched up against the steel units on the other side of the kitchen, her face a mask of terror.

'You didn't give a shit about my daughter. Grooming wasn't serious enough. You're here now though, aren't you? You caused this! You failed me, you failed her!'

Joel exchanged another glance with DS Rose. He rubbed a layer of filth from his face where falling dust had mingled with his sweat. He took a moment to think. 'I think I understand why but you can help me—'

373

This time the roar of the weapon was close enough for the flash from the muzzle to light up the kitchen. The floor between the two detectives erupted and Joel's ears popped then whistled. For a few seconds he was deaf completely. The second flash reflected in DS Rose's wide eyes and a metal cupboard twisted inwards to his left, now with a muffled thud. Joel's hearing came back all at once and was full of shouting. The same man's voice but now further away. Then came the sound of chairs scraping and scattering, something big upturned. Then another two shots that sounded different, fired into a bigger space. The silence that followed lasted just a few seconds.

Break, drop, snap! Then moaning. The sound of someone in pain.

'No one else needs to get hurt!' Joel bellowed, lifting himself back to his knees, the sound of someone in pain pushing him to do something – *but what*? He couldn't even move.

'Where are they?' the voice shouted back.

'Who, Nicholas? Where are who?'

'You're a firearms commander. I'm surrounded, you said. The whole town would have heard me. There's no one else here, is there?'

'They're waiting for my instruction.'

'Bullshit! Seems I'm not the only one telling lies to get what I want.'

'And what do you want?'

'Nothing from you! I had to do my *own* investigation.' Another shot. Further away, then footsteps and a second shot much closer. Joel had his hands pushed firmly over his ears but it barely made a difference. The whole room boomed and shook and he had to lift his hands over his head as bits of debris rained down once again.

Break, drop, snap.

'No one had to get hurt. If Callie Evans hadn't involved my daughter with that . . . that piece of shit.' The footfalls

374

started up again to sound like a man pacing. 'And then her bitch mother lied to cover it up. She wouldn't come clean even when I threatened her family. I thought she might have realised when her daughter tried to kill herself, I thought Sharon might see how painful it would be to lose her. But Callie was going to get better. The girl who started it all was going to make a full recovery, to get on with her life. And the man who destroyed my daughter still walks the planet a free man! No one cares about that, do they?'

Joel was desperately looking around for anything he could use. Anything that might help. He wasn't sure what that might be, against a man with a shotgun. He needed time. He had to keep him talking. 'Hannah did,' he called out, grimacing as he waited for the reaction. When there was nothing he continued. 'Whatever happens here I want you to know that. Hannah never stopped working that case.'

'More lies! She'd moved on! Stopped working the case entirely.'

'So you killed her?'

'Not me!'

'No, you had Danny Evans do it, hyped up on lies,' Joel said. 'And Richard Maddox, you used him to get rid of Danny, then set it up like a suicide. But you did that badly so we would see through it, right? Because we were supposed to be looking at an old man with no previous as the killer.' There was a silence where Nicholas didn't respond straightaway. Joel could still hear moaning; it seemed fainter now. The breathing was heavier in contrast. Joel held his breath to listen, only releasing it when he was sure they were the moans of a fully grown man. It could only be one person. 'You don't need to hurt Richard, you're not so different. You've both been let down by the police. Both of you have had your lives tipped upside down.' Joel was pulling open cupboards as silently as he could. He discovered an old tea urn, some stainless steel pots that were tarnished black. Nothing he could use.

375

'I don't care about Richard Maddox. He's pathetic. He was a means to an end. He's better off dead,' the man shouted. There were more sounds of movement. Footsteps moving further away.

'You never did find who was responsible, did you? We did. He was arrested this morning. The man that groomed those girls, that blackmailed your daughter, is sitting in a police cell right now. You'll get your justice.'

The footsteps now moved closer. 'You think that's justice? You think that's what I want?'

'That's what all this is about, isn't it?'

'Flushing him out. I knew that when people started dying, you would look into what happened to the girls again. I knew you would throw everything you had at it – death brings a lot of attention. And I was right. The name of that piece of shit you arrested will come out now and I'll know who he is. Then I get to show him what I've done, what he can expect.'

'What you've . . .' Joel faded out. DS Rose had shifted to her knees, still pressed against the stainless steel units. *That's why he kept the photographs*. He was going to show Christopher Hennershaw what happens to people like him. They get strung up, a shotgun forced into their mouth and they get to sit and wait for someone to turn up and pull the trigger. Danny Evans, Marcus Olsen . . . they might have been practice runs even for when he could get his hand on the main man. 'We spoke to your wife.' Joel came back a little louder. 'She told us you haven't visited Emma. She said you talk about her like she's dead. But she's not dead. Your wife and daughter are still hurting . . . just like you are, Nicholas.'

Joel had opened and closed the last cupboard. He was still empty-handed. He stood up, dusting some of the larger pieces of ceiling off himself as he did. He needed to get into that room. He could still hear groans of pain, but they were getting quieter, like maybe the man was losing consciousness. He needed to know where Jamie was too. Joel was going to have

376

to try to take control and the mention of Nicholas's daughter was either going to give him that chance or prompt Nicholas to shoot on sight. It was time to find out.

Joel retrieved the bag he had swept up from the boxroom. He had thrown it down when the shots had started but it was still by his side, with a layer of dust and debris. He took out the shoes. The dust had penetrated the bag to dim their polished shine. Joel lifted his hands up, holding a shoe in each, and stepped out into the view of the function room. 'I'm not armed!' he blurted. 'I'm no commander of anything, I was bluffing. Your wife said you would want these.' There was movement directly ahead. A man standing out in the hall instantly snatched a long, dark object up to point it directly at Joel. Then he took a step back. Joel reacted by stepping forward.

'Stay right there!' Nicholas shouted, but Joel didn't. His steps forward were slow and pushed Nicholas back. Joel made it to the end of the short corridor, far enough that he could see, to his left, an elderly man lying on his side – a man who matched the one he had seen on that video footage. Richard Maddox managed to tip his head enough to see Joel enter. Both his hands were reaching down towards his shin and his chest was rising and falling rapidly, like he was having to gasp for his oxygen. That would be why his moans were quieter. There was blood on the floor and on Richard's hands but Joel couldn't see the source.

'He's hurt,' Joel said, 'but you can still help him.' He took another two steps in.

'Shut up!' The gun was raised higher so Joel felt like he was looking right down into its black heart. He was at least blocking Nicholas's way into the kitchen. Maybe enough that, if this went badly, DS Rose would be able to throw herself through the gap in the door they'd come through.

'Richard's nothing to do with any of this. He's a victim of your manipulation. He doesn't deserve to die here, not like this. Let me help him.'

'Manipulated! Is that what I did?'

'Of course. It's all about control for you, isn't it? You're good at it too. You had people killing for you without question. But you can't control this anymore. You can't control me.'

'I can shoot you.'

'I'm a copper. Shoot one and we come back stronger. That's the mistake you made with Hannah.'

'There'd be no coming back for you.'

'I saw some things in your house. A folder. My wife, she works in marketing. She bored me with a presentation once, practice before she did it for real, and she talked about understanding the impact of colour. Blue paper. You wrote your messages to Richard, to Danny, on blue paper. It makes whatever's written seem more trustworthy, genuine. That's right, isn't it? The attention to detail is impressive and that's just one example. These men never stood a chance, Nicholas, you were too clever for them. They don't both have to die because of that.'

'They had a chance. They could have said no.'

'No, they couldn't.'

'Olsen got what he deserved from Danny. He had pictures of Callie too.'

'He did, but he didn't groom her for them. I assume he didn't tell you who did either. Was that another thing you couldn't control? And you sawed his head off for it. You're not very good when things are not going your way, are you?'

Nicholas shrugged, and the gun shook with it. 'Minor setback. You always get them. Richard here invited his friend to the party too. He might have been able to live had he not.'

'He still can. This is lost. How many people do you think you might have to shoot to get this back under control now? My mates know I'm here. I might have bluffed about being surrounded but it's only a matter of time until it happens for real. All you can do is help yourself, and you still have one lifeline.'

378

'Oh? What's that then?'

'Jamie Evans. Tell me where he is. Tell me he's still alive. That goes in your favour.'

Richard twitched on the floor, his moan suddenly louder. Nicholas reacted by dropping the barrel to point at him. 'Don't even think about it, old man!' Richard fell silent, and Joel took the opportunity to step back. He had walked beyond where Richard was laid out on the floor, and he could no longer see him. 'Why would I tell you anything?' Nicholas said.

'Because like I said, there's a whole team of armed police on their way. And all they know about you is that you killed one of their colleagues.'

Nicholas spat on the floor. 'She met with my wife. Behind my back, skulking around like some poisonous shadow over my family.' The rage returned all at once. The gun had dropped a little but it snapped back up now. 'She was trying to make her leave me. I thought she was trying to help us, to find who had done that to my . . . to my daughter, but she was just there to try and take away anything I had left.'

'I think I know why you haven't been to see Emma.' Joel managed another half-step backwards. Still he couldn't see Richard. Nicholas stepped forward to keep the same distance between them.

'You don't know anything.'

Joel lifted the shoes he was carrying higher then squatted down slowly to place them on the floor between them. Then he moved further back towards the door. He could see Richard now, still down to his left. 'It's not because you don't love her, it's because you love her so much you can't see her like that.' Joel stood up again, holding out his hands still, showing they were empty. 'Barker McClean,' he said, gesturing at the shoes and referencing the worn tag he had seen behind one of the tongues. 'A gift from your daughter before it all fell apart.'

Nicholas's gaze dropped to the shoes, but the shotgun was still raised to point at Joel's midriff. Joel took another step back. Nicholas moved with him. He was close to Richard now, too. 'I think you blame yourself . . . and I know what that's like.'

'You can't know.' Nicholas spat again This time it was involuntary, his rage still just below the surface, his eyes piercing Joel's.

'I'm only just back,' Joel said. 'I had a month away from work and for some of that I didn't think I would come back at all. I got a call to a young woman who was up on top of a multi-storey car park, sitting over the edge. Nineteen years old, her whole life ahead of her. She'd argued with her girl-friend, who had announced that she wasn't gay anymore. She had a fella, in fact. Standard call-out, I've seen calls like it a million times before. But I turned up after a run of shifts where I'd seen bad things happen and I was jaded. Just tired of it. Just like I think you are now. I told that girl that she was nineteen years old, that she had her whole life to find the right person to share it with, to be happy. I told her it will come, of course it will; happiness comes for us all.' Joel had to stop, his voice breaking where it was all getting on top of him, the emotion from that day, the dull pain in his ears, the tension in the room. The shotgun pointing at his chest. 'I finished what I had to say and she took a long look at me and then she just dropped. It's happened before, I've lost people, but this one was different. She was listening to me, she wanted to be talked down. But she looked me in the eyes and she saw right through me to where she knew I didn't believe it, didn't believe what I was telling her.' Joel was so lost in the memory he let his eyes blur.

'Some stranger? And you think you know how I feel? This is my—'

'I have two daughters,' Joel cut him off. 'They're younger. Younger than her, younger than Emma. But they'll get older, we can't stop that happening no matter how much we want to. And they'll see the world for what it is, they'll see the

380

darkness, and there might be times when it gets the better of them. And when that happens I will be the first person they turn to, to tell them that it's all OK, that they're going to be OK. But what if I can't make them believe that? And what if they're sitting looking over the edge of a multi-storey car park? I know the pressure, the fear of being a father who lets down what they love more than anything in the world. And if it happened and I had someone to blame, I can't imagine what I would do.'

The shotgun lowered. It was subtle. The man almost seemed to sleepwalk another step closer. Joel stayed put. Nicholas's eyes dropped to the floor. Joel was just about to start the appeal phase, his negotiator training still there when he needed it, but Nicholas suddenly lifted the gun back so it was level with Joel's chest. He stepped forward again. There was intent in his movement. The barrel was almost close enough to touch Joel.

'What would you do if someone was going to lock you up, stop you seeing your daughter again? You would fight to the last, wouldn't you?' Nicholas's face cracked with emotion. 'I could blow you away and get out of here.'

'You could, but you won't,' Joel said, hoping he sounded far more convinced than he felt.

'Why won't I?' The gun twitched.

'Because this was all about justice and about Emma. Everything for a reason. There's no reason to murder me. Or Richard. The only way to see Emma again is to put that down. Let me deal with the man who did that to your daughter.'

Nicholas pulled the gun higher, enough that Joel could look directly down the barrel and through the iron sights to where the man stared back. The gun was shaking, it was heavy, he wouldn't be able to hold it for long. 'No!' he said, 'you lot had your chance!'

'Callie's fine. You attacked the wrong girl!' Joel blurted, his hands outstretched.

381

'You're lying!' There was no shake now. The gun was still levelled.

'The girl in the next bed over. Callie's mother swapped their names. An innocent girl, nothing to do with any of this. It's over. Whatever you were trying to do, you failed. Give it up.' Joel was pleading with him now. He hadn't wanted to bring up Callie, he couldn't be sure how he would react, but it was all he had left. Nicholas hesitated and the gun sagged. He stepped back, now too far away for Joel to reach him. But Joel had nothing else left. He was preparing to lunge.

Richard must have seen his opportunity.

Joel just saw him as a blur on the floor. He was quick – just the glint of a blade – and Nicholas's reaction was instant. He dropped the barrel to point towards Richard and Joel threw himself at it. It went off, the *boom* filling the tight space and then the only sound left was a high-pitched whistle. Joel went down, now holding the weapon with both hands, pushing it into Nicholas as a way of trying to get some control. He was aware that Richard was underneath them; he must have brought his knee up for protection and it dug into Joel's stomach and winded him. Joel scrabbled with his feet to get some grip, trying to keep pressing forward, pushing the barrel of the gun away from where Richard lay.

Boom!

The sound of the second shot registered with Joel like it was through sound-deadening but he felt this one: the gun bucked in his grip, and he scraped his knuckle against something sharp. He let go. The gun didn't matter anymore. Nicholas was caught under him too. He bucked and twisted, trying to get free, and Joel could see enough of his head to swing at it with his big fist. It was a glancing blow. Nicholas took it and scurried away on his hands and knees, the light catching a large blade in his hand. He must have taken it off Richard. The blood that dripped from it would be his own, a wound in his calf preventing him from standing.

382

Another blur. This time it flashed across the room from his left. DS Rose led with her right like she was kicking a field goal. Nicholas's head was at the perfect height. The thud of the blow found its way through to Joel's muffled ears, as did the thump of the man hitting the floor, taking a row of stacked chairs with him. He remained still.

Joel planted a hand on the floor to get his balance. He felt it almost slip from under him; the floor was slick with blood. Richard was still laid out beside him. But he wasn't moving.

'Richard? Richard?'

There was no answer.

383

Chapter 61

Dover Police Station. Joel sipped at another rancid cup of something boiling. His ears whistled and popped as he worked his jaw and the sound of swallowing was as loud as the taste was foul. They were back in their makeshift office, the meeting room vibe even stronger now with all the chairs around the central table occupied. The table top was washed in a bright white from strip lights directly above, while darkness clawed at the window.

Perhaps the vibe wasn't so much meeting as disciplinary hearing. With all eyes on Joel. The Major Crime DCI was there with his own inspector and two sergeants. Superintendent Marsden had made it down too. DS Rose was the only one on his side of the table, close enough for their elbows to touch at a time when Joel wouldn't blame her for making a show of backing away.

Joel was the only one with tea. He had offered it to everyone else but it seemed machine tea had a terrible reputation across the force. Joel wondered if he and the tea now had that in common.

The DCI had been talking. He finished and sat back, his arms crossed, his cheeks glowing a shade of red that had been deepening the longer he talked. He was a squat man. No real neck and thick, hairy arms forcing their way out of a short-sleeved

384

shirt a size too small. He looked like he was battling to control his hands, opting to wring them constantly, a grip that only broke when he was really angry. Which had happened a lot. Joel's close proximity to a fired shotgun was something he could use – a blessing in disguise perhaps. The DCI had ranted about protocols and standard operating procedures, about the right people for the right job, using the phrase 'who the hell do you think you are?' on three separate occasions before ending with a demand for an explanation. So Joel had sipped at the rancid brown water as a way of taking his time.

'I'm so sorry. I didn't hear a word you just said,' Joel said with a shrug.

It seemed the DCI was done. He had no appetite to repeat his speech, and instead directed his glowing cheeks towards Superintendent Marsden to announce that he would be over-seeing the search of the offender's home and all evidence capture. He would also need full reports from both DI Norris and DS Rose before they went off duty and both officers would also need to ensure they were contactable. Marsden said how sure she was that both her officers remained very willing 'to do what's necessary', and at this the DCI huffed, threw his hands up in a gesture towards Joel and said, 'I think he's done enough for one day, don't you?'

Joel reacted like a phrase had finally managed to make it through his damaged ears.

'Thank you very much, sir. Just doing my job,' he said, with added cheeriness.

The DCI sat back. And he stared. The message seemed to be that the new centralised investigation team was excused to leave while the old guard of Major Crime would stay and mop up their mess. Joel didn't move, enjoying an elongated slurp at his foul drink. DS Rose stayed put too. It was Ma'am Marsden that spoke next.

'Can I have the room? Joel, Lucy, just you two, please.'

The DCI's cheeks glowed hotter than ever. He muttered

while getting up and was still muttering as he stepped through the door. Marsden waited until they were alone. Joel had tried to read her a couple of times when the DCI was having his rant. It was noticeable that, as the highest-ranking officer in the room, she had sat back and let him lead.

Now she cracked a wide grin.

'So that's what I would call a steep learning curve!' she said.

'You could say that,' Joel agreed.

'Your hearing seems to have come back all of a sudden, DI Norris.'

'I don't think I damaged the ear, I just got a bullshit filter fitted.'

'I think you might need one of those if you're going to continue working Major Crime jobs.'

'That's an option then?' Joel said.

Marsden held her smile. 'What do you think, Lucy?'

'Politics, Ma'am. Someone very wise once told me how they'd made a career out of avoiding it. I think they had a point.'

'Very wise indeed,' Ma'am Marsden said. 'There will be a fallout too. The Evans boy was found right as rain but he was taken off the street when we had knowledge of a potential threat towards the family. We need to be prepared for that. The attack at the hospital too. We need to be ready for the questions coming our way.'

'You mean *my* way?' Joel said.

'Not at all. From what I know, you two have done an incredible job with what you had at your disposal. What you didn't have . . . well, that will be down to me and I'm big enough and ugly enough to take any criticism there might be. Major Crime will want to make something off this. You let me worry about the politics.'

'What about the girl? Maybe if Major Crime had taken this . . . Maybe she wouldn't be dead.'

'The Evans mother didn't tell us everything. If she had, maybe we would have been looking at Nicholas Luckhurst earlier, rather than chasing after Christopher Hennershaw. Let's not forget, you arrested Hennershaw the same morning the hospital attack took place. With all the information, you might well have been knocking on the Luckhurst door to make an arrest, rather than Hennershaw's.'

'What happened with him?'

Marsden's face flickered in a smile again. 'Charged. Guilty plea too. Seems you taking his Playstation was the final straw. His solicitor advised him to go guilty on the grooming and blackmail offences against those girls. The evidence was good, I hear, what with the search of his home being done right this time. And his solicitor thought this was the only way he would stand a chance of avoiding prison time.'

'And does he?'

'CPS remanded him. They were very happy too. He'll serve the time that he was licensed for and then whatever the judge adds at court. He'll be away for a good few years.'

'That's good,' Joel said.

'That's incredible, Joel. You two were tasked with finding a murderer. You did that while convicting a dangerous sexual predator on the side. You should be very proud.'

'And Richard Maddox?'

'He's going to be okay. Last I heard he was going into surgery to fix his leg. He had a lump out of his arm but it was all flesh. Looks a lot worse than it is, apparently. The fact no one died in that old club is another job well done.'

'It's a little difficult to think of the positives. The girl in the hospital, I don't even know her name,' Joel said. Marsden looked fixedly at him. She leaned in a little to respond.

'This time we do it right. This time we all take it more seriously, you included. This is the sort of thing that can get on top of you and that's OK. You tell me what you need to make sure you don't take that home with you. That girl's death isn't on you, not either of you, that's on Nicholas Luckhurst and he will get what's coming.'

387

'I'd like to see the families,' Joel replied. 'Both of them. The girl in the hospital but also . . . that girl that jumped. Sometimes the police are involved in things that go wrong and we just move onto the next job, but the families involved don't get to do that. Luckhurst couldn't move on, Danny Evans couldn't either, and look what it did. The families of those two girls deserve their time with me. They deserve to know everything. I couldn't give two shits about what some DCI thinks, but they matter . . . they're all that matters.'

'OK then,' Marsden said. 'We'll make those arrangements when you've had some rest.'

Joel lifted himself to his feet. After all the excitement, he and DS Rose had been sure to go straight back to the Luckhurst house and retrieve the key boxes – and the pen drive that Marilyn Luckhurst had used – before leaving that place. Joel had already dug through some of it but there was a lot more material still untouched. As well as the black folder there were pages of notes. Luckhurst's research on each of his targets had been thorough – obviously an obsession. Joel leaned on the box for support, suddenly aware of his own exhaustion.

'They never stood a chance, not any of them. You should see the notes in here. I know it will all come out in time but he knew to get Danny Evans in that room with Olsen at night when he had been drinking. He knew to get Maddox when he was sitting with his wife; he thought he would be more vulnerable to someone tugging at his emotions up there. He even has a picture of a card Richard Maddox left on his wife's grave, which hints at a story of how his wife named the dog, for Christ's sake. The bastard ringed it like it was the key to all of this, like it was the one thing he could use to make sure he got what he wanted. Marilyn was right about him. He's all about control. They never stood a chance – maybe we didn't either.'

'You still got him though.'

388

'I needed Richard's help.'

'Not so sure he was helping you as much as helping himself.'

'He had a knife. I didn't see it until the last moment. Where did that come from?' Joel said, turning back towards Marsden.

'His sock apparently. He took it from Glenn Morris's house. It was left there as part of framing Richard for his murder. Along with Glenn Morris's body. Seems Richard still has the fight in him.'

'Glenn Morris!' Joel almost laughed. It was more shock, upset even. 'We didn't even know about that one.'

'We would have though. And we would have been looking at Maddox for his murder if you hadn't been so dogged.' Marsden slapped the table and suddenly got to her feet. 'You did good. Any reviews or investigations into this will only show that up, so I for one welcome it. For now it's home time. Major Crime seem keen to do all the boring bit, evidence capture, witness statements and paperwork, so I say we leave them to it.'

'The DCI wants full reports. I'll find a terminal here somewhere—'

'They can wait and I want to see them first. We need to be careful with the content. We can fill in the details later. For now, both of you need to take care of yourselves.'

'But the DCI—'

'Is a lower rank than me. The meeting was not the time to point that out; sometimes you have to let men like that say their bit. But he could still benefit from a reminder. Would you send him in, on your way out, please? And make sure he's aware that it's just him I require for now.' Joel gathered up his things and moved to the door. 'And could you ask him to bring me one of those teas,' she said.

'They're terrible, Ma'am,' Joel said.

'Oh, I won't be drinking it. It doesn't hurt to remind some people that they may be able to take the lead in some meetings, but for others they're the tea boy.'

389

Chapter 62

Two weeks later

Joel ran his fingers over the weathered brass bolts that were visible in the thick wood of the ancient door. It struck him as a little odd that there was such an impregnability to British churches and how this contradicted the message of a warm welcome from inside. Today the welcome had indeed been warm. Only the vicar and an elderly woman tutting over paperwork were present and both were quick to understand the situation – as out of the ordinary as it might have been.

When he stepped away from the church the sun flooded over him, justifying his decision to leave his suit jacket in the car. It had meant his cuffs, baton and spray were out on show, digging into his solid chest and back in a spindly holder that he had only agreed to wear as a trade-off with DS Rose. She hadn't wanted to come here at all and had made it clear why: how it was an unnecessary risk, stupid even – the sort of decision that wouldn't have to go very wrong for it to be career-ending; and how she couldn't think of a single good reason for their diversion. Joel had only disagreed with her on the last part. There was a very good reason for their diversion and he was still standing where Joel had left him, his weight upon crutches under each arm, with DS Rose standing close by his shoulder. She still looked unimpressed.

390

'Just the vicar and an elderly-looking woman. Hardly an elite escape team,' Joel said.

Richard Maddox smiled. 'Dammit,' he said softly.

'Ten minutes,' Joel said, 'and I mean it.'

'Okay then.' Richard seemed to hesitate. He was looking straight ahead across the graveyard of Lympne Church. 'Is it strange to feel nervous?'

'Nervous?'

'This is the first time I've been up here since . . . Well, there's just a lot to tell her. I know what she'll say, about me being a hothead. She always told me it would get me in serious trouble one day.'

'I'm sure she'll understand.'

'It's just over a year ago now. I hated the person who took everything away from me, but not as much as the person who showed me what was left. I was duped. I am a hot-headed old fool. If I'd just taken a moment to think . . .'

'You were never supposed to think. Just react,' Joel said.

'Well, I certainly did that.' Richard still hesitated, and his eyes looked heavy as he turned them towards Joel. 'Tell me, Inspector Norris, is this the last time I ever get to come here? Is that why you broke so many rules to bring me?'

'Some rules are open to interpretation. Now that you are well enough to be interviewed, my job is to transport you from the hospital to custody. This is a stop for your comfort. You're still recovering from a gunshot wound to the shin, after all. The doctor told me you shouldn't sit still for long.'

'He did say that.' Richard's smile dropped away quickly. 'Is this the last time, Inspector?'

Joel sighed. 'I don't know. But I do know a little more about you now, Richard, you and Angela. I learned a bit from that too. Maybe we could all do with remembering that whenever you say goodbye to someone you love, it could be the last time.'

Richard nodded. 'I couldn't have put it better. You're a family man, right? Cherish what you have. Every minute of it.'

391

'Talking of every minute, nine minutes left.' Joel lifted his watch to tap its face. 'Don't waste this time talking to me.'

'Thank you . . . for this . . .' He moved off, ignoring the path and moving straight across the grass. His first few steps were careful, like he was unsure how his crutches would fare on ground that would have taken a lot of rain over the winter. He needn't have worried; the last few weeks that Richard Maddox had been in hospital had been mostly glorious – spring had well and truly asserted itself and now, as Joel watched him take a seat on a bench, the backdrop was a dramatic bright pink, where a cherry blossom tree seemed to have been waiting for his arrival to burst into full bloom. Its branches, tickled by a breeze, shook petals over the grave he was facing.

'If he runs, you're chasing.' Joel was snatched from his thoughts by DS Rose. She moved up to stand next to him.

'When you said you wanted to stay, we agreed that you would do all of the running after people.'

'Seems you don't remember much about that conversation at all, boss.'

'Boss! You know, I think that's the first time you've called me that. Finally giving me the respect I deserve?'

'If he runs, you're chasing,' she said again. When he replied it was through a wide grin.

'Fair enough.'

THE END

Acknowledgements

Writing can sometimes feel like a solitary act – and it is true that there are many hours spent actively avoiding contact with other people while plotting, procrastinating or wrestling the blinking cursor to get a story written down. But the words contained in these pages would be very different, inaccurate, misspelled or just plain wrong if it were not for the involvement of a number of other people and it is only right that I fess up and tell you all about them.

There is no other place to start than with Rachel Faulkner-Willcocks. Rachel is the Senior Commissioning Editor with Avon Books and is the editor who rolled my words in glitter for *The Friend*, but far more than that, she was the driver behind me getting published with Avon in the first place. Rachel took a chance when all I had to offer was a confused vision about 'some bloke being tied up with a gun in his mouth'. She certainly didn't have to; the world of crime-writing is much like the world of crime itself, very competitive and with any number of us trying to make a living out of it. I only hope she doesn't regret it now!

Alongside Rachel, Avon Books clearly work closely together and I would like to extend my gratitude to the team as a whole. Once a story has a first draft, Team Avon sweep it up with cheery gusto; improve it, give it a beautiful jacket, an alluring blurb and manage it right through to a final product

393

that is something we can all be massively proud of. I know I am.

Another person I would like to make public my sincere appreciation is Charlie Paine. A Senior CSI for an outstanding police force, Charlie has guided me through all the gory bits for fourteen books. We are now at the point where I turn up unannounced and she looks up, rolls her eyes and says 'here to talk about death are we? I'll put the kettle on', while I twist my toe into the floor on the threshold to her office. Details included in *The Friend* came from Charlie taking hours out of her rest day and ensuring a constant top up of tea in her beautiful garden. Time is our most valuable commodity and that she – and her wonderful wife – would give me so much is something I appreciate more than I can put into words.

The Friend also needed expertise from an NHS source, and – in the craziest of years for our medical heroes – I need to thank Charlotte Elias, Clinical Skills Tutor at Cardiff University. Charlotte gave up some of her precious time to listen to me whittle on about how a character was going to spend much of the book in a coma, how I didn't really know what that might look like and I didn't really know how it was going to end up. Fortunately, Charlotte has the patience required for her career choice and she provided me with incredible detail. Far too much, in fact, and I should say that if there are any inaccuracies around medical elements in this book, that is entirely my fault – I will have cut out the wrong bit!

Thanks also to DC Leggett, who I was able to bounce off the procedural stuff that I should definitely know already. And who misses me more than he will ever admit.

The only person left to thank is my wife. There's no winning here. I could put Kayleigh first and she would be embarrassed, I could miss her out entirely and be criticised, and as it is, I've put her last where she will no doubt suggest she was an afterthought. I think being mentioned last is apt. She's the silent hero after-all, who, when I'm stuck into this other world, quietly deals with the real one. And I love her more than nachos.